HANGMAN

Michael Slade

VIKING

VIKING

Published by the Penguin Group

Penguin Books Canada Ltd, 10 Alcorn Avenue, Toronto, Ontario, Canada
M4V 3B2

Penguin Books Ltd, 27 Wrights Lane, London W8 5TZ, England

Penguin Putnam Inc., 375 Hudson Street, New York, New York 10014, U.S.A.

Penguin Books Australia Ltd, Ringwood, Victoria, Australia

Penguin Books (NZ) Ltd, cnr Rosedale and Airborne Roads, Albany, Auckland
1310, New Zealand

Penguin Books Ltd, Registered Offices: Harmondsworth, Middlesex, England

First published 2000

10 9 8 7 6 5 4 3 2 1

Copyright © 2000 by Headhunter Holdings Ltd.

CANADIAN CATALOGUING IN PUBLICATION DATA

Slade, Michael
    Hangman

ISBN 0-670-89480-X

I. Title.
PS8587.L35H36 2000   C813'.54   C00-931622-1
PR9199.3.S52H36 2000

Visit Penguin Canada's website at **www.penguin.ca**

Printed in Canada

A riddle:
This is for Slade's wife
This is for Slade's mother
They're the same person
So this is for Lee

The Hanging

And naked to the hangman's noose
The morning clocks will ring
A neck God made for other use
Than strangling in a string.

—A. E. Housman

Hangman's Noose

Walla Walla, Washington State
February 14, 1993

At midnight on this snowy eve—Valentine's Day—the state of
Washington would hang Peter Bryce Haddon. For the umpteenth
time in the past few hours, the reporter Justin Whitfield glanced
at his watch. Within a minute he realized that his mind had failed
to register the digital numbers. Whitfield checked the clock.
11:51. Barring a last minute reprieve from the governor, the condemned would dance with the hangman on the end of a rope in
nine minutes.

Tick-tock . . .
Tick-tock . . .
The minute hand advanced.
11:52.
Time was running out.

Several hours earlier, the Seattle crime reporter had driven
inland from the coast through light flurries of snow. Cresting the
Cascade Mountains by Snoqualmie Pass to cross the Columbia
River beyond Yakima, he had reached the southeast corner of the
state, where Oregon and Idaho bordered Washington. Flurries had
thickened to snowfall, whitening Walla Walla by the time he

parked his car outside the state prison. Television trucks set up satellite dishes on a swirling, wind-swept field as darkness crept around opposing vigils huddled in the parking lot.

A chain-link corridor ten feet wide separated the two camps, which were already divided by an insurmountable philosophical difference. Protesters fenced in the pen marked AGAINST carried printed signs that read "Why kill to show killing is wrong?" or wrote "Choose life" in the ankle-deep snow. Others braved the bite of the wind to kneel in prayer for Haddon, or they marched in a circle, hugging themselves and stamping their feet to keep warm, chanting, "We are justice-seeking people singing for our lives."

Advocates fenced in the pen marked FOR were in a party mood. Outnumbering the fifty protesters three to one, most were younger than their adversaries. Teenagers wore white twine fashioned into little nooses around their necks. Chants of "Hang him, hang him" taunted the other camp as hand-printed signs waved in searchlight beams. "An eye for an eye," quoted from the Bible. "What if it was your child?" under a photo of the murdered girl. "Haddon should hang," illustrated with the crude stick figure of a hangman game, the eyes X'd out to denote death.

Tick-tock . . .

Tick-tock . . .

Justin had entered the prison.

A hundred plus reporters would gather tonight at the Washington State Penitentiary for a death lottery to select the twelve media witnesses who would watch Haddon hang. Only one reporter would spend private time with the condemned, and he, at Haddon's insistence, was guaranteed a seat in the gallows gallery.

A guard inside the prison had ordered Justin to spread his arms and turn away from him. First frisked, then stripped of everything in his pockets, including his pen and notepad, the *Seattle Star* reporter was led to Unit 6 to wait.

So loud was the jangling of the phone that Justin had jumped.

Replacing the receiver, the grim guard ushered him out, and he trudged through snow that tumbled between fences topped with razor wire to reach the death shed. At the door to the killing machine, Justin signed in, feeling colder within the chamber than he had outside.

Tick-tock . . .

Tick-tock . . .

Justin faced the gallows.

The two-level structure, built in 1931, had not been used since Joseph Self was hanged in 1963 for killing a cab driver. Of the seventy-three cons Washington had executed since 1904, forty-three had met the hangman on this gallows. Peter Bryce Haddon would make that forty-four.

What Justin faced was not the spare wooden platform of Wild West days. Only the western states of Washington and Montana still offered convicts the option of the noose, but neck-breaking these days had been spruced up.

Ranged behind huge picture windows with pull-down screens that kept witnesses from actually seeing the death, two levels faced the viewing gallery. The ground level, into which the hanged man would drop through one of two trapdoors in its ceiling, also contained the metal table and brown pad used to snuff convicts who opted for death by lethal injection. The upper level was the hanging room. Drilled into the ceiling of that white chamber were two brown closed-loop hooks for the thick Manila hemp rope. Boiled, oiled, waxed and coiled with a hangman's noose, the thirty-foot-long rope was measured for a scientific drop. How far a condemned must fall to ensure a snapped spine is determined by weight. Haddon, at 130 pounds, would drop seven feet.

Bang!

Snap!

Thump . . . thu—

Was that how Haddon would hang?

As Washington's first execution in thirty years, and the first hanging in America since Kansas sent two men to the gallows in 1965, this was a Big Story bathed in limelight. For weeks, Justin had followed the build-up to tonight, reporting last-ditch legal efforts to save the doomed man.

Yesterday, the state Supreme Court had dismissed a lawsuit by twenty-two "taxpayers" who were challenging the noose as cruel and unusual punishment. To contend that hanging was a torturous way to die, the plaintiffs had referred the court to observations made by the warden at San Quentin in California from 1942 to 1954. A participant in sixty hangings, he had described one drop in horrifying detail:

> The man hit bottom, and I observed that he was fighting by pulling on the straps, wheezing, whistling, trying to get air, that blood was oozing through the black cap. I observed also that he urinated, defecated and the droppings fell on the floor, and the stench was terrible. I also saw witnesses pass out and have to be carried from the witness room. When he was taken down and the cap removed, big hunks of flesh were torn off the side of his face where the noose had been.

Bang!
Whissstle . . .
Riiiip . . .
Oooooze . . .
Was that how Haddon would hang?

Today, while he was driving here, the reporter had caught the result of another lawsuit on his car radio. A convict waiting on death row had appealed, to the ninth Circuit Court of Appeals, a federal judge's refusal to let him videotape this hanging as evidence of cruel and unusual punishment for his constitutional challenge of the death penalty. In denying that appeal, however, the court had granted him permission to have a witness present at the execution, and had ordered that the blinds between the gallows gallery and the lower chamber not be closed until the hanged man had ceased to move.

That meant Justin would *watch* Peter die.

At 4:40 that afternoon, prison officials had moved Peter Bryce Haddon from his longtime cell on death row, in the Intensive Management Unit of the penitentiary, to a holding cell by the gallows on the upper level of the execution chamber. From there, his "last mile" would be just a few short yards to his midnight appointment with the hangman. Two different staircases rose to the upper level. Up one, Justin had gone to spend dwindling time with the condemned...

Tick-tock ...

Tick-tock ...

Until his time was up.

Having left Peter with the priest who would offer him last rites, Justin had descended the stairs to the gallows gallery, where now he sat, scribbling notes with a pen and paper provided by the prison, glancing nervously at the clock, which was creeping inexorably toward the hanging hour.

11:53.

Every surface in the gallery, from the concrete walls and floors to the iron bars on the doors to the steel table and chairs, was cold and hard. The smell of fresh paint lingered. The only sounds were occasional pops from the loudspeaker, air rushing in through a heating vent and the scratching of his pen. Then additional witnesses entered to fill the other seats: the father of the dead girl, a stony-faced Greek; the twelve reporters, two pale, as if fearful they might pass out and embarrass themselves; a man from the American Civil Liberties Union, acting for the con who filed the videotape appeal; three guards to keep order; and—out of uniform—a Seattle street cop named Madeline Thorne, who...

11:54.

. . . sat down beside Justin.

"Cheeseburger."

"Huh?"

A voice from his other side. Justin turned from Maddy Thorne to face a Seattle TV reporter named Sue Frye. Dark hair. Dark eyes. Perfect teeth.

"Double cheeseburger. A side of french fries. Ice cream for dessert. And a Coke," said Sue. "That's the most requested last meal on death row."

"Where'd you hear that?"

"Read it in the paper."

"Not *my* paper," Justin said.

"No, a cheesy tabloid."

Conversations whispered in the gallows gallery had all the surface solemnity of gabbing in church. Nervous tension, however, was dissipated by small talk and gallows humor.

"Guess the runner-up."

"Steak?" said Justin.

"Steak and eggs. T-bone. With the eggs scrambled."

"Me, I'd order something big, to really mess up the chef. Bouillabaisse. Beef Wellington. Homemade wedding cake."

"There've been some strange last meals."

"Yeah? Like what?"

"An apple. Bubble gum. And two boxes of Frosted Flakes."

"Comfort food?"

"Got to be. But who orders liver and onions before he's going to die?" asked Sue.

"Hannibal Lecter. With a fine Chianti."

"No booze allowed. They give you water instead. I hear Texas may ban tobacco from its prison system. The most active death chamber in the nation, and Texas may deny cons the last solace of condemned throughout our history: a final cigarette."

Justin shrugged. "Tobacco will kill you," he said.

"This waiting is killing me," said Maddy Thorne.

Justin glanced from Sue to her, then at the clock.

11:56.

Four minutes to go.

"One guy's order," Sue said, drawing Justin back, "was six pieces of French toast, with butter, syrup and jelly; six barbecued spare ribs; six pieces of burned bacon; four scrambled eggs; five well-cooked sausage patties; french fries with ketchup; three slices of cheese; two pieces of yellow cake, with chocolate fudge icing; and four cartons of milk to wash it down."

"The condemned ate a hearty meal."

"And then there's the con who ordered a last meal of dirt. Seems dirt's the active ingredient in voodoo rituals. Since dirt wasn't on the prison's menu of approved foods, he got yogurt instead. That's one zombie who won't return from the grave."

A tap on his shoulder.

Justin turned.

Madeline Thorne nodded her head toward the gallows level.

"What did *he* order?"

"Peter?" Justin said.

It was as if she couldn't speak his name. The same way some people say "passed away" and "at rest" instead of "died."

"Nothing special," Justin responded. "All Peter wanted was what the other prisoners were having to eat tonight. Salmon, scalloped potatoes, mixed vegetables and Jell-O."

"Typical," Maddy said.

"Typical," he agreed.

Tick-tock . . .

Tick-tock . . .

The clock on the wall advanced.

"Would you opt for this?"

Again she nodded toward the gallows level.

"No," said Justin.

"An ugly way to go."

"He's afraid of needles. Has been all his life."

"Still . . . I mean, *this* over lethal injection?"

"The little girl was strangled."

"So hanging is some kind of statement?"

"He's drawing a parallel between him and her."

"How so?"

"He's saying they're *both* victims."

Tick-tock . . .

Tick-tock . . .

11:58.

Thorne, though still in her twenties, had the hard edge of most female cops. Cropped close, her blonde hair masked dark roots. Good looks were marred by the squint around her eyes, which were creased from too much suspicion in her professional life. All the hardness in her was on view in her tenseness tonight.

"Last words," Sue said, pulling Justin back. He felt like the rope in a tug-of-war between these two women.

"Don't know any."

"Yes, you do. Who said, 'Let's do it'?"

"Gary Gilmore. Before he was shot by Utah's firing squad."

"And 'Forgive them, Father, for they know not what they do'?"

Justin frowned. "That I know," he said.

"You're no doubt thinking of Anthony Antone, sent to Florida's electric chair for arranging the hit on a private eye."

"Actually, I was thinking of another guy."

"'Adios'?"

"Who's that?"

"Killer named John Thanos. Lethally injected in Maryland."

"Thanos? Fitting. Thanatos was the ancient Greek personification of death."

"'I love you'?"

"What?"

"Last words," said Sue. "Some guy, whose name I can't recall, to the prosecutor before Nevada jabbed him."

"Where'd you get all this?"

"Bite I'm doing tomorrow. 'You can be a king or a street-sweeper, but everybody dances with the Grim Reaper.'"

"Who's that philosopher?"

"Robert Alton-Harris, gassed in California. But my favorite is, 'I'd rather be fishing' quipped by Jimmy Glass before Louisiana fried him."

A tap on the shoulder.

Maddy again.

Another nod toward the gallows level.

"Know what he's going to say?"

"Yes," said Justin. "We talked about that. And he asked a favor. In the piece I write on him for the *Star* tomorrow, Peter wants me to—"

"Shhhh," shushed Sue.

The upper-level window rattled to strike midnight. All whispering in the gallery ceased. The rattle meant Haddon had left the holding cell and was being led to the window for last words. Silhouettes appeared behind the screen, then the muffled voice of the prison superintendent asked the doomed man if he had anything to say. The blind was pulled up and there he quivered: a slight, blue-eyed convict Justin's age, wearing a light gray prison-issue shirt, baggy blue jeans with rolled-up cuffs and a pair of navy blue Velcro running shoes. It was like staring twenty feet up at a mannequin displayed in a second-floor department store window. Haddon's hands were restrained in front of his waist, and the guards on either side stood with their backs to the gallery. Nearby leaned a board with straps, for use as a body brace should Haddon faint.

Those below had to strain to catch his last words. Weeks had gone into rehearsing, preparing the rope and testing the trapdoor, but checking the loudspeaker was not a priority. The system popped and distorted what he had to say while the guards on both sides supported his arms. Had Justin not already been told what those words would be, he would have missed most of what Haddon said to the gallery.

"My last words are—"

Peter's voice broke.

"That I am innocent, innocent, innocent. Be under no illusion. This is injustice. I owe society nothing. I am—"

He choked the words.

"An innocent man. Something wrong is taking place here tonight."

Behind Justin, the father of the dead girl cursed in Greek.

The shade dropped suddenly and a backlight came on behind the gallows. Haddon's silhouette stepped back to one of the trapdoors, where he stood on a black square that had been painted in the middle. Guaranteed anonymity and trained to be quick, a volunteer prison worker placed a hood on Haddon's head. Then the shadow hangman looped the noose about his neck, tightening the knot directly behind his left ear.

Justin felt a wave of dread surge through him. He willed himself to watch carefully. The hangman appeared to be chewing gum. A nod from the superintendent was his signal to push the button. The trapdoor crashed open and struck a metal hook.

In a blink, Haddon's silhouette disappeared. His body plunged seven feet into the lower room, where, by court order, the blinds were open. It jerked to a halt six feet from the floor. The snap of the rope yanking taut could be the snap of his neck.

The witness from the ACLU leaped out of his chair, craning forward to get a better view. Was he let down by the hanging? It fell far short of what the union had predicted: a slow death by strangulation, or a hard one by decapitation.

Instead, the body seemed to unstretch as it turned counterclockwise. The black hood in the noose was cocked at an odd angle. The shackled hands clenched and one knee bent slightly. Muscles tightened in the torso, then went limp, and seconds later Justin witnessed life abandon Peter Bryce Haddon.

HANGMAN

The superintendent came down from the scaffold to shut the blinds.

At 12:07, the doctor pronounced death.

Outside, in the FOR camp, fireworks exploded and cheers rang out. Across the great divide, candles were lit as those AGAINST shed tears. And down from the black sky, white snow buried the gallows under a midnight shroud.

The Aftermath

Like enough, you won't be glad,
When they come to hang you, lad:
But bacon's not the only thing
That's cured by hanging from a string.

—Hugh Kingsmill

The Hanging Judge

The Hanging Judge was in fine form for his last day on the bench. No meaner man had ever sat in lordly judgment over his fellow man than Mr. Justice Kincaid, or "Kinky" to the bar. He was a little guy, less than five feet tall, who surely had his bottom whacked by many a wet towel in gym showers at school, and later took his latent anger out on those unfortunate enough to end up in his court. Had he sucked on a lemon before climbing to the bench, his ashen face could have been no more puckered and pinched than the withered glare that glowered down at the convict.

"Mudge," growled the Hanging Judge, "you have been found guilty of a most heinous rape..."

Our social-studies teacher shifted uneasily on his seat. Flanked by twenty ten-year-olds in the gallery of the court, he no doubt had second thoughts about this idea: guiding his class on a field trip to the criminal courts, so we could go home to tell our parents about the exciting rape case Mr. Pritchard took us out of school to watch. Some parents get bent out of shape over education like that.

"Mudge," threatened the Hanging Judge, "it is now my duty to pass sentence on you... "

The skinny convict shuddered in the dock.

The homely woman beside me tensed.

Actually, the rape was not a "most heinous" crime. In years to come, we would dub it a "he said, she said" squabble, culminating in a most unusual verdict by the jury: "Guilty with a strong recommendation for leniency as according to the evidence there was insufficient resistance by the complainant." But Mudge, unfortunately, had drawn Kincaid.

The Hanging Judge had earned his name by hanging a lot of cons (a sentence he got kinky relish from having ordered carried out), not to mention his penchant for strokes of the lash (which he would tack on to a prison term wherever the law allowed). Time, however, had blunted Kinky's brutal fangs and claws, first removing the whip of corporal punishment from his grasp, then dismantling the gallows, though hanging was still on the books. And now, an unfair amendment to the Judges' Act was forcing him into retirement at the far-too-early age of seventy-five. His last chance to vent his spleen was Mudge trapped in the dock.

"Mudge," thundered the Hanging Judge, "you are the scum of the earth!" Kinky's last sentence would see the old boy off in style. "You are a sexual predator of the most insidious kind!" Kinky brushed aside the fact that Mudge had no prior record. "You are a jeopardy to every decent woman in your hunting ground!" Kinky ignored the recommendation of the jury. "If Parliament had not seen fit to remove it from the law, the lash would await you in custody!" Mudge's knees were knocking; his bones were rattling. "A fitting punishment for filth of your ilk is fifteen years in the penitentiary!" Kinky swept a dismissive arm toward the pit in the prisoner's dock, where iron steps descended to the holding cells below. "Take him down!" he ordered.

As poor, bewildered Mudge turned to stumble down the steps, the homely woman seated beside me leaped to her feet.

"You cruel cocksucker!" she yelled at the judge.

Must be Mudge's mom, I figured.

Mr. Pritchard, our socials teacher, blanched.

"You mean motherfucker!" Mrs. Mudge bellowed.

Mr. Pritchard turned positively white, undoubtedly imagining us running home to tell our parents what the angry lady said when the teacher took us off to court to watch the rape case.

"You miserable, rotten, sadistic old bastard!" she hurled at Kinky. Meanwhile burly court officials waded into the packed gallery to get hold of her, trundling her, kicking and screaming, out of Kincaid's court. The last we heard from her was "Nazi *cunt!*" echoing in from the hall.

Mr. Pritchard was in dire need of smelling salts.

Down the iron steps trod downtrodden Mudge.

So ended Mr. Justice Kincaid's last case, and all that separated the old bull from pension pasture was a shovelful or two of retirement-from-the-law bullshit. To mark Kinky's last day on the bench, counsel for the Crown rose at the prosecution table and managed to come up with a suitable laudatory remark: "No one could ever deny that Your Lordship has been a very courageous judge."

Then junior Crown counsel was on his feet. "I associate myself with that remark of my learned friend."

Then Mudge's counsel rose at the defense table. "I, too, associate myself with that remark from my learned friend."

Then the court clerk, who had served the judge for too many years, and who—I would later learn—admired alcohol, rose unsteadily to his feet and turned to face Kincaid. "And I associate myself with those remarks of Mrs. Mudge."

I howled with laughter.

The only laughter under Kinky's glare.

And became—I am told—the youngest person ever thrown out of court.

It wouldn't be the last time.

I had found my calling.

The arena of the courtroom was my kind of battleground.

Jeffrey Kline, Esq.

Barrister-at-law.

Counsel to the scum of the earth.

Counsel for the damned.

No doubt the reason I recall what lured me to the law is that the Hangman stalking me tonight brings the Hanging Judge to mind. Kinky, in his own way, was a serial killer too.

Almost twenty years have passed since Mrs. Mudge exploded at that sadistic judge. The memory highlights the danger to those who practice criminal law from the wretches who suffer the consequences of what we do in court. Imagine Mrs. Mudge with a gun.

Looking back on my breakthrough murder case, I see that as the lesson I was destined to learn tonight. The case began with a hanging—*two* hangings actually—the hanging of Peter Bryce Haddon way back in 1993 and the hanging of Mary Konrad in Seattle sixteen days ago, on Halloween. If the Hangman succeeds tonight, it will *end* with a hanging too. *My* hanging, here in this house in the East End of Vancouver.

There!

Is that it?

The snick of a key in the lock?

Showtime, folks!

Is the psycho at the door . . . ?

Halloween

"Once upon a time," said Granny O'Grady, sitting with Mary in her lap on the porch of the farmhouse in eastern Washington, "there was a mischievous Irishman named Jack. One day, after he had too much whiskey to drink, Jack tricked the Devil into climbing up a tree for a juicy red apple. No sooner was the Devil in the treetop than Jack carved the sign of the cross on the trunk so he couldn't get down. Only by promising Jack that he would never claim his soul was the Devil able to escape. Eventually, Jack died and his soul went to heaven, but he was turned back from the gates because of all his pranks. When Jack tried to go to hell, the Devil rejected him too, shouting, 'Go back where you came from. I'll keep my promise to you.' But Jack was lost in the smoky dark and couldn't find the path, so he called out, 'How do I do that when I can't see the way?' The Devil responded by tossing Jack a live coal from hell. Jack, who had been eating a turnip, put it inside to make a lantern. Ever since then, on All Hallows Eve, Mary, my darling, Jack of the lantern has roamed the earth in an endless, ghostly search for his final resting place."

"A turnip?" said Mary.

"A turnip," Granny repeated.

"Then why carve jack-o'-lanterns out of pumpkins now?"

"Because of potatoes."

"Potatoes?" said Mary.

"*Lack* of potatoes, actually."

"I don't understand."

"Once upon a time," said Granny O'Grady, "a long time ago in Ireland, our ancestors were farmers known as Celts."

"Daddy plays Celtic music."

The old woman tweaked Mary's nose. "Because they were farmers, Celts worshipped Baal, the powerful sun god who made crops grow. But Baal had power only half the year, and come the end of October, the winter god began his six-month reign. He was the Prince of Darkness. He was the Lord of the Dead. He was the god who killed crops and brought cold, black nights. His name was Samhain, or Summer's End."

"How long ago, Granny?"

"More than two thousand years."

Grandmother and granddaughter sat rocking on the porch. Before them stretched the origins of Halloween in the crops gathered from the orchards and fields of O'Grady Farm. The fertile valley into which the apple trees dipped blazed fiery orange with autumn's color. Leaves falling from branches and pumpkins plumping in patches and shocks guarded by scarecrows were orange, orange, orange. Black was the shade of the cat in the small pioneer graveyard, and come night, black would be the vault of the sky, into which would rise the face of an orange harvest moon.

"November 1," said Granny O'Grady, "marked the end of autumn and the start of winter, so that's when Celts held their ancient harvest festival of Samhain. It was a supernatural time when barriers between them and the underworld vanished. Of all the nights of the year, sunset October 31 to sunrise the next morning was most feared. Evil spirits summoned by the Lord of the Dead were everywhere. Ghosts, goblins, devils and demons were about, so it was a night when dark forces were at work. Witches gathered in covens to celebrate black sabbaths...

"Cackle, Mary."

Mary cackled.

"That's the sound of a witch. Hiss, Mary."

Mary hissed.

"That's the sound of a demon. Sigh, Mary."

Mary sighed.

"That's the sound of a ghost. To drive the evil spirits away, Celts gathered together around blazing bonfires."

Mary imagined the huge fire her dad would light that night, down in the field next to the big red barn. The burning wood would crackle and hiss like witches and demons, the sharp smell of woodsmoke would hang in the night and sparks would fly up like fireflies into a black sky bursting with fireworks.

"Hoping to blend in with the spirits and not be noticed, Celts who ventured into the dark wore beast heads and skins, or costumed themselves to look like the demons they feared. Some of the demons tormented Celts by playing tricks on their homes to drive them mad, and the only way to stop that was to offer them treats of apples or sweets."

Fidgeting in Granny's lap, Mary was bursting at the seams to don her goblin garb and join other farm kids for the hayride tonight that would bounce them from door to door along the valley, where each homeowner would face the little demons' threat of "Trick or treat."

"Black is the shadow," said Granny O'Grady, "of death, mystery and magic. Black is the color of cats and bats and witches' cloaks. Evil spirits made evil people into cats, so Celts threw black cats into the fires of Samhain. Evil spirits lurked in black crows and ravens, so Celts hung straw-filled scarecrows on crosses in their fields. A coven of witches numbered thirteen, twelve witches and a grand master, so the number thirteen brought Celts bad luck. Ghosts crept from graveyards to haunt Samhain, so tombstones were used to weigh them down."

"Potatoes, Granny. You forgot potatoes."

"*Lack* of potatoes, Mary. Famine in Ireland. So Irishmen left the old country for North America, and with them brought the Celtic traditions of Halloween. The pumpkins they found on arrival were better than turnips, so that's why we use pumpkins to carve jack-o'-lanterns today."

With a Hershey bar in one hand, a Coke in the other, Mary Konrad, dressed like a witch, green face and so on, stood crying in the darkened living room of what would soon no longer be her Seattle home, gazing out at the city street spooked up for Halloween, as Mary O'Grady, the girl she had been, recalled the happier hauntings of her youth.

How had life gone so wrong?

Tears gushed again.

All because of a summons.

And Halloween.

"The Romans," said Granny O'Grady thirty years ago, "had a harvest festival to honor Pomona, their apple queen. Orange, too, was the color of Pomona's celebration, so when Rome conquered Britain, Pomona joined Samhain. That's why apples play an important part in Halloween, and why we Irish have Snap Apple Night."

Apples were an important crop at O'Grady Farm, so after the hayride and trick-or-treat, and after the bonfire and fireworks, the O'Grady family held its own apple festival, inviting neighbors from miles around. The adults drank apple cider and the kids drank apple juice, and Celtic music coaxed everyone to dance an Irish jig, and teens took part in time-honored games that predicted their romantic futures.

Snap apple, of course. Played with apples hung from the ceiling by strings, the boys below jumping like rabbits for a bite. The first to chomp was the first who would marry.

But marry whom?

Marry Mary?

That was predicted by bobbing for apples. Each girl set her marked apple afloat in a tub of water, then the boys, hands behind their backs, dunked for them. The girl who launched the apple a boy grabbed with his teeth was the girl he would marry.

Four years in a row, Bill Somerset had chomped Mary's apple.

If there was any doubt about Bill and Mary, it was dispelled by the apple-paring test. Mary peeled an apple without breaking the skin, then swung that paring three times above her head, before she threw it over her magical shoulder. "By this paring," she wished, "let me discover the initial of my one true lover."

The peel formed a W.

For William.

For Bill.

Looking back from now to then, Mary remembered another superstition. "Never strip every apple from its tree," said Granny O'Grady. "That's unlucky. An apple or two must be left hanging for the birds. If an apple is found in the orchard come spring, there will be a death in the family."

The spring Mary married Bill an apple remained on one tree, and two days after the blossom wedding Granny died.

If Mary could turn back the hands of time, she would still be married to hard-working farmer Bill, having never left the valley where she grew up. But Mary was the lusty half of that relation-ship, built like those sexy country queens on record covers, so she had tired of cock-crow dawns and work that hurt her looks, and she eventually forsook Bill for the bright lights of Seattle.

It was the sad tale of many a country tune.

Had Mary not moved to the city, Mary would not have been summoned. Had Mary not been summoned, she would not have been mugged. Not mugged in the city sense of being waylaid on the street, but mugged morally in the sense of being forced against her will. Had she not felt intimidated by the pressure of the others to buckle before Halloween slipped away, she would not have made the biggest mistake of her life, and she wouldn't feel this uncontrollable urge to eat, eat, eat. If eating had not ballooned her up to twice the size she was when she married Dag, her second marriage would not have hit the rocks. Dag would not be drinking. The house would not be for sale. And Mary would not be crying her heart out now, tears streaking the green makeup on her face that masked the black shiner around her eye from Dag's fist.

The Hershey bar was gone.

Mary drained the Coke.

Then Mary waddled from the window to the entry hall to grab another chocolate bar from the bowl of treats.

Eating made her feel better.

Eating made her fat.

If only her eating disorder were anorexia.

With Mary, however, guilt forced her to munch, munch, munch.

To distract her mind from the despair she felt about her life, Mary Konrad had thrown herself into Halloween. The entry hall of the front door was now the creepy haunt of a wicked, withered witch. Black paper lined the ceiling and walls, and black lights made everything white glow unnaturally. Against the black, she had hung a skeleton of rattling bones and an army of eyeballs dangling from strings. Each eye was a ping-pong ball painted with a black pupil and a blue iris besieged by a network of red veins. A huge black cauldron boiled with dry ice, and from stereo speakers came whispers, sighs, groans, sobs, shrieks and screams.

Hanging the skeleton had made her cry.

With an Oh Henry bar in one hand and a Milky Way in the other, Mary returned to the living room to draw the blinds. The first of the trick-or-treaters were out on the sidewalk, three small ghosts in flapping sheets coming her way, followed by an adult wearing Grim Reaper robes, the hood a black maw that masked his or her face.

Death approaches, Mary thought as she shut out the night.

I wonder if the kids in the sheets know *why* it is Halloween?

That was the curse of the city.

Disconnection from roots.

People went through the motions without asking what they were doing.

Halloween in the city had become as commercial as Christmas.

Spend, spend, spend.

But underneath, bankrupt.

Back in the hall, waiting for the knock of the ghosts on the door, Mary plunked the pointed hat on her head, stirred the cauldron to swirl up more mist and recalled what Granny O'Grady had told her on the porch.

"Christianity came to the Celts with the Roman Catholic Church. What had been the Samhain festival of November 1 was declared from then on to be All Saints'—or All Hallows—Day. So the night before became All Hallows Eve, and that was shortened over time to Halloween."

Knock, knock . . .

Knock, knock . . .

Death was at the door.

Mary let out a cackle like the cackle she had once croaked for Granny.

"Come in, come in, my lovelies," Mary beckoned in a creaky voice.

The knob turned.

The door squeaked open.

A rusty hinge was taped to it for effect.

In stepped the first ghost, cautiously, eyes in the sheet slits fixed on Mary. The white sheet, the white eyes, glowed eerily in the ultraviolet glare. As the ghost approached the table of treats next to the bubbling cauldron, the shadow of the witch fell over it.

"Who's Samhain?" Mary asked, barking out lusty cackles.

The head in the sheet shook.

"Away with you!"

The ghost grabbed a Mars bar and vamoosed.

"Who's Pomona?" Mary asked the second spook.

"Dunno," said the hole in the sheet.

"Away with you, too!"

Off ran the ghost with a tiny packet of M&Ms.

"Do you know what Halloween means?" Mary asked the third specter.

Another shake of the sheet.

"Begone!" she croaked.

And it was with a Snickers bar.

The mist from the cauldron was really swirling now, filling the front hall with murky iridescence. Mary heard the hinge squeak as the door swung shut, then tensed as that was followed by the clicking of the deadbolt.

A hand appeared in the mist.

Pointing a gun at her.

"Ask me"—Mary jumped—"if *I* know what Halloween means."

The outline of the Grim Reaper materialized in the fog. Whoever it was had used the ghosts to hide behind. The voice came from beyond a mask buried in the hood. The closer Death came to Mary, the deeper into the dark maw penetrated the black light, until the mask jumped out at her.

What Mary faced was this:

The Lamp of Freedom

Vancouver
Tonight

Jeffrey Kline, Esq.

Barrister-at-law.

Hear my name in those terms and what do you think? Upper-class kid, West Side education, candy-ass school like Lord Byng or Prince of Wales, law degree from UBC out on Point Grey?

Dollars to donuts, you think I'm a silver spoon. But you're wrong.

The East End is me.

So let me tell you what it was like to grow up in Strathcona.

In the beginning, Vancouver was a Native campsite called Kumkumalay. Translation: "Big-leaf maple trees." In 1865, Captain Stamp selected the site for a sawmill. Shortly thereafter, Gassy Jack arrived. Gassy got his name from talking incessantly when he was drunk, and rolling in with him came the only barrel of whiskey for fifteen miles. He offered some idle mill workers all they could guzzle in a sitting if they would help him build a pub, and twenty-four hours later the Globe Saloon was awash in alcohol. With the harbor in front and False Creek behind, the bar, situated where five paths joined to form Maple Tree Square, soon became the anchor of Vancouver's skid row: a row of flophouse hotels and notorious booze cans named after the skid road used for dragging logs up to Hastings Mill. What spawned around the row was a rowdy, rough-and-tumble shantytown, where loggers, miners and fishermen could drink and get laid. A sailor boozing at Gassy Jack's became our first murder, and lots of those killed in this city today still die within a few blocks of Hastings and Main.

Got the picture?

The history of my 'hood?

And that was the golden age, before Strathcona went to shit.

A little geography will put me in place.

North to south you have the mountains, the harbor, the city and the river. South from the harbor to False Creek and beyond, Main Street cuts Vancouver into west and east. West is where the British spread in those early years, and where the powers that be in this town wheel and deal today. East is where the have-nots scurried to find a home, and where the down-and-outs currently huddle.

The West Side and the East End...

Worlds apart.

Lord Strathcona was a British imperialist who made a bundle off the Hudson's Bay Company and the Canadian Pacific Railway. Named for him, the 'hood, you might say, got the sweat off his balls and little more. Strathcona was the entry point for floods of immigrants: Japanese, Chinese, Italians and Jews, Scandinavians, Ukrainians, blacks, Hispanics and so on. A cosmopolitan pot-pourri, liberals might say. A welcome example of the brotherhood of man. A 'hood boasting the Ritter Project for those of low income, in one splendid apartment of which I grew up.

Hey, I was just a kid.

What did I know?

You want to call it renewal, go ahead.

To me, the Ritter Project was a squalid slum.

I never knew my father. He screwed my mom and ran. I hardly knew my mother. She OD'd on heroin when I was six. All I knew was Gram, who used to be a whore. A pro on the row who thought the worst of men. Still, I think Gram did her best for me.

We lived in this claustrophobic box high up in the tower. To call the elevator, you sparked two live wires together, then ascended through a gagging succession of smells, like bad cooking, vomit, piss and condoms used by teens at night on the stairs. A hot summer day would combine them into the worst stench of all and waft it up to our open windows. Close the windows and you would roast to death. Cockroaches were rife, and every light left unprotected was broken. As for graffiti, guess how I learned to read?

The tower was surrounded by several low-rises. All were hell-holes, but the tower was the worst. I remember one day the cops caught the kid next door shoplifting a coat, so he was driven home to be placed in the care of his parents. The cops arrived to find his father passed out drunk at the door, so pissed he hadn't been able to find his key. The kid found the key in his dad's pocket and helped him inside, the upshot being that the cops left the parent in the care of the child.

Actually, the kid was boosting stuff for his older brother. Since young offenders merely got a slap on the wrist, the hard-core punks stayed out of jail by using them as mules.

I envied the kid next door.

At least he had a dad.

Another day, the cops responded to a "shots fired" on the floor below. While searching for the shooter, they found two youngsters living alone in one apartment. A hunt revealed their mother shacked up with a biker over town. Garbage was piled four feet high in every room. A maze of corridors was how the kids moved around. To get rid of the smell, the project had to take the apartment out. Literally take it out—walls, ceiling, floor, guts and all.

We hoped that would put an end to the cockroaches, but it didn't.

Lord Strathcona Elementary was my school. The lord drove the last spike of the CPR in 1885, according to Mr. Pritchard in socials class. One day the kid sitting beside me was bored by such history, so he set fire to the hair of the kid in front of him. Mr. Pritchard broke his leg in a skiing accident. On crutches, he worked at the blackboard with his back to us. The kid on my other side pushed a pin through an eraser, then threw it full force to jab Mr. Pritchard behind the ear. I recall his crutches flying out like the wings of a bird. Next time we saw him, both legs were in casts and he was confined to a wheelchair.

Ergo, he took our class to court.

To drive home what happened to kids who refused to toe the line.

Three things struck me as we sat in Kinky's court. One, a court wasn't a solemn, somber, serious place. It was the best free show in town. Two, the lawyers were all chubby, while Mudge was a skinny and ill-fed runt like me. The fat cats of the legal profession had never missed a meal. And three, the lawyers were a network of pantywaists: powdered and pampered West Side boys, weaned off silver spoons. I knew I could take the whole lot down in an East End brawl.

A West Side brawl?

That's an oxymoron.

Then and there, I knew I could better them at the legal game.

The problem was how to get from the Ritter Project to the bar.

Britannia Secondary was my high school. Gangs were endemic to the East End. The H Squad (or Heavy Squad)—police armed with baseball bats—had crushed the Clark Park Gang by my time, and the consequent void was filled by gangs of ethnic refugees. Hispanics from Central America hefted *cojones* as big as grapefruit. Vietnamese boat kids were pirates at heart. The Chinese were trying to get into triads. And the Russian mafia was worse than Don Corleone's. Other whites were "sidewalk bikers" hoping to make the gang, for the Angels by then had absorbed Satan's

Choice, the Coffin Cheaters and Hell's Rebels. This being Canada, guns were rare. But then, a gun is the coward's weapon of choice. Too much distance between cause and effect. Those into wet work preferred a knife, thrilling to shivers that shuddered along the blade. Junk peddled on the street had sunk to a measly 1.5 percent, so T&Rs were the popular high. T stood for Talwin, a synthetic opiate analgesic painkiller, and R stood for Ritalin, a stimulant. A T&Rs was mixed by crushing two and two, and was mainlined like heroin. Ritalin gave it a nasty edge, which pumped the punks for vicious work with their flashing blades.

That was the minefield of my school.

Study, study, study—that was me.

Work, work, work to pay my way.

Stay alive; grab the chance; keep your nose clean.

And hey, I made it.

Read my card.

Jeffrey Kline, Esq.

Barrister-at-law.

Every chance I got to break away from school would find me sitting in a court gallery, absorbing more law than I did at UBC. The provincial courthouse was nearby on Main, and it was home to another "hanging judge." No capitals, he was lowercase, to distinguish him from Hanging Judge Kinky of high-court fame.

This hanging judge got his name from sentencing a shoplifter who was a deaf-mute. Sign language explained the proceedings to the accused. "Don't tell the accused what I'm about to say," the judge warned the translator before he passed sentence.

"The sentence imposed by this court is that you be taken from here to the place whence you came, and there be kept in close confinement until the first day of the next month, and upon that date that you be taken to the place of execution, and that you be there hanged by the neck until you are dead. And may God have mercy on your soul."

The judge grinned slyly. "I've always wanted to say that," he said. Then he passed the *real* sentence, a nominal fine, and told the translator to translate to the deaf-mute.

There must be a kick to be had from passing a sentence of death, for the next time I sat in that judge's court I witnessed a variation.

A member of a youth gang taunted the judge. "This is my first offense. You can't do nothin' to me. Let's get this over so I can party, eh?"

The judge pronounced the same death sentence that he had on the deaf-mute, then swept his arm toward the holding cell. "Take him down," he ordered.

No sooner was the stunned teen whisked away than the prosecutor was on her feet. "You can't do that, Judge. We don't have the death penalty, and the maximum for that offense is six months."

"The court of appeal will reverse me," agreed the hanging judge. "But I sure put the scare of hell into that little jerk."

You think I'm kidding?

I shit you not.

Except for the nuthouse, prison and the stock exchange, the legal profession has more psychopaths than anywhere else.

The word "fuck" plays a major role in court. I sat in on a new judge's first day on the bench. Having just thrown the book at an armed robber, he realized that he had failed to ask the convict if he had anything to say before sentence. So he asked him after.

"Yeah, I got somethin' to say," the con shot back. "You're a fuckin' asshole!"

The judge got up from the bench and was leaving court, then he stopped, turned and said to the man, "That, sir, was just a lucky guess."

Another day, I had a seat in Tin Ear's court. He was dubbed Tin Ear because he was hard of hearing. "Do you have anything to say before I sentence you?" asked the elderly judge.

"Fuck all!" replied the con in the dock.

"What did he say?" Tin Ear asked the court clerk.

"He said, 'Fuck all,' my lord."

"That's strange," retorted the judge. "I was sure he said something."

Another day, I was sitting in Prissy's court. The judge got the name Prissy because he didn't like dirty words. A complainant in a rape case was on the witness stand. She testified: "Then the accused said something disgusting to me."

"Stop!" ordered Prissy. "There are students in my court today. Crown counsel will give you pen and paper to write down what he said."

Scribble, scribble. The witness wrote.

The note with the offending words passed from the complainant to the court clerk, then up to Prissy, who shook his head with disgust, then down to the lawyers, who held it so I could see the words from the gallery, then across to the jury, where, juror to juror, it was passed along.

What the woman had scribbled was this: "Hang on to your hat, baby. I'm going to fuck you till your ears fall off."

Seated in the back row of the jury box was a buxom babe. Bouffant red curls tumbling down in ringlets. Green eyes buried behind false lashes. Bee-sting lips and tits out to there. She read the note and raised a brow that said all men are pigs, then nudged the juror beside her in the ribs and passed it on.

He was a geezer, Methuselah's age. Bald but for a fringe of hair, with a big Adam's apple. The trial had put him to sleep and he awoke from slumber to find the babe in the next seat slipping him a note. Reading it produced an effect like Viagra. He gave her a smile, gave her a wink, then folded the note and put it in his pocket, sitting back with a look of forthcoming satisfaction.

Sometimes I'd ride the bus to New Westminster so I could watch a yee-haw case from the rural Bible belt up the Fraser valley.

My favorite was the farmer who was charged with bestiality

after he got amorous with one of his cows. The offense was witnessed by the preacher next door. Testimony was that the farmer placed a milk stool behind the cow, then he stood on it to perform the act. Coitus interruptus was the result when the cow kicked over the stool to knock her lover on his ass.

A farmer in the jury box slapped his knee.

"They'll do that every time!" he chortled.

Ah, yes, juries.

Those flickering lamps of freedom.

Who can put it better than Britain's Lord Devlin? "No tyrant could afford to leave a subject's freedom in the hands of twelve of his countrymen. So that trial by jury," wrote the law lord, "is more than an instrument of justice and more than one wheel of the constitution: it is the lamp that shows that freedom lives."

The trouble with flickering lamps is that some snuff out.

And that, truth be known, is what led to my breakthrough murder case.

When you think about it, is trial by jury not an anachronism in this technical age? Twelve—why twelve?—folks are chosen at random to try an accused. Weighing evidence is new to them, and some—as a wag once delicately put it—are "unaccustomed to severe intellectual exercise or to protracted thought." Yet these twelve act as the sole judges of the facts, and they need give no reasons for what they decide.

In the beginning, a juror was a man compelled by the king to take an oath. The Normans brought the procedure to England in 1066. At first, a juror was a man who knew the facts, and the oath compelled him to tell the king the truth on penalty of damnation. King Henry II turned jurors into a jury, for if there was a dispute over land, the first man to get twelve oaths in his favor won. That was the origin of trial by jury, including the rule that the verdict of twelve must be unanimous. Later, juries evolved from facts known to evidence received.

So why twelve?

HANGMAN

Why not eleven or thirteen?

Because there were twelve Apostles?

The twelve disciples of Jesus Christ?

And does it not follow, if that's so, that there may be a Judas in the jury room?

Looking back on my breakthrough murder case, I see that anachronism is how it all began. Like I said, the case began with *two* hangings: the hanging of Haddon back in 1993 and the hanging of Mary Konrad in Seattle last Halloween.

Lawyers are like vultures. We circle overhead, watching the legal landscape for bones of the dead to pick. Our picking ground is the arena of the courtroom, where, if you're on the defense side of the bar, those trying to deny you a good feast are the guardians of the law. With meaty bones to pick and a worthy player on the other side to defeat, there is no greater thrill than a big *win!*

Sixteen days ago, last Halloween, I was a hungry vulture circling on the fringe.

Soon there would be gruesome bones to pick on the picking ground, guarded by a worthy player on the other side.

Though neither of us knew it then, Inspector Zinc Chandler and I were on a collision course, and the outcome of our courtroom battle would focus the Hangman's rage on me.

Is the handle turning?

Or am I seeing things?

Is this the climax of the case?

Is the psycho creeping in ... ?

Gallows Game

Inspector Zinc Chandler of Special X was standing at the curb in front of the hotel, waiting for Detective Ralph Stein to arrive, when a car pulled up and a tough, good-looking woman gave him the eye. Leaning over from the wheel, she rolled down the curb-side window. "Zinc Chandler, I presume?"

"And who are you?"

"Detective Maddy Thorne. I'm your date instead of Ralph."

A taxi honked behind her.

"Climb in. I don't bite."

The Mountie opened the door and sat in the passenger's seat. The car gunned away from the curb before he pulled the door shut. From the corner of his eye, Zinc looked the driver over. Muscular body, dressed in jeans and a black leather jacket.

"How'd you know it was me?"

"You look like a Canuck. Ralph said I'd recognize you by your hair."

Zinc's natural steel gray hair had been that color since birth. Its metallic tint was responsible for his given name. The business suit he sported tonight was of the same hue. Judging from the fes-tive costumes roaming the streets outside, he might be the most conservative-looking man in Seattle.

"So where's Ralph?"

"On a stretcher. Going to the hospital."

"What?" said Zinc. "I spoke to him at three. Don't tell me he took a bullet for the Job?"

"Nothing so heroic. But I'm sure it hurts as much. Halloween's a bad night, so we all work. Before leaving home this afternoon, Ralph scaled a ladder to clean his second-story eaves. Some of the slimy leaves he plucked from the gutter fouled the rung of the ladder directly beneath his shoes, so when he stepped down to descend—pardon the gallows humor—the step became a *giant* leap for mankind, to quote our first man on the moon. Broken ankles should keep Ralph in hospital traction for a few weeks."

"Ha!" said Zinc. It wasn't a laugh. "Your hospital system's a hell of a lot more compassionate than ours. In Vancouver, Ralph would be shown the door as soon as he was splinted and drugged."

"Anyway, that's why you're riding shotgun with me. I don't have Ralph as a partner, and you need to be fed and delivered to the airport."

"A cab's okay, Maddy."

"The fuck it is. This is Seattle. We're *hospitable* here."

"As Ralph is learning."

Which made her laugh.

The ice was broken, at poor Ralph's expense.

Maddy braked for a stream of monstrous pedestrians in a crosswalk. Headhunters, ghouls, cutthroats, rippers, zombies and evil eyes. One of the ghouls glared into the car and made a face at them. Zinc wondered if he and Maddy looked like thugs to the maskers, for The Job had definitely left its mark on both cops. Rugged and sharp-featured, his face was hard and gaunt. Forty years of life and two serious wounds—a bullet to the head and a knife in the back—had marred Zinc's once boyish good looks. Six foot two and almost 200 pounds, he had acquired his lean physique from working the family farm in Saskatchewan as a youth. Something about Zinc made people want him on their side, for instinct told them he would be a deadly adversary if the knife were at his throat.

He sensed the same in Maddy.

"Macha" female cops—like their macho male brethren—say "fuck" a lot. Listening to them is like going to see a Hollywood action film in which *every* character mouths "fucking this" or "fucking that" a zillion times before the credits roll. You know the director behind the film is a coked-up wreck, pacing back and forth as he gropes his own groin, boasting to the cast and crew that his will be the "fucking toughest film ever made." If Mr. Tough could see himself as others do, he too might question whether there was enough down there to grope.

The same applies to macha cops who utter "fuck" a lot. It comes across as a phony front meant to impress, and has the effect of undermining the actual toughness they possess.

But not Maddy.

She didn't give a fuck.

Zinc knew the word came to her as easily as "the" or "and."

This was a woman who definitely could take care of herself, and most likely take care of you in the worst situation.

She would be a *good* partner.

The crosswalk was clear of monsters and the signal had changed to green. Again, the car gunned away from a stop with decisive determination. Zinc suspected Maddy drove herself as hard as she did the wheels.

"Steak sound tempting? I know the best diner for beef."

"Steak sounds great. I'm in a carnivorous mood."

"Special X, huh? Ralph says you're a top dog with the Mounted's elite?"

"Ralph exaggerates."

"Ralph is down to earth."

"Literally, from what happened this afternoon."

This time, they *shared* a chuckle at poor Ralph's expense. If you're a cop, you find your laughs wherever you can.

"What does the X stand for?"

"External," responded Zinc. "The Special External Section of the Mounted Police investigates cases with links outside Canada. Because we also hunt the psychos, some say the X stands for Extreme."

"What brings you to Seattle?"

"A slew of cases. Some with the Bureau. Some with you. We have this deadly doctor with the fitting name of Dr. Twist. He was charged with murdering an elderly patient at his clinic for her money. He walked when he was acquitted by a Vancouver jury. We now have reason to believe he influenced that verdict by seducing one of the jurors."

"You mean he was screwing her *during* the trial?"

"Yeah, we caught it on tape."

"Naughty, naughty. The doc's a lady-killer in more ways than one."

"There may be trouble with the warrant that put in the bug, so we're looking for backup that's not a wiretap. Seems they snuck away to Seattle just after he was acquitted, so I asked Ralph to canvass local hotels. He hit pay dirt at the ritzy one where you picked me up tonight."

"They were guests?"

"For two days. Positive IDs."

"Bye, bye, juror."

"Bye, bye, doc."

"How do you know Ralph?"

"We jointly worked a case. A pimp recruiting teenage girls for sex across the border."

"Before my time."

"A few years back."

"Now, about that steak. What time's your flight to Vancouver?"

"Ten-fifteen."

"It's tight, but you'll make it if we go straight to the diner. I'll phone ahead and put the order in for two specials. How do you like your meat?"

"Medium rare," said Zinc.

As Maddy fished the cellphone out of her jacket pocket, it rang in her hand.

"Uh-oh," she said to the Mountie. "Thorne," she answered the caller. "Yeah, I know where that is. Right. Got it. I'll get there as soon as I can."

"Duty calls?" asked Zinc as she rang off.

"Yeah. A hanging. Want to come along?"

Judge to judge, cop to cop, professional courtesy rules. If a foreign judge visits a trial, he or she is offered a seat on the bench beside the judge presiding. If a foreign cop is present when a squeal comes in, he or she is invited to go see the stiff. Only another professional grasps the stress of the Job, so—since it's us against them—such courtesy offered calls for courtesy in return.

"Let's go, partner," Zinc said.

Patrol cars had cordoned off the block by the time Det. Madeline Thorne of Homicide arrived. The blue standing guard recognized her, and moved aside to clear the way so Maddy and Zinc could pass through. Slowly she cruised along the street in the unmarked car, closing on a knot of mid-block gawkers dyed red-blue red-blue by flashing wigwags on the roofs of the first-response vehicles snouted into the curb. The block was a blue-collar neighborhood serving the Boeing plant, and some of those milling about probably built planes. The houses were small and pushed together, and seemed to date from the Second World War. You'd think that war was still being waged by the boom of fireworks exploding overhead, raining down bursts of white, purple and green. The rat-a-tat-tat of machine guns peppered surrounding blocks when firecrackers were set off in series, and pungent fingers of cordite smoke gripped the dark. Screams of the dying grew louder as Maddy braked the car, gibbering up to ungodly shrieks as she angled into the curb, clipped on her ID and got out with the Mountie.

"Who lives next door?"

The question was asked by the crowd-control cop at this end of the walk to the murder scene.

"I do," said one of the gawkers.

"Then show some respect. Your neighbor's dead, sir. Silence those screams."

A beer drinker from the look of his ruddy face and rotund belly, the disgruntled man indicated a stereo speaker affixed to his house. "It's on a sensor. Movement sets it off."

"I don't care if Mr. Spock on the good ship *Enterprise* is at the controls. What I'm saying is let's have no ... more ... screams."

Beer Belly belched.

"The beam cuts across my walk and hers. It's you cops coming and going that prompts the screams."

"Is there a problem?"

Beer Belly turned.

And found himself eye to eye with the no-nonsense glare of a don't-mess-with-me woman.

"Who are you?" he asked the intruder.

Beer fumes billowed.

Maddy stood firm.

"Detective Thorne. Homicide. Who are you?"

"Joe," said the neighbor.

"Joe who?" she asked, pulling out her notebook and flipping it open to the page after the rubber band. She poised her pen.

"Hey, what is this?"

"Why'd you dislike her, Joe?"

"Dislike who?"

"Your dead neighbor."

"Who says I disliked her?"

"Actions speak louder than words. Would a neighbor who liked his neighbor hurl screams at her house on the night she died? Or would he be civilized enough to stop the racket himself?"

"You think *I* killed her?"

"Did you, Joe?"

"Hell, no."

"You act like it."

"It's Halloween."

"I *know* it's Halloween."

"All I'm saying is you got no right to spoil it. I paid a lot of money for those screams."

"Joe *who?*" Maddy said.

"All right. I'll kill 'em."

"Kill who?" Maddy asked.

"The screams," Joe answered. "You want to know who killed her"—he jerked his head at his neighbor's house—"speak to her husband."

Joe turned and jostled through the crowd clustered on the sidewalk in front of both his home and his neighbor's. He angled up the walk that led to his front door and cut the beam across the path that set off the screams. As Halloween shrieks shrilled from the outside speaker, several onlookers laughed amid the masquerade.

Some of the costumes showed a lack of imagination, a quick fix of plucking something off the shelf in Kmart or Wal-Mart or some such store. Others were creative. A woman balanced six-month-old pumpkins on her hips, each twin bundled in an orange felt Snugli, with triangular eyes, a similar nose and a mouth of pegged teeth stitched in black on each tummy. Green leaf hats were tied under drool-covered chins. A mummy swaddled head to foot with hospital bandages held the hand of an ogre with a third eye painted on its forehead. Creepy surgical tools made from kitchen implements like an old eggbeater, a spatula and a turkey baster hung from the belt of a witch doctor. Purple balloons enshrouded one tyke to make him a bunch of grapes. His mom carried a wine bottle. If Maddy were to award a prize for best getup, the winner would be a dad with his daughter sitting on his shoulders. He was chalked white, with sunken black eyes, and his left arm was gilded gold. A huge hypodermic was stuck in the golden arm. The girl astride his shoulders was costumed as the cutest little monkey you ever saw. Together, dad and daughter were a wasted heroin junkie with the monkey on his back.

"You," Thorne said, recognizing a familiar face in the crowd.

"Me, Detective?"

"Yes, you. Come here."

Justin Whitfield left the crowd, which strained to listen in. Maddy turned to Zinc and said, "Give me a moment," then led the reporter along the sidewalk, out of earshot.

"You got here fast."

"It's my job, Maddy."

"My job too. More than yours."

"Then you should listen to dispatch as diligently as I do. You'd be surprised by some of the scoops I've picked up by blending into a crowd milling at a murder scene. Particularly if it's a neighborhood clutch like this."

"The husband?"

"The husband."

"Fill me in," said Thorne.

"The happy couple moved here about a year ago. The honeymoon was over almost from the start. He's the sort of man who wants a looker on his arm. The kind who sees a pretty wife as evidence of his own virility. His wife was slim when they moved in, but she soon began to thicken. The heavier she got, the more he berated her. The story is she always had a chocolate bar in her mouth. I'd say something was eating at her, and the way she coped with it was through an eating disorder. He liked booze. They began to fight. The rows disturbed their neighbors. And last month he stomped out. What he shouted back at her, according to the neighbors, was 'I ought to butcher you for the fat pig you are.'"

"How long were they married?"

"About a year."

"Names?"

"The vic's Mary Konrad. Her husband's Dag."

"Know where Dag lives?"

"I'm working on it."

"Keep working while I take a look inside."

"From what I hear, the scene's a slaughterhouse. *I ought to butcher you for the fat pig you are.*"

"You ought to be a cop."

"So you keep saying."

"Anyone see the husband near the house tonight?"

"No, but he could have approached in costume. What better night to kill someone than Halloween? Only night of the year when you can walk around in disguise, and door securities are relaxed."

"Anything heard?"

"Yeah, a lot of screams. Trick-or-treaters crossed Joe's beam all night."

Another round of fireworks exploded overhead. *Boom, boom, boom!* The deafening din dampened conversation. The cop watched the reporter turn a kaleidoscope of colors. His sandy hair and blue eyes flared a rainbow spectrum. Justin was older than Maddy by several years: well into as compared to halfway through his thirties. A lightweight in build, he was no taller than her, and he wore the uniform of reporters everywhere: windbreaker, open-throat denim shirt, corduroy trousers and sneakers. For as long as Maddy had been a cop, they had worked like a team. A police reporter needs a deep throat with access to the facts, while a cop needs a private detective for off-the-record snooping. He was Thorne's leg up through the glass ceiling, and she had made him the *Star*'s star reporter.

"Here's the ME. Catch you later, Justin."

"I'll be waiting for a description of the abattoir inside."

"If it bleeds, it leads?"

"You ought to be a reporter."

"So you keep saying."

The medical examiner's car cruised down the street with an escort. Lumbering along beside it lurched three walking dead, jeans filthy from having crawled out of a muddy graveyard, bullet holes and knife slits dribbling poster paint from their zombie hearts, faces gray, lips black, and dirty hair squirming with spaghetti al dente as worms.

The car parked at the curb and Ruthless Ruth got out.

"Fitting escort," Maddy greeted her.

"Naw, they got it wrong. The chest wounds indicate murder. So there'd have been an autopsy and each should have a suture stitched from behind both ears up over the crown of the skull to show where I removed each of the little fuckers' brains."

Ruthless Ruth was the nickname Homicide detectives bantered behind Ruth Lester's back. Lester the Les was another sobriquet. Your average Homicide cop doesn't care about political correctness. Day in, day out, a Homicide bull (cow, too) wades through bloody messes left by what one human being has done to another, and he must be excused if he cynically calls something what it is, instead of by some wishy-washy term that has no meaning.

Homicide cops are crass.

And honesty is dying.

Maddy Thorne couldn't have cared less what went on at home in Ruth Lester's bed were it not for the discomforting fact that the ME wished her sex partner to be Maddy, and came on to the detective whenever they met. Lester was a mannish woman in both dress and appearance, her hands and wrists those of a strangler, her pants with blazer those of a sports jock and her ham face with no makeup and maximum butch about as feminine as Sly Stallone playing Rambo. Head to toe, then toe to head, Ruth gave Maddy the twice-over.

"Looking good, Mads. Very Homicide cop."

"Can't do the job if you don't look the part."

"Been inside?"

"No."

"Let's see what the fuck's going on."

The ME took her by the elbow to guide her along the sidewalk. The fingers examined the bones. Was that a sigh?

Homicide cops are the elite in all police forces. No one becomes a cop to work anything less than first-degree murder, and killers by definition are the tough ones on the street. Male or female, Homicide cops must be tough too, for much of the work involves intimidation. Maddy got her toughness from the rough breaks in her life. Her dad was ground to hamburger when she was two, sucked off his feet into the whirling blades of a jet engine. Her mother remarried within a year, so the child was raised in Seattle with two stepbrothers from her stepfather's first marriage. He was a cold man who belittled his sons and resented her. By fourteen, Maddy had lost her virginity to one of the boys. It wasn't rape. Both teens had consented. It wasn't incest. Blood relatives they weren't. What it was was Maddy yearning for someone's love.

Tough love.

C'est la vie.

It had toughened Maddy.

What doesn't break you makes you stronger, she thought.

The boy was three years older.

And later he had died.

But as tough as Thorne could be as a Homicide cop on the street, she was frilly and pink compared with Ruthless Ruth. Of late, Maddy had suffered debilitating migraines that were aggravated by the stress of her job. Last night she had turned in early with codeine painkillers coursing through her veins. She must have overdosed, for the nightmare that followed had her stretched out naked on a cold slab in Seattle's morgue. It was after-hours on the graveyard shift. Not a sound to be heard in this realm of the dead, until a door opened, a door shut and a lock clicked. A shadow crept over Maddy's flesh as someone approached, then a hand began to probe her body from head to foot. Though she tried to move, rigor mortis froze her; Ruthless Ruth looked down at her with lust in her eyes and ran that intimate hand up Maddy's thigh. "Looking good, Mads," sighed the pathologist.

Maybe it was the migraine.

Maybe it was the drugs.

Whatever it was, Ruth gave Maddy the creeps.

Zinc, still standing where the Seattle detective had left him, read the body language between the two women and thought it best to wander over and introduce himself.

"Zinc Chandler," he said, holding out his hand. The mannish woman had to release her grip on Thorne's elbow to shake it in return.

"Ruth Lester," she said. "I'm the ME."

"Good to meet you. I'm Maddy's new partner."

Ruth glanced at Maddy, then back at Zinc. "You're a Homicide cop? How is it possible that we haven't met before?"

"I work in Vancouver. With the Mounted Police. Maddy and I had a dinner date until she caught this murder."

"He doesn't mean 'partner' like Ralph," Maddy cut in, slipping Zinc a warm smile for Ruth to see. "He means 'partner' in the looser sense."

Leaving the ME to make of that what she wished, the detective added, "A client awaits. Shall we all go in?"

Turning on her heels, Thorne led Ruth and Zinc up the walk.

The house was similar to the one in which Maddy had grown up. They climbed three steps to a pillared porch littered with jack-o'-lanterns. Flanked by evil orange grins, a blue stood guard at the door. "Brace yourselves," the woman warned as they entered the spooky haunted house in the hall. Their teeth aglow with black light, they angled left through the door to the living room.

Dying room was more like it.

"Sorry," said yet another female cop within. "I puked on the floor."

The ME whistled. "We've come a long way, baby."

At first Maddy missed the gist of what Ruth was saying, then the pathologist added, "He doesn't count," with a nod at Zinc, and that's when it struck her how far they'd come indeed. Excluding the Canadian, every player in this room—victim, blue, sawbones, dick—was female.

"'Bout time," said Thorne.

They sidestepped the vomit on the floor to move toward a ceiling beam that separated the living room from the dining room beyond. This beam was supported at both ends by wall struts and angle braces, like a double gallows. Screwed in the center of the beam was a pulley, and hanging from the pulley was a hangman's noose, and cinched within the hangman's noose was the neck of a woman. A heavy woman dressed in black, with the face of a witch.

"That's how they used to hang 'em before the long drop," said Ruth. "Her neck wasn't broken. Death was by slow strangulation."

"How do you know?" asked Maddy.

"Petechial hemorrhages above the ligature."

"Your eyes are better than mine."

"See those tiny blood spots in the whites of her eyes? If not for the green makeup, you'd also notice them on her face. Strangulation congests blood in the head, causing the eyes to bulge and blood vessels to rupture."

"So blood gushed from her mouth?"

"No, that's different. A closer look and you'll see her tongue's cut out."

Ruth's coming on to Maddy was annoying, but Maddy hadn't shut her down with a slap, for the truth was Ruth was the best ME around, and if she sought to impress Maddy, so much the better.

Women network better than men.

"Impress us, Ruth."

Lester winked at Thorne. "A pulley on the beam. A pulley on the floor. The killer tied the victim's hands behind her back, then fed the rope through the pulleys to ease traction, then hoisted her up with the noose around her neck. He'd need a pulley system for a heavy woman like this."

"Sounds like he knew her."

"Or stalked her," Zinc suggested.

"Whatever the reason," said Maddy, "this hangman came prepared. Screwing that pulley into the floor left those shavings."

"A lot of work," Ruth said, "to lynch somebody. There's the tongue. See it? In that pool of clotting blood under the foot."

"Nagging wife?" Zinc posed the question.

"Don't ask *me!*" That's *your* department, said the ME's frown.

"What's your take, Ruth?" This from Maddy.

"The pressure of the noose on her throat forced out her tongue. Her lips were lacerated by the slash that cut it off. The mouth wound bled profusely down her chin."

"She looks like a cross between a vampire and a witch. Something said by the victim must have pissed the off hangman."

"That would explain the tongue. But why sever the leg?"

"Damned if I know," Maddy said. "It obviously has something to do with the puzzle on the wall."

All eyes turned toward the bloody game.

The body hanging from the beam was missing a leg. The killer had used a hacksaw to cut it off. Draining blood dripped from the stump under the black dress to pool on the floor. The hacksaw lay beside the tongue in the pool. The severed leg had been kicked over against the wall. The muscles had contracted and the bone stuck out an inch. A chunk was chipped from the bone where it had snapped off the thigh. Blood that oozed out of the leg had been used by the hangman to draw the grisly gallows game on the wall.

The game was this:

GUESS IN TOMORROW'S PAPERS

HANGMAN

A as in Abattoir

Seattle
October 31

The way Maddy explained it to Zinc was this.

Justin had been a reporter a few years longer than Maddy had been a cop. He had covered the first case she had investigated. As it turned out, the squeal became a headline shriek, and this resulted in legs up the ladders of both careers. Since then, under strict rules, Maddy and Justin had worked hand in glove, feeding each other information of mutual benefit, and bouncing crimes around to place them in perspective.

Zinc understood.

He had the same relationship with Alexis Hunt, who would be waiting at home for him in the bed they shared in Vancouver.

Every cop needs a confidant *outside* the Job.

It keeps you sane.

"That's not how you play hangman," Justin Whitfield said.

"No," replied Maddy.

With Zinc in the back seat, the three of them sat in the detective's car, sipping Starbucks coffee from take-out cups. They were parked a few blocks away from the crime scene to avoid the stares of the sidewalk crowd.

"The way to start," Justin said, "is you draw an *empty*

gallows. Everything down to the end of the rope in this diagram."

Maddy had sketched a copy of the gallows game on the living-room wall into her police notebook. Justin traced the scaffold with his finger as he related how to play.

"The person who draws the gallows also thinks up a word puzzle, and he writes down a dash for each letter in the mystery."

"He becomes the hangman."

"Uh-huh," said Justin. "The challenger guesses a letter in the word puzzle. If the guess is a good one, the hangman fills that letter in above the appropriate dash."

"Or dashes," said Maddy, "if the letter occurs in the mystery more than once."

"If the guess is a bad one—"

"The hangman starts the hanging—"

"By drawing a circle for the head of the missing hanged man in the hangman's noose."

Justin traced the circle beneath the rope in the notebook sketch.

"Yeah," said Maddy. "It's coming back. The *right* way to play is the challenger gets five wrong guesses to solve the mystery. Head, body, both arms, then one leg. Every wrong guess adds to the hanged man. If the hangman gets to complete the drawing before his adversary can crack the word puzzle, the hangman wins the game. But if the challenger solves the mystery before a sixth wrong guess adds the other leg, he beats the hangman."

"What you've got here is a killer playing hangman *in reverse.*"

Justin traced the head, body, both arms and one leg in the notebook sketch.

"He starts with the man already hanged—"

"Woman," said the detective. "The vic's female."

"Are we talking the game or the crime?"

"Both," said Maddy.

Justin shook his head. "You want to *liberate* the game of hangman?"

"To avoid confusion."

"Isn't that what I'm doing? A man for the game. A woman for the crime. That way we keep straight which is which."

"Okay," she capitulated. "The killer starts with the man already hanged—"

"Then removes a leg."

"You mean he doesn't draw it?"

"Right," said Justin. "Hangman in reverse. Part of the body is removed, not added on."

"The game's a cheat," said Maddy.

"How so?" asked the reporter.

"The leg was butchered before we got to guess."

"Three words of five, five and six letters. What three words solve this puzzle?"

"I have no idea."

"So it's not a cheat. He knows you won't solve the mystery right away. And his game *is* hangman in reverse. If guess-before-he-adds is the right way to play, isn't cut-before-you-guess the reverse?"

"Whose side are you on?"

"Come on, Maddy. A story like this doesn't pass by every day."

"Say we make a guess."

"You have to, don't you? If you don't and he kills again, there'll be hell to pay."

"Say our guess is good. What then, Justin? Do we get another guess before he strikes again? And if that guess is sound, as are the next few, might we not solve the puzzle without a mistake? In which case, hangman in reverse *is* a cheat."

"Who says the hangman must be fair?"

A car crammed full of illuminated jack-o'-lanterns drove by. A horde of wicked grins glared out at them through steamy windows. The driver wore a jack-o'-lantern over his head.

"More to the point," said Zinc Chandler, "is the conundrum

of the chicken and the egg. Which came first? The crime or the game?"

"Ahhh," said the reporter.

"Run with it," said the detective.

"Was this woman killed to play the hangman game?" asked Zinc. "A *random* victim, so anyone would do? All the killer wanted was a corpse to pose the puzzle, a means to grab attention to taunt the police. Which means the word game has nothing *unique* to do with her. She's merely the first random victim of a serial killer."

"If the game came first," said Maddy.

"Right," said Zinc.

"So checking this woman's background is a dead-end waste of time."

The Mountie nodded.

"And if the crime came first?" asked the reporter.

"Then the game may hide a motive *unique* to her. It could be the hangman game is a double-blind. It taunts the police with that unique motive hidden in the puzzle, and masks the fact the hangman was specifically after *her* by making the woman's hanging look like a serial killing."

"In which case, checking her background isn't a waste of time," said Justin.

"And there could be an alternative twist," said Zinc. "What if the killer is hunting serial victims with the *same* unique motive? The victims wouldn't be random and the crimes would still come first, but outwardly it would appear that playing the hangman game is the motive behind a random killing spree. Not only would the real motive be specific to this victim, but it would be specific to every victim in the spree."

"A triple-blind?" said Maddy.

"Possibly."

"You really know your stuff."

"I told you, Special X is the psycho hunting unit of the RCMP."

Justin took out his notebook and licked his pen. Ballpoint ready to fill a page, he turned to Maddy and asked, "What's it like inside?"

"An abattoir."

"That bad?"

"Take it from me."

"Was the leg amputated while she was alive?"

"No," said the detective. "Not enough blood. If her heart was pumping, there would have been arterial spurts and venous sprays. What we found was passive dripping from her severed thigh."

"How much?"

"Half a pint."

"Doesn't sound like a bloodbath."

"It looked like a lot on the floor."

"Why just half a pint?"

"That's all there was to drain. According to Ruth, of the six to eight pints of blood in the human body at any given time, only a fifth is available to drain away from wounds."

"Where's the rest?"

"Capillaries."

"A fifth is more than a pint."

"Don't forget the hanging sacs of both arms and a leg, and the blood trapped in the head by the hangman's noose."

"How big was the pool?"

"Eighteen inches across."

"An abattoir? A slaughterhouse? Sounds like hype, Maddy."

The cop sighed. "You're jaded, Justin. Blood pools don't just form a surface skin. Active clotting goes on for an hour after death. The pool inside was still warm and congealing. Body parts—her tongue and her leg—were strewn about the room. Tell me a better way to describe the scene."

He paused to think of a word.

"Try *yuck!*" said Maddy.

The car full of jack-o'-lanterns cruised by again, going the opposite way. The grins on this side were those of happy pumpkins. Jekylls hiding Hydes.

"How was the leg cut off?"

"Hacksawed," she said.

"Details?" he asked.

The pen jotted notes.

"According to Ruth, the leg was disconnected by sawing through skin and muscles, as well as most of the femur bone. The bone broke when the blade was three-quarters in, like happens if you saw an unsupported board. When it snapped, a chunk was chipped out of the bone left in the dangling leg. The cut was high on the thigh, close to the ball-and-socket joint. The saw severed the rest of the flesh and the leg was tossed aside. Do you want *more* details?"

Maddy drained her coffee as Justin wiped mist off the windshield.

"The leg's a clue to which came first, the crime or the game," said the Mountie.

"How so?" asked Justin.

"Cut the leg off while she is alive and I'd say that shows hatred toward her personally."

"Or the killer's a sadist."

"Cut the leg off after death and it must be tied to the hangman game."

"Or the killer didn't want blood all over him."

"Why cut off that single limb unless it's linked to the puzzle?" asked Zinc.

"You're forgetting the tongue," Justin replied.

"That was to keep her quiet."

"Hardly necessary. A gag would do. Sound effects from the hall and the speaker screams next door covered any noise."

"I think it's the husband," Maddy said. "Most murders are committed by someone known to the victim. He and the vic were embroiled in a bitter divorce. He threatened to butcher her, and that's what happened. The cut-out tongue suggests getting even with a scold. And what better way to hide his motive than by posing as a serial killer? Thus the hanging, and the leg, and the madman's game. I wouldn't be surprised if the puzzle is gibberish."

"You'll want the husband's address. I got it from a neighbor," Justin said.

"Screaming Joe?"

"No, the other side."

The reporter flipped back in his notebook to find the address. The detective used a penlight to copy it into her notes after the sketch of the hangman game.

"Time of death?" asked Justin.

"Ruth won't commit. Blood settled by gravity had begun to discolor the hands and foot, so judging from that lividity, a good guess would be about an hour and a half before we saw the body."

"If that's the time frame, the same neighbor may have seen the killer."

"Where?"

"On the sidewalk out front of the vic's home."

"When?"

"About an hour before that time of death. Or two and a half hours before you went in."

"Description?"

"Sort of," Justin said. "The suspect was dressed in a hooded robe like the Grim Reaper. Whoever was in the costume wore a mask. The mask—and I quote—'was like a skull face, but wasn't a skull. It was the face in that famous picture.'"

"What famous picture?"

"She didn't know."

"Height?"

"Average. Hard to tell with the hood."

"Weight?"

"Unknown. Hard to tell with the robe."

"Color?"

"Black. The robe, not the person."

"She see the hands?"

"No, covered by gloves."

"Anything else?"

"The suspect carried a bag."

"What makes the neighbor think that may have been the killer?"

"Circumstantial inference from what she witnessed later. Her son is only two, so they went out to trick-or-treat early. As they walked from their house toward the front sidewalk, three kids in costume, followed by the Reaper, turned up the walk toward the house of her neighbor. She thought the Reaper was the parent of the kids, and led her son the opposite way at the sidewalk T. Later, she passed the same kids *without* the Reaper. And no one answered next door when the witness and her son knocked."

"Time she saw the suspect?"

"About five-thirty."

"Time she knocked on the door?"

"About six o'clock."

"The murder was called in at 6:53. Some trick-or-treaters saw the body through the open door. The killer must have been inside when the neighbor knocked at six, then escaped in costume, leaving the door ajar."

"It fits," said Justin as Maddy entered the timetable into her notes.

"Was the neighbor suspicious when no one answered the door?"

"No, she assumed Mary was answering the call of nature."

"The neighbor's name?"

"Gustafson. Sara and Rolf. Rolf's off traveling. He sells lumber."

"Okay," said Maddy, closing her notebook. "First I'll track down Mary's husband, then I'll talk to the neighbor."

"What of what you've told me *can't* I use?"

"The only hold-back evidence is the Hangman word puzzle. You can mention the game itself, but not the number of words or how many letters in each. If that got out and the game is valid, there could be copycat trouble."

"Are you going to guess in the papers?"

"Yes," said Maddy. "If only to throw the husband off guard. But as you warned, if the game is real, we can't afford not to."

"I get the scoop?"

"Of course, Justin. The best first guess must be a vowel."

"I read somewhere it's a consonant."

"Which one?"

"Don't recall."

"You're a big help."

"Which vowel?"

"Start at the start."

"*A*," said Justin.

"*A* as in abattoir," said the detective.

The Wolf Man

"You missed your flight," said Maddy.

"I lost track of time."

"There's a couch at my place."

"Thanks," said Zinc. "But if you don't mind, I'll tag along. This case has its hook through my cheek."

"Mind?" said Maddy. "You put me at ease. Without Ralph, I'm minus a partner tonight. You'll do fine if Dag gets rough."

"I'll stay in the background. It's your show."

"A Horseman for backup. That's *real* cavalry."

They parked the unmarked car within a block of the address Justin had provided. Dag Konrad was living in a four-floor, run-down, red brick walk-up in an older part of Seattle. A "Monster Mash" was well underway on one of the upper stories, judging from the boisterous drunks who staggered down the stairs as the cops went up. While Bobby "Boris" Pickett sang about a "graveyard smash," a smashed Dracula slopping a Bloody Mary almost pitched headfirst down the steps, but with his other hand he managed to grasp the bodice of the Vampirella with him, liberating both breasts as he passed out at her feet.

The cops stepped over him.

"My dress!" cried the vamp.

"His slip's showing," Maddy said as they brushed by.

The party was in the apartment registered to Dag Konrad, husband of the vic. *Out* of the flat too, for it had spilled into the hall. Dag, it seemed, was not crying in his beer over breaking up with his wife. If he knew Mary Konrad was dead, it appeared to be cause to celebrate, for the Wolf Man who was pointed out to them as the fellow they sought was dancing wildly to the tune after "Monster Mash." Crowding the dance floor was an array of monsters old and new, with classics like the Phantom of the Opera and twin brothers dressed as Dr. Jekyll and Mr. Hyde bumping butts with a pantheon of modern mutants, Jason, Freddy and the ghostly one out of *Scream.* "Wild Thing" brought forth the wolfishness in Dag, for as he guzzled beer so foam frothed around his hairy mouth like rabies, his wayward hand pinched bottoms and he dry-humped passing thighs.

A man that oversexed, thought Maddy, undoubtedly has hair on his palms.

A wife gone fat would be a real-life monster for a sexist like Dag.

Chandler stood ready at the door while the Homicide detective entered the apartment. Maddy gradually worked her way through the gyrating masquerade toward the werewolf, wondering if she'd need to load her gun with silver bullets. She inched between the Frankenstein monster and the Fly, around Pinhead and the Creature from the Black Lagoon, the closer she got to the Wolf Man, the bigger he loomed. Dag was a hairy and muscular man in his own right, his bare torso darkened with a matting of macho fur, the jeans below torn calf-high like the ones Lon Chaney, Jr., wore in the film. The hair on his head was combed back in a pompadour. Black eye pencil was smudged around his bleary eyes. Adhesive attached unraveled spun yarn to his face, slanting up from the point of his jaw to his sideburns, and from where his eyebrows joined to his receding temples, and then straight up from the bridge of his nose to his widow's peak. A line of false teeth spiked up from his lower lip, the canine fangs dripping froth down his jutting chin. As Maddy jostled toward him, she was stripped by his squinty eyes. Then, with a thumb covering the mouth of the bottle in his grasp, Dag gave the beer a shake to fizz it up, gripped the bottle between his thighs like a big, brown penis and let it blow to spew foam at Maddy. Arching back his hairy head, he howled like Wolfman Jack.

"Police," said Maddy, disgusted, and she held up her badge.

A change, like in the movie, came over Dag. Hard to tell if he was turning into a man or transforming into a beast more rabid than his costume. Maddy's leg was ready to knee him in the groin. Smash that bottle and Dag would be neutered in the process, which would tame him like any unruly dog.

"Hey, it's a party."

They had to shout to be heard.

"This isn't about noise."

"Bitch," snarled Dag.

Maddy gripped the butt of the gun in the holster at her waist. If the neutering failed, she might have to put him down.

"Not you," added Dag. "That tub o' lard who's my wife."

"Let's talk outside."

"This about Mary?"

"Outside."

"Okay."

"You lead the way."

The bottle went limp between his thighs and fell to the floor. Poison Ivy, from one of the *Batman* films, played spin the bottle with her high-heeled boot. Dag stumbled drunkenly through the dancers, not as nimble as when he was doing the dog. The cop followed him to the door and out into the hall.

Zinc, lurking on the threshold, had scared off the overflow. Flanking the door were plastic skulls stuck on stakes as a warning. The epitaph on a tombstone at the foot of one read

HANGMAN

ROTTER
DIED OF BODY PARTS FAILURE
(FELL OFF)

Leaning against the wall was an open coffin, in which lay a horrified Bride of Dracula with a stake through her heart.

"Wha'd'ya think I did?" Dag slurred his words.

"You tell me," Maddy said over the music echoing from the
flat.

"I'm drunk."

"Uh-huh."

"You shou'n't be talkin' to me."

"Off the record."

"Honest?"

"Cross my heart."

"I'm drunk."

"So you said."

"Want that clear."

"Where were you between five and seven tonight?"

"Here."

"Doing what?"

"Lookit my face. Took a lotta time to gum it all on."

"Anyone with you?"

"Nope."

"Anyone call?"

"Naw."

"Any way you can prove you were here?"

"Wha's this about?"

"You tell me."

"Can't be Mary."

"Why?"

"Di'n't see 'er today."

"When did you last see her?"

"I was drunk."

"So you said."

"I want that clear."

"Everybody's a lawyer."

"I need a lawyer?"

"Do you?"

"You tell me."

"Why do you need a lawyer?"

"Who says I do?"

"You," said Maddy.

Dag looked confused. "I don't need a lawyer."

"If you say."

"The bitch provoked me."

"When?"

"Yesterday."

"So?"

"So what?"

"So what happened?"

"Aren't you s'posed to warn me or somethin'?"

"What good would that do? You're drunk, remember?"

"I am."

"You are. That's settled."

"I did it."

"Did what?"

"I was provoked. Mary said she'd take me to the cleaners for spite."

"So?"

"So what?"

"So you did what?"

"Let her have it."

"You mean you killed Mary?"

"Huh?" said Dag.

"Mary's dead. She's been murdered."

That seemed to sober the Wolf Man up fast, *if* he was drunk.

"I want a lawyer."

"I thought you didn't."

"One little punch and you're tryin' to stitch me up."

"Sir—"

"This is America. I got rights. You shouldn't question me when I'm drunk. You got a duty to warn me if I'm a suspect. I got a right to silence. And to have a lawyer present. And if I can't afford one, you got to provide it."

"Sir—"

"*This! Is! America!*"

"You got me there."

"You think I'm stupid? I watch TV."

"You want a lawyer?"

"Fuckin' right."

"Can you afford one?"

"No," replied Dag. "Get me Johnnie Cochran."

Maddy sighed. "Johnnie who?" she said.

Kline & Shaw

Vancouver
Tonight

It was my law associate, Ethan Shaw, who drew the article on the Hangman to my attention. At ten o'clock in the morning on November 1, fifteen days before the peril I find myself in tonight, I sat in our storefront office on the west side of Main, staring through

LAWYERS
KLINE & SHAW

stenciled backwards on the reception-area window, while outside the flotsam and jetsam of Vancouver's skid row ebbed and flowed, to and fro, from the cop shop across the street and the courthouse kitty-corner. Halloween, as always, would be good to the law business, so there I sat, waiting by the phone for legal aid to throw some new cases my way.

Yes, I said the "west side" of Main.

I suppose you're thinking, The East End kid made good. No doubt you recall me saying Main Street marks the divide between the affluent West Side and where I grew up. Well, the divide isn't *that* marked. The west side of Main is still skid row, so what I saw passing by as I gazed out was the grungy client base of Kline &

Shaw. Junkies, boozers, hookers, strippers, con men and such. The Needle Exchange was just up the street, so hypes by the handful jitterbugged by on their way to swap outfits against HIV. The ambulance parked out front said another had died. A nut we called the Windmill churned his arms near the courts, whirling them frantically in an effort to keep people away, shouting "Mother lovers!" at the top of his lungs. A crackhead was down on her hands and knees in front of our door, checking cracks in the sidewalk for crack others may unknowingly have dropped. Ethan had to sidestep her to open the door.

"Another uneventful day at Kline & Shaw," I said as he entered.

"Any calls?"

"Nope."

"No million-dollar mortgage?"

"Just a mountain of bills in the mail."

"Where's Suzy?"

"Sick."

"Not again. How am I to function without a good secretary?"

"She wants a raise."

"Don't we all."

"She's working to rule."

"No, she's not. The rule is we start work about nine a.m."

"I was here. Where were you?"

"I stopped by Mom's. Her toilet was plugged. It took Roto-Rooter to clear it."

"I wish they'd clear the pipeline to legal aid. All I want is a six-month trial from a big Halloween murder."

"Move to Seattle."

"Why?"

"The Hangman," Ethan said. With that, he dropped the morning tabloid that was nestled under his arm onto Suzy's desk.

"Hangman Lynches Woman," blared the headline.

"Leg Cut Off in Hangman Game," teased the subhead.

"By Justin Whitfield," accredited the byline.

Our local paper had picked the story up from the *Seattle Star.*

"I've read it," Ethan said, and disappeared into his office.

People find it hard to believe Ethan and I share space. We're not partners—we're associates. Partners combine incomes and jointly pay the bills, then split profits equally. Associates keep what they each make, after jointly paying the bills. Either way, Ethan and I are an odd couple. Ethan's blond and skinny, a runt of the litter, with disheveled hair above eyes bleary from too much time spent boozing in the Blarney Stone after work. When he's stressed, one eye twitches. Not from lack of rest, but from a mild case of Tourette's syndrome. Me, I'm as different from him as black is from white. I wish I could say I am handsome, but I'm not. That is unless your taste runs to Mike Hammer tough. Survival through high school saw me in the gym, boxing muscles into my physique and roughing up my baby face in the process. My hair's dark and short. My eyes look mean. And it's a look I use to advantage in court. Spooking witnesses is the name of the game. But does that mean there's no beauty inside the beast?

Mike Hammer.

Cool name.

I must read one of those books.

What Ethan and I have in common is the East End. He was raised there by his mom; I was raised there by Gram. We met at Lord Strathcona. We endured Britannia High. And we were two grubby-faced urchins surrounded by West Side silver spoons at UBC Law School. I think it was preordained that Ethan and I would end up back here on the skids. Our wallets are joined at the hip. Like Siamese twins.

Don't harbor any illusions about Kline & Shaw. I don't want you thinking our law firm is two noble men who forsook uptown riches to return to their roots, preferring to run a rundown storefront office serving the underfunded needs of poor, disenfranchised wretches. Believe me, I can relate. I was one of them for too many years. But I didn't fight my way up from the East End to end up a legal-aid lawyer serving the skids. I fought my way out of that cockroach-infested slum to become the best goddamn criminal lawyer there is, a man living on the West Side in a mansion of cedar and glass, with a client base of the richest and heaviest bad guys around.

If your life is on the line,
Time to call for Jeffrey Kline . . .

So what happened?

Why am I still here?

The first thing you've got to understand is that law is about connections. If your parents live on the West Side and you're a silver spoon, you're connected in some way through them. You go into Mommy's firm or bill Daddy's business friends. Or you capitalize on a client base of other silver spoons like you. West Siders go mostly into civil law. That's where the real money is, and they follow it. East Enders have always been left with criminal law. Criminals, for the most part, make up our connections. Small-time hoods and grifters are our client base. Big-time bad guys will always go for flash, so they get cherry-picked by mavericks working white-collar crime and the stock exchange, leaving us with the dregs funded by legal aid.

The East End bar.

Lawyers like Kline & Shaw.

When we went into law school, Ethan and I, legal aid was a springboard to the West Side. Graduate with debts up to here from student loans, without a single connection to launch your practice, and your best bet was a call to legal aid to say there was a new gun in town, so start sending cases. Elect for a jury trial whenever you had the option, and thanks to that new milk cow, the Charter of Rights and Freedoms, you could squirt an endless stream of money from the bottomless public purse. Work, work, work until you paid off your debts, and soon you could afford a move up the food chain. It was only a matter of time until you struck gold, since the law of averages was with you. Pan enough dreck and you were sure to get a Big Case, a small-time punk who hit the big time, and if you were good and got him off scot-free, you could use the win to hook clients flush with cash.

Law is about connections.

Law is about hooks.

When we came out of law school, Ethan and I, the milk from the milk cow was dribbling dry. Politicians here had made a big mistake when they gambled that the Pacific Rim was where the future lay, so when Asia took a dive in the global marketplace, we—unlike the rest of North America—went into recession. Penny-pinchers grabbed hold of the public purse, and the first to suffer the stinginess of politics in the nineties were those who did-n't vote: our client base.

The legal-aid system crumbled.

And took us with it.

Son of a bitch!

Just my luck.

The net effect of that crumbling was the scene in Kline & Shaw last November 1. Ethan had disappeared into his office right of Suzy's desk, and there would while away the day at cheap paperwork. Everything from landlord and tenant to immigration to divorce to real estate to wills and estates to creditors' remedies to motor-vehicle claims. Meanwhile, our secretary was on strike. I sat at Suzy's desk, surrounded by a mess of bills we could ill afford to pay, not a single client referral from legal aid in the mail, daydreaming that I was retained to act for the Hangman down south, and hoping that across the street in the courthouse cells the Salvation Army was filling out a referral form in my name: the Big Case that somehow would catapult me away from all this.

Jesus Christ!

Not only was I still saddled with student loans; not only did I still live in the East End in a rented house; not only was my office once a hippie head shop that still stank of patchouli oil; not only did I after seven years of university, a year of articles to an ambulance chaser and several years of practice here on skid row—still make God knows how much less than a plumber... but now some drunk who was staggering by had turned into our entrance alcove to piss on the door to Kline & Shaw.

I saw red.

I threw down the newspaper piece on the Hangman.

I stormed from the desk, tromped to the door and yanked it open.

The drunk pissed on my shoe as I clutched him by his grubby coat.

I bunched my fist, cocked my arm and was into a punch to launch his head into outer space, a reaction of the sort Mike Hammer would respect, when I spied a cop across Main Street, in front of the police station, eyeballing me.

I'm a defense lawyer.

Cops hate my guts.

So at the last moment, I pulled the punch to save myself from murder one.

The cop cocked his finger at me like a gun.

I tipped an imaginary hat on my head.

The drunk staggered away with his penis dangling out.

Another depressing day at Kline & Shaw.

The only sure cure I know is a walk uptown. So in I went to my office left of Suzy's desk, and there I packed my secondhand briefcase with a file requiring a factum for the court of appeal. No, not a murder—a measly B and E. I popped in to tell Ethan where I'd be, and then, since I'm also janitor for Kline & Shaw, mopped up the pool of piss at the door before escaping north toward the harbor inlet.

A black hooker wearing an orange scoop-necked blouse and tight orange crotch-cleaving shorts stood at the corner of Powell and Main, in front of a strip bar called Number 5 Orange.

"Trick or treat?" she said.

"A day late," I replied.

"Honey, it's never bad luck to have black pussy cross yo' path."

"Later," I lied.

"I be here," she cooed.

I turned west on Powell to enter Gastown, where Gassy Jack once served booze at Maple Tree Square; a statue of him on a whiskey barrel commands the five roads converging there today. Water Street ran along the inlet with the mountains beyond to the financial district, marking uptown. I angled along Granville, pausing at the Birks clock (beneath which lovers have rendezvoused since 1907) to retie my shoe, then turned west on Georgia and strolled a block over to the old courthouse, now the art gallery.

To me, the old courthouse epitomizes law.

That's where I witnessed Kinky. The Hanging Judge.

Our history of murder and hanging.

Including the architect.

The Rattenbury case is one of the crimes of the century. Look it up in any blood history. Rattenbury was a turn-of-the-century British architect who made his name in British Columbia. The courthouse and the legislature are his legacy. Polite society threw him out in 1924 for having an affair with Alma Pakenham, thirty years his junior. The outcasts fled to England to marry in 1928, and set up house in Bournemouth. Within six years Alma was bored, so she placed an ad in papers for a houseboy, the upshot of which was that a dim-witted youth named George Stoner ended up doing service in her bed. George got jealous of Rats, what Alma called her husband, so he bashed the old boy on the head with a mallet and did him in.

The next day, Alma confessed to save George. Then George confessed to save Alma. Their trial at the Old Bailey was a cause célèbre. Husband 67. Wife 38. Stud 18. Alma was acquitted. George was sentenced to hang. So Alma stabbed herself to death beside a Bournemouth stream where the lovers used to go. Ironically, George didn't hang. The sentence of death imposed on him was commuted to life without Alma.

That's the kind of case I dreamed would come my way.

A cause célèbre.

With lots of press.

Enough to catapult me away from depressing skid row.

Standing in front of Rattenbury's courthouse at noon that day, facing the stone lions flanking the steps up to its soaring pillars and listening to the noon-horn blast the first four notes of "O Canada" over the harbor at 115 decibels, I imagined I was an attorney in Seattle defending whoever the Hangman was against that state's gallows.

As luck would have it, the Hangman was about to cross the border.

Soon, there would be bones on *my* picking ground.

And if the Hangman gets me tonight, the next bones will be mine...

Lady-Killer

Doesn't anyone believe in romance anymore?
   In love at first sight?
   A tempest worthy of Shakespeare whooped and rained outside the windows of her townhouse at the foot of the mountains as Jayne Curry, surrounded by candles and sipping a glass of red wine, worked on the Web site she would launch to relate her side of the story. *Tap-tap-tap* . . . her fingers tapped the keyboard of her computer in counterpoint to the *tap-tap-tap* . . . of a wind-blown branch that rapped against the nearest pane.
   The first time I set eyes on him my heart began to flutter. I had waited my entire life for such a man. He was handsome in the classic sense, a full head of salt-and-pepper hair graying at the temples, the profile of a Greek god from a marble bust, his lean body tall and confident in a charcoal suit. When he turned to cast a gaze around the gallery, I'm sure every female present felt like me.
   The doctor had sex appeal . . .
   Here she would import a headshot of him from the graphics file, a photo she had surreptitiously snapped for her fantasy wall, a montage of irresistible males around her bedroom mirror. Those visiting her Web site could judge for themselves.

HANGMAN

Tap-tap-tap went her fingers.

Tap-tap-tap rapped the branch.

Blow any harder and it might break the glass.

The doctor turned away from me when the presiding judge took the bench. The lawyers introduced themselves to her, then Chief Justice Morgan Hatchett ordered the court clerk to read the indictment.

"John Langley Twist, you stand charged that on the eighth of January of this year, in the city of Vancouver, in the province of British Columbia, you did commit the first-degree murder of Lena Hay."

I was shocked.

This man a killer?

No way, I recall saying to myself.

Then, seconds later, the doctor confirmed my first impression.

"Having heard the charge, how do you plead? Guilty or not guilty?"

"Not guilty," the doctor said in a voice that rang with truth.

The clerk turned to the judge. "The accused pleads not guilty."

"Proceed," the judge ordered.

With a wooden box of names in hand, the clerk addressed the dock. "These good persons who shall now be called are the jurors who are to pass between Our Sovereign Lady the Queen and you at your trial. If therefore you would challenge them or any of them, you must challenge them as they come to the book to be sworn, and before they are sworn you shall be heard."

My heart skipped a beat when I was the sixth name called . . .

Her fingers stopped tapping.

But not the branch.

Tap-tap-tap . . . Its rap kept time with the click of her high heels across the hardwood floor as Jayne left her writing desk to refill her glass from the bottle of Beaujolais on the table. The table was set for two—as it was every night this lonely heart dined alone—with fine linen, a silver service and red roses in a crystal vase. Warm glow from the candlesticks mingled with that from the other candles throughout the room, bathing her with after-glow to soften her age. Tonight, Jayne wore a dinner dress the color of the wine, V'd for décolletage to please her imaginary beau. Rachmaninov set the mood for wishful love.

Bastard, she thought.

And drained the glass of wine.

And refilled the glass.

And carried it back to her desk.

In retrospect, I wish I had asked the trial judge to excuse me from jury duty. But how could I have said, in front of the entire panel, that my reason for asking to be excused was that I found the accused to be a dashing, attractive charmer, as I'm sure did every other female—including the judge—in that court? So I kept quiet and was chosen to take the jury oath.

"Do you swear you shall well and truly try and true deliverance make between Our Sovereign Lady the Queen and the accused at the bar, whom you shall have in charge, and a true verdict give, according to the evidence, so help you God?"

"Yes," I said.

And that is what I did.

The case outlined by the Crown counsel in his opening to us was weak from the start. Dr. John Twist owned a geriatric clinic in the city. Lena Hay was a patient of his, an elderly woman who died from an undetermined cause shortly after she changed her will to leave her substantial estate to Doctor Twist's clinic. What led the police to investigate were similarities between that death and two others, also elderly widows who changed their wills to benefit the clinic shortly before they died of natural causes.

The only autopsy done was on Lena Hay.

The forensic pathologist, Gillian Macbeth, could find no sign of foul play. What she did find on Hay's body was a needle prick, which a bitter nurse fired from the clinic told police was caused by Doctor Twist secretly injecting Lena at midnight with some drug.

The clinic had no record of that injection having been given, and no drug had been dispensed by its pharmacy. Potassium, maintained the Crown, is the drug of choice of murdering doctors. The effect of a shot of potassium is it knocks out the heart, and it can't be detected at autopsy because potassium is in the body naturally.

That was the case.

Would you convict . . . ?

Again her concentration was broken by that branch insistently rapping on the window. *Tap-tap-TAP.* It was rapping harder. Through snakes of black rain squirming down the glass she could see the skeletal limb clawing at the pane. Because she was dressed in her finery, she didn't want to go out, but if the storm blew the branch at the window any harder, her reluctance would result in a shattered hole.

Better safe than sorry.

So Jayne stood up.

What she was writing for publication through the Internet had reached a crucial point. How much of her lonely life should she reveal? Should she inform the world that she was called Plain Jayne at school, and that she remained a wallflower at every dance, fantasizing she was the belle of the ball in the arms of the best-looking boys? Unmarried and nearing fifty, she still romanticized alone at night, attending the theater by herself for *Romeo and Juliet* or *My Fair Lady*, and the ballet by herself for *Sleeping Beauty.* When she stayed home, it was to read books like *The Bridges of Madison County* and *Wuthering Heights,* or any novel by Danielle Steel.

No! thought Jayne.

I won't do it!

Why should it be *me* who bares *my* soul when *he*'s to blame?

Fueled by resentment, Jayne sat down again and began to tap the keyboard furiously.

That first day of the trial, while I sat eating a bag lunch on the steps near the law courts fountain in Robson Square, the shadow of someone fell over me and paused. I looked up to see a black silhouette against the sun, and instantly knew it was the doctor looming above.

"You're on my jury," he said.

"Yes," I replied.

"Good. At least one member will treat me fairly. You know what Robert Frost said about juries? 'A jury consists of twelve persons chosen to decide who has the better lawyer.'"

Then he was gone, and I shielded my eyes against the blinding sun . . .

Tap-TAP-TAP!

That damn branch!

After that, everywhere I went when the trial was recessed . . .

Tap-TAP-TAP!

John Twist . . .

TAP-TAP-TAP!

Was there . . .

The fury she felt over how the accused doctor had set her up suddenly focused on this branch threatening to break into the sanctuary of her home, much the same way John Twist had plundered the passion of her heart, and then her yearning body. Jayne Curry leaped up from her desk and crossed to the security panel on the wall beneath the upper landing of the split level, punching in the code that disarmed the alarm. Then she left the two-story vault of the combined living and dining room for the staircase in the entry hall that ran up to her bedroom. At the top of the stairs, the arch to the right brought her out onto the landing, from which she gazed down on the sea of candles flickering around the glow of the computer screen.

Her ruby nails scraped the banister as she kicked off her high heels and stomped toward her bedroom door, which was halfway along the landing. Entering, she traversed her boudoir, passing between the canopy bed in which the doctor had seduced her and the mirror encircled by her montage of dreamboat men in which she had watched John Twist take her from behind while the secret bug planted by police recorded her undoing. In the walk-in closet, she found a full-length, hooded raincoat to protect her from the storm, and then, carefully removing her expensive dress so she was in her underwear, she pulled on the coat, tied the belt and went downstairs.

The hall continued past the stairs to a door that opened on the L-shaped backyard. Jayne grabbed a pair of gardening shears from the tool shelf, then, with her other hand, tugged on a pair of rubber boots. The hood up, she opened the door and ventured out into the wind and rain besieging her home.

Rounding the corner, Jayne splashed up the arm of the L beside her townhouse. The wind whipped the flaps of the coat away from her garters and nylons. The rain invaded the hood to spatter and spoil her makeup. Cold goosebumped her skin as she seized the branch nearest to the assaulted window and severed it viciously with the shears.

In her haste, Jayne overlooked the footprints in the mud and failed to notice how the bark was rubbed off the branch, as would happen if a gloved hand had bashed the wet limb repeatedly against the glass.

She dropped the cutting in the muck and returned to the back door. Shedding the boots and shucking off the soggy coat, she relocked herself inside, replaced the shears on the shelf and shivered in her underwear back to the main room.

What was that?

Nothing?

Just the storm?

She looked around.

Spooky.

Too many candle shadows.

A night like this, you hear and feel things that aren't there.

Like phantom breathing.

And eyes watching you.

Which make you fear you locked yourself in with something evil.

Creepy.

She shuddered.

Enough turmoil, she sighed.

What Jayne would do instead of working longer on the Web site was run herself a bubble bath and settle in with a bottle of wine and drown her sorrows in the usual fashion. But before she turned off the computer for the night, Jayne padded across the hardwood floor in her stocking feet to punch the alarm code into the keypad on the wall under the split-level landing overhead.

That's when her toe touched wet on the floor.

Her first thought was that the wet was from her, some drops of rain shed as she moved. But when she felt her hair, she found it dry, which you'd expect, thanks to the hood. When she felt her body, she found it dry, too, as you'd expect, thanks to the coat. She crouched in the shadows to feel her legs, also finding them dry, what with the boots, and that's when she saw the spreading pool.

A leak? thought Jayne.

But how can that be?

The puddle on the floor was beneath the overhead landing, so not only was this spot covered by another level, but Jayne had walked the landing herself a few minutes ago, when she went up to her boudoir to fetch her coat.

In stocking feet, she recalled.

I kicked off my shoes.

So if the puddle isn't from me...

Still crouched in the shadows, she began to turn her head.

And if it isn't from a leak...

Her eyes traced the trickle that fed the pool.

The explanation must be...

She caught a glimpse of the feet sneaking toward her.

I'm trapped...

HANGMAN

She looked up.

With an *intruder!*

A split second before the noose cinched about her neck.

The rope running up to the landing above, looping over the banister before it descended to the Hangman's grip down here, was hidden in the shadows of a soaring indoor palm. The Hangman yanked on the rope to jerk Jayne a few inches off her feet, then yanked again to raise her a foot off the floor, before tying the loose end around the bottom of the post supporting the landing.

Jayne instinctively grasped the strangling rope with both hands, but she didn't have the strength to pull herself up. Instead, she thrashed in the air like a puppet bouncing on a string to the whims of a berserk puppeteer. Her nails tore to the quick as she clawed frantically at the noose biting into her throat, gouging red furrows from her flesh. Her heart pounded in her chest as her blood pressure spiked, panic flooding her bloodstream with adrenaline. Mewling gagged from her mouth as she gasped for air, but struggling against this stranglehold was to no avail. Blood engorged her face, which lack of oxygen turned cyanotic blue, as vessels burst in her bulging eyes, reddening the whites. Her tongue protruded between her teeth from the cinching of the noose, while trickles of blood from popping veins ran from her nose and ears.

One minute...

Two minutes...

Three minutes she danced.

The shadow of the Hangman embraced her like the shadow of death. Arms flailing, legs kicking, chest heaving desperately from asphyxia, the hanging woman silently screamed for air...

Air...

Aiiiiirrrr ...

As consciousness began to ebb, Jayne's muscles twitched involuntarily and general convulsions took hold. Her bladder and rectum voided, soiling Jayne's silk underwear.

She was beyond caring.

She was abandoning life.

And the last memory she would take to the great hereafter was the look of contempt on the Hangman's face as the knife in one crooked arm slashed horizontally across the hanged woman's tongue.

Twelve Angry Men

Vancouver
November 7

"Henry Fonda," Zinc said.

"I agree."

"Lemmon did a fine job."

"He's always good. But each time the camera panned away from him, I thought we'd see Walter Matthau in the jury room."

Zinc Chandler laughed. "Pass the popcorn, Alex."

Alexis Hunt handed him the bowl.

"Mmmm, good," Zinc said, stuffing his mouth. "For such a nerdy-looking guy, Orville Redenbacher pops the best."

"He's no longer popping."

"It's a lie. Next you'll say Aunt Jemima no longer flips pancakes, Betty Crocker no longer bakes cakes and the Colonel no longer fries chicken."

"Sorry, Zinc." Alex took the bowl.

"How did Orville pop off?"

"Drowned in a bathtub a few years ago."

"People drown in bathtubs?"

"Hey, you're the cop."

"If I knew we'd be eating popcorn from the grave, I'd have picked two horror movies instead."

The rain against the window made it cozy, the fire dancing cheerfully on the hearth, the critics snuggled together on the loveseat in front of the TV. Of late, Tuesday had become Movie Night for them, the ritual being they alternated going to the video store and returning with a double feature of flicks connected by theme, director, actor or locale. Their favorite link was an original and its remake(s) viewed back to back. Last week, Alex had selected *The Shop around the Corner* and *In the Good Old Summertime,* and she would have rented *You've Got Mail,* but it was out. That balanced Zinc's picks of the week before: no fewer than six Dracula movies, so they could crown the king of counts from among Schreck, Lugosi, Lee, Palance, Langella and Oldman.

No contest.

The best was obvious.

Tonight, the Tuesday critics compared *Twelve Angry Men.*

"Best heavy?" Alex said.

"That's a tough one."

"Tougher than best hero, that's for sure."

"Lee J. Cobb," Zinc said, casting his second vote for the 1957 version.

"I disagree. George C. Scott."

"Come on, Alex. Scott chewed up the scenery at the end."

"And Cobb didn't?"

"Put the films in perspective. Acting styles were different in the fifties."

"The emotions weren't. They remain the same. Both actors sat on the same trial in both films. A kid from a broken home in the slums stabbed his brutal father to death with a switchblade."

"*Allegedly* stabbed his father," Zinc corrected.

Alex fed him popcorn to shut him up. "You want my reasoning?"

The Mountie nodded.

"Both Cobb and Scott played the same character in both films. The vengeful self-made man tortured by the memory of a son who defied his authority to break away from his rule. So bitter was that rift that father and son have been estranged for years. This patricide case rekindled those repressed emotions in the juror played by Cobb and Scott, presenting him with the opportunity for vicarious revenge. On the hottest day of the year, the jury retired to a sweaty jury room to take a vote on whether or not to convict the slum kid and send him to the electric chair."

"It's lethal injection in the '97 version," piped in Zinc.

"Death is death."

"No, it's not."

"Save that argument for your turn, Ebert."

Zinc took the bowl of dwindling popcorn to finish it off while Alex argued her case.

"The first vote was eleven to one for conviction. The only juror holding out was the man played by Henry Fonda and Jack Lemmon. The voice of reason. Then one by one, he began to win the others over for acquittal, which locked him in a verdict tug-of-war with the most recalcitrant juror, played by Cobb and Scott. Finally, that juror was the one left standing alone, overwhelmed by the realization that he would have killed an innocent youth to get back at his own defiant son.

"I put it to you," Alex said in her best lawyer's voice, the one she learned from her father, a Portland judge, "that it matters not whether that juror cracked in 1957 or 1997—such repressed emotions would explode to push him over the top. Scott, therefore, may chew up the scenery all he wants."

Zinc handed her the empty bowl.

"Everything about the remake is wrong," he said. "What modern jury has only men?"

"*Twelve Angry Persons* sounds phony," she teased. "And the judge is a woman."

"That's what I mean. The remake tries to force a square peg into a round hole. Modern gloss can't hide the fact that the plot is from the fifties. Each and every change pulls the punch of the story. Lethal injection is not the bad death of the electric chair. Replacing worse with better lessens pressure on the jurors. Men today are encouraged to release emotion, so George C. Scott's imploding is over the top. Tough guys back then didn't cry, so Lee J. Cobb unraveling still shakes us today."

"Have you ever served on a jury?"

"No," said Zinc. "Canadian cops are disqualified by the Jury Act."

"I have," said Alex. "What an experience. It was more like *Twelve Angry Men* than it wasn't. There's no doubt the author of both films also served on a jury. He captured the ordeal."

"You believe the characters?"

"All twelve ring true. Aren't they as evident today as they were then? The O. J. Simpson trial was *Twelve Angry Men* in reverse. Instead of passion giving away to reason, it went reason to passion to end in travesty. The evidence was there for proof beyond a reasonable doubt, but race blinded the jury from reaching a sound verdict. Every citizen is subject to jury duty, yet we get no training whatsoever in how to achieve justice. Should we entrust a person's life to trial by his 'peers,' when a jury of them consists of twelve strangers who gather together to reach a decision influenced by the emotions, passions, mental quirks and human failings they take into the jury room?"

"The judge's daughter," Zinc said.

"Guilty," pleaded Alex.

"You're implying you like the remake better than the original?"

"No, I'm saying *Twelve Angry Men* should be shown in school. We should be taught how to plumb ourselves for bias, so if we're later called upon to be jurors, we can overcome prejudice and think harder about what really matters."

"I'd be a good juror."

"Would you, Zinc?"

"I'd sure as hell reach my decision on the facts and nothing else."

"Like you did in choosing Lee J. Cobb over George C. Scott?"

"That was based on acting."

"Was it really?"

"You think I was influenced?"

"Subconsciously."

"By what, Alex?"

"The fact that George C. Scott looks a lot like your dad."

That punch came out of nowhere to knock Zinc back into his past. Again he was standing in the farmhouse of his youth, maybe ten, perhaps eleven years old, he and his brother, Tom, dressed for bed. Pop was seated at the table with his drinking buddies, pouring stiff rounds of Canadian Club. The farmer fixed his rheumic eyes on Zinc and slurred:

> Shall there be gallows in England when thou
> art king, and resolution thus fobbed as
> it is with the rusty curb of old father
> antick, the law?

"Think lively, son. Name the bard."

"Shakespeare, Pop."

Her workday far from over while her husband held court, his mother turned from scrubbing dishes at the sink and sighed. "Run along, boys. And say your prayers."

"Got one for you, Chandler," old MacKinnon said. He owned the farm next to theirs.

"A buck?"

"Two."

"Three."

"Four," the two men wagered.

Ed MacKinnon thumbed through the thick anthology that settled their bets. Blinking to focus his bloodshot eyes on the poem, he read:

For they're hangin' Danny Deever, you can
hear the Dead March play,
The Regiment's in 'ollow square—they're
hangin' 'im to-day.

"Kipling!" hooted Pop with triumph. "Pay up, you cheap son of a bitch."

"Shit," MacKinnon grumbled. "Two out of three?"

Lying awake in the bunk bed he shared with Tom, Zinc had listened for hours to them carousing in the kitchen, wagering who could identify the most obscure poem. The Plowmen Poets got so drunk they could barely communicate, and that's when Zinc's dad began to bully his mom.

"Look at her, boys. Ravaged by time. The prettiest girl in Saskatchewan the day we wed. Now she's sagging tits and a spreading ass."

Oh, how he hated Pop for that, feeling his punctured heart bleed for his mom. Why did she take it? Because she was afraid? Or did she endure him for the sake of their sons?

Come morning, Zinc knew what to expect. Hungover and sleep-deprived, Pop made him run the gauntlet of the bards, whacking him with quote on quote to bring him to his knees and flaring at his mom if she tried to intervene.

"Stand back, woman," bellowed Pop. "I'll not raise an illiterate lout.

The hungry judges soon the sentence sign,
And wretches hang that jurymen may dine.

"Think lively, son. Name the bard."

"Pope, Pop," he said.

Then came the time Zinc stood up to his father, telling him face to face that he didn't deserve his wife, telling him eye to eye that he was a piss-tank bully, but the beating he took in return made his mother scream, so he didn't mouth off again to save her pain.

Got Pop back, though.

With his job.

Chandlers had worked that Saskatchewan farm for a century. Zinc's dad raised two boys to inherit the land, and he never forgave his elder son for abandoning it to become a Mountie. Pop had hated cops since the Depression, when he was clubbed senseless during the Regina Riot. Father and son had never reconciled, and Pop's last words on his deathbed were "At least Tom . . . turned out . . ."

. . . a man . . .

That memory bled into the jury room in *Twelve Angry Men*, except that Juror Number 3 was no longer George C. Scott. "It's the kids," Pop said in Scott's role. "The way they are—you know? They don't listen. I've got a kid. When he was eight years old, he ran away from a fight. I saw him. I was so ashamed, I told him right out, 'I'm gonna make a man out of you or I'm gonna bust you up into little pieces trying.' When he was fifteen he hit me in the face. He's big, you know. I haven't seen him in years. Rotten kid! You work your heart out . . ."

Alex was right.

Scott looked like Pop.

Is that why Zinc chose Cobb over him?

Because of bias?

What if Zinc were a juror and Scott was on trial?

Might he convict instead of acquit because he was Pop's son?

"You're right, Alex. I was biased. Which is, I guess, the reason we did away with the gallows. Not because killers don't deserve to be hanged, but because the legal system—"

His cellphone rang.

Grabbing it off the table, the Mountie answered the call. "Chandler," he said.

Zinc jotted notes.

"I'll be there in half an hour."
Zinc punched off.
"See you later," Alex said.
"Want to come along? There's definitely a book in who just got herself killed."

Death Row

Door after door, house after house, was strung in a continuous line along the rain-slicked street. Until the 1970s, this two-block stretch sandwiched between a pair of creeks that rushed down from the North Shore peaks above to the harbor below had pocketed miniature homes built during the war. Except for a few holdouts on the next street, the building boom of the age that gave us disco, bell-bottom pants and platform shoes had razed the past to leave its mark. A red door, a beige front, a false brown gable, each townhouse was a clone of its neighbor, born of the same blueprint, as Siamese twins are from the same genes.

Zinc turned the car away from the creek and drove along the row.

Too many houses.

Too few parking spaces.

The row of identical houses prompted Alex to hunt for details. Something in her psyche rebelled at human molds, at any attempt to string individuals into paper dolls. Squinting through the windshield as Zinc parked the car, she searched for clues that exposed the lives lived behind similar masks. A TV flickered blue beyond half-closed blinds. Was the image pornography from Red Hot

Video or Disney on the Family Channel? Rainwater overflowed the gutters next door. Had the lazy resident neglected to clean the eaves? Surely, since his Christmas lights were still up. The smell of foreign spices was pungent in the air as Alex swung open the car door and forded the river of rain rushing along the curb. Sniffing the air while she popped her umbrella on the sidewalk, she couldn't place the ethnic cuisine cooking in the house with the tinkling wind chimes.

"Irani," said Zinc, reading her mind or her twitching nose.

"Smells good."

"It is."

"I'd like to try it."

"Lots of Iranian restaurants on the North Shore. Those who turned refugee when the ayatollah overthrew the shah settled where the geography reminded them of home."

"I thought Iran was desert."

"So did I."

Alex took out her notebook and a pen. While Zinc held the umbrella, she drew a sketch of the street on a fresh page, jotting details as they splashed toward the crowd and cop cars besieging one door. At the top of her notes she wrote "Death Row."

Those who make murder their business have choice at a fork in the road. One route leads to danger, the other to relative safety. Zinc had embraced adventure by becoming a cop; he thrived on the adrenaline rush in hands-on crime and the thrill of chasing human foxes. Alex had opted for the safety of a true-crime writer, and, like forensic techs, lawyers and judges, she got her kicks vicariously.

To look at her you wouldn't suspect that she was what she was. Dark-side habitués, like female cops, invariably develop a hard edge. More than a decade younger than Zinc, which put her nearing thirty, Alexis Hunt was a honey blonde with blue eyes the color of a tropical lagoon. What she lacked in curves to hourglass her figure, she more than made up for with ballerina's grace. Alex in motion was the flow of a tide. Alex in Zinc's bed was an erotic writhe. She could be a dancer. She could be a model. So how did she end up at this aftermath of blood?

It all began with two cannibals and a boy in a lifeboat. It was a warm summer day in the Oregon of her youth. Alex, then ten, liked to laze up high in the canopy of leaves, sunlight stabbing her treehouse through gaps in the green. As birds chirped above and bees buzzed below, words wafted up with the clink of ice in gin and tonics from the lawyers lounging by the pool.

This was before her dad became a judge.

"Here's a bone to chew on," said Jackson Hunt, addressing the partners in his firm. "I came across a case from 1884 in which three men and a boy were shipwrecked and forced to brave the open sea in a lifeboat. Eighteen days adrift and both food and water gone saw Dudley and Stephens suggest the boy be killed and eaten. The third man balked at their plan. Two days later, starving and thirsty, the two plotters killed the boy. The three men feasted on the body until they were rescued four days later."

"Jackson."

"Yes, dear?"

"Five minutes to lunch."

His wife was flipping burgers on the barbecue.

"Dudley and Stephens were tried for murder. By a special verdict, the jury made three findings. One, the men probably would have died within four days had they not eaten the boy. Two, because the boy was in a weak condition, he probably would have died before them. And three, except by sacrificing one for the others to eat, the chance of survival at the time of the killing was unlikely. The verdict was then referred to a bench of judges to decide whether a defense of necessity was justified in law."

"Who likes their meat rare?" called his wife.

The lawyers shook their heads.

"No one, dear," Jackson said. "You see the dilemma?" he continued. "Both accused were able to *choose* between two undesirable options. One choice involved breaking the law. The other involved an evil of such magnitude to them and the third man that they felt justified doing so."

"Bullshit," said one of his partners. "You can't divorce morality from law."

"Is it immoral to kill one to save three?"

"If you and I were shipwrecked and there was only one plank, a plank that would sink if we both grabbed hold, should I have the right to drown you so the plank is mine?"

"If several are overtaken by common disaster, is there no right in anyone to save the lives of many by sacrificing one?"

"No," said his partner.

"So it's the duty of all to die?"

"Alex," her mom called. "Time for lunch."

The girl dropped the rope ladder to the ground and slid down from the treehouse as her dad advanced another legal argument.

"A dam is about to burst and flood a valley. The calamity will wipe out a town of a hundred people. By opening a sluice I can relieve the pressure, but that will flood a nearby farm and probably kill the farmer. I'm faced with a choice between breaking the law by drowning him or allowing the greater evil of letting a hundred people die. Make that a million, if it helps. Don't you think the law should excuse me if I elect to save the many?"

His partner saw an opening and went for the jugular.

"What if the farmer sees you opening the dam? An action he suspects you know will cause his death? If he has a rifle at hand, would he not be excused for shooting you in self-defense? And what about the boy eaten by the men? If he was strong enough to resist, would he not be excused for killing the cannibals in self-defense? If A can kill B of necessity, and B can kill A in self-defense, there is no rule of law, just anarchy."

"You're beat, Jackson," said another partner.

"What if the boy was a pirate about to be hanged when the ship wrecked? What if the farmer was in jail on death row?"

The partner arguing with Jackson chuckled. "I know you won't give up. That's what I like about you. It makes us lots of money."

"Come and get it while it's hot," the chef called from the barbecue.

"So?" said Jackson's adversary as they abandoned the pool. "What did that bench of judges do with the cannibals?"

"*Dudley and Stephens.*" Jackson winked. "Look it up."

That was the day Alex decided that she, too, would be a lawyer. Intrigued by the dark side of her father's work, she focused on abnormal psychology. The passing years saw her dad become a judge of the Oregon Supreme Court, while she completed a master's degree in preparation for law school. Tragedy, however, altered the course of her life.

First, her mother perished in a car crash on the I-5. Then, three months later, her father suffered an epileptic fit in court. The neurosurgeons were unable to get all the cancer, so Alex faced a choice between law school and him. She took her dad to the West Coast town of Cannon Beach, and there she nursed him through his slow death. To occupy her mind during that ordeal, Alex turned her master's thesis on America's premier serial killer into a true-crime book.

House of Horrors: The Case of H. H. Holmes caught the morbid imagination of enough readers to launch her career as a writer. It also inspired two psychos to create horrific Castle Crag.

The invitation seemed innocent enough. A group of crime writers would fly somewhere secret for a mystery weekend; there, they would match wits with a homicide detective from the Mounted Police. Who the victor was would determine how much was given to charity. So off Alex flew for a good cause, hoping a little R & R in Canada would ease the pain of her dad's death. But instead, she found herself trapped in the deadly maze of her own book as one by one the writers fell victim to the murder mansion on Deadman's Island.

How she got from there to here was charted in her subsequent books. She had escaped from the island with a thrilling story and a new boyfriend, for the Mountie sent to match wits with the writers was Insp. Zinc Chandler of Special X.

What Justin Whitfield had in Maddy Thorne, Alexis Hunt had in Zinc.

An inside source.

Her own Deep Throat.

The white police cars parked in front of townhouse 11 were jaundiced yellow by the sickly glow of sodium-vapor streetlights. Waiting ominously at the curb was a black station wagon manned by dark-dressed undertakers from the body removal service. Mist billowed from the outside vent of a clothes dryer next door, and lights peering through the fog were ringed by eerie halos. Mounties in blue windbreakers kept the curious away from death's door, where a cop with a clipboard stopped the couple.

"Inspector Chandler," Zinc said, his buffalo head badge in hand.

The officious rookie logged him in.

"She's with me," Zinc said, indicating Alex.

"Sorry, Inspector. No unauthorized entry is the order from my sergeant."

Zinc snatched the clipboard and signed Alex in. "I'm sure your sergeant will find that sufficient authority."

Cops call them bunny suits, the duds piled on a chair inside the door. The phrase made Alex think of plunging cleavage and cottontails and Hef working the room in silk pajamas. Only Keystone Kops fail to take precautions against tainting evidence, so the two paused in the entry hall to don disposable headgear, overalls and booties. The bunny suits made them look like astronauts, a simile reinforced by what they saw in the two-story vault off the hall.

Six of the seven in the room wore the same white suits as Zinc and Alex. They could be performing an experiment on a shuttle in outer space. Weightlessness seemed to lift the seventh off the floor. What could be an oxygen hose rose from her neck to the landing above. Was she a species from another galaxy, this creature dressed like a vamp in skimpy underwear, with a legless torso and a bug-eyed blue face?

Beam me up, Scotty, Alex thought.

What brought her down to earth wasn't the grisly grab of the crime. Having survived that charnal house on Deadman's Island, Alex was as baptized in blood as any morgue attendant. Instead, what yanked her back to reality was Rachel and Gill.

"Who tampered with the body?" asked Gill Macbeth. The forensic pathologist was standing on a ladder with her profile to Alex, examining the face of the hanging corpse.

"I did," replied Rachel Kidd. The sergeant gazed up from the foot of the ladder, where she sidestepped the pool of blood on the floor.

"Something covered her face."

"A mask," said the Mountie.

"Why did you remove it before I arrived?"

"To see who she was."

"That couldn't wait?"

"Not if the victim was who we thought. If so, we had a suspect to find at once. Before the Lady-Killer could alibi up."

"Well, the effect is you interfered with my job. Asphyxia may result from suffocation. *Or* from gagging or choking. *Or* from constriction of the neck. *Or* from compression of the chest. *Or* from suspension. A cover blocking the airways of a hanging victim must be seen in situ."

"Get off your high horse, Gill," said Kidd.

Macbeth glared down at the sergeant. "You seem to make a habit of messing up cases, Rachel."

Kidd shot daggers up at the pathologist. "If the cause of death has you baffled, Gill, I feel confident it *wasn't* suicide. Blue face. Bugged eyes. Reddened whites. Purple lips. Clenched fists. And discolored nails. It looks like asphyxia by hanging to me. As for the mask, that came later. *After* the killer slashed her stuck-out tongue."

"What mask?" Zinc said, playing the lightning rod to draw attention to him.

The social dynamics in this room were poisoned by estrogen. Gill Macbeth, in her forties, resembled Candice Bergen. Having spent her fertile years building a career, she had turned her mind to motherhood as her clock ticked down. Gill was pregnant by Corporal Nick Craven of Special X when Rachel Kidd arrested him for murdering his mother. Younger, prettier and the first black promoted up the ranks, Rachel, it turned out, had charged the wrong man. That freed the killer to bomb the cruise ship on which the Mounties held their Red Serge Ball. Gill lost her last chance to have a child when the explosion dumped her into a cold sea, the shock of which caused her to abort. Alex wrote about the case in her third book, which Rachel viewed as a tandem attempt by Gill and Alex to undermine her career. So while the others around the body focused on Zinc, the sergeant cast a look that could kill at the writer.

Men find it more therapeutic to kick each other in the balls.

"Chandler!" effused the coroner, a portly, hard-drinking sot. Custer would not have looked more relieved had reinforcements arrived.

The constable serving as exhibit man held up a plastic pouch. The mask within was this:

"*The Scream*," said Alex.

"By Edvard Munch," said Gill.

"That's not *The Scream* I know," said Zinc.

"Munch did a lithograph and an oil. This is the lithograph," Gill replied as she descended the ladder to join the others at ground level.

Zinc took the pouch from the exhibit man, reversing the mask to see the blood smeared around the mouth inside.

"This was on her face?"

"Yeah, when I arrived. One reason," Rachel said, "why I called you. It's like the mask Seattle police say the Hangman wore."

"Who found the body?"

"A neighbor walking his dog. The front door was blown open by the storm. He called in, got no answer and took a peek."

"Looks like a sex crime."

"I doubt it," said Gill. "Unless the killer has a fetish for underwear. The victim soiled herself when she was hanged, caking her panties to her buttocks. If she was raped, why's she wearing them?"

"The setup is definitely a puzzle," Rachel said. "Got to be careful. Nothing is what it seems. The table is set for two with candles, roses and wine. Romantic music. Sexy underwear. The inference is the victim invited a heartthrob here for dinner, and he or she was a monster who preyed on the hanged woman."

"The Lady-Killer?" said Zinc.

"Possibly. That's why I've got an APB out for him. And why"—she snapped a scowl at Gill—"I checked to make sure the hanged woman was Jayne Curry."

"Has Twist been located?"

"Not yet," Rachel said. "Though he's the prime suspect, I think she dined alone."

"Miss Lonely Heart?" said Alex. "Like in *Rear Window*, the Hitchcock film. Jimmy Stewart broke his leg and was confined to his apartment. To pass time, he spied on his neighbors through the rear window. He gave each a name based on what he saw. Miss Lonely Heart spent each night alone, pretending her lover joined her for dinner at a table set for two."

Rachel nodded. "The same with Jayne Curry. That's why she fell for the doctor, isn't it?"

"What's your theory?" Zinc asked.

"She was ambushed."

"Having dinner?"

"No, sitting at the computer."

The sergeant pointed to the glowing screen across the room.

"She was building a Web site about the trial, and whoever lynched her left it on. If it was Lady-Killer, why not delete her work?"

"Leaving it up makes it look like the killer wasn't him."

"Perhaps," said Rachel.

"So what's your take?"

"I think she dressed up in her finery for a Miss Lonely Heart dinner. Then she worked on her Web site at the computer. We found a recently cut branch outside that window, with two sets of indiscernable footprints in the mud. I think the killer bashed the limb against the glass to lure her out. She went upstairs to remove her expensive clothes. Her shoes are up on the landing and her dress is on the bed. With just a raincoat over her underwear, she disarmed the security system before she went outside. While she was cutting the branch with shears around the side of the house, the killer used the open door to slip in here. The victim returned and left her coat, boots and the shears at the back door, where we found them wet with rain. She entered this room in her underwear, probably to reset the alarm, and was ambushed by the killer."

Rachel directed Zinc back to the hanged woman. The other bunny suits at work were forensic techs. As one dusted the wine glasses on the table for fingerprints, the other measured the dis-

tance from the nearest leg stump to the pillar supporting the landing overhead. Secured around the pillar was the rope that had
been looped up over the railing to lynch Jayne Curry.

"The killer hanged her, slashed her tongue, then put on the
mask. Finally, after she was dead, her legs were cut off. The killer
kicked them across the floor to the wall behind you, and then used
the victim's blood to scrawl that game."

Zinc and Alex turned to face the wall between the entry hall
and this room.

"That," said the sergeant, "is the main reason I called you."

A pair of legs sheathed in nylons and garters lay against the
baseboard.

On the wall above, scrawled in blood, was a hangman game:

E as in Enigma

Vancouver
November 7

Those who make murder their business seek refuge in gallows humor. Take the job *too* seriously and your retirement will be spent in a rubber room. The corpse still hung from the balcony as those investigating the murder took a welcome break. The coroner was telling a story. Gallows humor, for sure.

"I ran into the strangest suicide of my career in a bar. To make sure his method of self-destruction did him in, the fellow hit upon what he thought was a foolproof plan. First, he found a hanging tree with a stout branch jutting out over a sheer cliff plummeting down to the sea. Then, to ensure that he suffered no pain, the would-be suicide swallowed an overdose of liquid morphine. Finally, to keep from strangling to death if his neck failed to break, he loaded a revolver to shoot himself in the head."

The coroner chortled to let them know the punch line was coming.

Scotch perfumed his words.

"The fellow tied one end of a rope to the jutting branch, then noosed the other end around his neck. The gun he carried as backup accidentally went off as he jumped over the cliff. The bullet struck the rope, almost severing it, then the jerk of his body snapped the remaining strands. Sixty feet below, he plunged into the sea, gulping salt water as he submerged. The gulp caused him to throw up the morphine, and, suicide thwarted, he swam ashore. That's how I met him in the bar, guzzling a hot toddy to get warm."

The listeners laughed as Zinc's cell called him back to work. He moved away from the group to answer his phone.

"Chandler," he said.

"Hi. It's Maddy Thorne. You left an urgent message with Homicide for me to call?"

Traffic in the background. She was in a car.

"That was quick," Zinc said.

"I'm off duty. But who's off duty these days with pagers and cells?"

"Sorry," said the Mountie. "Duty calls. Looks like we have a second Hangman victim here."

"Where's here?" Excited.

"North Vancouver. I'm staring at the victim as we speak."

"What's the link?"

"A *Scream* mask. And a hangman game."

"Jesus!" Maddy said. "We guessed wrong."

"Are you on a cell?"

"Yes."

"Is it secure?"

"Maybe not to the CIA. But it's digital."

"That's good enough," Zinc replied. "You guessed right. An *A*'s filled in."

"Which word?"

"Third word, second letter."

"Son of a bitch! The bastard won't play fair."

"If it's him. And not a copycat. How tight a lid did you put on the hangman game?"

"Strictly need-to-know. Hold-back evidence. You heard what I said to Justin. He could mention the game, but not the number of words or the number of letters in each. I doubt there's been a leak. We've kept the puzzle on a tight rein."

"So just the Hangman, Justin and Seattle police know the content of the word game?"

"Yeah. Plus you."

"I haven't told anyone. It's not my case. I didn't even tell the woman I live with."

"Looks like we have a cross-border serial killer," Maddy said.

"Looks like," agreed Zinc.

"The *A* doesn't solve the puzzle, but it answers a question. We wondered what would happen if we guessed the letter right."

"No quarter," said the Mountie. "The killer killed again. And will keep killing, I suspect, until the puzzle is solved."

Laughter broke out at his end of the phone as the coroner cracked a joke. A police siren passed Maddy at the other end.

"You mentioned a mask? Someone got a look at your killer?" she asked.

"No, the killer placed the mask over the victim's face."

"Why?" wondered Maddy.

"No reason I can see. Unless the Hangman *wants* us to link both hangings. Your APB last week said the Halloween killer might have worn a mask of *The Scream*. You get that from the neighbor who saw the Reaper approach Mary Konrad's door?"

"Yeah," said Maddy. "Remember what Justin told us? The neighbor described the mask as being like a skull face, but not a skull. It was, she said, the face in 'that famous picture,' which she couldn't name. Later, she was shown *The Scream* and identified it as the suspect's mask."

"You know there's more than one *Scream*?"

"I do," said Maddy. "The oil painting. The lithograph. And a stylized version in the Wes Craven horror film."

"Ours is the lithograph."

"That's what the neighbor picked out. If you send me a copy, I'll double-check."

Zinc took out his notebook and jotted a reminder to do that. "How's your case going?"

"It's not," said Maddy. "The task force working it has no solid leads. HITS did a computer search for possible links. Nothing came back. If a serial killer's on the loose, the hangman game seems to indicate Halloween was the first murder. The only suspect with a specific motive is the vic's husband."

"What do you know about her?"

"Mary Konrad was a country girl from eastern Washington. A weak personality. No enemies. Left her first husband years ago to move to Seattle. Worked at office jobs. Still good-looking when she met and married Dag. Then, after the wedding, she got fat. You remember Dag? The world's hairiest sexist. There's a guy who needs a babe to show the world he's a stud. Dag took to drinking and punching his wife as she ballooned up. An ugly divorce was underway when Mary got killed. The house in which she died was up for sale. Dag gets to keep *everything* now that Mary's dead. He has a strong motive and a weak alibi. We have suspicion, but no proof."

"Could Dag have done it?"

"To my mind," Maddy replied. "The Reaper was seen approaching the house at five-thirty. No one answered when the neighbor knocked at six o'clock. The murder was called in around seven. We didn't get to Dag's apartment until after ten that night. His alibi is that between five and seven he was putting on his makeup. It took some time to do, what with all the Wolf Man hair, but no one backs up the time frame he offered us. What if he put on the makeup *earlier* that day, and covered it with the *Scream* mask and robes to go kill Mary? Halloween provided the perfect opportunity for him to approach her house in disguise, and to escape in costume after Mary was hanged."

"Forensic turn up anything?"

"No, the scene was clean."

"Sex attack?"

"Negative. Her clothes were on, as you saw, and swabs for semen didn't analyze."

"What about the rope?"

"As common as they come. So are the pulleys used to hoist her up and the hacksaw that cut off her leg. The cuffs used to pinion her wrists can be purchased in any bondage shop."

"The killer must have gone prepared for that *specific* victim. Choose a woman not overweight and he wouldn't need the pulleys."

"That's what makes me believe the Hangman is Dag," replied Maddy. "He's the only suspect with a specific motive. He slashed Mary's tongue because his wife was a nag. The hanging and the severed leg are a blind, so that when we combine them with the hangman taunt, we'll think a serial psycho is loose. What better way to hide a specific victim than in a random spree?"

"And victim two?" said Zinc.

"The Hangman could still be Dag. He knows he's a prime suspect for his wife's murder, so he goes after another woman far from home and does everything he can to link both crimes."

"Dag needs checking."

"That's what I'm going to do."

"Send me what's relevant from your file and we'll check on him up here."

"You'll have it tomorrow. Now what about your vic?"

"That case your partner Ralph was helping me with in Seattle?"

"You mean the juror who screwed Dr. Twist?"

"Right. The case we discussed the night you picked me up."

"Don't tell me!"

"Uh-huh. She's the victim."

"I'm all ears," Maddy said. "Fill me in."

"Jayne Curry. Fiftyish. Unmarried. Lives alone. A 'lonely heart' type. She was working in her home when the Hangman lured her out. He slipped inside and waited for her to return. The noose was cinched around her neck in a surprise attack, then she was hoisted off her feet before she could react. No pulleys, just the rope looped up over a railing. No cuffs, so her arms were free to flail. Her tongue, as in your case, was severed with a blade, and after death both legs were cut off. They, too, were kicked across to the wall on which we found a hangman game drawn in blood."

"Both stick legs missing?"

"Yes. Hangman played in reverse."

"How big's the vic?"

"Petite," said Zinc.

"No need for pulleys. Sex attack?"

"The victim's dressed in underwear, but that can be explained. Her outerwear got soaked when the Hangman lured her out into the rain. The pathologist doubts her panties were removed."

"Find a hacksaw?"

"Not so far. We do have indistinct footprints outside."

"Good. We can compare the size of the prints with Dag's shoes."

"The Hangman placed the *Scream* mask over the face of the victim, then, as in your case, left the front door open in a storm so she'd be found."

"Is Dr. Twist a suspect?"

"Big time," said Zinc.

The professional bunny suits were getting back to work. Alex, notebook in hand, wandered over to rejoin Zinc by the hall door. A path of contamination, cleared by Ident forensically and safe to walk through, was marked on the floor. As Zinc talked with Maddy, Alex scribbled notes.

"Remember what I told you about our cause celebre? Twist was charged with drugging a rich patient at his medical clinic, shortly after she bequeathed her entire estate to him. The allegation was he did the old lady in with a shot of potassium."

"There was a recent piece in the *Seattle Star.*"

"Much of what we're about to discuss hasn't been released. Can I rely on you to keep it secret?" asked Zinc.

"My lips are sealed," said Maddy. "As yours were with our case."

"The doctor's a lady-killer. He's catnip to lonely women. Twist is handsome, charming and funny. To visualize him, think of Cary Grant. We know at least two other widows died shortly after leaving him their money. Until that case, we didn't have enough to charge him."

"The case on which he walked?"

"Yes," said Zinc. "The main witness for the Crown was a nurse Twist fired from his clinic. She testified that a needle mark the pathologist spotted on the body was made by a mysterious injection the doctor gave the deceased at midnight. The nurse chanced upon the event, which she wasn't supposed to see. After she reported to us what she had witnessed, investigators searched records at the clinic. There was no mention of the midnight injection, and no drug had been dispensed from the clinic pharmacy for that patient."

"Why potassium?" Maddy asked.

"It slips through detection at an autopsy because it's found naturally in a human body."

"So it all came down to the nurse?"

"Whom Twist had fired."

"A motive for revenge."

"The doctor took the stand in his own defense. He said he fired the nurse because he disagreed with her strong stance on euthanasia. He couldn't have her working in his geriatric clinic. The clinic would be liable if she killed a patient."

"The firing was *after* she saw him give the injection?"

"Yes," said Zinc.

"You think he knew the nurse saw him?"

"Probably."

"So he set her up with a motive for injecting the old woman in case she ratted on him?"

"He's clever, Maddy. That's why we haven't been able to pin a conviction on him. Jayne Curry was on the jury trying the doctor for murder. Sheriffs began to notice something was amiss in court. It began with flirtatious glances between Curry and Twist. Seductive smiles from her. An eyebrow arched from him. Jurors filed into the courtroom in the same order each time. A dramatic pause occurred in the procession before Curry entered, then she would step into the jury box and lock eyes with Twist. The looks became more blatant as the trial continued, and they took on a hint of sexual conspiracy. The sheriffs brought it to the attention of the judge when Twist was seen talking with Curry at lunch on the steps near the law courts fountain."

"Was there a mistrial?"

"No," said Zinc. "In the jury's absence, the judge warned Twist not to have contact with any jurors. But to avoid disrupting the jury, the judge didn't raise the matter with them."

"Strange," said Maddy.

"Twist's a lady-killer. The judge was a woman. He charmed her too."

Horns at the other end. Traffic was heavy.

"The jury was out for days before it brought in a verdict acquitting the doctor of first-degree murder. That night, an off-duty cop spotted Twist and Curry walking arm in arm. We began surveillance of both of them, and obtained a court order to bug their homes. Two days later, the mike in her bedroom recorded them having sex. From conversation afterward, it could be inferred that they had done it before, and that they became lovers *during* the trial."

Maddy tsk-tsked. "Bedding a guy you're trying for murder comes with a lot of baggage."

"What's even more important is Twist's story about the nurse. What he told Curry in bed—and probably had during the trial—was that his relationship with her was like *Fatal Attraction*. The nurse went weird on him after a one-night stand, and when he tried to break it off, she flipped out completely. It was the nurse who must have stuck the needle in the deceased, the night before the day Twist fired her. For revenge, she went to the police and framed him for murder."

"Was that his evidence in court?"

"No," said Zinc. "Not a word about having sex with the nurse. The reason he gave Curry was that it would make him look guilty. The Crown alleged he was a lady-killer who used his charm on women, so how could he tell the jury he slept with an employee, then fired her when she fell for him?"

"Even though it gave the nurse a stronger motive to frame him?"

"The trouble was, Maddy, the nurse is a lesbian."

"So he didn't have sex with her?"

"It was a lie. A lie Jayne Curry probably took into the jury room. And that gave us reason to go after her for obstruction of justice. "Canadian law makes it illegal for jurors to discuss what went on in their jury room. Except when questioned by police investigating jury tampering, or when testifying in court in an obstruction case. The bug in Curry's bedroom gave us cause to question all Twist's jurors."

Another siren passed Maddy at the far end of the phone.

"From the first straw vote taken by the jury, Curry steadfastly maintained Twist was innocent. She theorized it was the nurse who killed the old lady. The vote was two undecided, eight for conviction, two for acquittal. Curry became a belligerent advocate for the accused, and as deliberations progressed, she turned difficult. Agree with her and she was stable. Challenge her and she threw a nasty tantrum.

"Curry did everything she could to undermine the convictors. One buckled when it became clear that nothing logical said for conviction would sway her. Either you voted with Curry or the jury hung. More collapsed when she falsely warned them they would have to reveal how they voted in court if the verdict was a deadlock. They didn't want a killer on bail singling them out.

Arguing and acrimony wore others down. Mental numbness set in and they no longer spoke up. The last day was rife with emotion. The jury room was a hothouse. Curry accused a man of trying to railroad the doctor because of his intelligence and good looks. Comments got more and more personal, until those arguing for conviction finally gave up. The holdouts seemed to change their minds all at once. One juror described Curry's effect like this: 'Had she been different, so might the verdict.'"

"A soap opera," Maddy said. "A Harlequin heroine standing by her man."

"Eve and the forbidden fruit in the Garden of Eden," said Zinc. "Her attraction to the deadly doctor was intoxicating. She fell in love with a fantasy who didn't exist. Twist saw his chance to have a juror in his pocket. Every time Curry turned around, there he was, smiling at her like Rhett Butler. She saw the doc as a victim only she could save, falling into romantic escapism from her lonely life. Reality hit when we charged her with obstruction of justice. That's when she met the Mr. Hyde hiding in Dr. Twist."

"He dumped her?"

"And the lovestruck juror woke up."

"You went after her to get another crack at him?"

"The Crown filed a notice of appeal to quash the jury verdict acquitting Dr. Twist of murder. The main ground for seeking a new trial was 'improper communications and contact between juror Jayne Curry and the accused whom she was trying prior to the delivery of a verdict in court.' The court of appeal would be hard pressed not to order a new trial if there was sufficient proof the verdict was affected by matters other than evidence heard in court. A conviction for obstruction would prove Curry was not an impartial juror, so a guilty verdict in her case would result in a retrial of Twist for murder."

"I smell motive," said Maddy.

"The case against Curry was this: By engaging in a sexual fling with the man she was trying, she breached her oath to deliver a true verdict based solely on the evidence. The doctor told her that he was innocent, and that the real killer was a nurse with whom he had had a bad sexual encounter. That's why the nurse framed him for the murder she committed. Curry believed Twist's lie to be true, and she took that evidence, which didn't come from the doctor's mouth on the witness stand, into the jury room. She was the antithesis of what a juror should be, and her participation tainted the deliberations that led to the verdict. Curry was privy to information the other eleven didn't have, and it compelled her to influence them to acquit her secret lover. No way could she find the accused guilty and send him to jail. The trial wasn't fair, so justice was obstructed."

"You had her," said Maddy.

"Imagine you're Jayne Curry. A lonely heart all your life. Facing years in jail for saving the skin of a cad who played you for a fool. How betrayed you feel is evident from notes you made to launch a site on the Internet to sway public opinion. 'I didn't obstruct justice. I merely fell in love. I'm the victim of a deceptive lover, vengeful police and a justice system run amok. What I did wasn't a crime. No one told me not to have contact with Dr. Twist. The verdict I rendered was just. The Crown's case was weak. Why must I suffer for love?'"

"Offer me a deal," said Maddy, "and I'll rat on Dr. Twist."

"That was in the works."

"Bye, bye, false lover."

"Now imagine you're Dr. Twist. A jury has acquitted you of first-degree murder. What stands between you and freedom is Jayne Curry. If she is convicted of obstruction, you will be tried again. If she cuts a deal with the Crown, your jury tampering also means a retrial. Without Curry, you're scot-free. There is no admissible evidence to overturn your acquittal. Just weak inference and a bugging order with technical flaws. You're a cold psychopath who has killed before. What would you do?"

"I'd snuff Curry."

"Surely her death would point to you?"

"Not if the crime was committed by a genuine serial killer. A killer who hanged a woman in Seattle a week ago. A killer who left clues known only to him and the cops at both murder scenes."

"The tongue cut out is a nice 'twist,' eh? Does it mean 'Now you won't talk'?"

"Dr. Twist struck first in Seattle because he wasn't known here. His trial made him a cause célèbre in Vancouver."

"Fat Mary Konrad was his kind of victim."

"The Lady-Killer stalked her?"

"That's his style," said Zinc.

"Which explains why he came prepared with pulleys and such."

"With a random victim hanged to establish the Hangman, the cunning doctor then went after Jayne Curry."

"Twist needs checking."

"That's being done."

"Send me what's relevant from your file and we'll check on him down here."

"We need a joint task force."

"Yeah," said Maddy. "If the Hangman isn't Dag Konrad or Dr. Twist, we're looking for a cross-border nut hunting randomly. Or a psycho stalking women linked by some hidden motive."

"I'll be in Seattle on Friday."

"What for, Zinc?"

"You'll laugh if I tell you."

"I could use a laugh. Traffic is at a standstill. The sirens you heard were responding to a pileup on the I-5."

"My girlfriend's a writer."

Alex looked up from her notes.

"The Northwest Writers' Festival has come up with a unique idea for a fund-raiser. An event restricted to cops, lawyers, forensic techs, private eyes and crime scribblers."

"Homicide got invited. The party on the boat?"

"My girlfriend roped me into going along. Amtrak to Seattle, sail to Vancouver, and those from Seattle Amtrak home."

"Where'd they get the boat?"

"It's a cruise line. Training trip for the crew. A comp for the festival."

"A booze-schmooze cruise."

"Undoubtedly. With all night to kill. Come along, and we'll kill some time comparing files."

"Maybe," said Maddy. "So what's your guess?"

"The word game?"

"Yeah."

"I'll follow your lead. The first two words need vowels. In tomorrow's papers, let's guess *E*."

"So," said Alex once Zinc finished the call, "that was Maddy?"

"Yes," he said.

"The *same* Maddy at whose abode you slept when you were in Seattle?"

"Don't tell me you're jealous?"

"Of course not, Zinc. The same way it wouldn't irk you if I met some stranger at a book event and shacked up with him for the night."

"I slept on the couch."

"Did she sleep on the couch too?"

"Really, Alex. You know me better than that."

"How'd you miss your flight?"

"I got caught up in the case."

"In *Maddy's* case?"

"Yes."

"So you slept at Maddy's house?"

"It wasn't a house. It was an apartment."

"Oh! Pardon me. That makes a *big* difference."

"I see her as a cop. I don't see her as a woman."

"Even in her baby dolls?"

"She wasn't wearing baby dolls."

"Oh! Was she in the nude?"

"Stop it, Alex. You know you're the only woman for me. You have no cause to be jealous."

"I'm not jealous."

"Yes, you are."

"No, I'm not."

"Could have fooled me."

"The only person fooling you is Maddy, Zinc."

"She's a cop."

"Not a woman?"

"Not to me."

"What does she look like?"

"Well, like a cop."

"A *female* cop?"

"Of course."

"Is she good-looking?"

"If you go for the type."

"What type is that?"

"You know."

"No, I don't. But I'll soon see. And God help you, Zinc Chandler, if the cop you spent the night with, and just invited on *our* cruise, turns out to be built like a stripper or looks the least bit sexy to me."

The Tyburn Jig

Vancouver
Tonight

"Hangman Strikes Here," blared the morning tabloid from the newspaper box out front of the CNIB stand in the lobby of the law courts. The headline was seventy points at least. The size saved for catastrophes like Kennedy getting shot. The stand used to be staffed by clerks who were sight impaired, fitting since it was run by the Canadian National Institute for the Blind, but the woman who sold me both papers that morning of November 8—the day after Jayne Curry was hanged in North Vancouver—could see as well as, if not better than, me. It was naive to hope an honesty system would work with lawyers as the stand's main customers.

Honor among thieves?

I crossed to the elevators near the court registry and joined the throng of barristers on their way up. The sweet smell of money wafted off their power suits, and the number of chins on their plump, ruddy faces attested to their success. All were civil lawyers from the veal-fattening pens uptown, multi-floored international firms packed into phallic towers. Hundreds of minions chained to computers tracking billable hours were fed an endless stream of files to churn out needless paper for gullible clients who swallow padded accounts.

HANGMAN

Those let out for a little fresh air were the lackeys who followed their senior counsels lugging briefcases bulging with thick files.

The lawyers looked down at me like I was shit on their shoes.

Lard loathes lean and mean.

The elevator arrived and we packed in. I punched 3 for the law library. I told you my only sure cure for skid-row blues was to escape uptown. Here, I could fantasize that this is where I belong. Back when I got hooked on law in Kinky's court, I would amble over to Rattenbury's courthouse to watch jury trials. That courthouse has since become the art gallery, so now I amble two blocks south to the new law courts. Every lawyer, fat or lean, is equal in the law library, so I planned to spend the day reading cases uptown instead of in my grungy office at Kline & Shaw.

The elevator opened and we surged out.

By then I was gagging from those cloying colognes fat cats slap on to disguise the pungent stench that fear of losing sweats from them.

A long corridor ran the length of level three. A gallery of photos lined one wall: headshots of judges stretching from recent days back to when they still wore horsehair wigs. The entrance to the library separated appeal court from trial-court judges. As I moved toward the barristers' lounge, I traced recurring family names through several generations, as silver spoons were passed down from father to son. What hit me was how the faces grew tougher the further back I went, for those were the times when hangmen dropped forty-four cons down the elevator shaft at Oakalla Prison Farm.

Hangmen, I thought.

The barristers' lounge opened off the hall beyond the last photo. A sign by the door warned laymen away. Signs within asked lawyers to PLEASE TURN CELLPHONES OFF IN COURTROOMS, and cautioned us beneath a drawing of a black-masked burglar to PLEASE . . .

WATCH YOUR BELONGINGS. ALL ARTICLES LEFT AT OWN RISK. A Canadian trial lawyer wears British court regalia, minus the wig. At more than a thousand bucks for a basic set of robes, those left unattended vanish in a second.

Like I said: Honor among thieves?

Though it was nothing more than an alcove beyond the coat rack, Brian and Ken's Coffee House did a bustling trade. WELCOME. STARBUCKS IT AIN'T . . . BUT THE COFFEE'S GOOD AND THE PRICE IS RIGHT, read the sign. No false advertising there. Where else can you get a twenty-five-cent cup of caffeine?

The cupboards above the coffeepots were covered with cartoons. Snipped from newspapers and magazines, most were jokes about juries and hanging. I laughed as I stood in line.

I drained the dregs from the pot and carried my cup of coffee through to the lounge. The lounge was full of Queen's Counsel in shiny silk robes, wheeling and dealing to settle million-dollar lawsuits "on the courthouse steps," and barristers without QCs in dull "stuff" robes, trying to bail new clients out by phone before rushing off to court to defend those in the dock. I found a seat at the eye of the hurricane, and then sat down with my coffee to read about last night's hanging.

Catchy name.

The Hangman.

Trust Americans. They've always had a knack for nicknaming serial killers. Son of Sam. Murder Mac. The .22 Caliber Killer. Zodiac. Candy Man. The Sunset Strip Slayer. Forces of Evil. The Night Stalker. The Boston Strangler. The Score Card Killer. The Sunday Morning Slasher.

Having squeezed every fact from both papers, I crumpled my cup and tossed it at the basketball hoop of the wastebasket, then left the lounge for the library to cobble together a defense for an upcoming, run-of-the-mill drug case. As I wandered the shelves collecting law reports, the word "hangman" shanghaied me from the Lawyers' Leisure section.

HANGMAN

Dance with the Hangman: The History of Hanging from Jack Ketch to Albert Pierrepoint.

The book lurked among other books published to entertain: legal biographies, anecdotes, histories and such.

A light bulb went on in my mind.

I reached for the book.

Whoever the Hangman was, this killer was on a mission. A lynching in Seattle, a lynching in Vancouver—together they meant a killing spree. What began as a crime down south had become a tale of two cities, and one of those two cities was *mine*. No longer would my daydream be that I was an American lawyer. The killer of the decade had crossed the border, so now I could fantasize that I was *me*. If and when the Hangman was caught and tried, every gunslinger north and south of the line would want that client, so what could I do to make that gunslinger Jeffrey Kline?

Attracting the killer's attention was my bright idea.

Whatever the Hangman's mission, it centered on hanging. The killer had gone to great trouble to hang both victims, and to play the hangman game with police. In choosing America for the first lynching, the killer embarked upon a self-defeating course of action. With criminal law scattered among fifty-one jurisdictions, the fifty states and the federal government, the hangman never became a national icon down there. "Judge Lynch" was the law across the Wild West, but he was a different man in each county, and hanging went into decline in 1890, after Yankee ingenuity thought up the electric chair. The hangman as a named and feared executioner, hanging cons around the country and the commonwealth, was a *British* horror.

Welcome to British Columbia, Hangman.

Do you feel at home?

Tingling with excitement, I carried the book to where I was working and shoved my legal research for the drug trial aside. With pen and paper ready, I cracked *Dance with the Hangman*. What I planned to do was write a background article on hangmen for the local papers, the subtext of which—aimed at the Hangman—would be "I understand your mission. Jeffrey Kline is your kind of lawyer."

A few pages into the book, I came across a useful hook. A hook is what a lawyer uses to kick off a jury submission.

A century or two back, a boat full of Christian seafarers wrecked and sank in a storm. The survivors landed as castaways on a remote island. Fearing it was inhabited by headhunters or cannibals, they set out to explore their new home. On moving inland, they almost immediately caught sight of the rotting corpse of a man hanging on a gallows. No greater comfort could they have found. The hanging meant other Christians lived nearby.

Good hook that. A nice ironic touch. Was the Hangman's mission one of biblical retribution? An eye for an eye? A tooth for a tooth? Hey, I understand.

Next, a little horror to titillate readers. For six centuries or more, Tyburn Hill was the execution site in London. Speakers' Corner in Hyde Park is close by today, and maps still show the short road of Tyburn Way. At the hands of hangmen like the notorious Jack Ketch, it's estimated 50,000 people were publicly executed there.

Ketch was hangman from 1663 to 1686.

Hangman was a versatile job in his day. Hanging by the neck until dead was for common people, and Merrie England saw the ladder and rope in constant use. The condemned scaled a ladder placed against the gallows beam, and there was jeered by the public while Ketch cinched the noose. Then the hangman "turned him off" to dance "the Tyburn jig." Carts replaced the ladder during that century. With nooses hanging loose about their necks, prisoners were trundled by cart to Tyburn Hill as crowds along the route cracked jokes, partied, drank and pelted them with offal. Arriving at the gallows, the prisoners were strung up by Ketch, who then whipped the horse-drawn carts away so they could dance on air.

HANGMAN

Tyburn's Triple Tree had three gallows beams. Cart after cart could be emptied with ease. Often the condemned's bowels and bladder let go, so Ketch was also known as "the crap merchant." A euphemism for hanging was "pissing when you can't whistle."

Those who really pissed off the Crown were hanged, drawn and quartered. Ketch would hang you by the neck until you *weren't* dead, then cut you down and rip you open so he could draw out your bowels and roast them in front of your eyes. To finish, he would hack off your head and butcher you into quarters. The four pieces, stuck on poles, were displayed around London as a warning. Your severed head was a trophy to mount on Traitors' Gate.

"Quartering?" I wrote.

"The cut-off legs?"

So hated was the hangman that Ketch himself was hanged in Punch and Judy shows. Children were kept quiet with threats of "Jack Ketch will get you." The last witch, Alice Molland, was hanged in Britain before Ketch died, in 1685. So enduring was Ketch's gruesome legacy that every hangman after him was referred to by the public as "Jack Ketch."

My pen was flying.

On I read.

Another hangman of that time was John Crosland. How he came to get the job is the stuff of legend. A father and his two sons were tried and convicted for horse-stealing at Derby Assizes. Gallows humor ruled sentencing that day, so the judges offered to pardon one of the three men if he would consent to hang the other two.

The offer was made to the father, who hurled it back at the bench. "What!" he shouted with contempt. "A father hang his sons? How can I put to death the life I gave? No, let me hang by the neck a hundred times instead!"

The offer was made to the elder son. He too spat it back at the judges. "How could I live with *myself* if I hanged my own family?"

The offer was made to the younger son, and John accepted at once. So fine a job did he do of hanging his father and brother that John Crosland went on to become the hangman for several counties, an office he held to a ripe old age.

"Important point."

Notes were coming fast.

"Hangman isn't a job. Hangman is a calling."

"What makes someone conclude his mission in life is to hang people?"

The last execution at Tyburn was in 1783. From there, the Tyburn jig moved to a scaffold in front of Newgate Prison, in Old Bailey. Thenceforth, a convict strung up for slow strangulation was said to be "dancing in Bailey's ballroom."

Hmmmm, I thought. The Old Bailey. Now the name of London's Central Criminal Court.

I made another note.

"Hanging and the courts?"

The hangman who served the longest was William Calcraft. He was in office from 1829 to 1874. Death by slow strangulation was Calcraft's trademark. For work on the scaffold, he always wore dead black. In 1831, he hanged a boy of nine. There were times when Calcraft took pity on a strangling condemned, so he would pull down on the wretch's leg to help him die faster. Thus the origin of the saying "You're pulling my leg." Sometimes, relatives took up that task. Thus "hangers-on."

A memorable hanging occurred in his first year as hangman. Calcraft was to execute David Evans for murdering his sweetheart. The rope snapped as Evans dangled from the gallows, plunging him unnerved but unhurt to the ground.

"Shame! Shame! Let him go!" shouted the unruly mob.

"I claim my liberty," declared the half-hanged man. "You hanged me once. You have no right to hang me again."

Evans staggered to his feet, struggling to get away. Down came Calcraft to haul him up for another try.

"It's against the law," cried Evans, "to hang me a second time!"

"You are mistaken," the hangman replied. "There is no such law that you must be let go if there is an accident and you are not properly hanged. My warrant is to hang you by the neck until you are dead. So up you go, and hang you must until you *are* dead."

Evans hanged, protesting to the end.

"The Marquis of Queensberry rules don't apply on the gallows," I wrote.

"The same with the Hangman.

"The Hangman killed again, though police correctly guessed the letter *A*.

"The guess in this morning's papers was the letter *E*.

"Will the Hangman kill again if that guess, too, is right?

"I wish the cops would release the Hangman's word puzzle so I could take a stab at solving it.

"How many words?

"How many letters in each?"

The custom in Calcraft's time was that a hangman owned his victim's clothes and the rope used to hang him. That "Jack Ketch" made a pretty penny off the perquisites of his office. He sold the garments of those he hanged to Madame Tussaud's waxworks and other exhibitions. The notoriety of the convict put to death determined the price it cost relic hunters for a piece of the rope, sometimes as much as five shillings an inch.

Calcraft carried out the last public execution in 1868. A large crowd assembled in front of Newgate Prison. The corpse was left to hang for the usual hour. As the hangman was cutting down the hanged man, he was taunted by the mob with cries of "Come on, body snatcher. Take the man you killed." The public spectacle had seen its day. Henceforth, the jig was danced in private *within* Bailey's ballroom. Later, the Old Bailey was built on the prison site. Do the ghosts of the gallows haunt London's criminal courts?

I made another note.

"Hanging as public deterrent."

Hindsight, of course, is 20/20. As I worked in the library on November 8, I wondered if the article I hoped to publish could be fashioned into a double hook. Perhaps the Hangman would conclude that Jeffrey Kline was a lawyer who understood the mission and, if the killer was caught, should therefore be the gunslinger to defend the accused in court. Too many "woulds" and "shoulds" made that a long shot, so was there more to be gained by *provoking* the psycho? What if the article induced the Hangman to contact me? Once the killer was hooked, I could reel in the case. Say I made the piece read as if I understood the mission, but I included mistakes that cast doubt? Would that lure the Hangman in to set me straight?

A deadly game in hindsight, as events tonight are proving.

Hanged, drawn and quartered.

Prophetic words.

Is that the fate the Hangman has in mind for me ... ?

Scribblers

The galley proofs of *Perverse Verdict* were spread across Justin Whitfield's desk in the newsroom of the *Seattle Star*. The room was a wide-open space humming with manic activity as reporters writing to deadline banged away at keyboards to fill computer screens with copy, or transcribed interviews from hand-held recorders, or jotted notes while cradling phones in the crook between shoulder and ear. The cubicles in which they worked were scattered around concrete pillars holding up the ceiling. Bulletin boards pinned with maps, work schedules and union notices covered the supports. A bank of windows along the west wall overlooked Elliott Bay, with Puget Sound beyond. The sky out there was as joylessly gray as the carpet, cubicles, desks and upright surfaces in here, but not as gray as the hangover clouding Justin's mind.

Thank you, Jack Daniels.

God, how his head hurt!

Deadlines, stress and the urge to unwind.

Booze was, and always would be, the main hazard of his job.

If Justin had known the Hangman would strike again last night, he would have stayed in Vancouver and sworn off the sauce. Instead, he had imbibed with his brother in the airport lounge, watching planes come and go on the rainy runways of Sea Island while the waiter came and went with enough shots of bourbon and water to drown both men. Ethan drank like a lawyer. Justin drank to keep up. So by the time he caught the last flight to Seattle from Vancouver at close to midnight, the reporter was in no condition to report. Having missed the Hangman scoop despite being in the city where the crime went down, Justin first heard about the second killing on the radio in the taxi driving him home from SeaTac Airport.

Shit! he thought.

Just my luck!

With dawn had come no respite from the pain in his head. It was an ordeal simply to get to work. Work itself was self-flagellation. The piece he had just finished for tomorrow's edition was, understandably, not up to par. It lacked the insight he brought to a story by personally haunting the murder scene, and his pipeline from Maddy could provide only sketchy secondhand details. As for the crispness of his prose, the craftsmanship of the wordsmith reflected the hangover addling his brain.

The *Star*'s star reporter was fading today.

A shout from across the newsroom caught Justin's ear. An editor, jumping up, was waving his fist for the story. Time to check the stillborn copy into city desk, so Justin punched a button to send his Hangman article there.

That done, he switched hats from writer to editor.

The galleys covering his desk were page proofs for his soon-to-be-published true-crime book. As such, they marked the point of no return for last-minute changes. How they read was how *Perverse Verdict* would end up in print, so Justin turned his fuzzy attention to weighing Ethan's margin-scribbled comments.

Justin was proofing this passage when the phone on his desk rang:

The scene in the prison the night of the riot in 1984 was worthy of Dante's *Inferno*. For prisoners in protective custody, it was a living hell.

The riot began in Cell Block Three as guards were searching inmates for drugs before the night lockdown. Using fists and feet, twenty cold-blooded veterans of incarceration overpowered ten guards, then stormed the prison control center a hundred yards away, breaching it by smashing through inch-thick glass with fire extinguishers. The glass, installed just two weeks before, was supposedly unbreakable.

Command of the control center gave the rampaging convicts control of the jail. It contained electronic switches and keys for all the cells. First, they opened the hospital to empty it of drugs, then they unlocked Cell Block Two, known as The Predator. The Predator secured the most vicious, hard-core cons in Washington State.

The party got bigger and bigger as the rioters ran amok. From cell block to cell block, they moved through the prison, releasing doors to free their friends or to get at their enemies. The trail they left was littered with pills, bottles, capsules and hypodermic needles. The drugs they crushed were mainlined indiscriminately, including diuretics that made them pee. They destroyed the prison as they went, gutting the control center to leave it a shambles, torching the hospital so billowing black smoke filled the sky, battering steel doors and concrete walls with pickaxes stolen from a maintenance shed. Armed with baseball bats from the prison gym and homemade knives honed razor-sharp in the workshop, the frenzied mob quickly degenerated into a rabble of stoned psychos out for blood. The blood they craved was that of "skinners" and "rats," jailhouse terms for the sex offenders and informers who were kept in protective custody in Cell Block Four.

If you have hate in your heart and the keys to the jail in your hand, there's no stopping you from slaking your thirst for gore.

Skinners and rats are always afraid, but no fear is more ferocious than for fear that the guards will lose control. Peter Bryce Haddon was already unnerved from his first week in custody under a death warrant for the sex killing of a nine-year-old girl when he heard the heavy-duty cons in a take-no-prisoners mood unlock the door and come storming into protective custody.

The first guard to intercept them was beaten to a pulp. "Take that, screw!" the cons shouted as they took bats to his skull, slugging him until his face was a crimson goo and his scalp slipped askew like a cheap toupee.

"That snitch is mine," someone yelled as the first informer was dragged from his cell, clutching a Bible and sniveling for mercy in the name of one saint, then another.

Haddon almost fainted when the screaming began, a shrill shriek that soared to the whine of a dentist's drill. The rioters pinned the rat to the floor in the hall so all could see, and those whose turn was yet to come watched horrified as the snitch was scorched from foot to head with a blowtorch. The blue flame was held on his twisted face until the flesh bubbled and melted. When it was over, the head had been reduced to nothing but a charred skull.

A tattooed monster went to work on the rat in the cell next to Haddon's. He hauled the man out, whirled him around and cuffed one wrist to the bars, then he made him watch as he slowly cut one finger halfway through the joint. "Pull it off," he ordered, "or I'll cut your throat."

Haddon winced as the mutilated informer tore off his own finger. The savage con wrenched the severed digit from his bawling victim to crush underfoot like a discarded cigarette. Then he sawed deep into another finger, demanding the snitch pull himself apart again, and once that hand was stripped to the palm, made him rip the half-sawn fingers off his other hand with his teeth.

The gibbering of another informer yanked Haddon's attention away. The rat was gripped in a hammerlock by a huge psycho known as the Hulk. The Hulk had in his fist a piece of angle iron which he had stuck in one ear of the squirming snitch and was forcefully screwing back and forth to drive the rod through the man's brain and out his other ear. Death spasms animated the puppet in his grasp as, gripping the bar on both sides of the head like pumping iron, he carried the corpse from cell to cell to show those quaking in terror what to expect from him.

The clink of a key in the door to his cell pulled Haddon's attention back.

"Okay, baby-fucker. It's your turn."

That was around the time I arrived at the prison, landing in a chopper chartered by the *Seattle Star.* A full moon shone down on the burning buildings as firefighters shot water in through broken windows to quell the flames. Police in riot gear and National Guardsmen armed to the teeth besieged the jail. Rescued inmates stumbled out, eyes swollen and covered in blood from head to foot. Most were unrecognizable; many were in shock. Naked and shivering, a con slumped outside his burnt-out block, jabbering about the horrors he had seen inside. "They killed! They butchered!" he yelled as another con staggered out. "They butchered! They killed!" yammered the second man.

Deep within the dark, smoke-filled, sodden ruin, tactical squads moved cell to cell to reclaim the prison. What they encountered was utter destruction. Steel-barred cell doors torn off hinges. Reinforced concrete walls six inches thick sledgehammered apart, with wires dangling. Toilets smashed and water ankle-deep along the halls, forcing them to wade around broken glass, debris and smoldering mattresses. A stench of fear seemed to rise from blood streaks in the water. When they got to Cell Block Four, they found a foot-wide swath of caked gore running twelve feet along the wall to end above the propped-up bodies of three men. Their slashed throats testified to the orgy of violence continuing inside. Wails from Peter Haddon's cell corroborated the warning.

Haddon's clothes lay tossed out in the hall. His light gray prison-issue shirt and baggy blue jeans. His socks and navy blue Velcro running shoes. His T-shirt and underwear soaked from dread. Four cons, none of whom could lay valid claim to being human, had locked themselves in with him. They were known in prison as the Back Door Boys, and as the tactical squad moved into

Cell Block Four, the last thug was pounding at Haddon's back door.

"Nut him!" someone shouted as the squad came down the hall.

Slight, naked and wide-eyed, Haddon was standing up. The grunting con behind him wasn't as huge as the Hulk, but he was big enough. Muscular arms ran under Haddon's shoulders to lock fingers behind his neck, holding him in a vise grip while he was sodomized. A pair with their pants around their ankles held his legs apart as a fourth con squatted in front of his groin. Like a living jockstrap, Haddon's hands tried to cup his genitals in a frantic attempt to save them from castration. Crisscrossing his abdomen, hands and thighs with red slits, the squatter slashed a knife back and forth around Haddon's exposed crotch.

The squad had almost reached the cell when Haddon squealed. The pair spreading his legs each grabbed a wrist and held his hands away. The con with the knife grasped his penis to jerk him into the air, then swept the blade across in a groin-level arc. The shriek from Cell Block Four was heard outside.

I was there when they brought Haddon out on a stretcher. His testicles came out in a plastic cup. He didn't undergo surgery to have them reattached. By the time he arrived at the hospital, his mangled manhood was dead.

Imagine his fear the moment before the knife gelded him. It sends shivers down my spine. If there was justice in this brutal world, Haddon's sentence would have been commuted to life. But it wasn't, and nine years passed, during which his appeals ran out. Finally, the death warrant was executed, when, on February 14, 1993, the state of Washington hanged an innocent man.

That was the passage Justin was proofing when the phone on his desk rang.

"Newsroom," he answered.

"Justin Whitfield, please."

"Speaking," he said.

"My name's Alexis Hunt. I'm a writer in Vancouver researching the Hangman case."

"Uh-huh," said the reporter.

"You sound suspicious."

"Competition tends to get my back up."

"I'm not a reporter. I write crime books."

"So do I. I'm proofing one now."

"Is it your first?"

"Yes."

"I've written several. If you have any questions, feel free to ask."

"*Deadman's Island*, right?"

"Yes," said Alex.

"I've read your stuff."

"And I've read your reporting. It's first-rate. That's why I called."

"You've got five minutes. No more. We're on deadline here."

"The depth of your scoop on the Halloween hanging hints at an inside source. I suspect you've also seen the Hangman's word game. It's under wraps, so you can't print it. But when the case is solved, you'll be first with the story."

"One minute down. Four to go."

"My boyfriend is Insp. Zinc Chandler. He's the Mountie investigating last night's hanging. Needless to say, I have a good source too. But my source is good for only half the case. I lack a similar source for the half down there. As I see it, your situation is the reverse."

"So?"

"So I think we should consider teaming up."

"Woodward and Bernstein?"

"They got the Pulitzer Prize."

"There's a joint task force in the making. Chandler will get everything you need from down here."

"It's one thing for him to give me the scoop about what he controls. It's another for him to tell me what was told to him in confidence."

"True," said Justin.

"The same with you. I'll bet your piece on last night's hanging proves me right."

"I'm still listening. Are you through?"

"The Hangman case is huge. There will be lots of competition. Either I'm just one of many out to scoop you, or we forge a partnership that's greater than the sum of its parts and scoop the competition."

"How many words in the puzzle?"

"An odd number," said Alex.

"How many letters in the first word?"

"Uh-uh. Your turn."

"The same number as in the second," said Justin.

"Which is one less than in the third."

"The guess in the *Seattle Star* after the Halloween hanging was the letter A. How many A's were filled in last night?"

"That you'll have to get from your source."

"Okay, Alexis. You pass the test."

"Call me Alex. My friends do."

"What are you proposing?"

"That we meet face-to-face. I'll bring my file and you bring yours. It may work out. It may not. But if it does, we're both better off."

"When and where?" said Justin.

"This Friday. On a boat. Did you get an invitation to the Northwest Writers' Crime Cruise?"

The Scream

Vancouver
November 8

To the eye of a judge's daughter, it was still a courthouse. Though banners promoting the Toulouse-Lautrec exhibit hung between the Ionic columns soaring from the grand stairway up to the words VANCOUVER ART GALLERY beneath the cupola, Alex wasn't fooled. This edifice wasn't built to hang paintings; it was built to hang people.

The fence at the top of the stairs was a blatant clue. It secured the original entrance to safeguard the art. A public building that bars the public from its doors is suspect. Long flanking wings ran east and west, with access to the gallery now off Hornby Street, where Alex spotted another clue as she rounded the corner. Someone had tried to cover it with a blending color, but the word POLICE was still etched above the door that once led to the holding cells beneath the prisoner's dock. The accused went in presumed innocent and came out, after trial by their peers, as cons destined for the gallows.

The Rattenbury courthouse.

Back when the law had fangs.

Replaced by the kinder, gentler law courts a few blocks south after Canada did away with the noose in 1976.

To the mind of this judge's daughter, clues were everywhere. Convicts went to the gallows because they left clues behind for detectives to follow back to their human source. Convicts were saved from the gallows because police left clues behind for lawyers to twist into reasonable doubt. A lesson Jackson Hunt had taught his daughter well was always to keep an eye peeled for that telling clue that hid the solution to any mystery.

Clues...

Clues...

Clues...

Always watch for the clues.

The clue that lured Alex here today was the clue of the mask from *The Scream*.

A green awning guided her in from Hornby Street. The walkway was flanked by a pair of evergreens. The fountain beyond dated from those deadly days when the noose was loose; it was raised in 1912 by the Imperial Order Daughters of the Empire as a colonial monument for King Edward VII, now KING DEDWARD EVIL, thanks to graffiti additions. With changing times the relic had become a civic nuisance, and it was trundled about until it had ended up here as a butting bowl for cigarettes. The entrance to the gallery was by a door in the colonnade which ran from the rear of the west wing to the south wing, known as the Annex. Another relic from the past greeted her inside: a plaque thanking the Women's Auxiliary for its support of the old gallery from 1943 to 1979. The ladies had been retired in less sexist times, for the gallery was now *run* by five women, with the support of a lonely male.

Alex maneuvered through paintings on dollies to reach the reception desk. Once signed in and issued a security tag, she continued on toward the Annex stairs, past a vase of sunflowers arranged like Van Gogh's, except they were plastic. On her way up the marble staircase, Alex glanced out the windows of the second-floor landing to enjoy the autumn colors in Robson Square.

Outside, street kids lounged casually on the steps of the rear portico, beneath columns rising to the roof line of the Annex, inscribed across which was PLACED UPON THE HORIZON (CASTING SHADOWS). True, you can't get much artier than that, though Alex suspected whoever foisted that nonsense on the taxpaying public had smoked too much weed.

Phelan Phelps was a work of art too.

Alex found the librarian in the midst of a made-for-TV movie shoot on the third floor. How any man in this day and age dared sport an ascot at his throat she had no idea, but poofed and puffed beneath his chin, Phelps was a cravat-sporting kinda guy. The billow of paisley was nestled in the neck of his Dior shirt, which was striped with threads of spun gold complementing the gold links through his French cuffs. His fine-boned hands were manicured to perfection, and his coif was manicured too. One look at Phelps and you knew the librarian *knew* his art.

"Mr. Phelps?"

"Yes?"

"Alex Hunt."

"Alex? My, my. I expected a man."

Was that disappointment in his silky voice?

"You got my message?"

"Yes."

"About Edvard Munch?"

"Thank you."

"Pardon?"

"For pronouncing his name 'moonk.' I tire of those who pronounce it 'munch.' Munch is what we do to candy bars." He cast her a smile akin to the one in history's most famous painting.

"Am I interrupting?"

"Certainly not. I while away time waiting for you among these philistines."

"What are they filming?"

"I don't think they know. I'm told it's a court-room drama set in Savannah, Georgia. The courtroom is supposedly on the ground floor, so special-effects wizards raised scaffolding outside to plant a garden with appropriate vegetation beyond the windows. I'm sure they're currently plotting how to change the weather."

"Why not film in Georgia?"

The librarian shrugged. "The Canadian peso makes it cheaper to move Georgia here?"

The Annex, Phelps explained as they descended to the library on the second floor, attends to the administrative needs of the gallery next door. Since one of those needs is money, and Vancouver is Hollywood North, the new gallery decided *not* to renovate two of the old courts, which could be rented to movie companies for easy cash. The courtrooms retain the majesty of the past, with "banjo" windows and wainscoting and carved judges' benches. Neither has a prisoner's dock since both were civil courts, so they meet the requirements of American justice.

"Let's hope this lot doesn't expect money back," sniffed Phelps. "They contracted for a courtroom and a cell in the basement. Did you notice the tap gushing water outside?"

"Yes, beside the lion. Washing the front plaza."

"No, it was bilging water from the basement after last night's storm. The cell for the film is currently flooded."

Damn, thought Alex.

She had misread the clue.

The library that once supported the courts now stored the art gallery's books, prints and history. High windows faced east to greet each new day, and except for parallel rows of shelves advancing from the door, the librarian and his assistant had the vault to themselves.

"A conspiracy is afoot," said Phelps, "to relegate me to the basement. The board wants to entice Gucci and Saks Fifth Avenue into my realm. Have you read Wells's *Time Machine*? I was born an Eloi. Am I to live as a Morlock?" He raised a plucked eyebrow.

"I get it," replied Alex.

Phelps U'd her around to the bookshelf facing the side wall. He paused for effect as he reached for a text and stopped short.

"The name of that artist, Ms. Hunt?"

"Moonk," she replied.

He plucked *Munch: The Scream* from the bookshelf.

"Painting or lithograph?"

"Lithograph," Alex said.

Phelps opened the book to page 88 and held it out:

"What you see," Phelps said, "is the most recognizable image of fear, pain and outrage in the history of art. To see *The Scream* is to hear its cry. No need to take Art History 101 to grasp what Munch is saying. What he achieved in his signature work is the direct communication of hysteria.

"The painting dates from the fall of 1893. The lithograph from 1895. From the first day it was displayed in Berlin at the close of that century, Munch's howling homunculus has provided the screaming meemies in stressed people everywhere with the perfect image of how they feel about whatever is driving them up the wall. Whatever the cause, here's one thing you can do: clap your hands over your ears and scream your head off.

"We recently had an exhibition of Munch prints here. With it came a side exhibit called 'The Scream and Popular Culture,' a collection of kitsch demonstrating how this image has become *the* universal icon of angst. 'A scream a day keeps the shrink away,' read the caption on a poster with multiple images of Munch's print. *The Scream* was on sale as a key chain, a stress ball, a mouse pad, a fridge magnet, a tie, an inflatable doll and a whoopee cushion that—*Eeeeeeeee!*—let out a scream when you sat on it. Macaulay Culkin adopted the pose in the ad for *Home Alone*. An American bank printed checks with *The Scream* on them. A feminist button featured the image with a quote from Margaret Atwood: 'Men are afraid of being laughed at.... Women are afraid of being killed.' Whatever your angst, be it fear, pain or outrage, *The Scream* vents it. Who today doesn't have things to scream about? Taxes, traffic, school, politicians, Monday morning, bullies, abuse, advancing age, a worsening sex-per-week ratio. One look at *The Scream* and you think, Yes, that's how I feel! Which explains why—except for the Mona Lisa—Munch's howler has become the most published, appropriated, caricatured, parodied and down-right popular high-art image since we evolved from apes."

Phelps let out an exaggerated sigh. "So much fuss about a

picture of a woman who has lost her earrings."

Alex laughed.

"I stole that line," said Phelps.

"Oscar Wilde?"

"No, Dame Edna. The question you posed in your message was, What does *The Scream* mean? Well, that depends on your point of view. Thanks to pop cult, it means everything and nothing today."

Phelps began to close the book. "I trust that answers your question?"

Alex stopped him. "Actually, I was hoping for Art History 101."

"How deep do you want to go?"

"To the bottom," she said.

"May I ask why?"

"You've read about the Hangman? Police believe the killer wore a *Scream* mask in Seattle and left a similar mask on the victim here. Obviously, Munch's icon speaks to the Hangman. I've come to you for an inkling as to what it says."

"*The Scream* as a clue to murder?" Phelps's interest was piqued. "The place to start is with the artist's place in history. Edvard Munch, 1863 to 1944. Munch marks a pivotal point in Western art. 'I paint not what I see, but what I saw,' he wrote. That distinction is subtle but crucial, Ms. Hunt. Before him, painters viewed the world around them for inspiration. After Munch, they turned inward, to the landscape of their minds and souls.

"In a world where God is dead, only the individual remains to fill the void. What Freud did was liberate the tormented self. What Munch did was illustrate the torment released from our heart of darkness. Obsessive and nightmarish, his work augured the twentieth century so completely that even with its end a hundred years later, the howls of outrage, pain and fear captured in Munch's *Scream* still echo. Does the Hangman hear the screamer's shriek as his own?"

MICHAEL SLADE

"Do we know Munch's inspiration?" Alex asked.

"Yes, an ancient Inca mummy on exhibit at the Paris World Fair of 1889. Excavated in Peru, it was found bound in a fetal position inside a large clay jar. With its gaping eye sockets and open mouth, it had survived the ravages of time with its fear intact. A macabre reminder of the horror of death, that relic made a deep, lasting impression on Munch. A few years later, the artist fashioned that antiquity into his icon of angst."

"*The Scream* is Death incarnate?"

"That's why it works." Phelps flipped to notes in the appendix of the book. "For Munch's esthetic inspiration, we have his own words."

Alex read the note above his finger: I walked along the road with two friends. The sun went down—the sky was blood red—and I felt a breath of sadness—I stood still, tired unto death—over the blue-black fjord and city lay blood and tongues of fire. My friends continued on—I remained—trembling with fear. I felt a loud, unending scream piercing nature.

"How *The Scream* works is as fascinating as why," said Phelps. "The diagonal lines of the bridge leading to other people cannot hold back the sagging curves of the sky or the wavering lines surrounding the overwrought mind of the Screamer. The upright figures he/she/it passed a moment before on the bridge are disinterested peers central to the horror. They refuse to acknowledge the overwhelming anguish they just witnessed. See how they have turned their backs on the screamer?"

"I see a woman."

"I see a man," said Phelps. "What the screamer represents is an ascxual wraith, an apparition of a living being portending his or her death. The eyes are wide open, but peripheral vision is lost.

148

The hands are clasped over what must be ears on a skull-like head. The narrow ellipse of a mouth screams directly at the viewer. The body lacks the ramrod uprightness of the figures in the background, and as it loses human anatomy, the torso twists like a worm into an S-curve conforming to and extending the curves of the warped landscape. The net effect is a pathological loss of self.

"*The Scream* captures a psychotic experience. It is an objectivization of subjective sensation. The open issue is what caused the loss of identity? The bridge leading to nothing is a simile for death. But is it death in the past or death in the future that wrenches this scream from the screamer?"

"What's the original worth?"

"Fifty to sixty million dollars. It was stolen from Oslo's National Gallery in 1994, on the first day of the Lillehammer Winter Olympics. Ransoming it was a foolish crime. How do you sell history's second most famous painting?"

"The thieves were caught?"

"Yes, when they tried to collect the ransom."

"Was Munch insane?"

"That," said Phelps, "is for you to decide. He was raised in a dysfunctional Norwegian home. His mother died of tuberculosis when Munch was five. His father was a religious fanatic who raved about the Bible. When the boy got tuberculosis, the fever brought visions of hell. Munch was fourteen when his beloved sister, Sophie, died of the same disease. An obsession with death was the only constant in Munch. When his father was on his deathbed, he bequeathed Munch his Bible to save his son's doomed soul."

"A healthy life," said Alex.

"His images say it all. A pathological sense of isolation broods at the heart of his art. What Munch shows in *The Scream* isn't an expression of his state of mind, but proof of it. 'Could only have been painted by a madman,' he scrawled on one version of *The Scream*. The picture is autobiography raised to the level of universal pain. Munch suffered a nervous breakdown and went to a

Danish clinic, where the cure was electric shocks."

"Hmmm," said Alex.

"The lithograph is part of a series titled *The Mirror*. When the Hangman looks in this mirror, what does he see?"

"I wonder," said Alex.

"I hope I've helped," said Phelps.

Clues...

Clues...

Clues...

Always watch for the clues.

The Echo

Jeffrey Kline, barrister-at-law, was mistaken when he thought, In choosing America for the first lynching, the Hangman embarked upon a self-defeating course of action. The hangman never became a national icon down there. The hangman as a named and feared executioner, hanging cons around the country and the commonwealth, was a *British* horror.

Not so.

It's true that America has no pantheon of hangmen to rival Ketch, Calcraft, Marwood, Berry, Billington, Ellis and Pierrepoint. But that's because America prefers to focus on the condemned as the celebrity of the gallows. The Last Meal—the best on the prison menu—is basically an American tradition, and in the early days of the Wild West it was followed by the local madame sending the best of her brothel in to satisfy the doomed man's other appetite. Whether by their own or society's desire, American hangmen went to great trouble to stay out of the public eye.

Can Britain boast that a future head of state hanged a ne'er-do-well? America can. When Grover Cleveland was the sheriff of New York's Erie County, the soon-to-be twenty-second and twenty-fourth president of the United States personally sprang the trap for the killer Patrick Morrissey.

As for the act of hanging itself, Yankee ingenuity developed the "jerk 'em up" gallows. The invention had neither a drop nor a trapdoor, replacing them with a heavy weight attached to the end of a noosed rope looped up over a horizontal beam. When the elevated weight was released to plunge to the ground, the con was yanked high into the air so all could see him die. The jerk-'em-up gallows was ideal for the paying spectacle of a "sheriff's ball." Like the ball on Bedloe's Island in 1860.

Albert E. Hicks—Hicksie to his friends—was tried and convicted of piracy on the high seas. Hicksie was a notorious Manhattan underworld thug who murdered three men on an oyster boat bound for Deep Creek, Virginia, before it reached port. Because piracy was a federal rap, it was thought he couldn't be hanged in the city of New York, so the execution was set for an island in the outer harbor. Since access to Bedloe's Island was restricted to those with boats, the hanging was perfectly placed to charge admission. The "sheriff's ball" earned the federal marshal more than a thousand dollars.

As for the hanging, it was quite an affair. Two hundred marines surrounded the scaffold on three sides with a hollow square. Ten thousand customers anchored within sight of the gallows. A man named Isaacs placed the noose around Hicksie's neck, then, from the privacy of his booth beside the scaffold, the hangman cut the rope that held up the weight. Down it plummeted and up jerked Hicksie, hanged high in the sky for all to see, where it took the strangled man eleven minutes to die. Such a good location did Bedloe's Island prove to be that a quarter-century later it was selected as the site for the Statue of Liberty.

In America, you can say the foundation of Liberty is hanging.

The room in which the Hangman sat thinking about Hicksie and the jerk-'em-up gallows was dark except for a beam of light focused on a print of *The Scream* hanging on the wall. The shriek of the screamer echoed in the killer's mind, for Munch's icon of angst captured the pain and outrage the Hangman felt tonight, an outrage screaming for such eye-for-an-eye revenge that death would come as a blessing to tomorrow night's victim.

The jerk-'em-up gallows.

What should I use? the Hangman wondered.

The boom?

The anchor?

The halyard winch?

I'm coming for you, fucker.

The Yardarm

Bart Busby was a bully.

Always had been.

Always would be.

Bart knew that bullies were created, not born, and that he was the Frankenstein monster of a brutal family. His earliest memory was of his ma screaming at him that she hated his guts. She made it clear from then on that she had never wanted a child, and that his birth had stolen opportunity from her. She could have been a movie star, or a game-show queen, or any number of other glittering celebrities. But instead, she had ended up a Cinderella drudge, struggling to manage a waitress job, housework and him, while her precious youth was going, going and then gone. That's why Ma spent money on herself and not on Bart. Because he owed her everything for ruining her life.

Bart's relationship with his pa was even rougher. "Spare the rod and spoil the child" was Pa's favorite motto. Pa worked for Boeing as a riveter, one of those guys who fastened sheets of metal together, a line of work he despised as being beneath him. But if he had to labor at such a shitty job all day to feed his family, then by God, he expected Bart to toe the line. If Pa came home from work to find Bart hadn't done something Pa expected should be done, he'd whip off his belt and thrash the boy until his buttocks bled. Bart still had the scars to prove it.

Whenever Bart was thrashed with Pa's belt or Ma's tongue, he would take it out the next day on someone weak at school. Bart had several whipping boys he liked to pick on. Bottle Bottoms was a runt who wore thick glasses. Bart would seize them from his face to taunt the little wimp, then push him back repeatedly with a series of chest shoves, telling him he should be in a school for the blind. Nicknamed after Quasimodo, the Hunchback of Notre Dame, Quasy was a humped kid burdened with a deformed spine. Bart would follow him at school and kick his behind, asking if being a cripple made it easy for Dad to bugger him standing up.

Bart knew he was a bully, and he was proud of the fact. Pushing others around gave him satisfaction. The experience of watching someone else writhe in pain or feeding off their fear of him built Bart up. If they sniveled and cried, so much the better, for it felt good to see their blotchy faces, streaming tears and snotty noses. Mix in a bit of blood, and that was best of all.

There were other benefits too. Extorting things of value allowed him to replace the allowance denied by Ma. Because his victims were all outcasts and geeks, the approval of the in-crowd was guaranteed. He sensed the support of like-minded kids, and their silent approbation was thunderous applause to his ears.

So positively reinforcing was being a bully that Bart continued being one into his adult life. He was adept at selecting those who made the best victims, for Bart was an expert at picking up the signs. Those who were sensitive, quiet and cautious; those who were anxious, isolated and alone; those who habitually withdrew from confrontation; those so depressed they found no joy in happy occasions... all were easy pickin's for Bart to bully. He had a macho distaste for weakness of any kind.

Take, for instance, the wuss he encountered earlier today, on the final leg of a two-week selling trip to Oregon. A skinny, bespectacled, asthmatic Jew, the wuss was the proprietor of a family bookstore in Astoria. Bart, on the other hand, was a large, intimidating ex-football player, currently marketing office machines with the hard sell. The Jew's wife was behind the till, so Bart made a point of telling him what a nice set of tits she had. The guy cringed. He was a bookish nerd. So in a false, convivial style, Bart proceeded to tell him in explicit detail how he would fuck a woman like her. All the while he had his eyes locked on her titties, a trick that invariably made a weak bitch squirm, and he ended by wiggling his tongue in a most suggestive way before giving the wuss a little wink of male conspiracy.

"Bet that's how you fuck her, huh? And who's that over there? Not your daughter?"

The wuss, like all true victims, fumbled the play. He tried to switch Bart off by laughing and making *himself* an object of fun, but Bart already had his eyes on the girl's budding boobs. Finally, the wuss got rid of him the only way he could: by buying a new copy machine he didn't need.

God, that felt good.

But nothing would ever feel as fine as convicting that kiddy-diddler of murder punishable by death. Bart had never had respect for any of his peers, so was it not ironic that he was chosen as a juror to give that scumbag trial by *his* peers? Pa had been a vicious asshole at home, but people outside the family thought he was some kind of saint. To them, Pa was a hard-working, charitable man, and from that Bart had learned how to put on a front. The front he presented to the court got him on the jury, and as a juror he was free to exert another lesson learned from Pa: Make sure no one ever gets the better of you. And in that jury room, Bart made sure no one did.

Peter Bryce Haddon was Bart's kind of victim. The defendant was slight, wide-eyed and scared. Knowing it would jitter Haddon and make him look guilty, Bart made a point of staring hard at the accused throughout his trial. The case had dragged on interminably, and my, how Bart had enjoyed watching the jumpy diddler squirm.

After the verdict, and after the sentence, he read in the *Seattle Star* that Haddon was raped and castrated in a prison riot. As far as Bart was concerned, that was *real* justice. The diddler had raped and taken the cherry of that little girl, so tit-for-tat, the same was done to him. Besides, what use did a wuss have for balls?

That incident had inspired the name of the boat Bart owned before the boat he was boarding now. In days of old, when sailors set out to sea, they took with them a clutch of cabin boys to bugger for sport and relief. Because the boys were virgins in the ways of nautical love, they spent the first day at sea stripped of their pants, sitting on greased pegs jutting up from the flat of a bench. After a day of rocking back and forth with the waves, the "peg boys" who would serve the crew were loosened up.

Prison made Haddon a peg boy, so to speak, and in homage to what happened to that wuss in the riot, Bart had named his last boat *The Peg Boy*.

After that, he thought being a prison warden would be the ideal job for him. How Bart would enjoy bullying the scumbags who got banged up for doing stupid things that he was too smart to get caught doing. It would be like tormenting rats in a cage. He would make them do *very* hard time.

When he later read in the *Seattle Star* that Haddon had hanged, Bart was proud of himself. As far as he was concerned, that was ultimate justice. The diddler had strangled the girl he had raped, so tit-for-tat, the same was done to him. Besides, what use did a wuss have for life?

Not only did the hanging give Bart another fantasy—for years after, he thought being the state's hangman would be the ideal job for him—but the execution also inspired the name of the sailboat he was now boarding. In days of yore, the British navy used to hang pirates from the yardarm, the horizontal spar at the head of a mast to which the top edge of a square sail was rigged. Bart's boat was a thirty-nine-foot center-cockpit sloop with triangular sails, so it didn't have a yardarm topping its mast. That didn't matter. The name had meaning for Bart. In homage to what that wuss had suffered on the gallows, Bart had named his current boat *The Yardarm*.

The Yardarm was moored on the west shore of Lake Washington. Seattle sits between the Pacific waterway of Puget Sound and the inland lake. The glacier-gouged basin is $19^{1}/_{2}$ miles long and generally $1^{3}/_{4}$ miles wide. Lake Washington is overlooked by towering, snow-capped Mount Rainier. Its more than fifty miles of shoreline are fairly smooth, and only a few bays indent it here and there. Its beaches are narrow and the shore drops off quickly, plunging to the lake bottom at two hundred feet. Two pontoon bridges cross it in the middle, one of which joins southern Mercer Island to both shores. Seattle owns the west shore, but not the east. That belongs to Bellevue, Renton and numerous small towns. The northern reaches of Lake Washington offer fine sailing, so here is where Bart moored the sloop that he called home.

When Bart returned from a selling trip he liked to go for a sail. There was something about venturing out on the lake at night that satisfied the bully's insatiable need for control. At night, Lake Washington was his alone. Wuss sailors, who took their boats out only in daylight, were safely tucked in bed with their teddy bears.

Having parked his car onshore behind the long-term moorage, Bart lugged his suitcase down the ramp and out onto the deserted dock under a moonless, starlit sky. The clouds of the last storm were scudding away, clearing the air for the next storm, which was already brewing at sea. At ten to fifteen knots, the chill night wind rippled the black depths of the beckoning lake sparkling with reflected city lights. As Bart hoofed along the finger to which *The Yardarm* was tied, halyards slapping her mast and waves lapping her hull welcomed the skipper aboard.

Aye-aye, Captain, thought Bart.

Starboard to the finger, his sailboat was moored stern in. Unhooking the lifeline to climb aboard, Bart heaved his suitcase over the gunnel and stepped down into the sunken cockpit. "Center cockpit" meant the steering area of the sloop was between two cabins, the main cabin forward and a private cabin aft. With his sea legs compensating for the rocking hull, Bart unlocked the companionway doors to the forward cabin, sliding open the overhead hatch before he entered. Inside, he flipped a switch to ALL to juice both batteries so he could fire up the diesel engine.

Climbing back out to the open cockpit between the cabins, Bart raised the cover of a hatch built into the floor and reached in to turn on the light in the engine compartment. First, he checked the oil with a dipstick, then he unscrewed the cap on the heat exchanger to confirm the coolant level, and finally, he opened the seacock so brine could flood the cooling system. Satisfied with the engine, Bart switched off the light and closed the hatch.

In the center of the cockpit stood the binnacle, a vertical mount with the steering wheel on its aft side, a black transmission lever on its port side, a red throttle lever on its starboard side and a glowing compass on top. After removing the canvas cover protecting it, Bart inserted a key into the instrument panel. He checked the transmission with one hand to make sure it was in neutral, pumped the throttle several times with his other hand, then cranked the key in the binnacle to fire up the engine.

Like a newborn babe whacked on its bottom, the thirteen-horsepower Volvo diesel coughed itself into life. As it *chug-chug-chugged* in the dock slip, again Bart swung down into the main cabin to turn on the running lights and the autopilot. From a recess in the cabin wall, he withdrew a flashlight and the winch handle, then, jack-in-the-box that a single crewman was, he popped back up to *The Yardarm*'s cockpit.

Dropping the winch handle into a side pocket on the binnacle, Bart flicked the flashlight on to see if the batteries were still strong, and that's when the sudden beam caught the clue.

Illuminated by the torch was a fresh scratch on the lock of the aft cabin.

Bart unlocked the aft cabin and shone the beam of the flashlight in. Like a spotlight on a theater stage, the beam plucked details out of the dark. It caught the rudder post angling up dead center from the cabin floor to the ceiling, the metal tube wrapped with Manila hemp rope for a nautical look. It caught the maritime junk on the shelf across the transom, a clutter of shackles, stainless-steel bolts, bungee cords, a whistle and an empty wine glass. It caught the twenty-dollar bill Bart had dropped on the quarter-berth when, before the selling trip, he had searched his wallet for a business card.

Had Bart been an Alex Hunt when it came to clues, he might have searched further in his response to the scratch. The money, however, was enough for him, since surely a thief would have stolen it had someone broken in. Convinced the scratch on the lock resulted from a *thwarted* theft, Bart extinguished the flashlight beam and locked the aft cabin.

The Hangman was left in the dark.

Barnacle Bart was ready to sail.

From the cockpit, he sprang back onto the dock to untie the fore, aft and spring lines, then, after shoving the boat away from the finger and slightly ahead, he leaped back on and put her in gear by pushing the transmission lever from NEUTRAL to FORWARD. His other hand advanced the throttle, and slowly *The Yardarm* chugged out of the dock slip toward the open expanse of Seattle's largest lake.

Once the sloop was clear of the west shore marina, Bart crabbed along the starboard side to gather in the fenders, clipping the lifeline back in place before he returned to the wheel. More throttle and Bart left the big city behind.

Waves made the wheel kick and wind tossed Bart's thinning hair. Headlights crossing the Evergreen Point Bridge to the south were a noose of pearls around the neck of the dark lake. Venus glimmered bright between galleon clouds sailing the black beyond of outer space, and a shooting star streaked green as it burned itself to death. Seen through the tracery of rigging overhead, the stars seemed to swing in time with the swells buffeting the boat. Glittering with pinpricks of reflected light, the bow wave pitched and splashed as the stem rose and fell, biting the fathomless water so a billion bubbles streamed by to join the wake that frothed astern. Hoist the sail and its silhouette against the starry sky would stand aloft like a monstrous shark's fin.

Time for a bracer, thought Bart.

A quarter-berth is a much-needed space-saver on a boat. The aft cabin of *The Yardarm* had less depth than the height of an average man, which meant such a guest would have to sleep curled up in a berth shorter than he was if the cabin ended at the companionway doors. What a quarter-berth did was add length to a cabin's depth by extending itself as a cubbyhole past the doors and under the cockpit floor. With head to the transom and feet in the hole, a man could sleep full-length in quarters shorter than he was.

When Bart had shone the flashlight into the aft cabin, the Hangman was curled up knees to chin in the quarter-berth cubbyhole beside and back of the doors. Had Bart entered to peer around into the nook, he would have faced the business end of a 9mm Glock.

Now, as Bart engaged the autopilot to slip below, the killer listened intently through the doors.

Once the skipper was off the deck and the cockpit was clear, the Hangman crept out of the aft cabin into the chill night. A gloved hand closed on the winch handle stored in the binnacle pocket as the *Scream*-masked killer took up an ambush position beside the main cabin companionway.

Having hit a button to engage the autopilot to the cockpit steering wheel, Barnacle Bart slipped below for a tot or two of rum. From its hiding place in the bilge of the bow, he fetched a bottle of Mount Gay sugar-cane brandy. The finest rum there is comes from Barbados, and having bullied that Jew into buying a machine he didn't need, Bart was in a party mood.

Straight from the bottle, three slugs of Mount Gay warmed his gullet.

"Yo-ho-ho," Bart sang to what, unknown to him, was his wraith in the cabin mirror.

The festive mood was broken by two interruptions in a row. The first was the jangling of *The Yardarm*'s phone. Bart let the machine answer the call with the greeting he'd recorded before his selling trip.

"You've reached Bart Busby. I'm on the road until the night of November 9. Leave a message and I'll get back to you."

"Mr. Busby, this is Nate Frank. I'm canceling that copier you strong-armed me into."

The line went dead.

Fucking kike, thought Bart. I'll tear the bra from your wife's tits in front of you.

There was a time, back in the good old days, when he could do that without worry. Bully a wuss and Bart knew the wuss would cringe away. But not anymore. The world was topsy-turvy. Bully a wuss at school or work today, the chances were, judging from stories in the news, the guy would pull a machine gun and mow you down along with a hundred other people.

As with AIDS, you had to adapt.

So that's why Bart pushed the button to replay the message. This time, he'd concentrate on the Jew's tone, to assess whether he was a wuss on the edge or merely a wuss with false courage once Bart was gone. In which case, he would crumble quickly when the bully returned next trip.

The machine played ten messages before the Jew's, one of which was a beep that marked the Hangman's call last week from a public phone. No message, just a beep, because the call was made to ascertain when Bart would return to his boat.

Bang!

What was that?

Bart turned from the machine.

Bang!

Outside.

Something loose in the wind?

Bart hurried to the companionway to scramble back out to the cockpit. As he scaled the stairs through the open hatch above, the bully saw a zillion stars up in heaven. Where he was going, there would be no stars at all.

Ironically, Bart's first thought was that the boom had somehow slipped off the gallows. A boom was the spar extending back from the mast at the foot of a sail, and a gallows was the notched support on the roof of the aft cabin that kept the boom from swinging when the sail was lowered.

That gallows, however, wasn't the gallows that he should be worried about.

For what had caused the bangs that drew Bart out was the companionway doors of the aft cabin slamming shut. Strange, since Bart was certain that he had locked them before slipping below deck for a tot. With that mystery in mind, he poked his head up through the hatch into the starry night, his torso emerging from the main cabin like a snail forsaking its shell, until the Hangman smashed the winch handle down on his skull.

Bart saw stars of another kind as the bully crumpled into the cockpit well.

With a knee on deck by the gunnel and leaning over the cabin roof just forward of the hatch, the killer waited in ambush for Bart to come up from below. *Whap!* The winch handle clubbed down on the bastard's head to lay him out cold, giving the Hangman lots of time to truss him up.

There were different ways this could be done. Free the boom from the gallows and it could be used to lynch Bart by noosing him with a line that ran up to the head of the mast and came back down. Fasten the loose end of the line to the stern end of the boom and Bart would be yanked up into the air if the boom was shoved to either side, out over the lake. The pull of that "jerk 'em up" gallows, however, would not be that high, so the hanged man's legs would probably dangle in the water, making it difficult to proceed with what the Hangman had planned for Bart.

An alternative would be to fasten the loose end of the line to an anchor with lots of chain. Throw enough metal overboard to counter Bart's weight and the anchor sinking down into the depths of the lake would yank him up the mast. That method, however, created a problem of logistics. How do you hide that much equipment onboard without piquing suspicion?

Better to use the winch.

And hoist Bart like a sail.

The word "wuss" was a major term in Bart's lexicon. "Wuss" was an amalgam of "wimp" and "pussy," and for a man of Bart's intellect, "wuss" fit poets to a T. The only poem Bart had liked before he dropped out of school was Samuel Taylor Coleridge's "The Rime of the Ancient Mariner."

> Water, water, everywhere,
> And all the boards did shrink;
> Water, water, everywhere,
> Nor any drop to drink.

In effect, the Mariner was a bully like Bart. The cocky seaman proved that to his shipmates by shooting their good omen, an albatross, with his crossbow. That brought a curse upon the ship, which killed all aboard except the Mariner. The seaman's horror was seeing the crew come back to life.

HANGMAN

They groaned, they stirred, they all uprose,
Nor spake, nor moved their eyes;
It had been strange, even in a dream,
To have seen those dead men rise.

The helmsman steered, the ship moved on;
Yet never a breeze up-blew;
The mariners all 'gan work the ropes,
Where they were wont to do;
They raised their limbs like lifeless tools—
We were a ghastly crew.

Bart had missed the point of that poem back when he was in
school. What pleased him was that it presented a welcome break
from all that wuss poetry about clouds, trees and nature shit. But
now, as he came back to consciousness from the clout on his head
to find what seemed to be an animated corpse working the rigging
of his ship, Bart recalled the Ancient Mariner and what had happened to him. Suddenly, fathoming the theme, this bully was
deathly afraid.

With Bart laid out cold in the cockpit, the killer had crossed to the
binnacle to put the transmission in neutral by easing back on the
black handle. Flicking a switch in the main cabin had doused the
running lights. Once *The Yardarm* no longer had "way," the sloop
creaked and groaned as it floundered on the choppy lake. Lit by
little more than a canopy of stars, the drama unfolding beneath
the mast was nothing but a shadow play against the dark of night.

Injure your neck and a physiotherapist may "hang" you in
traction. You will be seated in a chair with a halter supporting your
head, one strap under your chin and another cradling the back of
your skull. The halter will be connected to a hanging line, and your
neck will be put in traction by adding weight of ten to fifteen
pounds to the other end. The halter suspends without strangling.

The Hangman cinched Bart's unconscious head into such a halter. The winch for the main halyard used to hoist the sail up the mast was on top of the main cabin, just forward of the cockpit. The halyard line ran from the winch to a pulley at the foot of the mast, then up the mast to another pulley at the masthead, then down the mast to where it was snap-shackled near the foot. The Hangman loosened the halyard line looped around the winch and scrambled forward to unclasp the other end from the mast, pulling it back to the cockpit to snap the shackle to the halter webbing Bart's head. A few turns of the line around the winch to tighten the free end and the killer was ready to hang Bart by inserting the bloody handle into the top notch of the winch to crank, crank, crank.

As the winched halyard shortened, the cold-cocked bully was slowly hauled by the neck out of the cockpit well and forward over the roof of the main cabin until his head hit the foot of the mast. Crank, crank, crank and he began to rise as the halyard hoisted him like a sail toward the masthead pulley. When Bart's feet were in the air a foot above the forward cabin, the Hangman secured the winched end of the halyard by dropping it into a pinch cleat. Nylon ties lashed the hanged man's wrists and ankles to deck stanchions on both sides of the boat, so Bart returned to consciousness to find that he was dangling by the neck with his arms and legs spread-eagled as upside-down Vs.

The animated corpse from the "Ancient Mariner" was a horrible sight. The face had a wonky eye and looked like a screaming skull, and by the faint light of the heavenly stars was as eerie as hell. Judging from the sheen, which could have been an astral aura, the rest of the body was sheathed in a coverall of black plastic. Were Bart not so groggy from the ambush clout to his brain, he might have deduced that was so the apparition would leave no forensic clues behind for the cops to trace. Touch a match to the second skin and—*poof!*—it would be gone.

Having hanged Bart from *The Yardarm,* the Hangman moved aft to lower the Zodiac with davits down onto the lake. The inflated rubber dinghy was powered by a Honda 9.9-horsepower outboard engine. The Zodiac, tied alongside the boat for now, would provide a getaway after this was over. The Hangman would put the sloop into gear by shoving the transmission handle to Forward, then would lock the autopilot on a collision course with the west shore. Advance the red handle for a touch of throttle, and long after the Hangman had fled in the Zodiac, *The Yardarm* would run aground in Seattle.

But that would be later.

After this revenge.

Bart pissed himself when he saw the living corpse pull a knife from a carryall on the roof of the cabin. He tried to plead with the horror as the starlit blade slashed his piss-soaked pants away from the lower half of his body, but the halter strap under his chin had shut his yap. The demon cast the tattered garment into the lake. For a moment Bart feared the monster would go for the family jewels, but then he heard a sound below like the unzipping of a zipper. He strained his terrified eyes down to their lower lids in time to witness his stomach and intestines spill out through a horizontal cut across his belly just above the level of his navel.

The pain hit like a torpedo.

Bart screamed deep in his throat.

"Bully," snarled the Hangman through the muffle of the *Scream* mask. "That's for what you did to an innocent man."

Below his heaving ribcage, Bart's guts had tumbled out from their own weight, and they hung swaying between his legs with the rocking of the waves. The odor off them was as foul as Bart's character, for the knife that had slit through skin, fat and the muscle of his abdominal wall had nicked the bowel as well. The yellowish fat on the coils glistened sickly. Because the small intestine doubled back on itself, the grisly mess dangled to his knees but didn't hit the deck.

Again the Hangman reached into the carryall.

Had Bart had functioning bowels, he would have shit himself.

The hand-held, cordless reciprocating saw weighed three pounds. Powered by a nine-volt in-handle battery that jiggled the blade at twenty-seven hundred strokes per minute, the tool looked like an electric knife, except it was able to cut through wood and mild steel. Cutting the flesh and bone of Bart's limbs would be like sawing butter.

The Hangman went to work on the left leg first. A cut from the outside in severed the femoral artery and then the femur bone, spurting blood like a geyser from the combination of heartbeat and gravity. Muted by the halter, Bart—conscious all the while—screamed and screamed and screamed.

> Blood, blood, everywhere,
> And the size of Bart did shrink;
> Blood, blood, everywhere,
> For the Hangman's eyes to drink.

In days of yore, in Britain, from whence Americans imported hanging, those who really pissed off the Crown were hanged, drawn and quartered.

Sharks

Sharks can smell blood in the water, so the sharks were out this morning.

In the early hours of the new day, *The Yardarm* ran aground on Sand Point. With Pontiac Bay to its north and Wolf Bay to its south, Sand Point juts like a nose into Lake Washington. The county had created an airstrip here in 1920, and four years later, that was taken over by the U.S. Navy. When the air station was shut down in 1970, the city of Seattle claimed Sand Point for a park. Had the government not locked up the land during Seattle's early years, it would probably be a residential enclave today. Instead, Magnuson Park boasts one and a half miles of largely undeveloped shoreline on the west side of Lake Washington. Here, tree-framed vistas of misty blue water front panoramas of the Cascade Mountains to the east and the glaciated cone of Mount Rainier to the south. Grass tapers down to a narrow gravel strip of a beach, and there, at a relatively isolated spot where plants and trees were left alone to attempt a return to primeval forest, *The Yardarm* and its bloody cargo, still dangling from the mast, ran aground in the dark before dawn.

The man who found the sloop was in a broken-hearted funk.

Like Bart, he had come home from a business trip last night, a day earlier than planned, to surprise his new wife, which he did when he caught her in the throes of sexual ecstasy in their still-unpaid-for marital bed with his best man.

To drown his sorrows, the poor guy had moped to an all-night liquor store and, fortified with a bottle of Wild Turkey, driven east on NE 65th Street, across the Burke-Gilman Trail, which once was the old Burlington Northern railroad grade, and Sand Point Way into Magnuson Park. There, he had abandoned his car to walk the beach on foot, drinking straight from the bottle as Bart had done, until, pissed to the gills, he had ended up here, where, against the first flush of dawn across the lake, he witnessed a sight of such carnage that he sobered up fast.

Luckily, with him was his cellphone.

Did he call the cops?

Not on your life.

The call he made was to Sue Frye's TV station, as it offered a cash reward to any Seattleite who phoned in an exclusive news tip.

The bigger the story, the bigger the reward.

So that's why Sue Frye and her camera crew arrived *before* the cops at the scene of the Hangman's third murder, and began feeding live video of what they found back to their TV station for immediate broadcast to the waking city.

Vancouver

"Zinc?"

"Mmm."

"Are you awake?"

"I am now, Alex."

"Do you still love me like you did when we fell in love?"

Opening his eyes, he rubbed away the sleep. "What brought this on?"

"Tonight's your date with Maddy."

"No," he said. "Tonight's my date with you."

"Is she coming?"

"I have no idea. She didn't say she was. All she said was maybe. Since I suggested we use the cruise to meet and discuss files, I haven't heard anything different from her."

"Are you disappointed?"

"Of course not, Alex. I'm going on the cruise to have fun with you, not to work on a case. I get enough work at work, thank you very much."

"That's what nags at me."

"Huh?"

"Why did you stay overnight in Seattle with Maddy when you knew I was waiting at home in bed for you?"

"The case caught my interest."

"It wasn't your case."

"It is now."

"But it wasn't then. And you know what the doctor said about losing sleep. You don't want another epileptic fit."

"Alex, I got sleep."

"Yes. At Maddy's."

"You're not being fair. You've got me coming and going. Where did this sudden streak of insecurity come from? I love you and no one else. End of story. So rest at ease, and we'll live happily ever after."

"What does Maddy look like?"

"A shriveled-up prune," said Zinc.

Where would Zinc Chandler be today if not for Alex Hunt?

In the aftermath of the Cutthroat shootout, he had returned from Hong Kong with a bullet wound to his head that might have ended his career as a Mountie. For the rest of his life, Zinc would pop several caps of Dilantin a day to ward off epileptic seizures. Four years had come and gone while Zinc worked the family farm in Saskatchewan, waiting for headquarters to approve his return to duty. There he lived the daily regimen of a Spartan and a Stoic, to mend himself body and mind.

Dispatching Zinc to Deadman's Island had seemed a good idea. Special X was embroiled in a high-profile media circus—an American feminist had been butchered by a psycho who thought he was Jack the Ripper reincarnated—so Chief Superintendent Robert DeClercq could not spare an active investigator to keep his promise to provide a real cop for the detection game of a mystery weekend that had been auctioned off to aid charity. The secret buyer was specific about how he/she desired the interactive game to be played. Twelve crime writers from Canada and the States would be flown to an isolated island off the Pacific Coast to match wits with the cop for a prize of cold cash. The set-up was to echo Agatha Christie's *And Then There Were None*. Since Zinc was still waiting for his call to duty, DeClercq's offering him as the real investigator seemed the obvious answer to his predicament. So that's how the Mountie had found himself surrounded by scribblers in a float plane docked in Vancouver harbor, waiting for the last straggler to arrive before flying off to Deadman's Island for a deadly weekend.

Etched in his mind forever was the first time Zinc saw her.

Barely discernible through the rain was the city's downtown core. Huddled like a waif at its feet was the shack of Thunderbird Charters. From the shack to the float plane out on the water stretched a gangway and a hundred-foot dock. The woman sea-legging down the gangplanks struggled against the storm, suitcase lugged in one hand, umbrella opposite fighting the wind to block the slanted rain. She wore a black tight-waisted jacket over black jeans tucked into black cowboy boots, and a black trenchcoat that flapped around her like Zorro's cape. Though her blonde hair was pulled back in a ponytail and clipped with silver heart-shaped barrettes, her features were masked by wayward strands dancing about her face. As she neared the plane, she looked up, and Zinc's heart was gone.

Eyes so blue you could dive in to swim in tropical lagoons. A narrow, delicate chin around a most kissable mouth. The grace of an angel in her every move, and the sensuality of a fallen woman in her sleek form. Boarding the plane was the fantasy of Zinc's dreams, so how he wished—God, how he wished—that he was the man he had been.

"Sorry I'm late, but cross-border shoppers clogged Peace Arch. I'm Alex Hunt," she told the others as the engines coughed to life. Zinc touched his forehead subconsciously to hide the indent the surgeons had left in removing the slug from his brain.

They say the strongest relationships are forged on the anvil of war. Courage under fire fuses the deepest bond, and everything in life after that is reduced to a footnote in your biography.

What Zinc and Alex went through that weekend was as hellish as any war. Having lured the crime writers to Deadman's Island on a false pretext while Special X hunted for him back on the mainland, the Ripper killed them off one by one in fiendish ways. Necessity forced Zinc and Alex to make a last stand, confining them to a single room through the long night before the grisly climax.

The woman who spent that vigil with Zinc had transformed herself into an Amazon warrior. Grace replaced by grim determination, Alex crouched beside the door with a knife in each fist. Hair matted and sweaty clothes clinging to her body, she glared with such ferocity that he knew she would have no compunction about stabbing their stalker in the back.

Zinc was out of Dilantin, and it was only a question of hours until the scar in his brain overwhelmed him. Stress and lack of sleep shortened his endurance, so it was a matter of life or death that the Mountie get rest.

He and Alex lay on separate beds in the dark. The cyclonic storm outside was tearing at the roof. Locking themselves in here for the night was the only refuge they could muster. The springs of the bed next to his creaked, then Zinc sensed Alex moving silently across the gap between them, until she hovered over him like a guardian. Her scent was so intoxicating that shivers ran up his spine. Her breath was as soft as a feather's breeze.

She kissed his forehead.

She kissed his wound.

She kissed his lips and said, "Sleep."

Sleep he did.

A fitful sleep.

But sleep nonetheless.

The Ripper had stabbed Zinc in the back during the final conflict, and it was a toss-up whether the Mountie would live or die. If the man who flew to the island was but a ghost of his former self, the man carried off on a stretcher was a fading mirage.

They say those who endure a near-death experience see a blinding white light. Zinc witnessed such an aura during his struggle with death, and all that kept him from advancing into the brilliant glare was Alex Hunt calling him back from somewhere behind. When Zinc awoke in the ICU of a West Coast hospital, he saw that "somewhere behind" was the chair beside his near-death bed. Whether he saw that light or not didn't matter. Perhaps he imagined it because of what "they" say (and who, by the way, are those mysterious "they"?), but what he did not imagine was Alex softly calling to him not to slip away through all those in-the-balance days while he was unconscious.

Zinc had come around to find his guardian angel in tears.

"I love you," Alex said.

"And I love you," said he.

On Zinc's release from hospital, she had taken him home with her to Oregon. There, on the windy, crashing shore of Cannon Beach, where she had previously cared for her cancer-ridden dad, Alex had nursed her unconsummated lover back to health. Each day, with sea-spray fountaining around Haystack Rock, they combed the untamed beach together from end to end. When Zinc was strong enough to add sex to his rehabilitation, Alex seduced him like he had always dreamed of being seduced, the instinctive lover who tuned up his body like a Rolls-Royce mechanic.

It was *almost* worth getting wounded!

The bullet to his brain had scrambled Zinc's mind, however. If you were to ask him how much rain fell in November, and the response he intended was "The rain in November would have drowned Noah," he might, if he didn't concentrate, reply, "The rain in Spain falls mainly... No, that's wrong."

Crosswords are good. Chess is better. But nothing hones the deductive mind like a Golden Age puzzle. The 1920s and 1930s were the Golden Age of the classic detective story. The three great practitioners of the art of deception were Agatha Christie, Ellery Queen and John Dickson Carr. Of these, perhaps the most devious mind was Carr's. His forte was the locked-room puzzle, the impossible crime.

To sharpen Zinc's mind in Cannon Beach, Alex went back to Carr. She would extract the locked-room puzzles from his classic books—*The Three Coffins, The Crooked Hinge, The Plague Court Murders*—and set them up at home as challenges for Zinc to unravel. To add spice to the game, she made herself the prize, shedding a garment for each clue guessed and donning one for each one flubbed. Come night, this version of strip poker picked up where it had left off, and if he cracked the mystery, she was his.

Zinc soon got adept at solving such puzzles.

Eventually, thanks to Alex, Zinc was patched up. When the call to return to Special X finally came, it meant Alex had to abandon Oregon for British Columbia if she was to live with him. Knowing how important it was to Zinc as a man to return to the force, and being the one with a portable occupation, she sold her house, packed up her belongings and crossed the Canadian border.

Where would Zinc Chandler be today if not for Alex Hunt?

And what would he do if he lost her?

Now, as Alex moved into his arms, the phone by the bed rang. On reflex, Zinc reached out and punched the speaker button. "Chandler," he said to the activated mike.

"Zinc, it's Maddy Thorne." Her husky voice filled the bedroom. "You get Seattle stations on cable, don't you?"

"Yes, all of them."

"Turn on KVOT."

In addition to the set on which they had watched *Twelve Angry Men,* Zinc and Alex had a TV on the wall at the foot of the bed. Plucking the remote control from the bedside table, Alex clicked it on and entered the cable channel for that Seattle station.

A moment later, the gray room flickered with blue light. The image that appeared onscreen was an aerial view of the city taken from a chopper. The word "Live" was superimposed in the upper corner, and in the lower corner was "Breaking News." At first, Zinc wondered if this was the morning traffic report, for there was the Space Needle on the horizon and here was traffic on a bridge across Lake Washington, people commuting into the city. But then the camera closed in on what appeared to be a park jutting out into the water, revealing police cars and cops on foot converged around a sloop that had run aground.

A body hung from the rigging, minus both legs and an arm.

"What do you see?" Maddy asked.

"An aerial shot of a boat."

"See a good-looking woman raising her hand?"

"The one on the phone?"

"That's me."

Alex scowled.

"Don't peek down my neckline," Maddy said through the speaker.

The image onscreen switched to a land-based shot of the sloop. The sun was breaking to the east, not up like it was now. "Recorded Earlier" replaced "Live" in the upper corner. Standing in front of the boat and facing the camera was a dark-haired, dark-eyed woman flashing perfect teeth.

"Sue Frye," she said, "reporting to you *live* from the scene of the Hangman's third hanging. Those sirens you hear in the background are police cars responding. A KVOT watcher phoned in this news tip, so you are the first in Seattle to witness this sickening crime. What do you make of *this?*"

"Oh, no," said Zinc.

"What do you see?" asked Maddy.

"A media shark named Sue Frye feasting on blood in the water."

"Guess what happens next."

"She shows what we don't want seen."

"The hold-back evidence is held back no more."

As if on cue, the camera panned away from Sue Frye to close in on the butchered body hanging from the mast of the sloop. In a weak attempt at good taste, the remains were shot as a silhouette against the blazing bloodball of the rising sun. Both legs and one arm were shortened to dripping stumps, while the other arm was lashed to a deck stanchion with rope. The camera followed a drip of blood down to the cabin roof, then off that roof toward the deck beside the starboard gunnel, but stopped short to focus on a bloody hangman game scrawled on the cabin wall:

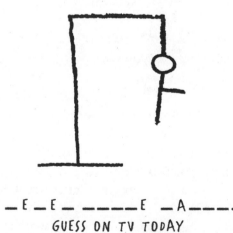

_ E _ E _ _ _ _ _ _ E _ A _ _ _ _

GUESS ON TV TODAY

HANGMAN

"Three *E*'s," Zinc said.

"Another good guess."

"So the Hangman won't stop killing until we solve the whole puzzle."

"If then," said Maddy.

"Let's hope," said Zinc.

The camera dropped for a quick shot of the severed limbs on the bloody deck beneath the hangman game, then the focus returned to Frye.

"Here come the police," Sue said as the cameraman swiveled around. The face of an angry uniformed officer filled the lens. "Take your hands off me," shouted Sue. The image onscreen jumped all over the place while the sharks were repelled.

Zinc took the control from Alex and pressed the Mute button so he and Maddy could talk.

"Who's Sue Frye?"

"Local legend. She's been around awhile. Made her name covering this state's return to the noose back in 1993."

"Now she's got a scoop with another hanging, eh?" said Zinc.

"Broadcasting the hangman game to the public is a rough turn of events. We won't be able to separate copycats from the real McCoy."

"Look on the bright side. A viewer might solve the puzzle."

"Does it mean anything to you?"

"No," said Zinc.

The *whup* of the chopper drowned Maddy's voice at the far end of the call, then she appeared as large as life on the silent screen. Maddy looked up and scowled at the telephoto lens, waving the helicopter away like a malarial mosquito.

"You just mouthed 'Fuck off' on live TV," scolded Zinc.

"Another pass and I'll empty my gun at the fucking pilot."

"So this victim's male."

"Uh-huh," said the detective.

"Anything else different from the Hangman's female crimes?"

"Lots," she replied. "The vic's a traveling salesman named Bart Busby. It's his boat. The Hangman didn't use a noose this time. Strung the guy up with a harness instead. That meant he was alive and conscious for what followed. Unlike the previous killings, this vic's guts were pulled out. Then his limbs were sawn off before he died. And finally, his jaw was slashed to ribbons after death."

"Sounds personal."

"*Very*," said Maddy.

"I didn't see any guts on TV."

"They shot the corpse in silhouette. The guts hang down in front of the mast."

"How tasteful."

"Trust Sue Frye."

"What could be Bart's connection to the Hangman's female victims?"

"No idea."

"Another blind?"

"If it was Dag Konrad or the Lady-Killer."

"You're checking Dag?"

"As we speak. And the good doctor?"

"We think Twist crossed into the States the night of the Vancouver killing."

"Interesting."

"He may still be there."

"You're coming down tonight?"

"Yes, by train."

"If I can get free, I'll join you for the cruise. I suspect we may spend all night comparing theories and notes."

"What about the guess?"

"I hate to give it to Sue."

"You can bet the Hangman's watching her now."

"The second word of the game is missing a vowel."

"*A. E.* Let's be consistent."

"*I* it is," said Maddy.

"Liar," Alex said as Zinc punched off the speakerphone.

"What have I done now?"

"She doesn't look like a shriveled-up prune."

Lawyer's Luck

A minute before seven a.m. on November 10, six days before the climax that is going down tonight, the phone rang in my East End home as I was about to shower. Naked, I left the bathroom for the den, catching the call on its seventh ring.

"Hello."

"Jeff, it's Ethan. Turn on KVOT."

"Hey, I'm naked and it's cold in here."

"Overnight, the Hangman struck again in Seattle. A camera crew beat the cops to the scene. They got a shot of the hangman game and the word puzzle drawn in blood. You've got thirty seconds to catch it broadcast on KVOT news."

"You at home?"

"Yeah."

"I'll call you back."

The TV was in the tiny box I call my living room, and since I'm the last person on Earth without a phone that moves, I had to abandon Ethan if I was to turn it on in time.

Ten minutes later, a blanket wrapped around me, I phoned him back.

"What a case," I said. "A gunslinger's dream. What I

wouldn't give to land a client like that."

"You in the office this morning?"

"Later, around noon. Got to finish research at the library first."

"There's something I want to discuss."

"I'm listening, Eth."

"Face to face. Not on the phone."

"Will it wait until noon?"

"Yes, I want to drop by my mom's on the way in to work."

"More plumbing problems?"

"Family problems, Jeff."

"Okay, noon at the office."

"See you then."

As I put down the phone, I studied the palm of my hand. Before running to catch the news I had grabbed a pen from my desk, and finding myself without paper when the puzzle appeared on the tube, I had used my skin to record the Hangman's word game.

Written on my hand was:

_ E _ E _ _ _ _ _ E _ A _ _ _ _

What the hell did that mean?

Having quickly showered, shaved and gulped down a breakfast of Eggo waffles, I drove directly to the law courts through a sunny haze, then parked my car in the cheaper lot toward False Creek.

I rode the elevator up to the law library with a pair of big-firm, paper-pushing fat cats. Their ruddy cheeks had cracked veins from too many liquid lunches. The one with two chins was telling the one with three chins a joke.

"This lawyer parks his BMW on the street, Sid."

"How gauche," Sid replied.

"As he opens the driver's door to climb out onto the road, a car wheels around the corner and takes off the door."

"Ouch," winced, Sid as if bodily hurt.

"'My Beamer! My Beamer!' shouts the lawyer while a passing cop car screeches to a halt."

"The cop didn't chase the hit and run?"

"It's a joke, Sid. The cop gets out and runs over to the shouting driver. The vanity plate on the Beamer flaunts 'Lawsuit.' 'You lawyers are so materialistic,' sneers the cop. 'Your arm's been torn off, but all you can think about is your car.'

"A look of horror crosses the lawyer's face.

"'My Rolex! My Rolex!' cries the poor fellow."

The fat cats laughed.

I laughed too.

Especially when both pushed back their sleeves to check the time on Rolexes.

I wore a cheap Timex.

So the joke wasn't on me.

"Criminal law is one of the few professions where the client buys someone else's luck. The luck of most people is strictly non-transferable. But a good criminal lawyer can sell all his luck to a client, and the more luck he sells the more he has to sell."

That's William S. Burroughs.

I can't put it better.

That, in a nutshell, captures my profession.

The way I saw things that Friday morning, Jeffrey Kline was a lawyer down on his luck, and if he was ever to climb to the top of his profession, he—*me*—would have to make his own luck.

The Lord helps those who help themselves.

Is that how it goes?

The library was bustling at that time of morning. Harried counsel, robes flapping like gospel singers in full throat, gathered last-minute case authorities for court. Sunbeams shone through the windows along Hornby Street, dubbed "Horny Street" in disco days because it was lined with clubs. The last tenacious autumn leaves clung to trees along the sidewalk.

I sat where I had worked on Wednesday and emptied my briefcase.

The Hangman had caught me by surprise by striking again so soon. On a pad of legal-size paper I jotted a rough timetable:

Seattle.	October 31.	Halloween.	Mary Konrad.
Vancouver.	November 7.	A week later.	Jayne Curry.
Seattle.	November 9.	Two days later.	Bart Busby.

What distracted me on Thursday from finishing my self-promoting newspaper piece on hangmen was a chickenshit domestic-assault trial in provincial court. No matter, since I thought I had a week to bait the hook, but now it seemed the Hangman was on an accelerating schedule.

Even more disconcerting was where the killer had struck. By returning to Seattle for the third hanging, the Hangman had slipped from my grasp if he got caught. Arrest him north of the border and his lawyer could be me. Arrest him south of the line, in American jurisdiction, and the client I hoped to attract would go to a Seattle gun.

Time was of the essence.

I had to lure him back.

So again I fetched *Dance with the Hangman* from the Lawyers' Leisure shelf.

"Calcraft *hanged* them. I *execute* them."

That telling distinction was voiced by the man who succeeded Calcraft as Britain's public executioner from 1879 to 1883. Before William Marwood, hanging was a process of slow strangulation. The condemned was hauled up or "turned off" a ladder or cart to dance the Tyburn jig until the noose eventually throttled him to

death. What Marwood recognized was the fundamental impor-
tance of weight plunging through distance as a means to cause
"instantaneous" death by snapping a hanged man's spine. On
demonstrating his "long drop" to British officials, he was offered
the job of hangman over a horde of other applicants.

Marwood turned hanging into a science. A deep pit was dug
beneath the scaffold so he could give those he hanged a drop of
between seven and ten feet, according to each convict's height and
weight. Because of how a rope is made, he learned to position the
noose knot beneath the left ear. That way, his client's head would
be suddenly jerked back when his body reached the full extent of
its plunge. If the noose knot was placed on the right side, the head
would be jerked forward, resulting in strangulation instead of a
broken spine. And so the condemned could not raise his hands to
grab hold of the rope, Marwood devised a belt that pinioned his
wrists to his waist.

A thought occurred to me.

I scribbled notes.

"Why does the Hangman strangle instead of snapping spines?

"So his victims suffer?

"For something they did wrong?"

So proud was Marwood of his occupation that he had business cards printed:

WILLIAM MARWOOD

PUBLIC EXECUTIONER

HORNCASTLE, LINCOLNSHIRE

So pious was Marwood that he would kneel down and pray
for the soul of the convict he was about to hang. "I am doing
God's work according to the Divine command and the law of the
British Crown," he told one and all. "I do it simply as a matter of
duty and as a Christian. I sleep as soundly as a child and am never
disturbed by phantoms. Where there is guilt there is bad sleeping.

I live a blameless life. Detesting idleness, I pass my vacant time in business. It would have been better for those I executed if they, too, had preferred industry to idleness."

"Hangman" was a term Marwood detested. He referred to himself as "the public executioner." Before long, his name was known in every household. Children playing in the streets had a riddle:

"If Pa killed Ma, who would kill Pa?"

The answer?

"Mar-wood."

Except when performing a hanging, this hangman was an inveterate joker. Once, at a jail with steps leading up to the gallows, Marwood slipped as he was climbing to prepare the noose. He quipped to gathering officials: "Somebody will be killed coming up these steps, if they don't mind."

"Gallows humor?" I wrote.

"The Hangman's hangman game?"

Marwood made hanging a science.

Berry made hanging an art.

A former cop who sought the job after he was hurt in a pub fight, James Berry hanged 134 convicts between 1884 and 1892. He was the first executioner to work out a regular scale of drops according to the weight of the person being hanged. The lighter the build, the longer the drop. In his memoirs, Berry wrote:

> The rope I use is thirteen feet long and has a one-inch brass ring worked into one end, through which the other end of the rope is passed to form a noose. I always adjust it with the ring just behind the left ear. This is best calculated to cause instantaneous and painless death, because it acts in three different ways towards the same end. In the first place, it will cause death by strangulation, which

was really the only cause of death in the old method of hanging, before the long drop was introduced. Secondly, it dislocates the vertebrae, which is now the actual cause of death. And thirdly, if a third factor were necessary, it has a tendency to internally rupture the jugular vein, which in itself is sufficient to cause practically instantaneous death.

"What effect does hanging have on the hangman?" I wrote.
"Does it warp his psyche?
"Can it drive him insane?"

In 1885, Berry journeyed to Exeter to execute John Lee. A wealthy matron named Emma Keyse had employed Lee as a footman. When she reduced his wages, he gave her a beating and cut her throat, then tried to burn her body to cover up. Berry's attempt to hang Lee is undoubtedly the most puzzling event that ever occurred on a British scaffold.

The gallows at Exeter Prison was built in a coach house by convicts. Three times Berry positioned Lee on the drop, pinioned his legs, tugged the white cap over his head and cinched the noose. Three times he stepped back to pull the lever, and three times the trapdoors failed to open. After each attempt, Berry retested the gallows and found that the drop worked properly without Lee on it. When Berry was unable to carry out the sentence within half an hour, unnerved officials postponed the execution until advice could be sought from the Home Office. Because of the ordeal Lee underwent, his death warrant was commuted to life imprisonment. Freed from jail in 1905, he went on tour as "The Man They Couldn't Hang."

Why the gallows refused to work remains a puzzle. Some say the wood was wet and expanded to jam against the frame when Lee stood on it. Years later, a convict confessed to sabotage. Prisoners, he said, had raised the gallows, and prisoners maintained it. According to him, he inserted a wedge so the trap wouldn't drop, and then removed it when he was summoned to help Berry with the tests.

Whatever the cause, the hangman was shaken. Like Marwood, Berry prayed for those he hanged, and he thought this was the hand of God intervening to stop him from killing an innocent man.

He suffered a nervous breakdown.

He became a lay preacher.

He toured the country to advocate the abolition of hanging.

At his funeral, Berry was said to be an "evangelist."

Another thought.

Another note.

"Is the Hangman preaching?"

The man who succeeded Berry was James Billington. Before his death in 1901, Billington hanged 147 people. Fascinated by hanging by the time he was a boy of ten, little Jimmy experimented with dummies and a model gallows in his backyard. Later, when he got to perform the real thing, James let the greatest mystery in the history of crime "drop" through his fingers.

Dr. Neill Cream, the compulsive Lambeth Poisoner, fed strychnine to London prostitutes a few years after Jack the Ripper's autumn of terror. The Ripper's identity remains unsolved. Billington had the noose around Cream's neck, and was in the process of pulling the trapdoor lever, when the doctor cried out through the hood, "I am Jack the—"

Bang!

Drop!

Snap!

"If I had only known he was going to speak," said the hangman later, "I should have waited for the end of the sentence."

"Hanging is so final!" I wrote.

Like Marwood, Billington was known for his gallows humor. On finding the chamber of horrors in a waxworks empty of customers, he took a place among the lifelike effigies of notorious killers. Minutes later, in came other patrons. Perplexed by the fact that one figure wasn't listed in the catalogue, a woman stared at the unknown exhibit until it winked at her. "This one's alive!" she cried, drawing others. When her husband tried to soothe her with "Nay, lass, it's a dummy," Billington pointed at him and shrieked in his face. Patrons fled in horror as the owner rushed in, but all he found was a mild-mannered gent viewing the exhibits.

If ever there was a man ill-suited for the job of hangman, it was John Ellis. So fond of animals was he that if he liked a chicken he'd raised, he wouldn't eat it for dinner. Ellis became hangman because of a dare. "I think what first suggested such a profession to me was when some friends and I were reading about an execution, and one of them said to me, 'You would never have the nerve to hang a man.'

"I said I would—and did."

Ellis hanged some of the most famous murderers of the twentieth century. Crippen in 1910. Drinking later in a pub, Ellis said he could have sold the rope for five pounds an inch! Smith in 1915. This "Brides in the Bath" killer seized each successive wife by her feet to drown her for her money. One murder saw Smith buy a cheap tin bath and return it later, asking for his money back as it was of no further use. Major Armstrong in 1922. He poisoned his wife with arsenic weed killer. As Ellis pulled the lever, the major cried, "I'm coming, Katie," the name of his murdered wife.

"Hang" and "execute" were words Ellis never used. He "put them away." When he retired in 1924, having served as hangman the same length of time as notorious Jack Ketch, he had put 203 away.

In 1932, Ellis was home with his family, sipping tea. For no apparent reason, he leaped from his chair, tore open his collar and rushed to the kitchen for his straight razor. "I'll kill you," he bellowed. His wife ran from the house. "I'll cut your head off," he cried as his daughter fled too. The police responding found him lying face down in a pool of blood, with two self-inflicted slashes across his throat. The ghosts of the gallows had put Ellis away.

"What effect does hanging have on the hangman?" I wrote again.

Harry and Tom were brothers. Al was Harry's son. The Pierrepoints, you might say, made hanging a family affair. From 1901 to 1956, the three pulled the lever on more than eight hundred convicts. Harry hanged 107. Tom got three times that number. The execution shed was called Uncle Tom's Cabin—a family pun. Uncle Tom worked a farm with horses, chickens and goats. When young Al came to visit as a boy, he liked to taunt the billy goat so it would charge. What a thrill to see the tether yank it to a halt. In class, Al was told to write an essay on this topic: "What I should like to do when I leave school." What he handed in began, "When I leave school I should like to be the Official Executioner… " That wish came true in 1943, when Uncle Tom retired as "Number One" on the official list.

The war and its aftermath kept Al busy. Not only were there home-grown murderers to hang, but there were spies, saboteurs and war criminals. More than two hundred Nazis died on his scaffold, and Al hanged as many as twenty-seven a day.

Lord Haw-Haw. Heath. Haigh. The Beast and Bitch of Belsen. Al's clients were the rogues' gallery of the day, but his most important hangings were the pair from 10 Rillington Place.

On November 30, 1949, Timothy Evans walked into a Welsh police station and reported that he had found his wife and fourteen-month-old daughter dead in his London flat at 10 Rillington Place. Police found the strangled bodies in a backyard shed. Evans, a mentally challenged laborer, stood trial for murder. John Reginald Halliday Christie, the man who lived in the apartment below, was the Crown's main witness. Evans's defense was

HANGMAN

"Christie done it." The jury disagreed. And so, on March 9, 1950, Al Pierrepoint hanged Timothy Evans.

Three years later, Christie vacated his flat. The tenant upstairs came down to clean up and found three naked women dead in a papered-over cupboard. He called the police, and their digging uncovered two more women buried in the yard and Mrs. Christie's body under the floorboards.

It turned out that Christie was a necrophiliac. "Can't Do It Christie" and "Reggie-No-Dick" were his names at school. From 1943 to 1953, he had lured the women home to gas and strangle so he could rape their corpses. He kept their pubic hair in a tin for masturbation later. In one of his statements, he also confessed to killing Mrs. Evans.

Al Pierrepoint could—and did—hang Christie on July 15, 1953, but what Britain's hangman could not do was "unhang" Evans. That case led to an inquiry, which helped spur legislation. The British abolished hanging in 1964, and two years later Timothy Evans was posthumously pardoned.

"Hanging is so final!" I wrote again.

"What effect does hanging an innocent convict have on the hangman?"

So engrossed was I in researching this that I had lost track of time. If Ethan and I were to meet at the office at noon as planned, so much for making any more notes in the library.

I packed up and left.

When I look back on those notes I made the morning of November 10, I'm gratified to see how close I came to solving the mystery.

Perhaps if I had published the piece, the Hangman would have noticed, but as things turned out, printing it wasn't necessary.

I didn't know it yet, but my luck as a lawyer was about to change...

Family Ties

Vancouver
Tonight

Our on-again, off-again secretary was back at her desk at Kline &
Shaw, surrounded by the unpaid bills that threatened to bankrupt
our financially precarious law firm. That was six days ago, when
I walked in from doing hangmen research at the library. Suzy
Wahl was frowning—not a welcome sign—which crinkled the
eyes and wrinkled the brow of what was a pixieish face. Her
chewed nails were those of a cannibal eating herself alive. One
nibbled hand lifted the phone receiver to her ear, while the other
poked a shrinking finger at the number pad.

"Why the gloom?"

"Ethan."

"What's he done?" I asked.

"The phone you see in my hand is in peril of being cut off. As
are the lights overhead and my food supply. But Ethan has me calling around to find and purchase a pair of tickets so you two can
cruise."

"What?"

"You heard me."

"Not that *writers'* cruise?"

"The very same."

"Put down the phone. I'll take care of this."

As I stormed toward my associate's office, savvy Suzy waited for me to throw open the door, then called out, loud enough for Ethan to hear, "Tell him to put the cash you save toward a raise for me."

Ethan was drafting a will.

Startled, he looked up.

"No way," I fumed. "What a waste of money."

The flyer for the crime cruise had been mailed to every law office in Vancouver and Seattle, and to all police departments in both jurisdictions, and to every private eye lurking on the fringes, and to West Coast writers who thought they were hotshot armchair sleuths. Someone had come up with this cute idea to raise money for the Northwest Writers' Festival. Let's have a mystery cruise restricted in attendance to those who feed off crime. Guests with uniforms should wear them, like a masquerade. Come in costume if you wish, or "dress to kill." There'll be an onboard murder committed for all to solve, and a prize awarded to the guest who guesses correctly. Then we'll dance the night away under a dome of stars.

Whoop-de-do, I thought. That's the sort of shindig I despise with a passion. The law's full of them. Backslappers' bashes.

Since the day Captain Cook planted the Union Jack on these rainy shores, the legal profession in British Columbia has wallowed in backslappers' bullshit. On a west coast, the waterfront homes are on the west side, so that's where those born to rule have always settled. Imperialists control the law, as they have always done, so functions put on by West Side lawyers in the name of the whole profession reflect their values and are dull, dull, dull.

The one exception was the East End Bar.

The East End Bar was formed by two defense lawyers and the city prosecutor—all of whom had their offices on the east side of Main—after they soundly concluded that the stuffed shirts of the legal profession didn't know how to party.

Every so often, the East End Bar would gather for a blowout soirée in a cheesy Hastings Street hotel with fake Polynesian decor. Plastic palm trees and such. Those who assembled were in for a no-holds-barred roast, with anyone in the room a potential target for off-color jokes. The meal was rubber chicken and the booze flowed in a flood, and as the evening progressed, the level of behavior degenerated. Food fights were common, and buns flew freely; the person at the podium was offered a garbage can lid as a shield to protect himself. Outside, near the parking lot, lurked two cops who hated lawyers, waiting to bust every drunk who tried to drive away. As stories spread throughout the profession about what was going on, tickets to those slugfests became the hottest admission around. Soon scalpers were fleecing West Side boys crossing Main to slum. Hanging about the courts, I heard the rumors too, and could hardly wait to partake in that fun. But all that was history by the time I got called to the bar.

What killed the East End Bar was feminists.

The way I heard it was this:

The East End Bar was awash with booze one October night when a clutch of recently called feminists took umbrage at the smutty roasting of Corky Calhoun. Corky had already passed out at the head table. His partner, Hughie Small, was at the podium relating how Corky was such a good lawyer that he once got a client's buggery charge reduced to one of "following too closely," when the leader of the party-crashers marched to the microphone. A buxom woman, with wire-rim glasses like those John Lennon wore, she venomously berated the drunks as "teenage boys with hard-ons."

"Act like a teenage girl with a wide-on," Hughie replied, "and you'll fit in."

"I demand equal mike time," the outraged feminist dictated. "Tit-for-tat."

"I'm sure my cowering tats are no match for this lady's tits," Hughie shot back.

And that's when a buttered bun soared across the pigpen, with Hughie deftly deflecting it with the garbage can lid. Unfortunately, it smacked the irate woman on the cheek, bashing her wire-rim specs askew, so they dangled from one ear.

Letters to *The Advocate* and saber-rattling about sexual harassment and assault charges followed. And of course, political correctness was jackbooting in. The East End Bar was a dinosaur facing extinction, out of step with the cinched-in ways of homo sapiens, so the legal functions of today are like those of our fuddy-duddy past, rigidly hammerlocked by guardians of good taste.

That's why I refuse to attend backslapping bashes where other lawyers gather, and why I was angry to find Ethan wasting funds we couldn't afford on hobnobbing with bores.

"I won't sign the check."

"Cool down and take a seat, Jeff."

"What's wrong with you, Eth?"

"I told you this morning on the phone. Family problems."

"Your mom?"

"Partly. She's not well."

"What's the other part?"

"My older brother."

I blinked. "Your older brother? That's news to me. All the time I've known you and you've never mentioned him."

"There's a reason."

"What?"

"Can I trust you, Jeff?"

"Jesus, Eth. When wasn't it you and me against the world, buddy?"

"Sorry."

"You should be."

"It's just that... "

I spun my hand like a wheel. "Get it out."

"Is it legal and ethical *not* to give cops the name of a serial killer?"

"As a lawyer?"

"And a citizen."

"You?"

"Me."

"Who?"

"The Hangman," Ethan whispered.

Suddenly, I grasped what rough shape he was in. If a man drinks every night, there's a stiff price to pay. What with the baggy, bleary eyes and puffy, ruddy face, my law associate, I now saw, was firmly in the grip of the grape and heading for a crash.

A crash could take me with him.

"You look like shit, Eth."

"I feel like shit," he said.

"If we had a shower, I'd stick you under it."

"When we're rich, partner," he replied with a wry grin.

That was a running joke in our office. Anything we didn't have—which was just about everything—we'd have "when we were rich."

"The Hangman?" I said. "You think you know who it is?"

My heart was beating fast.

My poker face was calm.

I had not told Ethan about the hangmen piece I was writing to try to lure the Hangman to the piss-splashed door of Kline & Shaw.

"Suzy," he shouted to the outer room. "Nip out and get us coffee."

"That's not in my job description," our rebellious secretary countered.

"Please," Ethan pleaded.

"Can't you wait? I'm sure they'll serve coffee on your fancy cruise."

"*Pretty* please."

"That's better."

Suzy got up and went out.

Ethan and I had the office to ourselves.

"I fear the Hangman is my older brother, Jeff," he confided.

You can imagine what went through my mind. For the preceding few days I'd racked my brain to find a way to make the Hangman notice me as a gunslinger, only to have the one person who believed implicitly in my legal ability tell me confidentially that he was linked to the killer of the decade by family ties.

"Why?" I asked.

"Because he's obsessed."

"With what, Eth?"

"The Peter Haddon case."

"Haddon? That rings a bell, but I can't place it."

"Back in 1993, he was hanged in Washington State Penitentiary for the rape and strangulation of a young girl."

"Right, Washington's return to capital punishment. The con that Seattle reporter proved was wrongly found guilty of murder."

"Justin Whitfield."

"Wait a sec. He's the reporter who wrote the piece on the Hangman's Halloween murder in Seattle last week. The article in the paper you brought to the office the following morning."

"Justin's my older brother."

Wherever this was going, I could hardly contain my excitement. A wrongfully convicted man hanged for rape-murder. A crusading reporter later proving him innocent of that crime. A reporter so obsessed with hanging that he became the Hangman, a murderer who baffles cops with a hangman game that hides his motive.

"Family ties?" I prompted.

"I was born in Seattle, Jeff. My parents divorced shortly after. My dad raised my older brothers and my mom raised me. She met Brad Shaw when he was in Seattle for a convention. He brought her back to East Vancouver to live common law. They later married, and I got his last name through adoption."

"Ever see Justin?"

"Not till he was out on his own. Mom loathed Dad and didn't want me under his influence."

"What makes you think Justin is the Hangman?"

"He witnessed Haddon's hanging in 1993. He was the only reporter Haddon would meet before he died. The two spent hours together the night of the hanging. The next day, this appeared in the *Seattle Star.*"

From his desk drawer, Ethan withdrew a dog-eared, yellowed newspaper clipping.

"Where'd you get that?"

"From my mom."

"And she got it from Justin?"

He nodded his head.

"Does she suspect?"

"We haven't discussed it. But I know she's worried. I told you, he's *obsessed!*"

Leaning forward, he handed me the clipping and I read:

"I'M INNOCENT!"—CONVICT'S LAST WORDS

HADDON HANGS

Justin Whitfield
Seattle Star

Walla Walla—He stood before us on the gallows of the state penitentiary, a moment before the hangman cinched the noose around his neck and dropped him to his death, to protest his innocence one more time.

"My last words are—"

His voice broke.

"That I am innocent, innocent, innocent. Be under no illusion. This is injustice. I owe society nothing. I am—"

He choked the words.

"An innocent man. Something wrong is taking place here tonight."

Then it was over. Peter Brice Haddon was dead. And now I am left with the nagging suspicion that the state of Washington hanged an innocent man . . .

"Whoa!" I said.

My heart skipped a beat.

The hand that held the clipping was the one I had used as impromptu paper to record the hangman game off the TV. Taking a shower had lightened it, but it had not erased the scrawl.

The ink tattoo was:

_ E _ E _   _ _ _ _ E   _ A _ _ _ _

"Justin has written a book about the Haddon case, Jeff. The title is *Perverse Verdict*. He sent me a copy of the manuscript and asked if I would proofread it for errors. Justin drove to Vancouver on Tuesday to see Mom and to pick up the pages from me. He was *here* the night of the second Hangman killing."

"Is that it?"

"No, there's something else. Just before you came in from the library, Justin phoned to ask if I'd be on the crime cruise tonight."

"Why?"

"He didn't say. Only that it's important."

The street door opened and closed as Suzy returned with coffee.

"That's why you want the tickets?"

Ethan nodded.

"To see if Justin is or isn't the Hangman?"

"I need your help, Jeff. There's definitely smoke, but is there fire?"

Suzy entered Ethan's office and handed us each a coffee. "I paid for them," she said. "There's nothing in petty cash."

From my pocket I withdrew a loonie and a toonie to reimburse her.

"Well?" she said.

"What?"

"Did you do it? Talk Ethan out of wasting money on a fancy cruise?"

"Suzy, dear," I said. "Be an angel. If you have to screw him, so be it, but *get* a pair of tickets from any guy who has them."

Jury List

Justin Whitfield awoke from a dream about his twin brother to find that he had overslept until ten o'clock that Friday morning. In his dream, it was the summer that he and his twin had erected a Cheyenne tepee beneath their treehouse in the maple at the far end of the backyard. They'd painted the tepee with Indian designs by coating their hands with various colors to press around the canvas cone in a Plains tribe pattern. Unknown to both his brother and the girl, his twin was secretly undressing in the tepee, the other half of the fraternal whole was up in the treehouse spying down on them through the gaping smoke hole.

"Yes," said the girl.

Yes, he thought as the teenage memory faded, and Justin awoke with a hard-on like the one he enjoyed in the dream.

"Weird," he said to himself. "Why, when I dream of sex, do I dream of underage girls? Especially *her?*"

Of late, the *Star* reporter had deprived himself of sleep. What with the tug-of-war between trying to scoop the media competition on the Hangman case and having to proofread the galleys of his soon-to-be-published book, not to mention the damage he did to himself by matching Ethan drink for drink in that airport bar in Vancouver, Justin had pushed himself to the point where you crash and burn. So not only had he overslept this morning, but the exhausted reporter had snored through several important phone calls.

After crawling out of bed to brew a pot of coffee, Rip Van Winkle punched Play on his answering machine.

Beep . . .

"Justin, it's Maddy. There's been a third hanging. Pick up if you're there. Sue Frye and a camera crew are already at the scene. The stiff's on a boat run aground on Sand Point.

"I'm waiting . . .

"I'm waiting . . .

"Remember the early bird and the juicy worm?

"Okay. All I can say is turn on KVOT."

Beep . . .

"Wake up, sunshine. It's your boss. The Hangman is prowling. Where the hell are you? Call back immediately or the story goes to Frank."

Beep . . .

"Maddy again. The worm's been gobbled. KVOT broadcast the hangman game. I've spoken to the Mounties. Our third guess is *I*. It hurts, but I gave the scoop to Sue Frye."

Beep . . .

Jolted by adrenaline instead of caffeine, the *Star* reporter forsook the kitchen for his living room. Every surface in here was covered with documents and pictures pulled from Justin's bulging Peter Haddon files, all fanned around the galley proofs of *Perverse Verdict,* which were piled high on a table in front of the TV. He grabbed the remote from beside a can of Coke and a bag of chips, clicked it on to bring the dead screen to life, then surfed the channels through mindless junk to KVOT.

Years had passed since she had covered the hanging of Peter Bryce Haddon, but time had failed to leave its mark on Sue Frye's face. Either she slept in a cryonics deep-freeze or she had recently gone under the knife of a plastic surgeon.

"In yet another exclusive for KVOT, Seattle police have asked me to reveal their next guess toward solving the hangman puzzle. Following previous guesses of *A* and *E,* the third is the letter *I.*"

The picture onscreen switched from Sue to one of a mangled body lynched in silhouette against the rising sun.

"It has been confirmed that the body found early this morning hanging from the mast of a sailboat beached on Sand Point was that of the sloop's owner, salesman Bart Busby..."

The mention of the latest victim's name on TV galvanized Justin to reach for a sheaf of papers beside the galley proofs. He shuffled through them until he found the jury list from Peter Haddon's trial. His eyes ran down the list until a name jumped out at him:

Ron Hughes, foreman
Denise Weston
Wally Berekoff
Darcy Desjardins
Miles Illington
Bart Busby
Carmen Landry
John Chwojka
Mary Somerset
Michael Eastman
Saranjit Singh
Rudi Goldman

Sue was back on the tube. "A KVOT viewer earned a reward this morning when he phoned in the news tip that brought you coverage of the murder first on this station. Now KVOT is offering an all-expense-paid trip to the island of Tahiti for the first viewer who cracks the baffling Hangman word puzzle.

"Our phone lines are open..."

Sue's orthodontic smile gave way to the gruesome hangman game scrawled on the forward cabin of *The Yardarm*.

As Justin picked up the portable phone beside the galley proofs, *not* to call KVOT with the right answer, his mind filled in the letters missing from the bloody word game.

Married Name

The skulls that had flanked the door on Halloween were gone, as were the tombstone in the hall and the coffin with the count's bride staked through the heart. Before Detective Thorne could rap on Dag's apartment door, the nosy neighbor in the adjoining suite stuck out her head, which was pinned up with hair curlers, and shouted, "I hope you're here to throw that bum out on the street."

"Is there a problem?" Maddy asked.

"You should have heard 'em. Rutting like minks. I didn't get a wink of sleep because of them. Dag Konrad is the neighbor from hell."

"You're sure it was him?"

"Of course I'm sure. The bed was pounding against my wall all night. Three of them! Really! There must be a law about orgies. The jerk bellows like a bull when he comes."

As if snorting out of his pen to meet the matador, Dag flung his door open and he stood there, no less hairy than he had been on Halloween, even though he was devoid of makeup today. His head hair and chest thatch were plastered flat with sweat that glistened on his skin while it fouled Maddy's nose. Stubble darkened his chin like a dirty shadow, and spikes of hair bristled down at her from his flared nostrils.

"Animal!" shouted his neighbor.

"Hag!" Dag yelled back.

"Evict him!" ordered the woman.

"Drop dead, bitch!"

"Asshole!" she cried, and slammed her door to have the last word.

"My alibi," Dag said, winking at Maddy.

There's a strut some men do after they've had sex, much like a take-a-look-at-*me* cock coming out of a hen house. Dag wore nothing but pajama bottoms held up with drawstrings, and from the front they made him look like a half-and-half satyr. The grin on his face was that of the cat that ate the canary. Bull, cock, goat, cat. Dag was a full barnyard this morning.

"I've been expecting you. Enter," he said, moving aside so Maddy could step into his dark apartment. It reeked of sex and cheap perfume, like every whorehouse she had tossed when she worked Vice.

A TV flickered in a bedroom to the left, casting a cold blue glow out at them. Against the wall shared by Dag and his nosy neighbor, a brass bed filled the frame of the door, and in that bed were two naked women with pumped-up breasts.

"Join the party," Dag said.

"Thanks, but no thanks."

"I've been in that bed since last night until late this morning."

"No offense, but I suspect those two are *paid* witnesses."

"And worth every penny."

"For sex perhaps. But not as an alibi."

"You'll want their names."

"That I will."

"Girls," Dag announced as they entered the bedroom, "meet Det. Madeline Thorne. The sexy redhead is Peaches and the luscious blonde is Cream."

"Out of bed," Maddy said, "and show me ID."

The bed creaked and rattled as the hookers obeyed, then the headboard banged the wall as the weight of all that silicone left the mattress.

Dag ogled the pneumatic pair as they bounced away for their purses, then drew Maddy's attention to the TV, where Sue Frye was reporting.

"That's how I knew you'd come after me. And here's why, as much as you may wish it isn't so, I can prove the Hangman doesn't live here."

Dag fingered a button on the VCR to convert the TV picture from one that came in on cable to one recorded on videotape. Onscreen, Peaches gripped the headboard for dear life while Dag gripped her hips from behind to pound her toward the wall, against which—*bang! bang!*—banged the brass bed. Sure enough, Dag let out the bellow of a bull, as if he had just been jabbed by a picador's lance, though truth was the one impaled with the lance was Peaches.

"What time did we start filming, girls?"

"An hour after you ordered in Chinese," responded Cream.

"You'll want to check the delivery time," Dag told Maddy. "The name of the restaurant is on the cartons in the garbage under the sink. Is seven o'clock last night a good enough alibi?"

The cop nodded. "*If* you were here," she said.

"You think we shot that scene some other night?"

"Why not?"

Dag grinned. "You do agree that hunk is me? Where would I find a body-double hung like that?"

"It's you," Maddy conceded.

"Hark," said Dag, cupping an ear. "Is that a voice you recognize?"

"Animals!" the nosy neighbor was heard to shout on tape.

"The walls in this dump are paper thin," Dag said matter-of-factly. "And what is that? I do believe it's a TV program."

As if to demonstrate how two could play this game, the neighbor next door had cranked up the volume of her TV on tape, so between the cries of ecstasy—fake or real, it was hard to tell—pounded from Peaches, Alex Trebek was heard asking questions on *Jeopardy!*

"What time did we stop filming?"

"We haven't," giggled Cream.

The ID Maddy took from Peaches confirmed that her name was Peaches Hoite. Cream's ID said her name was Shirley Creame.

Wonders never cease.

Dag ejected the tape from the VCR. He stacked it on two others and offered the three to Thorne. "I need 'em back for the Academy Awards," he said. "Match what you hear in the background with last night's and this morning's TV schedules. You'll find my alibi is water-tight."

Maddy pulled on a latex glove to accept the homemade pornographic tapes.

Dag scratched his belly and cocked his head.

"You got balls, you know. Coming here alone. What if I *was* the Hangman at the end of my rope? Look at me and look at you. If push came to shove, you'd be dead, Detective."

Maddy shrugged. "You say you're innocent. So what have I to fear?"

"Where's your partner?"

"Injured."

"You think I did that too?"

"No," she said, and managed a smile.

"I should have been a cop. I've got the knack. You think that's bullshit?"

"Yes," she said.

"Want me to prove it?"

"How?" she asked.

"By giving you the motive for the Hangman crimes."

"Bullshit, Dag."

"Try me, partner."

"Why was your wife killed?" Maddy asked.

"The same reason as Busby. Because she was on the jury that convicted Peter Haddon."

That shut her up.

"You do remember him? The guy the state hanged in 1993? The con that reporter later proved was innocent? Mary was on that jury. Under her married name. The name of her *first* husband. Mary Somerset. It was Bart Busby who secured the conviction. That guy was a bully in the jury room."

Takes one to know one, Maddy thought. "You're right," she said. "You should be a cop."

Dag puffed his hairy chest with pride. "Told you, Detective. I got the knack." Unconsciously, his hand dropped to give his balls a heft.

"I'm listening," Maddy said. Out came her pen and notebook to flatter him.

"Mary was a country girl from eastern Washington. Grew up on an apple farm as Mary O'Grady. Mary married a local hick named Bill Somerset. She tired of him and working the earth, so she escaped to Seattle. One day, as happens to most of us, she got a jury summons. This was back in the eighties, when she was twentysomething. Mary was a looker up to a year ago, but beauty didn't give her confidence to deal with men. When guys looked her over, their eyes locked on her body, and that made her feel physically threatened."

"Mary was submissive?"

"She liked her man on top."

"What happened in the jury room?"

"Busby fucked her over."

"How so?" Maddy asked.

"Mary's vote was to acquit Haddon. Busby's vote was to convict him. The final day of deliberation was Halloween. The pressure was on to reach a verdict so those jurors with kids could get home in time for the trick-or-treating. One by one, the acquitters buckled under Busby's bully tactics, until the only remaining hold-out was Mary."

"Eleven to one—they ganged up on her?"

"No," said Dag. "It was Busby's show. What's that fancy term for a person's weakness?"

"Your Achilles heel?"

"Bingo," he said. "Busby was a bully who grasped Mary's Achilles heel. He *knew* his victim, and how to get to her. When she was talking, he stripped her with his eyes. When she got up from the table, he did too, and he invaded her personal space to confront her man to woman. After the others gave in, when Mary stood alone, he accused her of having rape fantasies. That's why she was trying to hang the jury, he said. Because secretly she got off on the thought of Haddon raping the little girl."

"So she crumbled?"

"Mary wasn't strong. She didn't have the strength of her conviction," said Dag.

"In Haddon's case, the strength of her acquittal," said Maddy.

"She should have hung the jury. Like the Hangman's doing now."

Peaches snickered.

Cream joined in.

Gallows humor caused their big balloons to bounce about.

"Why didn't you tell me this before?" Maddy asked.

"I didn't connect the dots until Busby was hanged overnight. Besides, only a fool who's under suspicion of his wife's murder talks to the cops trying to loop a noose around his neck."

Maddy glanced at Peaches and Cream, still ajiggle with after-shocks.

"Why'd you marry? Mary wasn't your type."

"I made a mistake. It seemed right at the time. I was a reformed drunk and womanizer. Mary was an eyeful. She'd kept herself in shape. And she was looking for a man her love could save. The downside was that Mary couldn't save herself. She thought she had put the Haddon verdict to rest. Appellate courts had ruled the jury was right to convict. Haddon was hanged. Justice was done. Then just after I married her a year ago, that reporter proved Haddon was innocent of raping and strangling the little girl."

"Mary couldn't take the guilt?"

"So she began to eat. You saw the size of her when she died."

"And you fell off the wagon?"

"Yep," said Dag. "What can I say? I like 'em slim, with big hooters."

Maddy closed her notebook and put it away. "I'll leave you to your budding movie career."

"Before you go. Is there a reward?"

"For what?"

"Helping Seattle police solve the hangman game."

"Come again?" Maddy said.

"I already called it in to KVOT. I won the reward they offered for the solution. The hangman word puzzle spells Haddon's name."

Crime Cruise

Zinc was as easy for Maddy to spot as Dr. Livingstone was for Stanley in darkest Africa. The scarlet tunic glared as red as an open wound.

"Zinc."

"Maddy. Justin."

"Hi," said the reporter.

The Mountie shook hands and introduced them both to Alexis Hunt.

"Nice dress," Maddy said.

"Thanks," Alex replied. "Tonight's attire harks back to when Zinc and I met."

The two women looked each other over as if each thought the other a window onto Zinc's libido.

He felt naked.

This meeting took place at the top of the gangway up from the dock as those Vancouver passengers who had arrived in Seattle by Amtrak were boarding the boat. A long line of Canadian cops, lawyers, techs, scribblers and PIs snaked up to join their American counterparts already aboard, so the four moved toward the Champagne Terrace to clear the way.

"What a ship," said Maddy. "This cruise must cost a fortune. Where does a writers' festival get the cash for this?"

"Drugs?" suggested Justin. "Bank robbery?"

"Actually," Alex said, "money's being made off us. This is a fund-raiser. Not a fund-spender."

"Fooled me," Maddy said. "That you'll have to explain."

"Vancouver makes millions off a U.S. law. Foreign ships cannot traffic between two American ports. That's been the law forever. Since when, I forget. But one thing I know for sure is that whoever thought that up never cruised to Alaska. Most cruise ships are foreign, so they can't carry passengers north to that state from southern U.S. ports. Consequently, Vancouver is the dominant port of departure and has a lock on the lucrative Alaska cruise trade."

"Instead of Seattle," said Maddy.

"Which should have the business. There may, however, be a loophole in American law. Can a foreign ship sneak around the ban by docking briefly in Canada along the way?"

"You mean split the cruise?"

"In law, though not in fact. One cruise sails from Seattle to Vancouver. A *separate* cruise sails from Vancouver to Alaska."

"Will it work?"

"Who knows?" Alex said. "The cruise line that owns the ship we're on is going to run the blockade as a test case."

"We're guinea pigs?" said Justin. "Let's hope the U.S. Navy doesn't fire on us."

"Undoubtedly some lawyer dreamed this up," scoffed Maddy. "Lawyers believe loopholes are the *substance* of the law. They're willfully blind to the fact that a hole is *lack* of substance."

"Hear! Hear!" said Zinc.

"I still don't see how funds are raised from us?" said Maddy.

"The ship is on a dry run to acquaint the crew. We are aboard to make it seem real. Wealthy people love to support writers' festivals. It makes them look and feel like artistic patrons. This ship was sailing anyway, so someone rich who knows the owner of the cruise line got it comped to the festival. No overhead means the ticket price and whatever we drink is profits."

"Loopholes," echoed Maddy. "I'll bet they write it off."

"Does that make them writers too?" wondered Zinc, and everybody laughed.

There is no snazzier uniform in North America than that of a Royal Canadian Mountie in full peacock plume. As egalitarians, Americans dress to impress the common man (or the common person, if you prefer). Canada, however, is still under the Crown, so Canadians who dress to kill dress to impress the queen.

Zinc wore the classic scarlet tunic of the Mounted Police, except that both sleeves had black-bordered cuffs to signify his rank. A stripped Sam Browne without a side arm harnessed his chest. His blue breeches had a yellow stripe down the outside of each leg and were tucked into riding boots fitted with spurs. Flashes of gold glittered from buttons and regimental badges. The Stetson known around the world crowned his noggin.

At this stage of boarding, most passengers on the Champagne Terrace were American, so Zinc drew stares when he entered with Alex on his arm. A wolf whistle from Ruth Lester made the Mountie blush. Zinc thought Ruthless Ruth was whistling at him. Maddy knew Lester the Les was whistling at Alex.

With good reason.

Alex wore the same plain cream dress complemented by basic gold jewelry that she had on Deadman's Island. Here, like there, the occasion was a gathering of crime experts, and both invitations had stipulated "dress to kill." That evening would have been the most romantic of Alex's life had a real killer not embarked on a carnival of carnage. Here was an opportunity to begin again. That was the in-joke between Zinc and her. The net effect—déjà vu—was Alex looked as ravishing tonight as she had looked on the day she and the Mountie met.

Who says you can't go back?

"I feel like a horse's ass," the Horseman mumbled to Maddy. "Where's your uniform?"

"Give me a break. I wouldn't be here if we didn't have to compare files."

Sensible shoes, blue jeans, an open-throat blouse and a leather jacket were her party clothes.

"Save me a dance," said Maddy.

"Tough guys don't dance," said Zinc.

"Make that a minuet."

And lose a glass slipper? thought Alex.

As you would expect from a group tied together by crime, the topic that danced on everyone's lips was the hangman puzzle. That afternoon, KVOT had broadcast Dag Konrad's solution, so tonight the largest cluster hung around Sue Frye. Sue looked haggard from working since before dawn. Was her camera crew aboard for late-breaking news?

"I'm in the wrong medium," Justin complained. "Sue bled the scoop dry and I have yet to print."

"Justin and Sue are rivals," Maddy explained. "It goes back to the night Peter Haddon hanged."

"Let's grab a table before the crush," said Zinc. "Alex and I caught the news as we rushed for the train. We didn't have time to refresh ourselves on the Haddon case."

"Justin's *the* authority. That's why I corralled him," Maddy said.

Aft of the Champagne Terrace soared the Moby Dick Dining Room. Two deck levels high, it circled around a huge white whale diving from the ceiling. So as not to upset diners at their seafood repasts, obsessed Captain Ahab and his bloody harpoon were nowhere in sight. Beyond a wall of mammoth portholes, the lights of Seattle began to retreat astern as *The North Star* cast off for Puget Sound.

"I hope this cruise is less eventful than my last one," Alex sighed. "A bomb blew a hole in the hull and the ship sank under me. My leg was in a cast. I nearly drowned."

"You saved her?" Maddy asked Zinc.

"No, I was in Africa. With trouble of my own."

The table they selected was as far away from the grand piano as they could get. The woman tickling the ivories played showbiz tunes from *The Little Mermaid*. It was enough to make Zinc swear off cruising for the rest of his life.

"So," he said to Justin, "tell us about Haddon."

"What do you want to know?"

"First, bring us up to speed on the crime."

"Peter Haddon was charged in May 1983 with the rape-murder of Anna Koulelis. Nine-year-old Anna lived with her father in the house next door to the basement suite Peter had recently rented. George Koulelis owned a Greek restaurant in Seattle. Before going to work at the Athens Taverna, George took his daughter to school each weekday morning. During the break between serving lunch and dinner, he drove home to spend time with her after school."

"What about the mother?"

"She was somewhere in Greece. Since Anna had been born in the States, George got custody of her when his wife ran off to Europe."

"Who stayed with the girl at night?"

"A nanny arrived at five to cook for Anna and sit with her while her dad was at work."

"The girl was snatched?"

"Yeah, after school. The last witness to see Anna alive was a classmate named Judy. The two stopped at a local store for bubble gum and agreed to meet at four in a park to play with their Cabbage Patch dolls. That was at 3:30. Judy was in the park at four, waiting for her friend."

"Anna didn't show?"

Justin nodded.

"Where was she grabbed?"

"Supposedly at home. Her father returned at 4:35 to find her gone."

"Four thirty-five?" said Zinc. "That seems rather late if he was to spend time with her."

"Yeah," said Justin. "But he never budged on the time after he changed it."

"Changed it from what?"

"Four-ten," Maddy replied. "That was the time he gave in his initial statement."

"The time is crucial," Justin said. "Peter worked part time at a computer store. Even if his alibi was a lie—he told police he stopped for food and gas after he got off work—it was physically impossible for him to have arrived home before 4:15. Had Anna's dad stuck with *his* arrival time of 4:10, the case against Peter would have crumbled at the start. By changing the time he got home to find Anna gone to 4:35, George Koulelis opened a window of opportunity for Peter to have abducted his child. Instead of being eliminated, Peter became a plausible suspect."

"Why did the father initially think the time was 4:10?"

"He glanced at the kitchen clock as he walked in the door."

"Why did he change the time?"

"The clock, he said, was slow. He noticed it days later and threw the clock away."

"That satisfied detectives?"

"Yes," interjected Maddy. "Like you, the officers involved thought 4:35 was late if George drove home to spend time with Anna. They also noticed that he wore a new wristwatch. They suspected that he knew the time he got home was 4:35, but that he moved it back to 4:10 because he felt guilty about not being there when his daughter came home from school."

"The cops were wrong?" said Alex.

"As it turned out," said Justin. "From what we know now, it seems likely that George *did* get home at 4:10. Later, he changed the time to 4:35 so Peter would be charged. Which he was."

"Why was Haddon a suspect?"

"Blame that on the father too. When Anna couldn't be found

after a neighborhood search, the investigators asked George if anyone had acted strangely toward her. He told them about 'the weird kid' next door, whose basement-suite windows faced Anna's bedroom. The walkway to the Koulelis backyard was along that side. If Peter was home, he could have seen Anna walking her bike to the rear of the house before she went in to get her doll to go play with her friend in the park."

"Why was he 'weird'?" asked Alex.

"Peter Haddon was a cyber-geek. His goal in life was to become the next Bill Gates. When he wasn't working, he was off in the Zone, seated in front of a glowing screen down in his underground hole."

"Was he a pervert?"

"Only in George's mind. A glance out Peter's window would angle up under Anna's skirt."

The dining room was filling up with a motley crew of cruisers. The scarlet tunics of the Mounties seized the most attention, followed by the penguin getups of the Canadian barristers. It could be the set of a Sergeant Preston of the Yukon film, if only the Arctic was home to Antarctic wildlife.

"What was the detectives' theory on how the crime occurred?" asked Zinc.

Maddy took over from Justin. "Anna brought her bike home from school. The bike was found in the back yard. Something delayed her from going to meet her friend. Peter returned home sometime between 4:15 and 4:35. He waylaid Anna when she rushed out to go to the park and locked her inside the trunk of his car which was parked out back. By the time George arrived at 4:35, they had driven off."

"When was the abduction?"

"January 23, 1983."

"When was the body found?"

"Three months later. April 25, to be exact."

"Where was it discovered?"

"On the outskirts of Seattle. By a man searching a thicket of woods for his lost dog."

"What were her remains?"

"Mostly skeletal bones. Time and the weather had rotted what animals didn't eat. Tattered clothes covered the torso. Below the waist was bare. The way the body was sprawled suggested a savage sex assault. A broken hyoid bone indicated strangulation. Her underwear was found stuffed in her mouth."

"The lab find any traces?"

"Yes," said Maddy. "Two hairs, not Anna's, caught in the chain of a locket around her neck. Numerous fibers on what remained of her clothes. And semen stains on her underwear."

The conversation paused while vegetable soup was served, then picked up after the waiters moved to the next table. One of them almost stepped on the Stetson propped against Zinc's chair.

Justin picked up from Maddy. "Armed with the lab report, detectives sought out Peter. On first impression, 'the weird kid' did seem strange. Peter's eyes were dark and piercing. A nervous tic made him look guilty. The tic was actually a mild case of Tourette's syndrome, genetically inherited from his mom."

"They told him Anna was dead," said Maddy between sips of soup. "They asked if he would provide a sample of his hair and let them vacuum his car to eliminate him as a suspect."

"Which he did," said Justin. "And the samples went to the lab. And the lab report that came back confirmed their suspicion."

"Peter's hair matched the two hairs caught on the locket," said Maddy. "And six fibers recovered from the girl's clothes, including two on her underwear, matched five fibers in what was vacuumed from the trunk of Peter's car. That was 1983, so DNA tests on the semen stains weren't available."

"From then on," Justin said, "Peter lived in the shadow of the gallows."

Maddy finished her soup and set down the spoon. "Tunnel vision took over," she said. "The lab report linking Anna to the trunk of Peter's car, and Peter to the locket on Anna's corpse, convinced investigators that they had the right man. So married did they become to their pursuit of Haddon that they screened out evidence that didn't fit their only suspect. Such blind conviction meant the case put together against Peter was self-fulfilling. In effect, they made a case *after* the case."

"How far did they go?"

"The works," said Maddy. "Interviews conducted so they planted ideas. No record of troubling statements. Jumping to conclusions and never looking back."

"Was Haddon arrested?"

"Not right away. First, they tried to smoke him out with a false profile. The FBI sent a profiler to assess the crime. He toured the murder site and re-enacted the killing. His profile predicted that the perp would be an older, lazy, unintelligent man who lacked self-esteem, was physically disfigured and had a history of arson and voyeurism."

"Doesn't sound like Haddon."

"Not by a mile. So what investigators did was doctor the profile for a news release. The strategy was to make it seem as if Peter fit Anna's killer to a T, in the hope that he would panic and give himself away. No one considered the prejudicial effect of the ruse. Tailoring the false profile to fit him planted certainty of Peter's guilt in the minds of civilian witnesses. And in the minds of potential jurors too."

"Did he spook?"

"No. The people who spooked were the detectives. The FBI told them to allow two or three weeks for the killer's fear to fester. But when there was no reaction within a few days, Peter was arrested."

"Why jump the gun?"

Justin jumped in. "The excuse I was offered years later was this: 'Well, he didn't come running in to say "Here I am. I confess," did he?'"

"And now we know why, don't we?" said Maddy.

"Was Haddon grilled?"

"And how," said the detective. "All Homicide had was a circumstantial case. The window of opportunity and a few hairs and fibers. The hairs and fibers matched, but that wasn't conclusive. Other hairs and fibers could match too. What they lacked to cinch the noose was a confession."

A flurry of waiter activity whisked away the soup bowls, replacing them with the main course, a medley of *fruits de mer*. The conversation slowed as the four ate seafood, to the accompaniment of the clatter of cutlery on china. As the ship cruised up Puget Sound, past Kitsap Peninsula and Whidbey Island, isolated lights slipped by the portholes. Ahead, beyond Admiralty Inlet, stretched the Strait of Juan de Fuca.

"Interrogation wrung no confession from Peter. He steadfastly maintained he was innocent," said Maddy. "Every comment he made, of course, became suspect. Showing too much emotion or curiosity revealed guilt. Too little did the same.

"By then, news of his arrest saturated the media. Detectives were forced to justify their conviction, so they began cobbling a case around Peter. A cop driving the paddy wagon swore he overheard Peter admit to someone in back, 'I'm in trouble if they find out I had sex with an underage girl.'"

"How old was Haddon?"

"At the time of the crime?"

"Yes."

"Twenty-one."

"Old enough to hang," added Justin.

"What sealed his fate," Maddy said, "was the word of two snitches. The first to come out of the woodwork was a man charged with robbery who was locked in the cell with Peter on the night of his arrest. He ratted on him in exchange for leniency. His cellmate, the snitch swore, became distraught that night and, in a fit of agonizing over his plight, blurted out, 'Fuck, man. I killed that little girl.'"

Zinc shook his head. "I don't trust rats."

"The rat passed a polygraph."

"I'm leery of them too."

"So am I," said Maddy.

"And the other snitch?"

"He emerged the following day. A deal was struck to reduce his wounding charge after he swore he heard Peter confess through his cell wall."

"The *same* confession?"

"Yes. The night of Peter's arrest. The second rat was jailed next to him and the first snitch."

"The same words?"

"Almost. A slight variation. In his version, what Peter wailed was 'Fuck, man. I did it. I killed that little girl.'"

"And the polygraph?"

"It didn't catch him either. That was enough for Homicide," Maddy wrapped up. "Detectives had motive: lust for underage girls. Means: the car with the same fibers as those found on Anna's clothes. And opportunity: the 4:15 to 4:35 window.

"Peter was charged with murder.

"The next year, 1984, he stood trial."

"The trial was an eye-opener," Justin said. "I sat through it as a journalism student. The battle between the prosecution and the defense was more like a boxing match than a solemn inquiry into the guilt or innocence of a man. The hard-edged partisanship of the lawyers was scary. 'Fight him every inch of the way.' 'Don't let that sleazebag cuddle up to you in front of the jury.' 'Force him to call witnesses so we can gut them alive.' Those were comments I overheard from the state attorney."

"My dad was a trial lawyer," Alex said. "That was always a concern. How does an attorney vigorously prosecute an accused in an adversary system without overstepping the boundary of fairness to him? His term for the answer was 'noble cause corruption.' The belief that it is okay to distort justice because of the moral right-ness of convicting someone like Haddon."

"An honest lawyer?"

"There are a few," she said.

"The prosecutor danced circles around Peter's attorney. He had an answer for everything. The defense attacked the match between the fibers found in Peter's car and those on Anna's clothes. The fibers were simply there. No *common* source was known. Something shedding, like say a rug in Peter's car. Given the close proximity of both homes, the wind could have trans-ferred the airborne fibers of unknown origin to Peter's car and to Anna's clothes. Or maybe they were tracked about by someone they had in common, like the postman.

"The prosecutor's answer was Anna's underwear. How did the fibers end up there? Because she was raped on a blanket from the trunk of Peter's car? A blanket he got rid of after she was dead?"

"That is more likely," Zinc said.

"I agree."

"And then there was the similar hair."

"That didn't help," Justin said.

"But without the confession, there was no smoking gun."

"The defense attacked the snitches as rats without moral con-straints. They concocted that bogus confession to buy leniency. Their brazen performances on the stand should not be believed.

"The prosecutor's answer was, that the worst liar in the world can still tell the truth. The fact that both men concurred in what they heard, the fact that both statements weren't identi-cal, the fact that the confession echoed Peter's admission of underage sex overheard in the paddy wagon—these were sound reasons to accept the testimony given under oath. Did Peter's front collapse that first night in jail? Was it guilt that forced him to blurt out the confession?

"As the trial ground on, Peter seemed to slip into full-blown paranoia. All of it, we now know, was justified. By the time he took the stand in his own defense, he was a twitchy wreck of a man."

"His alibi sank?"

"It didn't hold water. No one remembered him buying food or gas. He could have returned home by 4:15. Then, if that wasn't bad enough, Peter's lawyer made a blunder that torpedoed his client. He called a backup defense of insanity."

"The fool," said Zinc.

"You've seen that done up north?"

"We, too, have dithering lawyers who can't make up their minds. They hedge their bets by splitting the defense. 'My client didn't do it. But if he did do it, he was insane.'"

"Mugwumps," said Alex. "That's what my dad called them. Their mug's on one side of the fence and their wump's on the other."

The four shared a laugh.

"Dr. Jupp is notorious as a shrink who loves the limelight. The defense can always count on him," Justin said.

"Peter's lawyer called Jupp," Maddy added.

"The psychiatrist testified that Peter was schizophrenic," Justin continued. "He could have raped and killed Anna in a delusionary fugue, and later repressed all memory of what he had done. By leading evidence of insanity, Peter's attorney not only conveyed the message that he was acting for a dangerous man, but he also made it look like he didn't believe his client's alibi. It struck observers as passing strange that a defense of insanity would be led for an accused who hadn't committed the underlying murder.

"So in the end, what began as a case of junk evidence against Peter turned into a courtroom battle dressed up in enough legal theatrics to overcome its basic weaknesses. All that stood between Peter and the hangman's noose was the common sense of twelve jurors. His life depended on their being true to the oath they took, and not playing out personal agendas in the jury room."

A man about thirty, with blond hair and bleary eyes, approached their table from the other side of the dining room.

"Am I interrupting?"

"No," Justin replied. "Everybody, meet my brother, Ethan Shaw."

Zinc, Alex and Maddy acknowledged him. One by one, the three introduced themselves.

"Crime isn't his field, so I doubt you've crossed swords, but Ethan is a Vancouver lawyer," Justin told Zinc.

"I practice with a criminal lawyer," the young man said. He pointed back at the table he had left, where a tough-looking fellow about the same age and wearing barrister's robes studied them. "Jeff Kline. Know him?"

"No," said Zinc. "But then, I don't get into court much these days."

"Join us?" Alex offered.

Ethan shook his head. "Actually, I came to spirit Justin away. Everyone's talking about the hangman word game. Jeff and I were discussing Peter Haddon. I told him Justin was the reporter who blew the whistle, so Jeff wants to hear the story from him." He turned to his brother. "How about dessert?"

"Go," said Maddy. "We have files to discuss."

"Mind if I tag along?" Alex asked.

She gave Zinc a look that said, Here's your chance to swing. If you love me, you must love me for *me*.

"Be my guest," Ethan said, crooking out his arm.

As Alex rose to be escorted away, Zinc noticed two things about the unsteady lawyer. One was the smell of Scotch wafting from him. The other was the twitch that winked one eye.

Gunslinger

I watched them come toward me, the three of them: my law associate, Ethan; a male who was surely his brother; and a woman who meant the Mountie in red was the luckiest guy onboard. They weaved through a sea of tables from him to me, which masked the fact that my office partner couldn't walk a straight line. Lucky for Ethan he had the beauty on his arm, for if not he might have ended up on someone's plate. That was six days ago, just before the onboard hanging that drew me into the case, which has resulted in the Hangman's stalking me tonight.

"Ditch him," I said as the trio reached my table. "He's too young for a fine-looking, grown-up babe like you."

"If I don't have to change his diapers, no man is too young for me."

"Too old and you end up changing diapers too."

She laughed.

I grinned.

It was a good start.

I scare most women.

They see me as a threat.

So it was refreshing to see her look me straight in the eye.

"You look Ethan's age."

"I am," I said.

"Which makes you the pot to his kettle, right?"

She was quick.

I like ballsy women.

"Alex Hunt," Ethan said, "meet Jeff Kline. Jeff, this is Alex. And this is my brother, Justin."

The man I had asked Ethan to bring over held out his paw. As we shook, I wondered if this was the hand that had scrawled the hangman puzzle.

"Sit down," I said.

They each took a seat, and as if on cue, dessert arrived. It was some puffed concoction smothered with fruit and sauce.

"Pavlova," said Alex.

"Really," I replied.

"For the Russian ballerina."

"Oh," I said. Believe me, you wouldn't catch me dead at one of those. Girls in fluffy miniskirts and guys in tight pants showing off their stones.

"She was the ballerina known for *The Dying Swan*. If I'm not mistaken, that was created for her. Early last century, when Pavlova toured Australia and New Zealand, a chef down under created this for her."

"You learn something every day," I said.

A forkful of Pavlova slipped down my barbarian's throat. It tasted like a ballerina's tutu. Give me an apple pie any day.

Ethan was getting miffed at me for playing cutesy with his date. "I told Justin you wanted to hear what he did after Haddon hung."

"Hanged," I said.

Ethan's face twitched.

"Hang a coat on a hook and the coat is hung. Hang a man on a gallows and the man is hanged. Unless he is as well-endowed as Pavlova's ballet partners. Then you can properly say he's hung, too."

Alex chuckled.

Classy chick.

One of those women who can take on both the high and the low.

"You learn something every day," Ethan responded coldly.

I didn't want to do it—hey, he and I have stood together for years—but the opening Ethan gave me was too good to let close. Not only did I slip it to Alex that I was in her league, but if Justin Whitfield was the Hangman, here was my chance to let him know I was his kind of lawyer.

"That's why you don't walk under ladders."

"What is?" Alex said.

"Hanging," I replied.

"I don't get the connection."

"In the early days of hanging cons on Tyburn Hill in London, the condemned climbed a ladder to the noose and was 'turned off' to strangle. The body was left to hang for an hour under the ladder. That's why we think it unlucky to walk under one today."

"You know a lot about hanging," Justin said.

He gave me that scrutinizing stare that reporters have copyrighted.

"The Hangman fascinates me."

"Why?" he asked.

"Because hanging is how the common law has always exacted judicial retribution. Pharaoh hanged his baker, the Bible says. It also mentions a gallows fifty cubits high. The gallows was brought to Britain by Anglo-Saxon invaders. It's fair to say the cross and the noose took hold at the same time. The Hangman goes to a great deal of trouble to hang his victims. When I ask myself why, the answer I get is biblical retribution. An eye for an eye. A tooth for a tooth. The Hangman isn't a killer in the usual sense—he's an executioner on a mission. What this Hangman is doing is what hangmen have always done: He's punishing the guilty, and he's deterring those who might transgress by driving home the consequences of not toeing the line."

Think about that, I thought.

If you're the Hangman, Justin, am I not the gunslinger you want if the cops bust you?

One who *understands?*

"You're mixing metaphors, Jeff."

It was Alex speaking.

She was turning the tables on me for making Ethan look ungrammatical.

"How so?" I asked.

"'Towing the line.' You can't mix driving a car with towing a barge. That's like saying, 'The president will put the ship of state on its feet.' You're mixing wheels and feet."

I grinned. "Alex, you're the lowest snake in the grass who ever stabbed a man in the back."

"See," she said. "You know better."

"Actually, it's you who got it wrong."

"Oh? How so?"

"A mixed metaphor is the use in the same expression of two or more metaphors that are illogical in combination, agreed?"

"Yes," she said.

"'To drive' can mean to operate a car. But it can also mean to send by force, agreed?"

"I suppose."

"When a judge condemns a convict to hang, what he says at the close of the sentence is this: 'And may God have mercy on your soul.' God lives in heaven, and He's our Maker, so heaven is where a soul comes from and where, if God has mercy, it goes 'home.' Thus when a hangman breaks a convict's neck, it can literally be said that the condemned is 'driven home.'"

Justin rolled his eyes. "God save us from lawyers," he groaned.

"And you're in trouble on another front," I added. "Somewhere along the way, you picked up the expression 'to toe the line' and wrongly fixed it in your mind as 'to tow the line.' It's T-O-E, not T-O-W. So while we both agree that 'to toe the line' means to conform strictly with a rule or law, you see the image of that metaphor as a person towing a barge along a straight and narrow canal with a tow line over her shoulder as she trudges the towpath alongside the water."

"I'm wrong?" said Alex.

"The origin of that phrase is this. The hangman on a British gallows chalked a line on the trapdoors as a guide to where the condemned should stand. Cons who did as they were told 'toed the line.' But cons who roughed up and refused to go peacefully were *driven home,* so to speak, strapped to a board.

"Sorry, Alex, but either way you lose. Both of my supposedly 'mixed' metaphors relate to hanging."

"You learn something every day," she said, adding her lesson to Ethan's and mine.

"That's how it's done," I said, with a meaningful wink at Justin. "Before your toe is on the line, / It's time to call for Jeffrey Kline."

"Ethan tells me you were present when the verdict came in?"

"Yes," said Justin.

"What was that like?"

The four of us had moved to the Captain Ahab Bar. As wine bottles flowed and ebbed to and from tables in the dining room, the Moby Dick crowd was getting drunk and rowdy. We had escaped to the quieter lounge to talk about Haddon. With candles on wooden tables, nets and harpoons on the walls, the bar was supposed to capture the flavor of Melville's Lahaina.

"You're a lawyer," Justin said. "You know what it was like. The almost-sickening tension in court as the jurors filed in. They were pale and nervous. Only one—Busby—looked at Peter. The foreman delivered the verdict in a tired voice. No sooner had he rendered it than Peter exploded in court. 'You call this a justice system?' he yelled at the judge. 'Where's the goddamn justice in it for *me?*'"

"Was Haddon removed?"

"The court adjourned for sentencing. Peter was crying as they led him away. The father of the dead child cursed Peter's attorney. 'No champagne this time, pal,' he said."

"Did you report the proceedings?"

"No," Justin said. "I didn't enter the case until the appeals ran out."

"Why?" I asked.

"I guess I believed in justice."

Justin, Alex and I were drinking coffee in the bar as the ship turned west. A compass sunk in the tabletop tracked direction. Already drunk and sulking because of my earlier put-down, Ethan was ordering one stiff drink after another.

"Easy," I said.

"Mind your own business, Jeff."

"Why did the appeal process fail?" asked Alex.

"The authorities were convinced that the right man had been convicted. Haddon's lawyer saw to that by leading evidence of insanity at his trial. That's how everyone knew for certain that Peter was the killer, and that became a strong dynamic in the state's pursuit of him through the upper courts."

"A psycho child-killer?"

The reporter nodded. "Peter's lawyer had overplayed his hand. The jury had legitimized the state's case with its verdict. The defense was forced to allege that Anna's father and the two snitches were lying, that the hairs and fibers didn't match or the lab had botched the job, that the wagon driver had not heard Peter admit to underage sex and so on. That gave the state its rebuttal. What the attorney for the appellant was alleging was a huge conspiracy involving civilians, scientists, police and prosecutors—all to railroad an innocent man."

"It does sound outlandish," Alex admitted.

"The courts thought so too. With so many bits of evidence pointing to Peter, it seemed too coincidental to be coincidence. Either he was guilty or he had the worst luck in the world. As it turned out, he *did* have the worst luck in the world."

"It's hard to overturn a jury verdict," I cut in. "Jurors are the triers of the facts, and once evidence is weighed by them to determine the facts of any case, an appeal court won't set the verdict aside unless you can undermine it."

"Which the defense couldn't. Once the verdict was in, the state's case hardened."

"Testifying under oath makes witnesses hunker down," I said. "Lying in court is perjury. That can send you to jail."

"A decade passed between Anna's death and Peter's hanging. In that time, DNA testing was invented. Semen stains were found on Anna's underwear, but the science wasn't refined enough by 1993 to get a workable sample to compare with Peter's DNA."

"Time ran out," I said.

"Because there was a deadline. Had Washington not revived the death penalty, Peter would have been alive when refined DNA testing became possible."

"So how do you fit in?"

"As it became obvious that the courts wouldn't come to Peter's rescue, his only hope became a pardon from the governor. By then, I was crime reporter at the *Seattle Star*, so he summoned me to death row and begged for my help."

"Investigative reporting?"

"In a way. I tried to interview the father of the dead girl about why he changed the crucial time he said he got home, but George Koulelis refused to let me in. Having struck out there, I tried to find the snitches, but both had been released from jail, thanks to having testified against Peter, and had disappeared back into the woodwork.

"Finally, in a last-ditch effort to influence the governor, I wrote the usual polemic about capital punishment. I began with a quote from Clarence Darrow, in the hope that America's all-time greatest lawyer could undo the damage Peter's counsel had done:

> Every human being that believes in capital punish-
> ment loves killing, and the only reason they believe
> in capital punishment is because they get a kick out
> of it. Nobody kills anyone for love.

"I finished with words to the effect that killing was a cruel, brutal, barbaric act. As state-sanctioned vengeance, it didn't deter crime, and it was the enemy of justice because it was so irrevocable, irreparable and ultimately final that it prevented correction of those mistakes that slip through the system.

"The governor didn't respond, but I got a lot of hate mail. And someone sent me a quote by Ambrose Bierce to counter Darrow's: 'A hangman is an officer of the law charged with duties of the highest dignity and utmost gravity.'"

"That was the end of the line?"

"Yes," Justin responded. "Peter asked me to spend his last hours with him. It was snowing on Valentine's Day when I arrived at the prison. I expected to find a psychological wreck. But what I found was a man facing death with dignity. You know that famous quote from Dr. Samuel Johnson in 1777: 'Depend upon it, Sir, when a man knows he is to be hanged in a fortnight, it concentrates his mind wonderfully.'

"That's what Peter was like in those final hours. Just before the priest came to give him last rites, he asked me as a last wish to prove he was innocent after he was hanged.

"I was in tears.

"I promised I would.

"That night I wrote an article that was published the next day in the *Seattle Star.*"

"This article?" I said. And from a vest pocket in my barrister's robes I pulled a photocopy of the newspaper piece Ethan had shown me earlier that day at our office:

"I'M INNOCENT!"—CONVICT'S LAST WORDS

HADDON HANGS

Justin Whitfield
Seattle Star

Walla Walla—He stood before us on the gallows of the state penitentiary, a moment before the hangman cinched the noose around his neck and dropped him to his death, to protest his innocence one more time.

"My last words are—"

His voice broke.

"That I am innocent, innocent, innocent. Be under no illusion. This is injustice. I owe society nothing. I am—"

He choked the words.

"An innocent man. Something wrong is taking place here tonight."

Then it was over. Peter Brice Haddon was dead. And now I am left with the nagging suspicion that the State of Washington hanged an innocent man...

"Yes," said Justin. "That's the one. Publishing it brought more hate mail. But among those damning letters was a troubled one tipping me anonymously to a cover-up at the lab."

"Which lab?"

"The lab that did the hair and fiber tests. From my secret informant, I learned there was a contamination problem at the lab back when it did the tests on the fibers recovered from Anna's clothes and the trunk of Haddon's car. An internal search for the source of that contamination went on for years, and finally the only solution was to move the lab."

"But testing continued?"

"All the while. Hard as it may be for some people to believe."

"Not me," I said. "It's like pollution. You don't see company employees running to the press to blow the whistle on the hand that feeds them." I winked at Alex. "Are those metaphors mixed?"

"The lab techs really mucked it up," Justin said. "The samples taken from Anna's clothes and Peter's car were contaminated with foreign fibers *at the lab*. Then scientists analyzed those samples to see if there were fiber matches, effectively creating the 'matches' that indicated Peter had driven Anna from her home to where she was killed in the trunk of his car. That's why the lab found fibers on Anna's underwear, the match that Peter's lawyer couldn't answer at the trial with an argument of random transfers."

"Junk evidence," I commented.

"Which made Peter a suspect and got him charged," said Alex.

"Got him convicted too," Justin added. "The junk evidence intensified in impact when the state attorney gave his closing address to the jury standing beside a chart mounted on an easel. Arrows linked photos of the car to shots of Anna's pathetic remains to connect the matches. 'Good old common sense will tell you that Anna was abducted in Haddon's car,' he said."

"What about the hairs snagged in the chain of the locket?" Alex asked.

"After the fiber bombshell exploded, I got another tip from my informant. Stored in the lab, I was told, were samples of hair snipped from Anna's classmates at the time her body was found. They were to be analyzed for the purpose of exclusion. Then Peter was arrested after his hair matched, and testing of those samples was never done."

"Was it later?"

"Yes, I forced the matter. And sure enough, hair from two of Anna's classmates matched as closely as had Peter's."

"Unbelievable!"

"Hardly," I said. "Didn't anybody watch the O. J. Simpson trial? That's what happens when lab techs play Sherlock Holmes. They get so caught up in trying to be of help to the police that they forget the fundamental rule of scientific method: They are to work vigorously to challenge and *dis*prove a hypothesis, rather than to prove it."

"That's the excuse I got for the oversight," said Justin. "The tech on the Haddon case had been too busy analyzing other samples that might strengthen the case against him."

Ethan was turning puke green around the gills. He looked like he was seasick on a tossing tide of booze. I feared he might hurl the dinner in his stomach at us.

"Fresh air, Eth?"

He ordered another Scotch.

"Next, I went after the snitches," Justin continued. "We have a recipe for disaster in the States. You don't have minimum sentences and a 'three strikes rule' in Canada, do you?"

"No," I said. "Many wish we did."

"The result has been the spawning of professional rats. The only way an American con can get his minimum sentence reduced is if a prosecutor recommends it. No recommendation and he comes out of jail dead in a box. A desperate situation calls for desperate measures, so cons will comb newspapers for the facts of sensational arrests, or even send relatives to pretrial hearings to get snippets of evidence that will make a false confession credible."

"Is that what happened to Haddon?"

"Yes," Justin said. "Nothing makes the heart of a professional rat beat faster than learning that an infamous accused will share space with him. Peter's arrest came before the three strikes rule, but the snitches had the same motive to work a deal: leniency."

"So how'd you crack 'em?"

"It took me four years. I had to wait until both were arrested again."

"Both?" I said.

"They were a team. The pair finally got popped in Florida and tried to work the same deal with prosecutors there. Too bad for them, there were guards within hearing distance of the cell, and the confession the pair swore they heard wasn't heard by anyone else."

"Polygraphs?" Alex asked.

"They beat them in Florida too. For pathological liars, passing lie-detector tests is a cinch."

A festival photographer entered the bar. I called her over by waving my arm. Here was my chance to get Justin Whitfield, the brother Ethan suspected of being the Hangman, in an innocent photo of the four of us.

Alex glanced behind her. She was sitting with her back to the starboard windows. "Are those the lights of Victoria coming up?" she asked.

We all looked forward off the starboard bow.

"Yes," said the photographer.

"Angle the shot so they're in the background," I suggested.

She stood aft to snap the picture; the three of us drinking coffee smiled naturally. Drunken Ethan attempted a plastered grin.

"Copies will be available as you leave the ship," she said, then left.

"We had to petition a court for the DNA test. My paper made the application," Justin resumed. "I took the stand to explain why I doubted the verdict and, under cross-examination, was accused of grandstanding by the state. 'What harm can there be in a test?' I replied. 'The case is closed. Haddon was hanged. The state has nothing to lose. But isn't there a lot to lose if the test *isn't* done? Public confidence in and respect for the law dictate that no stone be left unturned if we're to ensure justice didn't miscarry.'

"The state attorney responded, 'You went fishing and are down to your last worm.'

"'The question is, Do I use it or not?' I replied to the judge. 'I want to use it.'

"So she made the order.

"A Boston lab affiliated with Harvard was agreed upon. In terms of quality, the DNA left by the killer in the semen stains on Anna's underwear was almost as bad as it comes."

"Is that a pun?" I asked.

"No," he said. "Contaminants known as inhibitors were the stumbling block. In Anna's case, the problem was organic matter that was left behind as her body decomposed in the rain-soaked Washington woods. DNA analysis had failed in 1988 and 1992 because the degree of sophistication required to overcome the contamination wasn't available. DNA science had been refined since the year Peter was hanged, so I hoped enhanced technology would finally be able to extract workable DNA from the semen left by the killer.

"I won't bore you with the details," Justin said. "To neutralize the contaminants, forensic serologists combined four techniques. They diluted them, added enzymes, soaked them up with protein and extracted them. The purified DNA underwent two state-of-the-art tests: polymarker analysis, known as PCR, and DQ Alpha testing. These two tests, variations on the same strategy, compare biochemical traits or gene markers at various sites on the DNA chains in both samples: the killer's and the suspect's. If the genes match, the suspect is the killer. A mismatch on a single point and he is in the clear.

"The scientists scored the DNA off the underwear first. As I recall, the killer's gene markers came up B, B, AB, B, AC.

"Then, late one August night in the Boston lab, surrounded by four scientists and two state attorneys, I watched them score Peter's DNA.

"His gene markers came up A, B, A, AB, AC.

"'He's excluded,' the tester said.

"'Fuck me!' muttered one of the prosecutors.

"The genetic jury was in.

"No matter what their combination, those letters spelled acquittal."

Ethan put down his drink. Scotch slopped on the table. He was swaying in his seat as if he was going to pass out. The server came over to mop up the spill. "Due west," she said as she wiped the face of the inset compass.

"Monday morning quarterbacks," I commented. "DNA has made a lot of people smart... in hindsight."

"It worries me," Justin said, "that what I wrote about the case may have inspired the Hangman."

I cocked a hungry ear. This was what I was here to hear. The Hangman's masked confession?

"I don't feel good," Ethan groaned, slumping low in his chair.

"Too much booze," I said. "Did I not try to warn you? What you need, partner, is a breath of fresh air on deck."

"Come on," Alex said. "Let's take a walk."

"You and me?" he mumbled.

"Yes," she replied.

Wrapping an arm around him, Alex helped Ethan to his feet.

"Want help?" I asked.

"No, stay and talk. I'll find you later to catch up on what I missed."

With that, she led my wobbly associate out of the bar.

"You were saying?" I said.

"Huh?" said Justin, distracted.

"Something about what you wrote may have inspired the Hangman?"

Hung Jury

Strait of Juan de Fuca
November 10 (Six days ago)

While the killer was in the process of stalking his victim on the ship, Zinc Chandler and Maddy Thorne were comparing Hangman files. They sat in a quiet corner off by themselves, having abandoned the Moby Dick mob for a top-deck hideaway, a table in the Regal Lounge up on the Crown Deck. Stars by the billions shone in through the skylight overhead, for the storm predicted the day before had died at sea. It was buried somewhere out in the dark Pacific, beyond the narrows of the strait. The cruise would be smooth sailing. Or so they thought.

"You don't drink?" Maddy asked.

"Can't," said Zinc. "I took a bullet to the head a few years back. Doctor's orders. I've sipped my last booze."

"Headaches?"

"Screamers."

"Me too, lately."

"Mine are linked to epilepsy."

"I get migraines."

"Bad?"

"And how. The kind that crush your head in a vise."

"Must lay you low."

"To the mat. It's a bitch to be on call twenty-four hours a day with a disability like that."

Clinking his glass of Perrier against hers of Canada Dry, the Mountie offered a toast: "To no more headaches."

"Unfortunately, we share one with this damn case. What say we go back to square one and run through it again?"

"You first, Detective. The headache began in Seattle."

Rummaging in her file, Maddy found a photo of the first hanging and dropped it on the table.

"Mary Konrad—then Mary Somerset—was a juror at Peter Haddon's trial. Because he was wrongfully convicted, Peter hanged. Shortly after Mary married Dag a year ago, Justin exposed the perverse verdict in the *Seattle Star.* Mary fell apart from guilt and split up with Dag. Ten days ago"—she tapped the photo—"Mary was hanged. The Hangman left a hangman game at the murder scene. The game—we now know—hid Peter Haddon's name."

"Question," Zinc said.

"Shoot," said Maddy.

"If the perverse verdict was the Hangman's motive, why wait a year after it was exposed to take revenge on that juror?"

Maddy shrugged.

"Dag?" said Zinc. "He and Mary were in the throes of a dirty divorce. He loathed his wife for fattening up on guilt. If Mary were to die in a way that left him in the clear, Dag would lose nothing from the split and be rid of her."

"That's what I thought."

"You've changed your mind?"

"There's a problem," Maddy said.

"A fatal one?" asked Zinc.

"Dag's out of the picture unless we can break his alibi. He held an orgy last night to shoot a porn film starring him. The sound track recorded a TV blaring in the apartment next door. I checked the programs on the tape and found that they aired last night. Faking the alibi would require filming the visual earlier or later, having his cohorts record the audio track while he was off hanging Busby, and then somehow melding the sound with the image to fool our lab."

"It might work in a novel."

"But not in real life. Besides, if Dag dreamed up the Hangman to mask getting rid of his wife, and after hanging Mary went to Vancouver to hang Jayne Curry as a blind, why use 'Peter Bryce Haddon' as the answer to the hangman puzzle?"

"I see what you mean. It doesn't make sense. What Dag would want you to do is make the Mary Konrad–Peter Haddon and Jayne Curry–Dr. Twist jury connections, and assume the Hangman was on a mission of revenge against perverse jurors."

"In which case, the solution to the puzzle should be 'perverse verdicts' or something like that. What Dag would do is lead us *away* from the real motive, not pose 'Peter Bryce Haddon' to lead us back to Mary... and back to him."

"Right," said Zinc. "And hanging Busby would make even less sense. Having hanged Curry to lead you away, he wouldn't hang another Haddon juror to lead you back to Mary."

"No, he'd lynch a juror from a *third* travesty."

"I'm convinced."

"Scratch Dag?"

"Yes," said the Mountie.

"Your turn, Inspector. Let's do Curry."

While Zinc and Maddy were bouncing theories about in the Regal Lounge, the killer was hanging his victim several decks below. The ship was cruising westward in the narrows of the Strait of Juan de Fuca. The Olympic Peninsula in Washington State was a dark brood of mountains to the south. British Columbia stretched forever off the starboard side, where the glitz of Victoria had twinkled by.

Zinc finished his Perrier and set down the glass. From his file he fetched a photo of the second hanging and dropped it on the table beside the first.

"Jayne Curry was on the jury that tried Dr. John Twist. Thanks to Curry's romantic fling with the gold-digging doctor, the Lady-Killer was wrongfully acquitted of poisoning a defenseless old woman. That verdict is currently under appeal, but any chance of a new trial died with Curry."

"A strong motive," said Maddy.

"And Twist is cunning. I wouldn't put it past him to hang Mary Konrad as victim one. Having established a serial psycho taunting police in Seattle with a hangman game, he then crossed the border to get rid of Curry as victim two. The final twist was returning south to hang Busby. So here we sit, trying to puzzle out the Haddon motive, while Twist gets away with murder and avoids a retrial."

"I don't buy it."

"Why?" asked Zinc.

"Sandwiching Curry between two Haddon jurors makes her murder stand out. As with Dag, Twist would get more out of lynching three jurors from different travesties. That the puzzle answer is Haddon's name makes it worse. I find myself wondering why Curry is the anomaly of this case, which focuses my attention on her and Dr. Twist. Not a smart move for a cunning man."

"Okay, let's put Twist on the back burner."

"He's still in the States?"

"As far as we know."

"Agreed," said Maddy. "The back burner it is. We don't scratch the deadly doctor until he offers us an alibi as tight as Dag's."

While Zinc and Maddy were whittling down the suspects in their files, a *North Star* crewman was touring the stateroom decks below, cranking his key in the box at each safety station to confirm that security rounds were made on a regular basis. His cheerful whistle preceded him along the empty passageway dividing ocean-view and interior staterooms on the starboard side of "A" Deck, until the startled crewman spotted blood pooled on the floor of an exterior cabin with its door to the hall propped open.

The crewman radioed the bridge for help.

Meanwhile, in the lounge on the Crown Deck, Maddy dropped a photo of the third hanging onto the table beside the other two.

"The Hangman isn't Dag. The Hangman isn't Twist. Where does that leave us?" she asked.

"One thing we know: the victims aren't random. The Hangman isn't a serial killer in the classic sense. He, or she, didn't choose Konrad, Curry and Busby to play a fill-in role in some warped fantasy this killer is acting out."

"True," said Maddy. "Each was personally stalked. And each was hanged because she or he was on a jury that rendered a perverse verdict."

"The Hangman isn't a psycho in the lunatic sense. He... let's use 'he'?"

"Sure," said Maddy. "I don't go for all that word torture shit. We're deep in a manhunt. Not a person-hunt."

"He—the Hangman—doesn't have a motive that's rational to him alone. This killer has a motive we can all understand. The jury system—yours and mine—is supposed to protect the innocent and punish the guilty. Perverse verdicts happen when jurors fail to keep the judicial oath they took. And if a jury fails to do its duty—"

"The duty falls to *vigilantes* to correct."

"The Hangman's not a psycho. The Hangman's a vigilante. He's directly descended from the lynch law of the Wild West. The 'cowboy coil' and the hanging tree. What the Hangman is doing is—"

"Balancing the scales."

"He's a vigilante who goes straight to the source. The Hangman doesn't wreak vengeance on those who escape justice because jurors fail to do their duty. Instead, he exacts retribution from the cause of that injustice by lynching *the perverse jurors themselves*."

"The motive's more than that."

"Yes," said Zinc. "It's also personal. The Hangman's ulterior motive is to avenge Peter Haddon. That's why his name is the answer to the hangman game."

While Zinc and Maddy were interlocking the jigsaw pieces of the Hangman's motive, *The North Star*'s captain rushed down from the bridge to assess the implications of the hanging aboard his ship. One glance into the bloody cabin was enough to convince him that this was as bad as it could be, so he dispatched a crewman he could trust to be discreet to fetch a senior Mountie from the decks above.

Inspector Chandler, the sailor was told, was the top cop.

He went to find him.

"Back to square one. Let's put it together," said Maddy. "Peter went to the gallows for a crime he didn't commit. Wrongful conviction by a jury placed the noose around his neck. The Hangman is hanging jurors because of that travesty. The killer's motive is hidden in the hangman game."

"Question," Zinc said. "*Why* play the game?"

"What's your theory?"

"The Hangman is on a crusade. The hangman game has caught the public's attention. Lynching those responsible for Haddon's hanging isn't enough. The Hangman wants to scare the hell out of every potential juror who might do something similar in the future. Fail to perform your duty and this could be you."

"So the motive is bigger than Haddon?"

"In a way. But Haddon's the martyr whose death is behind the Hangman's rage."

Having passed Victoria and Port Angeles, the ship had left the Strait of Juan de Fuca behind. From here it would sail up the west coast of Vancouver Island, past the sound where Captain Cook had planted the Union Jack to claim British Columbia for the Crown in 1778. Rounding the top of the island sometime in the night, it would then cruise down the Strait of Georgia to

Vancouver, docking at dawn so those from Seattle could Amtrak home.

"We're slowing down," said Maddy.

"I wonder why?"

The Seattle detective placed the death photos of Konrad and Busby side by side. "After Dag made the jury connection between these two, I spoke with some of the jurors who convicted Peter. We've put the ones we can find under police protection."

"Their reaction?"

"Varied," Maddy said. "As you would expect from a group composed of a Boeing factory worker, a geriatric nurse, an accountant, a fisherman, a computer tech, an ad exec, a car mechanic, a shop clerk, a plumber and a mother who had a premature baby during the trial.

"Some blamed the system. 'My faith in jury trials is shaken forever. How can you expect twelve people to make a just decision if you don't give them all of the facts? If we'd had more to work with, the result would have been different.'

"Others accused themselves. 'People point fingers at us now and ask how could twelve rational jurors not have a reasonable doubt? How could we send an innocent man to the gallows? They don't understand what went on in that jury room. In hindsight, I made a mistake that will haunt me the rest of my life.'

"The one thing they agreed on was that Peter would not have been convicted if not for Mary Somerset—Konrad, to us—and Bart Busby."

Zinc sat forward. "Why?" he asked.

"The jury deliberated for several exhausting days. In the end, Mary threatened to hang the jury. As the only holdout for acquittal, she held Peter's life in her hands. A hung jury would have forced a retrial, at which the mistakes of the first trial could have been corrected, and what Justin later exposed might have come to light in time to save Peter's neck."

"But Mary caved in?"

"Without a rational reason. She simply gave up to stop Busby from bullying her."

Zinc picked up the photo of Mary Konrad hanging dead from the beam in her home. He studied it and said, "The Hangman is on a crusade to punish the jurors who doomed Haddon, and to scare the hell out of anyone who may pervert the course of justice in the future. Mary represents all jurors who have a reasonable doubt but lack the backbone to do their duty. By not hanging the jury, she hanged Haddon instead, and for that Mary became the Hangman's first victim."

"It fits," said Maddy.

Zinc continued: "The single word 'guilty' from Konrad's mouth was what hanged Haddon. That's why her tongue was slashed. Before Mary died, she told the Hangman that Busby was to blame. Busby became the Haddon juror the Hangman hated most. That's why—unlike the women—he was butchered alive."

"You look puzzled."

"I am," said Zinc. "If the Hangman suddenly hated Busby that much, why didn't *he* become victim two?"

"Because he was out of state in Oregon on a selling trip."

The sailor searching for the inspector had reached the deck below. After he combed it from stem to stern, his last stop would be the Crown Deck above.

Maddy took over from Zinc. "With Busby away from Seattle, the Hangman faced a problem: What if we linked Mary to the Haddon jury before Bart returned, and theorized that she was lynched in revenge for Peter's hanging? In a flash of insight, we might see Peter's name as the answer to the hangman puzzle and put the other Haddon jurors—*including* Bart Busby—under police protection."

Zinc picked up the photo of Jayne Curry hanging dead from the upper landing in her home. He studied it and said, "To prevent that, the Hangman struck again. The second murder was a smokescreen to blind you until Busby returned. Hanging another

Haddon juror would only increase the odds that you would make the connection. That's why the Hangman went to Vancouver to hang Jayne Curry."

"Not only did that hanging blind us to the Haddon motive, but it also advanced the Hangman's crusade to scare all potential jurors. If Mary hanged because she unjustly convicted an innocent man, Jayne Curry hanged because she perversely freed a guilty one."

"The *Scream* mask, the slashed tongue and the hangman game ensured that Seattle police would connect Curry and Konrad. While you followed the false lead of that red herring, the Hangman bought sufficient time for Busby to return. That explains why the Vancouver lynching is the anomaly in the case."

Zinc tossed the photo of Jayne Curry to one side.

He picked up the photo of Bart Busby hanging dead from the mast of his boat. He studied it and said, "Busby represents all jurors who break their oath to play out a hidden agenda in the jury room. He was a bully who liked to see people squirm. First he went to work on Mary, the holdout juror. Then, after Haddon was convicted through bully tactics—"

"Busby enjoyed the effect of what he accomplished for years. Peter was raped and castrated in a prison riot, and thanks to Bart's hijacking the jury, was eventually hanged for a crime he didn't commit."

"Ugly," Zinc said.

"It all fits," said Maddy.

"And makes me doubt whether courts are fit to try death-penalty cases."

"What happens now?" asked Maddy. "Is the Hangman's crusade over? The two directly responsible for Haddon's death are dead. The word game is solved. Everyone knows the answer. The lesson to learn from Peter's hanging is abundantly clear: Fail in your duty as a juror and this could be you."

"Do you think it's over?"

"All except whodunit."

"And who's that?" Zinc asked. "Someone related to Haddon?"

"That would explain the *Scream* mask."

"A primal scream?" said the Mountie.

"Or maybe it's another juror on the Haddon case. Look at the effect guilt had on Mary Konrad. She grew into an obese woman. What if another juror broke down under the strain of having been on the jury that sent Peter to the gallows?"

"So he—"

"Or she—"

"Wants the world to know who's to blame—"

"Or wants to get even with those who burdened him or her with guilt."

"A mad juror?"

"Why not?"

"Going after bad jurors?"

"That's how the Hangman knew what went on in the jury room. And why Mary—for her part—became the first victim."

"You don't have to be a juror to learn that in the States, do you? Canada has a law that makes it illegal for jurors to discuss their deliberations. From what I see on TV, however, American jurors are ready to blab a second after the verdict is in."

"True," said Maddy. "Which is too bad. If we had your law, it would narrow the suspects."

"What about another defendant facing death? Would that not give someone a motive to spook the jury pool? He takes Washington's only hanging to date and converts it into a scare tactic to save his own skin."

"If he's in jail, who does the hanging? A contract killer?"

"Or an accomplice. Or a lover on the outside."

"Ironic," said Maddy, "if the death penalty gave someone a motive to kill. It's supposed to work the other way 'round."

"What about a zealot against the death penalty?"

"Have you ever witnessed a hanging?"

"Indirectly," said Zinc. "On Deadman's Island, we suffered a lynching in the dark."

"But not an execution?"

"No," he said. "The death penalty was gone when I joined the Mounted."

"I have."

"What? Witnessed a hanging?"

"Yes."

"Who?"

"Peter Haddon."

"Holy shit!"

"I was at Walla Walla in 1993."

"How'd that come about?"

"Between you and me?"

"Whatever you tell me, Maddy, is in strict confidence."

Beyond the door to the Regal Lounge, the sailor searching for Inspector Chandler climbed to the Crown Deck.

"A cop and a reporter. You know how it is? Justin and I occasionally help each other out."

"Sure," said Zinc. "Symbiosis. Sometimes it's best to work hand in glove with the press."

"Justin was looking into whether Peter was guilty. This was in the months before Haddon hanged. The appeal process had almost run its course. Peter's last hope was for Justin to find something. What Justin required was some digging on the inside. I became a cop years after the Haddon trial. He asked me to check if the detectives who'd worked the case had influenced Anna's dad into changing the time he said he got home to find her missing."

"Did you?"

"Yes. That's why I became a cop. To ensure that justice was done in an unjust world."

"Any luck?"

"Nope. We *still* don't know. Anna's dad refused to waver from his testimony. The bulls who dealt with him maintain they did it by the book."

"Why'd you go to the hanging?"

"Justin asked me to. By then, he was obsessed with Peter's innocence. He feared Haddon was going to the gallows because *he* had fucked up."

"Justin?"

"Yes. By not breaking the story."

"You went as moral support?"

The detective nodded.

"How'd you get a seat in the gallows gallery?"

"Justin arranged for Peter to make me one of *his* witnesses."

"Must have been grueling."

"It was," sighed Maddy. "The execution attracted a horde of pros and cons. Those For and those Against were caged outside, in the prison's parking lot. Except for that surrounding abortion, there's no hotter moral rift in America. Zealots against abortion have shot doctors who perform them. From the zeal I witnessed in the shouts of those against hanging Haddon, I wouldn't be surprised if the Hangman was spawned among zealots violently opposed to capital—"

"Inspector Chandler?"

Interrupted, Zinc and Maddy turned. A *North Star* crewman was approaching their table.

"Yes?" said the Mountie.

"I was sent to find you. It's urgent that you come with me. Captain's orders."

Bleeding Heart

Pacific Ocean
November 10

"Urgent?" said Zinc. "What's the problem?"

The crewman glanced at Maddy.

"I'm a Seattle detective."

The crewman hesitated.

"Out with it," said the Mountie.

"There's been a murder, sir. The captain needs you below."

"A murder?"

"A hanging."

"That's in poor taste," said Maddy.

Both cops knew from the invitations that there was to be an interactive murder mystery on the crime cruise sometime tonight. Those who wished to play the game for a magnum of champagne would be summoned to the scene of the crime. There, they would face a mess of clues about the "body" and, from the evidence left by the murderer, would try to guess whodunit and why. The closest answer would win the booze. That's what Zinc and Maddy thought this was. A summons to play.

"Alex sent you?"

"No, sir. The captain."

"Give us a moment."

The crewman withdrew to the door.

"He's good," said Maddy.

"They use actors."

"Are you game?"

"Are you?"

"Why not?" said Maddy.

"If we win, the champagne is yours."

"Alex will be cross."

"She's behind this charade."

They followed the crewman from the lounge and down the stairs to the Sun Deck. The scene of the murder was to be in the solarium around the indoor pool, under the crystal canopy of the deck above. Through the open door to the solarium, Maddy and Zinc could see a mannequin sprawled by the water. Those arranging the murder were fussing with clues in final preparation for the passenger sleuths' arrival.

"This way," said the crewman, holding the elevator door for them.

"Where are we going?"

"To 'A' Deck, sir."

"'A' Deck?"

"Yes, sir. To one of the cabins."

Five decks down, the elevator stopped outside the dining room. The door slid open on a shouting match. A lawyer-turned-author was regaling the diners who were too drunk to leave the room with tales of his research safari to Africa. The drunks were involved in deep conversations of their own, and it was hard to hear with this guy at the mike yakking. The author was angry that his pearls fell before swine, so he used the amplification system to drown out the drunks. The drunks were pissed at the nerve of this little Hitler, and they began chanting, "Shut the fuck up!" In effect, it was nothing more than your usual squabble of lawyers. My, how they love the sound of their own voices.

Zinc looked for Alex.

Alex was nowhere around.

The crewman told the drunk who tried to enter the elevator to take the next one.

The door closed.

The lift continued its drop.

Zinc put one and one together and began to wonder if they would all be embarrassed. Alex Hunt was a sexy trickster. Many were the times she had sexually shanghaied Zinc. The clues were there to indicate she might be up to that. The stateroom assigned to them was down on "A" Deck. He wouldn't put it past Alex to leave the lawyers and Justin talking somewhere on the ship while she slipped away to their cabin. Dispatching a crewman to lure Zinc to the "murder" would be her kind of fun, and when he entered the stateroom, there she would be, in the nude with nothing but a blood red rose between her teeth.

"Take me," Alex would say.

And usually he would. That being one of the reasons why Zinc loved Alex to death.

But if that was how this game played out tonight, there would be red faces when Maddy entered the cabin with him.

Maddy, too, was puzzled by what was going on. The "murder" was a hanging, the crewman had said. With the Hangman on the loose, that was in poor taste. Would those who had organized the festival make such a mistake? It wasn't a faux pas befitting an arty crowd. Besides, if the mystery was planned for the solarium, why lead the Mountie and her down here?

It must be a prank.

But it wasn't.

That was evident the instant the elevator stopped and the door slid open on "A" Deck. *North Star* crewmen were everywhere, corralling passengers who'd come down to their staterooms or barricading the entrance to the starboard passageway. The crewman sent to fetch Zinc ushered the Mountie and the detective around the cordon and along the almost-deserted hall to where the captain stood by an open cabin door.

The captain was a lanky man uniformed in white. He had the bearing of ex-navy in his mastlike spine. Whatever perils he'd faced at sea were masked by the cut of his jib, but what he had witnessed in the cabin had rammed his even keel.

No introductions.

"The Hangman's aboard," he said.

The captain stepped aside so Zinc and Maddy could gaze in.

The stateroom was an oblong with two portholes in the far wall. The portholes were over twin beds with a floor space between. The flowered quilts on the beds matched a curtain that could be drawn across the cabin as a privacy screen. The curtain was pushed back to bare the curtain rod.

Tough as she was from all the death she had seen in her life, Maddy was shaken to her core by the sight of the hanging corpse. The body was hoisted a foot off the floor by a rope looped over the curtain rod and tied to the leg of one bed. The head in the hangman's noose was crooked to one side. The face was blue from asphyxia. The bulging eyes were bloodshot from burst vessels. Strangulation had forced out the tongue, which the killer had slit with a slash across the gaping mouth. Blood gushing from that wound had poured down the torso, soaking the victim's formal dress red. Both arms and both legs were slashed as well. The blood from those cuts had pooled on the floor, where it oozed around the body of a man crumpled unconscious at the feet of the corpse.

In the blood that crept from him toward the cabin door lay a knife with its blade pointing at the side wall.

On that wall, scrawled in blood, was a hangman game:

_ E _ E _ _ _ _ I _ E _ A _ _ _ _ _

GUESS ON TV TODAY

HANGMAN

"What in hell..." said Maddy.

She turned to face Zinc.

And found herself face to face with a likeness she knew well.

Shock had tightened Zinc's flesh hard against his skull.

Disbelief had shot his eyelids wide.

Outrage had twitched one pupil to the side.

His mouth was frozen open in the elliptic O of a silent shriek.

He was Munch's *The Scream.*

The victim hanging from the rod was Alex Hunt.

The Brig

Vancouver
Tonight

The practice of criminal law consists of fighting courtroom battles and recounting legendary war stories. How successful a lawyer is can be gauged by whether the battles making news are being fought by *him*, and whether the war stories he tells make up *his* reputation. If both focus on gunslingers other than him, then he's no more than a wannabe yearning for his mirage in the desert. That was me, six days ago on that fatal cruise, full of battles and war stories that other lawyers had fought and earned.

But all that was going to change.

I was talking death with a couple of American gunslingers from Seattle when Det. Maddy Thorne found me in a bar called the Brig. *The North Star* seemed to have more bars than passengers, no doubt to ward off the titanic chill of all those Alaskan icebergs that played chicken with the ship on its northern cruises. The Yank with the handlebar mustache—his trademark, I'll bet—was a slippery snake in the grass named Josh Hand. He referred to himself as "the Learned Hand," an attorneys' in-joke about a famous U.S. judge. Sporting a bolo tie with a steer's-head clasp, his sidekick was an urban cowboy named Russ Russell. He referred to himself as "the Rustler," but I fixed him in my mind

257

through alliteration. Russ Russell was the *sound* of a snake in the grass.

"Do you gamble, Jeff?"

The question came from Josh.

"All lawyers are gamblers," I replied.

Russ took a twenty from his wallet and slapped it on the bar.

The snake and the slither gave each other the eye. I felt like a mouse being sized up as a meal.

"As sentence stories go, Kinky's not bad. But when it comes to gallows humor and the bench, twenty dollars says I can better that."

"Better Mrs. Mudge going ballistic when the judge slammed her son?"

"Yep."

"With whom?" I asked.

"José Gonzales."

"A client of yours?"

"Nah," said Josh. "A bit before my time. Gonzales was sentenced back in 1881. In U.S. District Court. New Mexico Territory Sessions."

I glanced at the twenty.

It would buy a round.

I picked up the gauntlet Josh had thrown down.

"So let's hear it."

"Whoa," said Russ. "To coin a phrase, show me the money, pal."

I pulled a Canadian twenty from my wallet and put it down.

The Yanks stared at the colorful bill as if it should be hanging on a roll beside the toilet.

"We're not playing Monopoly."

"Place a bet," said Russ.

"With legal tender."

"Which I can take to the bank."

"See that?" I said, pointing out the window. "It's Vancouver

Island. We're in Canadian waters. So my money *is* legal tender here."

"It should be thirty."

"With exchange."

"Hey, big spender. Don't be cheap," I said. "That twenty's worth as much to me as yours is to you. Why should I gamble one and a half times your bet?"

"Whatever," said Josh. He stroked his mustache.

"It's only money," Russ said. He tugged his bolo tie.

"So," I said, "tell me a story that's better than Kinky and Mudge."

From the inside pocket of his rumpled brown suit, Josh pulled a folded photocopied sheet and said, "Read it and laugh, Jeff."

I angled the hand-off toward the light behind the bar:

> José Manuel Miguel Xaviar Gonzales ... in a few short weeks it will be spring. The snows of winter will flee away. The ice will vanish. The air will become soft and balmy. In short, José Manuel Miguel Xaviar Gonzales, the annual miracle of the years will awaken and come to pass. But you won't be there.
>
> The rivulet will run its soaring course to the sea. The timid desert flowers will put forth their tender shoots. The glorious valleys of this domain will blossom as the rose. Still, José Manuel Miguel Xaviar Gonzales, you won't be here to see.
>
> From every treetop some wild woods songster will carol his mating song. Butterflies will sport in the sunshine. The busy bee will hum happily as it pursues its accustomed vocation. The gentle breeze will tease the tassels of the wildgrasses ... and all nature ... José Manuel Miguel Xaviar Gonzales ... will be glad ... but you.

You won't be here to enjoy it because I now command the sheriff or some other officers of the county to lead you out to some remote spot ... swing you by the neck from a knotting bough of some sturdy oak ... and let you hang until you are dead.

And then, José Manuel Miguel Xaviar Gonzales ... I further command that such officer ... or officers retire quickly from your dangling corpse ... that vultures may descend from the heavens upon your filthy body until nothing shall remain but bare ... bleached bones of a cold-blooded, copper-colored, bloodthirsty, throat-cutting, chili-eating, sheep-herding, murdering son of a bitch.

I laughed out loud.

"Is that for real?" I asked.

"As real as this twenty you just lost," said Josh as he reached for my money.

I clamped the Learned Hand. "Not so fast," I said. "Mickey Spillane, I assume, is your favorite author?"

"Huh?" grunted Josh.

"He should be," I replied. "Judging from your way of judging, I, *the Jury* is right up your alley. As for me, I prefer a more objective judge."

He grinned slyly.

I grinned back.

The snake and the mongoose.

The mongoose and the snake.

"Point made," Josh said.

"Fitting," said Russ. "A Mexican standoff over a guy named José Gonzales."

Josh winked slyly.

I winked back.

HANGMAN

"Are you a gambler, Jeff?"

"All lawyers are gamblers, Josh."

"Then why don't you and I gamble on a judge. Next person through the door settles the issue. You tell him the tale of Kinky. I tell him the tale of Gonzales. And we let the luck of the draw decide."

"You're on," I said.

"Good. Release my hand."

The three of us turned our bar stools to face the entrance of the Brig.

"A buck says it's a man."

"You're on," I repeated.

"It must gall you," Russ said, "to no longer have hanging in Canada to bet against. A death-penalty case is the ultimate gamble. Just you and the state playing craps in court for your client's life. Betting cash is child's play compared to that. You gotta be one of us to know the execution thrill. Sex won't get your rocks off with half the blast that gambling with losing your client to the noose or the needle will."

"We still play," I said.

"How, without a gallows?"

"We use *your* gallows and our Extradition Act. As long as life hangs in the balance, the thrill is there to enjoy."

"Welshers," Josh scoffed.

"Cowards," Russ sneered.

"If there's one thing we hold in contempt, it's a killer without balls. The way I see it, if you want to kill someone in the States and beat our justice system at trial, that's your God-given right under the Constitution. But if you play, be prepared to pay. It's only a welsher who gambles in America, then flees to Canada to avoid the cost of losing."

"That's harsh," I said. "*You* set up the game."

"What game?" they asked in unison.

"Cheat the hangman, fellows."

The snake and the slither exchanged glances. They were silently trying to decide which one would ask the ignorant question.

"How's that?" said Josh.

"Let's go back to 1972. In *Furman* v. *Georgia,* the U.S. Supreme Court outlawed the death penalty in America. That was the ultra-liberal era of the Warren court in the United States, so the outcome of the *Furman* case was no surprise. The current extradition treaty between the U.S. and Canada had been signed the year before, in 1971. Foreseeing *Furman,* U.S. negotiators feared that capital punishment would be abolished in the States while Canada still had the gallows as the lawful sentence for murder. That's why the provision you think so unfair was put in the treaty. So *you* could demand *we* guarantee not to execute fugitives extradited *from* the States *to* Canada."

"Son of a bitch," said Russ.

"You gotta love the irony in that twist of fate," I said. "The treaty was ratified and came into force in March 1976. In late June of that same year, Canada's law makers voted to abolish hanging. A few days later, in early July, your Supreme Court reinstated the death penalty in *Gregg* v. *Georgia.*

"What goes around, comes around, as they say. Your chickens have come home to roost, as they say. You made your bed, now lie in it, as they say. You reap what you sow, as they say.

"So, hey, guys. We're all lawyers here. Isn't the name of the game to get our clients off however we can? And if America made a mistake by giving Canada a way to cheat *your* hangman—by demanding that *you* guarantee not to execute a fugitive killer extradited *from* Canada *to* the States—do you not think it just good counsel work to ram that mistake up your ass?"

"Whoa," said Russ. "Here come de judge."

All eyes locked on the door to the bar, for there stood the woman I had seen talking with the Mountie in the dining room after Ethan, Justin and Alex came over to join me for dessert.

She looked tough.

I like ballsy women.

"Hey, Detective," called the Learned Hand. "Would you resolve a bet for us?"

The cop came over.

"I'm busy, Josh." She eyed me. "Are you Jeff Kline?"

"The one and only," I said.

"Then it's your lucky day. Have I got a client for you."

I looked around.

"Where?"

"In the brig."

"We're in the Brig."

"The *real* brig. The ship's holding cell."

"Who?" I said.

"Come with me and you'll see."

I stood up and grabbed my twenty off the bar.

"You owe me a buck," I said to Josh. "First person in was a woman."

"In your dreams," he said.

"Welsher,' I replied.

Every ship has a brig of one sort or another. In the good old days of rum, sodomy and the lash, it was a rat-infested hole where prisoners languished until they were dragged out to be flogged, keel-hauled or hanged from the yardarm. On a ship as upscale as *The North Star,* the brig was a windowless cabin on the lowest deck, occasionally used to confine belligerent drunks or compulsive bottom-pinchers harassing women on the dance floor. What made it a brig was the bolt was on the *outside* of the door.

"Mind if I frisk you?" the detective asked.

"No," I said, holding out my arms.

Maddy ran her hands over and under my barrister's robes.

"My turn," I said as she finished patting me down.

"Touch me and I'll break your arm."

"I do believe you could."

"And would," she said, pulling back the bolt to unlock the door.

"Who's in there?"

"A surprise. Knock when you're through."

She opened the door, let me in, then shut the door behind me and engaged the bolt.

"Christ, am I glad to see you!"

Ethan made a wobbly attempt to stand, but his legs refused to support him.

"What have you done, Eth?" I said. "You look like a refugee from a slaughterhouse."

My office partner was covered with blood. Spatters dotted his face like terminal smallpox. His black robes were soaked with blood, as if he had been sleeping in a pool of gore. A bruise darkened his forehead around the temple, and his bleary eyes had the terrified look of a fox being hunted by hounds. Ethan sat slumped on one of the beds several feet from me, but the smell of alcohol off him reached the door. Light a match in here and the room might explode.

"I didn't kill her, Jeff."

"Kill who?" I asked.

"Alex Hunt."

"What!" I exclaimed.

"They think I'm the Hangman. She was *hanged,* Jeff. They found me passed out on the floor by her feet. Near a hangman game on the wall."

"Where?" I asked.

"In my cabin."

"In your *cabin?*"

Ethan nodded.

"Is this a joke? Are you putting me on?"

"Does it look like a fucking joke?" he exploded.

"Eth, you're drunk."

"I was drunk, Jeff. This nightmare is sobering me up fast."

"Why was Alex Hunt in your cabin?"

"I don't know. Wait... Yes, I do. We went out on deck for air. I felt better, but it was cold. She said we needed coats to walk the jogging track. We both had cabins on 'A' Deck, so we went down to bundle up. Alex helped me enter mine, then suddenly I felt the urge to puke."

I waited.

"Think, Eth."

"I'm trying, Jeff. It's a haze from all the booze I drank."

"You were in the john?"

"Puking up my guts."

"Where was Alex?"

"She was in the cabin."

"Waiting for you?"

"I suppose. Then... then... "

I waited.

"There was a knock on the door."

"Alex answered it?"

"I don't know, Jeff. She must have."

"Why?"

"Because she was on the floor."

"Dead?"

"Don't know."

"When was that?"

"When I came out from puking in the john."

"Then what?"

"That's all. I don't remember. Someone must have whacked me on the head."

"Your temple's bruised."

"My head feels scrambled. Any chance we could get a pot of coffee?"

"In a moment. First things first. Did you say anything to the cops?"

"I don't think so."

"That's a poor answer."

"I was drunk. I was stunned. I was scared, Jeff. I don't think I said anything."

"Eth, you're a lawyer. You know rule number one is never talk to the cops."

"Fuck me," he moaned. The seriousness of the situation was overwhelming his ragged emotions. "I didn't kill her."

"I don't care if you did. From here on, you leave everything to me."

He began to cry.

"Hear me, Eth?"

"Yes, Jeff."

"I do all the thinking. Trust me, buddy, and I'll save your life."

I let him cry himself out.

Then I knocked on the door.

The two of them were in the hall when I came out. The detective from Seattle and the Mountie from Vancouver. The Mountie locked eyes with me. We both knew the drill. Every murder trial is a game of chess, and this was the moment when both of us first engaged the player on the other side.

"Jeff Kline," Maddy said. "Zinc Chandler."

"Counsel," he acknowledged.

"Inspector," I replied.

I got his rank from the insignia on his red serge tunic. The Mountie, in his own way, looked as battered emotionally as Ethan did in his cell. The Horseman's heart was bleeding for Alex Hunt. We didn't shake hands. We were squaring off. Had we been wearing boxing gloves, we both might have banged them together before the first punch.

Sorry, Alex.

Mixed metaphors.

Chess game.

Boxing match.

Take your pick.

"I want to see the crime scene," I said, moving a pawn on the board, coming out of my corner.

"Why?" asked Maddy.

"Why not?" I said. "You don't have a monopoly on the evidence."

"And if we say no?"

"It will return to haunt you. I'll tell the jury at trial how you tried to scuttle my client's defense. We don't want another Haddon, do we?"

"No," said the detective. "I'll take you up."

"*I'll* take him up," the Mountie snapped at Maddy with an edge to his voice.

I glanced at her.

I glanced at him.

There was definite potential here.

Was that the sour smell of a turf war I whiffed?

To secure the crime scene on "A" Deck, the ship's elevators were out of use. We were forced to climb two flights of stairs, and on the way up I asked both cops if Ethan Shaw had said anything to them.

"Yes," said the detective.

"Yes," said the Mountie.

"What?" I asked.

"'Find Jeff Kline. I won't say a word until I talk to him.'"

Good, I thought.

A cordon of beefy cops blocked the entrance to "A" Deck from the stairwell. Sure enough, standing in front of a camcorder held by someone hired on the spot was a face I recognized from this morning. Ready to scoop the competition with another Hangman exclusive, the TV reporter Sue Frye was trying to wheedle her way through the door to the murder cabin.

A flash of a badge and we were in.

"Word travels fast," I said as the door swung shut behind us.

"Too fast," said Maddy.

"The ship has turned around. Where are we going?"

"Vancouver," said the Mountie.

"On whose orders?"

"Mine," he replied. "We're in Canadian waters."

"It should be Seattle," the Seattle cop commented dryly.

A turf war for sure, I thought with satisfaction. Divide and conquer.

The scene outside the door to the death cabin was like that in the center aisle of a church in which the wedding had been canceled at the altar by a reluctant bride or groom. Those milling around from "her" side were Washington State cops and techs summoned by the detective. Those milling around from "his" side were British Columbia counterparts gathered by the Mountie. Each side eyed the other suspiciously, as if only one-half had a right to be in the aisle.

"Stand at the door," the Mountie said, "and don't step in."

I got the distinct impression that neither cop trusted lawyers. One in front, one behind, they walked me along the passageway to the door and stood flanking me while I peered into the cabin. The tension coming off the Mountie was palpable. So strong was the feeling of hatred I sensed from him for whoever had killed his lover that I do believe he was capable of homicide himself. Blood will have blood, Gram used to say.

"Who found the body?" I asked.

"A crewman," replied the detective.

"Why'd he look into the cabin?"

"The door was propped open."

"Not closed? Not locked?"

"I said propped open."

"Where was my client?"

"There," said the Mountie. He pointed to the outline of a

human being in the flow of gore from beneath the hanging body toward the open door.

Except for two women examining the bloody remains, the cabin had yet to be invaded by both teams of forensic techs.

"Gill Macbeth I know. Who's the other doctor?"

"Ruth Lester," the detective said. "A pathologist from Seattle."

His and hers sawbones too, I thought. No doubt about it, the shit will hit the fan when the ship docks in Vancouver.

I indicated the knife in the blood on the floor.

"Has that been dusted for prints?"

"Not yet, Counsel. But rest assured we'll compare any with your client's," said the Mountie.

I glanced at the hangman game on the wall.

"The letter *I* has been added to what I saw on the news this morning."

"The killer can't spell," said Maddy.

"How so?" I asked.

"The *I* should be a *Y* if the word game is meant to spell Haddon's name. It's Bryce with a *Y*, not Brice with an *I*."

"Interesting," I said.

"You're sure?" asked the Mountie.

"I read the file enough times," replied the detective.

"I've seen enough," I said.

"Well?" asked the inspector.

"Well what?" I said.

"May we talk to your client?"

I shook my head. "Sorry," I said. "Anything he has to say will be said in court."

He shook his head. "Answer a question? How can you defend someone you know is guilty?"

"Ahhh," I said. "The perennial wonder."

"That's no answer."

"*That* is," I replied. I pointed to the name half-spelled in blood. "The writing is on the wall."

I was back in the brig, helping Ethan drink a pot of coffee.

"There's going to be a turf war fought over you," I said. "The Seattle police and the Mounties both want to charge you with Alex Hunt's murder. When we dock in Vancouver, they'll make their moves."

Ethan washed his weary face with one hand. "What a nightmare."

"It could be worse," I said. "Imagine yourself in the same fix without me as your lawyer."

He tried a smile, and failed miserably.

"The first battle we fight will be to keep you out of the States. What with the noose and the needle, they play hardball down there. Win that fight and we'll save your skin."

"What's the law, Jeff?"

Ethan was a civil lawyer. Extraditing someone from Canada to face execution in America wasn't his field of practice.

Nor was it mine.

Until now.

"Remember Charles Ng? Wanted by California back in the 1980s for at least a dozen sex-torture killings? Ng was arrested in Calgary, and fought extradition back to the States by claiming he was protected by the Canadian Charter of Rights. Since Canada no longer has the death penalty, he said it would be cruel and unusual punishment for a Canadian court to send him back to face the gas chamber in California."

"He lost, didn't he?"

"Sure," I replied. "What Ng had going against him was his citizenship. Lawyers for the States scared the Supreme Court of Canada with a floodgates argument. If Ng won, our country would become known as a safe haven for American killers on the run. Faced with having the dregs of the States as nose-thumbing tourists, the SCC ruled there was nothing wrong with shipping Yanks back to face their own legal system."

That didn't cheer him up.

HANGMAN

His coffee cup was shaking.

"It's one thing to send an American back to death in America, but it's a profoundly different matter to expose a Canadian to a penalty Canada has abolished. Under the Charter of Rights, we have the legal right to enter, remain in and leave our country. If extradited to face death, we would be denied the right to return home. Except in a box, and that doesn't count."

The cup was still shaking.

"Where does that leave me?"

"You told me this morning at the office that you were born in Seattle. In law, that makes you an American. The family was split, you said, when your parents divorced. Your brothers remained with your dad in Seattle, while your mom moved baby you to Vancouver so she could live with a Canadian she met at a Seattle convention. After he and your mom married, you got his last name through adoption. The question is, buddy, did you also get his citizenship?"

"No," said Ethan.

"How come?" I asked.

"Mom didn't know if the marriage would last. If it didn't, we'd go back to the States. She came north only because of Brad Shaw, so what he did was sponsor us for permanent residence. Me as an accompanying dependent of Mom. We were issued visas and were landed as permanent residents of Canada. There was no reason for me to become a Canadian citizen, so I kept my American citizenship."

"You fucked up, Eth. If only you had gone for *dual* citizenship, we could use your right to live in Canada as a Canadian to thwart America's right to execute you as an American."

He set down the coffee cup to keep from dropping it. Fear distorted his face.

"Don't worry," I added. "I'll figure something out."

"I didn't *do* it, Jeff."

"I know, Eth."

"It's a frame!" he said forcefully.

"By whom? Justin?"

He pinched the bridge of his nose as if in psychic pain. "He's my *brother*, Jeff."

"So?" I said. "Cain was Abel's brother too."

Ethan shook his head, trying to shake suspicion.

"I left him with you when Alex took me for a walk on deck."

"We spoke for a few minutes in the bar," I said. "Then Justin excused himself and left."

"Where'd he go?"

"I have no idea. What if he followed you and Alex down to your cabin, knocked on the door while you were throwing up in the can, knocked her out with a blow to the head, then waited in ambush for you to come out of the toilet compartment? He knocked you out, hanged her and left you to blame."

Ethan wasn't convinced.

He was in denial.

"Why kill Alex? That doesn't make sense. The Hangman hangs jurors, not crime writers, Jeff. I can see no reason for Justin to kill her."

"I can, Eth. He gave me one himself. When we were talking after you and Alex left, he told me she wanted to write a book about the Hangman jointly with him. He said she had phoned him from Vancouver early this week and suggested they meet tonight on this ship to consider a partnership."

"So?" Ethan said.

"Think it through. If Justin is the Hangman, as *you* suspect, what use to him would a writing partner be? He's obsessed, remember? The Haddon crusade is *his*. At best, he'd see Alex as competition. At worst, he'd see her as a threat."

"A threat to what?"

"His secret identity. Alex was sharp. We both saw that tonight. For all we know, Justin might have slipped up with her, and was fearful that clue might lead Alex to the skeleton in his closet."

"So he killed her?"

"Why not, Eth? What you have going for you, buddy, is *lack* of motive. Opportunity and means can be pinned on you, but without motive the cops will never be able to convict you. The Hangman hanged Alex out of fear she would unmask him. Since you had no reason to fear Alex would unmask you, the police have no reason to suspect you are the Hangman."

My law associate looked as if he was going to cry again.

"Jeff... "

"Uh-oh."

"I'm in *big* trouble."

"Are you holding back on me, Eth?"

"I have a skeleton, too."

"Motive?"

He dropped his eyes.

"How strong?" I asked.

"Strong enough to convict me. This morning, after I told you Justin was my brother, you asked why in all the time you've known me I never mentioned him. 'There's a reason,' I said, then we changed the subject."

"What reason, Eth?"

"I had *two* older brothers."

"Had?"

"Yes. One twin died."

"Died how?"

"Guess."

"Jesus, he was *hanged.*"

It shocked me that I knew so little about Ethan's background. We first met at school in the East End, and since our home situations were alike, I assumed he was an only Canadian child like me, also being raised by a single mom. His stepfather, Brad Shaw, was out of the picture by then.

"Spill your guts," I said.

It came out like a confession.

"I was born Ethan Quinn Haddon. That name changed to Ethan Shaw when my mom remarried. I was just a baby when we left Seattle. My dad thought I was fathered by another man, so I never met him before he died. My mom loathed my dad and didn't want me near him, so she saw the twins without me. The twins were raised in Seattle by my dad. One was named Peter Bryce Haddon. The other was Steven Mark Haddon. When Peter was found guilty of murder in 1984, Mark was a journalism student. He took a pen name and later made it legal. Steven Mark Haddon became—"

"Justin Whitfield," I said.

Hired Gun

"How can you defend someone you know is guilty?"

That's the question the Mountie asked of me, and that's the question every layman asks or wants to ask if he corners a criminal lawyer.

What's the answer?

Well, I'll tell you.

The *practical* answer is Peter Haddon. That's what I meant by saying, "The writing is on the wall." Enough people *knew* he was guilty to loop a noose around his neck and drop him through the gallows floor for a crime he didn't commit.

You think he's the exception?

Think again.

From 1900 to the present day, American jails have either executed or released from death row more than a hundred convicts who were found to be innocent. Canada bears the guilt of what it did to the three Ms: Morin, Milgaard and Marshall. Britain hanged Evans on the word of Christie, and might have done the same in more recent years to framed Irishmen if it still had the noose.

Courts, not lawyers, determine guilt. A lawyer has no right to prejudge a client. The *last* thing a client needs by way of defense is a lawyer doing a half-assed job because he thinks him guilty. If lawyers turn away clients they prejudge, many an innocent accused may be denied counsel. If the day arrives when that accused is you, should you not have the right to demand of your lawyer, "I hired you for your skill as an advocate in court, not to suffer the prejudice of your personal beliefs?"

If you seek medical help for cancer, you don't expect a doctor to turn you away because he thinks your death should help rectify the population imbalance between men and women. Nor do you expect him to refuse you treatment because your conservative politics are adding to the misery of the homeless on the streets. Instead, you expect him to be *professional,* and to put aside his personal beliefs while he does the goddamn job you want him to do.

So why not lawyers?

That, however, is only the practical answer to the Mountie's question. As I was standing in the doorway to Ethan's cabin, with the corpse of Chandler's lover hanging from the rod, I could—if I hadn't feared he'd haul off and slug me—also have given the inspector the *theoretical* answer.

When I became a lawyer, I took an oath. That oath imposed a duty on me to "uphold the rule of law." The rule of law is the reason we live in a free and democratic society. Without the rule of law, chaos and anarchy are the norm: you take what you want, you rape who you want, you kill who you want in that Darwinian jungle.

The rule of law means *everyone* has the right to a fair trial. A fair trial is one in which the prosecutor presents the case against, the defense lawyer vigorously tries to tear it apart and the judge and jury decide what's true from what they witness in court. A lawyer cannot lack the courage to honor his oath. The moment lawyers start refusing to take cases because of conscience, the rule of law begins to fall apart. To quote an American journalist, Edwin Yoder, Jr.:

The law will protect the good man and the righteous cause only if it also extends an even hand to the evil and iniquitous as well. That lesson, hard to grasp and still harder to embrace, is the heart of the rule of law.

A lawyer is duty bound not to "throw" a case. The apotheosis of advocacy is boldly to defend the case of the most unpopular or repugnant client. In such cases, the lawyer represents a principle and an ideal: the notion that the worst client in the worst case is entitled to be defended by all honorable means.

Can it be put better than Sir Thomas More's words in *A Man for All Seasons?* In the 1500s, More lost his head to King Henry VIII because the lawyer refused to forsake the rule of law so the king could marry yet another wife.

"How can you defend someone you know is guilty?"

I do it, says the lawyer, to protect us all:

> ROPER: So now you'd give the Devil benefit of law!
>
> MORE: Yes. What would you do? Cut a great road through the law to get after the Devil?
>
> ROPER: I'd cut down every law in England to do that!
>
> MORE: Oh? And when the last law was down, and the Devil turned round on you—where would you hide, Roper, the laws all being flat? This country's planted thick with laws from coast to coast— Man's laws, not God's—and if you cut them down—and you're just the man to do it—d'you really think you could stand upright in the winds that would blow then? Yes, I'd give the Devil benefit of law, for my own safety's sake.

Of course, I don't know a single lawyer who thinks like that, so that's why I didn't give the Mountie both barrels of bullshit. The player on the other side knew the legal game, so he knew why we lawyers *really* defend clients we know are guilty.

Lawyers are gamblers.

Courts are gambling casinos.

Clients are betting chips.

And the goal of the game is to *win!*

The harder the case, the bigger the *win!*

The bigger the *win*, the greater your reputation.

The greater your reputation, the more money you make.

The more money you make, the more inflated your ego.

The more inflated your ego, the higher you rise to the top.

And when you get to the top, you're the king of the world.

So was Ethan guilty?

Who gave a fuck.

I had a notorious case to *win!*

That's why, last Tuesday morning, November 14, four days after Alex Hunt was hanged on *The North Star,* and two days before the peril I'm in now, I strapped on the six guns and went to court.

Spread the word.

There's a new gun in town.

Turf War

"Something's up," said Nellie.

"What?" asked Zinc.

"I don't know. The Feds are acting cagey. It must be the consent."

The *Criminal Code of Canada* lay open on her desk, beside a file labeled with Ethan Shaw's name. Nellie turned the book around so Zinc and Chief Superintendent DeClercq could read:

> 477.2 (1) No proceedings in respect of an offense committed in or on the territorial sea of Canada shall be continued unless the consent of the Attorney General of Canada is obtained not later than eight days after the proceedings are commenced, if the accused is not a Canadian citizen and the offense is alleged to have been committed onboard any ship registered outside Canada.

Nervous Nellie was as fidgety as the Mounties had ever seen her. Nellie Barker was the deputy regional Crown counsel in charge of the provincial prosecutors at 222 Main. Her office was on the second floor of the Vancouver provincial courthouse in the heart of skid row, kitty-corner to the piss-stained door of Kline & Shaw. The fact that the Shaw of that struggling firm was in the cells downstairs charged with first-degree murder, and that the Kline of that street-legal storefront was sitting in Courtroom 102 waiting to defend him, did little to calm her nerves. Not when the case was shot through with this many holes, most of which were big enough to make Nellie bite her nails.

"Where exactly did this murder occur?"

"We don't know," Zinc said. "We're still investigating."

"Is there a problem?"

"A turf war, Nellie. The ship sailed from Seattle up Puget Sound, then out through the Strait of Juan de Fuca to the open sea. That means *The North Star* passed through American waters, then Canadian internal waters when it was in the strait, and finally Canada's territorial sea as it sailed up the west coast of Vancouver Island."

The jumpy prosecutor was bouncing around in her chair, burning off more calories than meals could replace. Barker, a bag of bones in her baggy blue suit, was so gaunt she looked anorexic. What made her a sharp prosecutor was her trepidation. Nervous Nellie could see trouble coming a mile away.

"Where *might* this murder have occurred? South of the border in the States?"

"Unlikely," Zinc said.

"But possibly?"

"At the moment. Until we have a witness."

"Inspector, I beg you, be more specific. Yesterday was the Monday holiday after Remembrance Day, so I took the long weekend off to be with my dad. He was at D-Day. It's a rough time for him. So I wasn't around when this case came in, and now I find myself caught in a Rubik's Cube. To make it easy for me, spell it out."

"It's a turf war, Nellie, over who gets to try the Hangman. The

Americans want Ethan Shaw for two hangings in Seattle. We want him for one in North Vancouver. The death on the ship is the only crime for which there is a suspect and evidence, so both jurisdictions are after this accused."

"Where was the victim last seen alive?"

"I don't know."

"Why?"

"Because it's a turf war. The body was found when the ship was on Canada's territorial sea. The American cops asked the captain to sail back to Seattle. Because we were then in Canadian waters, I countermanded their request and ordered the captain to sail *The North Star* to Vancouver."

"How'd the Americans react to that?"

"We reached a compromise."

"I'm listening."

"A joint Hangman investigation was already underway. We agreed to investigate the crime scene together, and to divide up the interviews of those aboard. There were a lot of people on the ship. Even now, days later, some statements have yet to be taken."

"What happened when you docked?"

"I arrested Ethan Shaw for first-degree murder on Canada's territorial sea. I drove him to the jail next door and booked him in. He was seen by a justice of the peace. Since Monday was a statutory holiday, the JP remanded him to appear in court this morning."

"And the Americans?"

"They left in a huff."

"With *their* witness statements?"

"Yes," said Zinc. "They were south of the border before we knew they were gone."

"So we have half the evidence and they have the other half?"

"For the moment."

"What does that mean?"

"We're meeting this afternoon to discuss exchanging witness statements."

"You haven't seen theirs?"

"And they haven't seen ours."

"This isn't a poker game."

"They're Americans, Nellie. Americans are used to getting their own way. The Hangman killed two people in the States and two in Canada. He was caught here, so we try him first. Holding back the statements is a strong-arm tactic. I'll be damned if I'll give them the Hangman on a silver platter."

"The last victim was your lover?"

"Yes," said Zinc.

"You're too close to the case."

"That's why I'm here," said DeClercq. "The reason the inspector is still involved is that no one knows better than him what happened on the ship."

"Where was the boat when you last saw Alexis Hunt alive?"

"In American waters," said Zinc.

"Have you any reason to believe she was killed in the States?"

"No," he replied.

"Do we have a statement from anyone who saw Alexis alive in Canadian waters?"

"No," he said.

"Do the Americans?"

"I don't know."

Nellie had nibbled a finger down to the quick. One day, she would come unstrung from stress.

"A court is waiting downstairs for us to appear. I sense trouble," said the prosecutor.

"Why?" asked Zinc.

"The caginess of the Feds. If this crime did occur in Canada, it might have taken place on the Canadian side of the border that runs along the middle of the Strait of Juan de Fuca. The Supreme Court of Canada has ruled those are *internal* waters, so"—she tapped the consent section of the *Criminal Code*—"no federal okay is required to prosecute a foreign citizen on a foreign ship."

"I know," said Zinc. "But I don't trust lawyers."

"How wise of you," Nellie said.

"Unlike you, I *do* think this is a poker game, and I think the smartest player usually wins. If it does turn out that Alex was hanged on our territorial sea, I want to make damn sure the necessary federal consent is in place. That's why the charge alleges the crime occurred there and not on internal waters."

"The *Criminal Code* says the consent of the attorney general must be filed within eight days."

"We have lots of time."

"That's what worries me."

"I don't follow, Nellie."

"Did you take it upon yourself to ask the Feds for consent?"

"No," said Zinc.

"Nor have we. So why did counsel for the attorney general of Canada phone this morning to ask us not to call the Shaw case until he arrived?"

"I have no idea."

"Something's up," said Nellie.

To understand what was up, you have to understand this: Canada, like America, has a federal system. That means power is divided between the federal government—known as the Feds—and the provinces or states. Canada has the benefit of being the younger brother (or sister, if you prefer) of America, so Canada gets to correct what it rightly or wrongly perceives as mistakes south of the border.

Mistakes like jurisdiction over criminal law.

If law and order is the goal of criminal statutes, you want your citizens to *know* what the law is. That means you want the law to be consistent from coast to coast. To that end, America made a mistake in giving power to enact crime statutes to the individual states, instead of to the Feds in Washington. Nowhere is the result more evident today than in capital punishment, where, depending upon the state beneath your feet when you commit murder, they hang you, gas you, shock you, shoot you or stick you with a needle.

Or if you're lucky, the state spares life.

When Canada came together in 1867, the fathers of Confederation "corrected that mistake" by giving the power to enact criminal law and procedure to the Feds in Ottawa, and the power to administer justice in accordance with that law to the provinces. Go anywhere in Canada and the criminal law is the same, which may explain why Canadians, at three o'clock in the morning, stand on deserted street corners and wait for the Do Not Walk sign to change.

At least that's the theory.

The Feds being Feds, however, they kept certain administrative powers from the provinces. If provincial prosecutors wish to try a foreign citizen for a crime committed on a foreign-registered ship in Canada's coastal waters—the territorial sea—they must seek the blessing of Ottawa. No federal consent, for whatever reason, and there can be no trial.

An even bigger power grab was extradition. Ottawa kept that power entirely for itself. Commit a murder in the States and it will be the Feds who decide whether or not to send you south to stand trial.

This the Americans knew.

The *rules* of the game.

And who plays poker better than Americans?

No sooner had *The North Star* docked in Vancouver than Zinc arrested Ethan Shaw for Alex's murder, effectively snatching him from the long arm of American law. That arm, however, was longer than the inspector suspected, for when the Seattle cops were back on their own turf, Ethan was charged with aggravated first-degree murder in Washington State and a warrant was issued for his arrest. Under state law, no decision had to be made on whether to seek the death penalty until thirty days after arraignment, but this was the Hangman they were going after, and it was an election year, so the hope of the state attorney was that a rope would please the people. That's why he opted immediately for death instead of life without parole.

Upping the ante.

Fed to Fed, the state's request to extradite Ethan was made to Ottawa by Washington, D.C. A little federal wheeling and dealing went on, most of it centered on a cop killer Canada wished extradited from North Dakota, and this culminated in a meeting of under-the-table minds. A copy of the arrest warrant from Washington State and a request by America under the Extradition Act for a provisional arrest warrant in Canada were faxed to the federal Department of Justice in Vancouver, where they were passed to Lyndon Wilde, QC, for action.

Because Monday was a holiday in both countries, for Remembrance Day in Canada and Veterans' Day in the States, today was the first opportunity for the Feds to go to court. Bright and early this morning, Wilde had placed a call to the office of Nervous Nellie Barker down in skid row, but the overstressed and underpaid provincial prosecutor had yet to come in to work. Having left a message for her to stand down the Shaw case until he arrived, Wilde walked to the law courts in the better part of town, and there he asked for an *ex parte* hearing before a Supreme Court judge.

A *secret* hearing in chambers.

A card up his sleeve.

A cab was waiting at the curb when Wilde came out. He didn't like parking his Saab in the grungy environs of provincial court, so he rode the hack east to skid row, climbing out in front of the squat concrete building at 222 Main, where he passed through security and took the stairs up one floor.

All eyes turned toward the federal prosecutor as Wilde knocked once and opened the door to Nellie's cluttered corner office.

"Am I barging in?"

"Of course not, Lyndon."

Nellie was as tense as a stretched elastic band.

"Officers," said the Fed, throwing a visual dagger at DeClercq.

"What brings *you* here?" asked the chief superintendent.

They had a history, the lawyer and the Mountie. It was a toss-up as to who loathed whom the most.

The roly-poly Fed approached Nellie's desk to lord his bulk over the provincial Crown. With a bow, he tipped an imaginary hat on his head.

"In my capacity as counsel for the attorney general of Canada, and acting on behalf of the United States of America, I have a provisional warrant for the arrest of Ethan Shaw, at the request of the state of Washington. That state wants him extradited to stand trial on a charge of aggravated first-degree murder, punishable by death, for hanging Alexis Hunt."

"What?" snapped Zinc.

"Are you deaf, Inspector?"

"I don't believe what I'm hearing."

"Shall I repeat it?"

"What about the murder charge I laid *here?*"

Wilde tossed his imaginary hat across the office, then replaced it with another one.

"In my capacity as counsel for the attorney general of Canada, and acting under Section 477.2 of the *Criminal Code*, I regret to inform you that the AG will *not* grant the consent necessary to try Shaw for murder on our territorial sea."

Zinc balled his hands into fists as he rose from his chair.

"Traitor!" he said.

It came out as a snarl.

Wilde spoke to him, but he locked eyes with DeClercq. "Do your duty, Inspector. Execute the warrant. I want Ethan Shaw in Supreme Court chambers at two this afternoon."

HANGMAN

Those who have followed the heartbreaking careers of both Mounties will know without being told why the chief superintendent was there. The commanding officer of Special X had himself lost loved ones to this cruel job, so he knew only too well the emotional maelstrom that had sucked Zinc in. Even more concerning, Alexis Hunt wasn't the first lover Zinc had sacrificed to his hunt for a psycho, and the last time—chasing Cutthroat in Hong Kong—had cost him a bullet to the brain. It had been doubtful whether Zinc would ever get through that grinder, and now the angry inspector was going through it again.

For the past week, DeClercq had been flat on his back with flu. A wiry man, tall, lean and somewhere in his fifties, with wavy hair, alert eyes and an aquiline nose, DeClercq had watched the bug turn him into a ghost of himself. This, however, was too volatile a situation not to keep in control, so, flu or not, DeClercq was here.

He gripped the inspector's arm. "Let the courts handle it, Zinc."

Zinc pulled away. "That's what I'm afraid of, Chief."

The Best Defense

Courtroom 102 was the usual zoo. Be it murder or stealing candy from a baby, every criminal case in Vancouver begins either there or next door in 101. Since 102 gets last names from *I* to *Z*, Ethan Shaw—two days ago—was to make his debut in that prisoner's dock.

The zookeeper that morning was a judge we called the Quip. The Quip thought he was funny. The Quip was in his element. The flotsam and jetsam of Vancouver came into his court like a tide, providing the Quip with fodder for his razor-sharp wit. At that moment, he was dealing with the black hooker who had propositioned me several days ago in front of the strip joint across the street from the courts. She wriggled provocatively in a chair facing the bench, as if trying to line the Quip up for a quickie over lunch.

"Madam," said the judge, "I know you're not used to hearing this from the men of your acquaintance, but would you please *stand up* for me."

The packed gallery groaned.

I groaned silently.

The Quip made the face of a stand-up comedian facing a rough crowd.

HANGMAN

The watchers who police the courts for anything they perceive as politically incorrect scribbled sour notes.

The crowd in the gallery was rough indeed. Junkies by the dozen, as you'd expect to find in *the* major gateway for Asian heroin, as well as Native court workers propping up mumbling drunks and street loonies with MPAs (mental patient advocates) trying to keep them from decomposing into nuts. Buzzing in and out of court like flies on shit were harried runners bringing files and taking files away, and lawyers for the Crown and for the defense, and duty counsel representing the lawyerless ones. A woman in the gallery clutched a pair of infants crying for feeding, while she cried for her husband locked in the cells.

The doors guarding the dock from the cells were run by two sheriffs; they were known affectionately as Laurel and Hardy. Laurel was the skinny one who manned a built-in desk, and Hardy was the fat one hunkered in a chair on wheels. The dock, a half-and-half cage of Plexiglas and wood, was on the left side of the court if you faced the bench. Feeding the dock with riffraff were two steel doors, one for males and the other for females and PCs.

To call an in-custody case, the procedure was this. A lawyer wrote the name of his client on the sheriffs' calling board. Laurel would phone the jail to have the prisoner sent to the dock. Hardy would get off his fat ass and enter the pen through a swing gate with the latch on the outside. Then he would unlock one of the steel doors, releasing the client from either the male cells or the cells for women and those in protective custody. The sheriff would stand with the prisoner while the case was heard, then send him or her back to jail. A square in one corner of the calling board advised the court how many jailed were still unprocessed. Comedians that they were, Laurel and Hardy had written, over the number in the square, "Now serving... "

An hour had passed since I put Ethan's name up on the board. He still had not been called.

Why? I wondered.

"Vertical prosecution" was the answer I was given by the black team. The provincial Crown counsel office, run by Nellie Barker, was forever trying to impose order on the chaotic zoo, and the latest attempt, also doomed to failure, was the team system. The black team was the bail team in remand court. Anyone arrested made a first appearance here to resolve the issue of release or detention, then the case was sent, according to the first letter of the accused's last name, to a court staffed by one of four prosecution teams. The white team took A to E, the green team F to L, the red team M to R, the blue team S to Z.

> If you think that sounds like high school, so do I.
> Boom-a-licka, boom-a-licka, bow-wow-wow,
> Chick-a-licka, chick-a-licka, chow-chow-chow,
> Boom-a-licka, chick-a-licka, who are we?
> The team that wants your ass in custody.
> YEEAAY TEEAAM!

It could be worse.

At first, they were "pods."

Pods made the prosecutors a laughing-stock in the courts. The members of a team were the "peas" in the pod. A prosecutor who switched pods was a "pod-hopper." There was a horror movie from 1956 called *The Invasion of the Body Snatchers*, and what snatched your body was a pod. The term "pod" was scrapped in favor of "team," but it was fondly remembered by the Quip.

The Quip was dealing with yet another theft charge against the Time Traveler, a skid-row drunk reeking of rubbing alcohol who, for some reason known only to him, had stolen his sixty-third wall clock. So jelly-legged was the TT with the DTs that Sheriff Hardy had to hold him up in the dock.

To everyone's surprise, the Quip was off the bench and down to the dock in a flash.

"Didn't I tell you to cut this crap?" he yelled at the drunk.

Through crusty, red-rimmed eyelids, the TT blinked at him.

"Ish 'at you, Larry?"

"You were a bum when you were my client, Moe, and you're a bum now. I ought to lock you up and throw away the key. Instead, I'm going to lock you up and dry you out. What have you got to say?"

"Thanksh, Larry."

"You're welcome, Moe."

The Quip turned to Hardy. "Take him away," he said.

Win one for the Quipper, I thought.

With puns like that, I definitely had the makings of a judge.

Like I said, a zoo.

The Quip was returning to the bench when he spied Nellie Barker coming into court through the barrister's door.

"The pod god arrives," he said.

Nellie walked to the black team's podium, near the door, and usurped the position of the remand-court team head.

"Calling the case of Ethan Shaw," she said.

You could feel a shudder of anticipation grip the gallery. Everyone knew the Hangman was about to appear in court. The reporters, including Justin Whitfield up from Seattle, poised their pens and pads. Sheriff Hardy fetched Ethan from the male cells while I rose from my seat and approached the bench.

"Jeffrey Kline for Ethan Shaw," I announced. "The spelling, Madam Recorder, is K-L-I-N-E."

That, of course, was for the media.

The Quip was about to say something off the cuff, but he must have decided to be judicious for once in his career.

Now Ethan was in the dock.

A hush came over the court.

My law associate looked like forty miles of bad road.

"Yes, Ms. Barker?" said the judge.

I thought Nellie was going to tell the court that Ethan's case was a "special assignment." That meant it would be a vertical prosecution up through the courts, with the same Crown counsel at both the preliminary hearing and the Supreme Court trial. What usually happened was that one of the color teams did the prelim, and if the case met the standard for committal (is there a substantial likelihood of conviction and is the prosecution in the public interest), it was sent to senior counsel uptown to try.

Instead, Nellie stunned me with...

"The Crown withdraws the charge of murder against Ethan Shaw."

Someone in the gallery gasped.

Ethan exhaled a sigh.

"You're quite the advocate, Mr. Kline," responded the Quip. "Without a single word, it seems you got your client off."

"May he step out of the dock?"

"Sheriff," said the judge.

Laurel undid the latch on the outside of the gate to the counsel area, then Ethan stepped out to join me in front of the bench. As we moved toward the barrister's door, a rush of reporters scrambled for the gallery exit to intercept us outside. No photos can be taken inside the building, so milling beyond the doors to the street were camera crews and anchors by the dozen.

"Smile," I cautioned Ethan. "We're on uncandid camera."

Andy Warhol got it wrong. It isn't fifteen minutes of fame, it's fifteen *seconds*. No sooner were we out on the street and in the public eye than I caught sight of the player on the other side. Parting the sea of camera crews like Moses did the Red Sea in the Bible, Zinc Chandler closed on us with his badge in hand and said, to send poor Ethan back to infamy, "Ethan Shaw, I have a warrant for your arrest. The state of Washington seeks to extradite you on a charge of aggravated first-degree murder. Come with me."

Another rubby had marked his territory at the door to Kline & Shaw. This time, I didn't stop to mop it up. Win Ethan's case, I thought, and I will never clean up piss again. No one pisses on the door of a law firm in fancy digs uptown.

Word spreads fast in the legal profession. If you chase ambulances, you listen for sirens. The phone had been ringing nonstop since Ethan's arrest on the extradition warrant that morning. Silver spoons in the fat-cat firms towering over the law courts kept calling to offer their uptown services to my client. A few were subtle, but most weren't. One spoon had the balls to warn me that I was skating on thin ice and might be reported to the Law Society for a conflict of interest by acting on behalf of my law partner. I told him we were associates, not law partners, and if I did decide to farm out Ethan's case, he would be the *last* shyster I would call.

Have Gun, Will Travel was the game Seattle attorneys played. Several, including my good buddies the Learned Hand and the Rustler, offered to be the American half of my "defense team." They said they'd come up to help block the extradition request, and if we lost that battle, I was to let them defend the trial of the decade in the States. I told them Canadian lawyers don't need a "defense team." We're trained to win murder cases by ourselves.

Leeches, I thought.

At half past one, I left Suzy to defend the fort and, stepping over the puddle of piss outside, turned toward the harbor at the foot of Main to walk the same route to the law courts I had the other day. The black hooker was back on the stroll at the corner of Powell, trying to earn money to hire a lawyer to defend her on the charge I had seen her face in remand court a few hours earlier. On one breast of her scoop-necked blouse she wore a red poppy.

"A day late," I said.

"Soldier, it's never too late to hide in my warm trenches."

"Later," I lied.

"I be here," she cooed.

Strolling up Granville, I passed the Birks clock. As lovers have done for the past century, an embracing couple rendezvoused on the corner for a late lunch and come what may. I wondered if the Mountie and Alex Hunt had met here too?

As always, I paused for a moment at the Rattenbury courthouse to gaze up at the stone lions and soaring pillars. I recalled the last day of the Hanging Judge, and how, as I was thrown out of Kinky's court, I swore to myself I'd return one day to argue a headline murder case.

Well, that day had come.

But gone was the tradition.

When the law was centered here, practicing was fun. The assize court was a masterpiece of past British rule, a cavern of ornately carved hardwood complemented with brass fittings and rich red drapes. The accused in the dock and the jurors in the jury box were guarded by Stetsoned Mounties in full red serge. Once the jurors had been sequestered to consider their verdict, counsel would join the judge in chambers for a drink or two, at which time the trial would be rehashed witness by witness to laugh at the funny moments, determine the turning points or place a friendly wager on the result.

The lawyers would then retire to the Crown counsel cubbyhole, which was squirreled away in the attic over the pillars supporting the roof. While the jury pondered, the court jesters partied, and if the Scotch ran out before there was a verdict, the cops were asked to make a booze run. Shortly after, they would show up with a brown evidence bag.

The night I remember most clearly from my days as a court watcher was the one when a troubled jury posed a question to the judge at midnight. The young defense lawyer was so full of Scotch that he had to be dragged into court with both arms around two seasoned prosecutors who could hold their booze. They propped him up at the counsel table as best they could and waited to see if the cranky judge would end his budding legal career for being drunk on the job.

In came the jury as the lawyer teetered from side to side. Then in came the judge, who was known as the Bounder for his habit of bounding up onto the bench. He caught his toe on the top step and sprawled across his chair, which rolled on casters to the jury side of the bench. There, he lay across its arms like Superman in flight, grinning at the jurors as he slurred: "Laddies an shenlemen of the shury. Ishh there a pro'lem? Ishh it becau ya think the shun of a bitshhh nex ta ya doeshn't have a brain in hishh head? Shorry, laddies, *her* head tooooo."

Whereupon he shwung his arm in a wide shweep that encompassed the twelve shtunned faces.

"Tha bashtard won' look like ashh mush of an ash-hole in the morning, sho I'm gonna ashk the shhhheriff to put ya up fer the night."

Whereupon he fell on the floor, shtruggled to his unshteady feet and shtaggered off the dais back to the bottle in chambers, unable to perform that feat as sober as the proverbial judge.

No sooner had the Bounder stumbled from court than the Crown attorney closest to the sloshed young lawyer leaned across and laughed. "Come tomorrow morning, you won't be the only one praying for an acquittal to keep this record out of the court of appeal."

That's what it was like in the free-wheeling days before the West Side silver spoons built their new law courts two blocks down the street. For some reason the main door is situated in the corner farthest away from the center of town, so it's rarely used—except for media shoots. This being my big case, I walked the extra block to make my grand entrance and played the earnest defense counsel rushing to meet the enemy for a mass of camera lenses.

"No comment... "

"No comment... "

"No comment... "

Wait and see, people.

What greeted me inside the automatic sliding doors were

thirty-five courtrooms on five tiers stacked up the right angle of a glass wedge. Coldly antiseptic was the overall feel, despite the greenery spilling from each level like the Hanging Gardens of Babylon. The tomb reflected the minds of those who built it, so sucked dry of humor and drama was this lifeless waste. By the time I scaled the zigzagged stairs to Courtroom 53, I was as bored as an East End kid could be.

Time to light the hair of a judge on fire.

Fun and games.

Like it used to be.

The courtroom gallery was packed as I made my way through the gate to the counsel area. Hardwood, brass and velvet had given majesty to courtrooms in Kinky's day, but the silver spoons had tastefully done this one up in concrete and felt. The court watchers in this bland shell were more upscale than those mobbed into remand court this morning, for that was the East End and this was the West Side. A chance to see the Hangman was not to be missed.

Short, stout, flush-faced and mustachioed, Lyndon Wilde, QC, reminded me of the trademark CEO on a Monopoly game. Definitely a West Side silver spoon. Because this hearing was in open-court chambers, it wasn't necessary for lawyers to robe. Wilde, however, had robed anyway, and he stood there at center stage in his striped gray pants, bulging black vest and starched white shirt with upside down V tabs. To please the gallery, he fiddled with a pocket watch on a gold chain.

"Lyndon," I said.

He ignored me.

I doubt the old fart knew who I was.

"Jeff Kline," I said.

I held out my hand.

I'm sure he shook it only to look civilized to the crowd.

His palm was dry.

He was confident.

My arrival had interrupted a quiet argument. Wilde was flanked by Chandler and DeClercq. There was no love lost between the prosecutor and the Mounties, for I had heard the story of Wilde's fall from grace when he lost big time to the chief superintendent in a cause célèbre trial alleging Corp. Nick Craven had killed his own mother. The result was that the province quit sending Wilde cases, so that's why he now worked for the Feds. Trying to thwart Chandler in his attempt to try Ethan for Hunt's hanging was like throwing gas on embers.

"*Why* won't the AG give us consent?"

Chandler had to stoop to stare Wilde in the face.

"Not here. Not now." Lyndon glanced at me.

"It's okay," I said. "Fight it out. Looks like the cops are on *my* side."

Out came the watch.

"Time for court," said Wilde.

And right on cue, in came the judge. The Mounties were forced to retreat from "the pit" as the associate chief justice climbed to the bench. Again it struck me how dull the law courts were. There would be no Scotch shared with counsel in this judge's chambers, for back when the silver spoons moved to this prissy palace, the law lords upstairs gave them a ruling to help maintain decorum. Henceforth, to make us teetotalers one and all in chambers, everything that went on behind closed doors had to be *recorded*.

Imagine that.

What party-poopers.

"The United States of America versus Ethan Shaw," announced the clerk.

"Mr. Wilde?"

"May it please your lordship. Ethan Shaw has been arrested under the provisional extradition warrant you issued this morning."

Quick Draw nodded. "Bring him in."

Associate Chief Justice Lance McGraw—Quick Draw

McGraw to the bar, on account of his tendency to make hasty decisions—was a horse-faced man with a lantern jaw and large teeth befitting his cartoon namesake. He watched the sheriff unlock the door to the holding cells below to usher Ethan into court and across to the prisoner's dock. Back in Kinky's and the Bounder's day, the prisoner sat in a raised, carved hardwood box, guarded by a Horseman in regal red, but the dock today had shrunk to a small plastic one, and the sheriff on guard wore boring brown.

Could the silver spoons do any more to foster contempt of court?

They sure earned mine.

"The clerk will unseal the sealed file," said the judge.

Showtime, folks.

I walked to the dock.

The best defense is a good offense, they say in America, and since I was at war with America, I took their sage advice.

"Jeffrey Kline appearing for Ethan Shaw, my lord. I wish to put on record at this first appearance that my client has been—and is being—framed. Ethan Shaw is the brother of Peter Bryce Haddon, a man wrongfully *lynched* for murder by the state of Washington in 1993. Now the state seeks to compound that crime by attempting to *lynch* my client."

Stirring in the gallery.

American reporters?

"A serial killer known as the Hangman is loose in the Pacific Northwest. His motive for hanging his victims, all but one of them jurors, is thought to be to avenge Haddon's hanging. To that end, the killer plays a word game with police, the answer to which spells out Peter Bryce Haddon's name.

"Bryce—as legally registered—is spelled B-R-Y-C-E.

"The warrant before this court involves a hanging that occurred on a ship cruising from Seattle to Vancouver by way of the Strait of Juan de Fuca and our territorial sea off the coast of Vancouver Island. The crime was committed somewhere along that route. The body was discovered in my client's cabin when the ship was unarguably sailing in Canadian waters."

Wilde was making notes.

No doubt he thought me a young fool for revealing my poker hand.

"I ask your lordship to note that "the body was found by a crewman when he spied it hanging inside through an *open* door. That means anyone onboard could be the killer. The open door gave everyone opportunity.

"My client was found unconscious on the floor, in blood pooling from slashes on the body. Nearby was the knife that caused those wounds, and I've been told the hanging rope was cut from a life preserver line out on deck. The open cabin door and the fact that no fingerprints were recovered from the knife means everyone aboard the ship also had means.

"That, my lord, leaves motive."

Among the press reporters jotting notes, I caught sight of Justin Whitfield.

Good, I thought as I withdrew from the breast pocket of my cheap business suit the newspaper piece he wrote on Haddon's hanging.

"Drawn in blood on the wall beside my unconscious client was the Hangman's word game with a letter added. An *I* was in the center of the middle word, so if Peter Bryce Haddon is the answer to the game, that means the killer spells Bryce B-R-*I*-C-E. The same way the name is spelled in this article"—I waved the clipping in the air—"by that reporter"—I pointed at Whitfield.

"—printed in the *Seattle Star* the day after Haddon hanged."

Hey, what can I say?

I've seen "Perry Mason" reruns on TV.

"Motive, My Lord? There is no motive here. If Ethan Shaw is the Hangman, out to draw attention to the wrongful hanging of his brother, why would he hang a victim in his own cabin on the ship, pointing the finger of suspicion at himself even if he hadn't been found unconscious in a pool of the victim's blood, then fill in the hangman game to make his motive perfectly clear *by misspelling the name of his own brother!*

"How does that make sense?"

The judge scratched his head.

Quick Draw was intrigued.

"Let me see that clipping, Mr. Kline."

I gave it to the court clerk, who passed it on up to the judge. Sitting smugly silent in his seat, Wilde gave me what he thought was enough rope to hang myself. Only a fool telegraphs his strategy to the prosecution before he calls his defense at trial. Time stood still while the judge read:

"I'M INNOCENT!"—CONVICT'S LAST WORDS

HADDON HANGS

Justin Whitfield
Seattle Star

Walla Walla—He stood before us on the gallows of the state penitentiary, a moment before the hangman cinched the noose around his neck and dropped him to his death, to protest his innocence one more time.

"My last words are—"

His voice broke.

"That I am innocent, innocent, innocent. Be under no illusion. This is injustice. I owe society nothing. I am—"

He choked the words.

"An innocent man. Something wrong is taking place here tonight."

Then it was over. Peter Brice Haddon was dead...

HANGMAN

"Mr. Whitfield?"

Among the reporters, Justin rose to his feet.

"Yes, your honor?"

"Why is Bryce misspelled?"

"I phoned the story in from the state prison. The person who took it down misspelled the name throughout the piece. The typos came to my attention after it was published."

"You may be seated."

Justin sat down.

"Yes, Mr. Kline?"

"Ethan Shaw was drunk, my lord. Too drunk to have perpetrated this crime. There is a bruise on his forehead"—I pointed to my client—"which doesn't match any blunt object found in the cabin, including the footwear of the victim. Whoever framed him took the club away. Given the misspelling in the hangman game, that person could be anyone violently opposed to capital punishment who read the story in the *Star* after Haddon hanged and mistakenly stored the wrong spelling in his memory.

"B-R-I-C-E, my lord. Not the way Ethan Shaw would spell his brother's name. That misspelling gives everyone aboard the ship *except my client* the hangman's word-game motive."

I paused to let the reporters scratch a few notes. Tomorrow, what I was saying to the judge would be front-page news.

Damn, I thought.

I forgot to spell Kline.

Sure as shit, someone would misspell it K-L-E-I-N.

"My lord," I said, "there is no case here. And if this extradition continues, it may clog the courts for years. My client wants to stand trial *here* and *now,* so he can be acquitted of this bogus charge. This morning, I appeared in provincial court at 222 Main to defend a charge of murder on Canada's territorial sea. The refusal by the attorney general of Canada to give his consent is all that stands in the way of an expeditious trial in these courts. I ask you to order the Crown to give the necessary consent, and to vacate this provisional warrant granted to the United States."

I took my seat.

Wilde stood up.

He flipped open his pocket watch as if to confirm the time I had wasted, then addressed the court with a patronizing jab at me.

"My young friend has much to learn about jurisdiction. The jury address we just heard is out of place. I am here to fix a date for an extradition hearing on the warrant issued by your lordship. This crime occurred on a foreign ship sailing from Seattle. The victim was an American. So is the accused. There is no evidence that this crime took place in Canada, and without that nexus, no jurisdiction to try Shaw here.

"Consent is a matter for the attorney general. He has decided that consent should be denied. That puts an end to the matter. Let's fix a date."

I was on my feet.

"My friend could get consent."

"No consent is forthcoming. Those are my instructions."

"Mr. Kline," said the judge, "that ends the matter of the necessary consent. No more tilting at windmills. Let's fix a date."

"My lord," I said, "I wish to read some law. Could this case be adjourned until tomorrow morning?"

"Mr. Wilde?"

"I'm in these courts, my lord."

The judge nodded.

"Ten o'clock, Mr. Kline."

Fire one, I thought.

The torpedo was in the water.

One Angry Man

Where would Zinc Chandler be today if not for Alex Hunt?

And what would he do if he lost her?

It was black beyond the windows of the TV room in which he and Alex had watched *Twelve Angry Men,* and it was black in here where Zinc sat alone in the dark, and it was black in the heart, mind and soul of this angry, grieving man. Following the theatrics in Supreme Court that afternoon, the inspector had made arrangements for Alex to be cremated, and now he sat slumped amid the ashes of his smoldering life.

God, how his head hurt from the bullet scar in his brain. With each thump of his broken heart, it screamed for release from the pain. He wished he could end this torment by eating the muzzle of his gun. One squeeze of the trigger and he could embrace oblivion, but then who would make sure that Alex got justice for the outrage done to her?

He would.

Count on it.

Her killer would pay.

Again and again, that final image replayed in his mind. Ethan approaching their table over dinner on the cruise, to take his brother Justin to meet Jeff Kline. "Go," said Maddy. "We have files to discuss." "Mind if I tag along?" Alex asked, as she gave Zinc a look that said, Here's your chance to swing. If you love me, you must love me for *me*.

Then she was gone.

Gone eternally.

And now Zinc was left wondering if Alex had died doubting that he loved her for *her*.

If only he had flown home from Seattle that night Konrad was hanged. If only he hadn't slept on the couch at Maddy's place. If only he hadn't told Alex that was what he did. If only he had recognized that she was worried about his commitment, this woman who had always seemed so sure of herself that he had never concerned himself with that phantom worry.

If only... if only... if only...

"Dammit!" he exploded.

And instantly had the urge to smash something to pieces.

His hand was around the neck of a lamp on the table beside the loveseat, about to hurl it against the wall with the full force of his anger, when the cellphone beside it called.

"Chandler," he answered.

"Special O. Guess who just landed at the airport on a flight from San Francisco?"

The Lady-Killer figured it was time to settle the score with that bitch of a lesbian nurse who had blown the whistle on him, effectively putting an end to the paving of his yellow brick road. Timing was everything when it came to murder, and tonight was the perfect time for her to commit "suicide." Doing her in earlier would have implicated him. Had she died before his trial, the suspicion would have been that he had silenced her as a witness. After the verdict, his big concern had been what to do with Jayne Curry, for the amorous juror might have been able to jeopardize his acquittal on appeal. His trip to the States had been to escape from her clinging for a while, then when Curry was hanged, he knew he would be suspected of being the Hangman, so he had decided to lay low until tonight.

Timing.

What made tonight the perfect time to settle his outstanding score with that whistle-blowing nurse was the lucky interlocking of subsequent events. Not only did he have a San Francisco alibi for the night Busby was hanged from the mast of his boat, but he was also not aboard the cruise ship when Alex Hunt was killed, and now it seemed certain that the cops had the Hangman in court. The Hangman's lynching of Curry had effectively put an end to the Crown's appeal, so his acquittal was no longer in jeopardy. His only motive left for doing in the squealing nurse was revenge, and even if that was in his cold, cold mind, would he be foolish enough to chance the risk?

Surely not.

Far more likely that she did herself in, for the gossip the doctor had heard as far away as California was that his former nurse was down in the dumps after being jilted by a younger woman who had stolen the old girl's heart.

Is that why she stuck the hypodermic currently in *his* pocket into her arm? To give herself a deadly shot of the poison in the glass vial that was also in *his* possession here outside her garage?

Is that why, before she stuck the needle in her arm tonight, she left the motor of her car running? So carbon-monoxide gas would fill the garage, ensuring her demise from one poison or the other?

Is that why—

His ears perked up.

Was this her coming home?

A car had turned into the lane leading to the rear of her modest house, and headlight beams were advancing through cracks in the fence toward her garage. Once the car drew near, a second motor kicked in, and the doctor heard the automatic door of the garage begin to clatter up.

The yard between her house and the garage was full of murk

and gloom. The door to the yard from the garage opened outward, and that's where the Lady-Killer lurked to ambush the nurse. The window nearest him was a blind eye until the car turned into the garage and knifed its headlights through the glass into the dark heart of the yard. Through the window, Dr. Twist saw the face of his former nurse above the steering wheel.

The eye went dark.

She had doused the beams.

The car door slammed shut; he heard the tapping of her approaching heels before the sound was absorbed by the clatter of the automatic door as it descended.

Good, thought Twist.

That will drown out her cry.

His gloved hand jabbed the needle of the syringe into the glass vial, then eased back the hypodermic's plunger to suck up the poison. The handle of the door from the garage turned as the doctor dropped the vial back into his pocket, and he prepared himself for action the moment the door swung open.

Her hand would be on the handle as it hinged away from the jamb, her arm preceding her body out into the backyard. A quick grab of her wrist from his position beside the door, and the needle would jab into her arm before she could react. Her cry of surprise would be a gasp, not a scream, lost in the ongoing clatter of the lane door. His glove would stifle any shriek before it came out.

Ready.

Set.

Here she comes...

"John Langley Twist," shouted a voice behind him, "you're under arrest."

The watchers of Special O had followed Twist from the airport, keeping Zinc informed of his whereabouts, and when Twist's final destination turned out to be the backyard of his former nurse—the nurse responsible for his murder trial—Zinc had set this trap.

Yes, the nurse had driven her car into the garage, but it wasn't her on the other side of the door. It was a cop who had slouched down in the passenger's seat, emerging to assume the nurse's role once the garage was dark. As for Zinc, he had crept into the backyard by the walkway skirting the side of the house from out front.

By dim light from the street and the glow cast by the windows of surrounding homes, the Mountie saw Dr. Twist coming for him. The hypodermic needle spiked down from his raised fist like the knife used to kill in *Psycho*'s shower scene. Zinc could have drawn the Smith & Wesson holstered at his waist, but he had yet to discharge the anger seething in him, so instead he took his rage out on the Lady-Killer.

Zinc blocked the stab with his left forearm, then swung his right hand in an upward arc behind the immobile limb gripping the syringe. Locking his right palm over the back of his own left hand, the inspector used the strength of both muscled biceps to wrench back the doctor's arm until a bone snapped. He threw the shocked man back against the garage, so the boards of the wall backed his head, then drove his knuckled fist forward to shatter Twist's nose. A knee slamming into his groin finished off the Lady-Killer, dropping him to the dirt as a bloody, broken mess. His pretty-boy face would set lonely hearts fluttering no more, and his conceit of a cock would need convalescence before it would stand up to cons in the pen.

Zinc would have kicked him, but he held that urge in check.

Twist wasn't on the ship the night Alex died.

So while he had vented his anger for now on this pathetic substitute, Zinc didn't want to be in jail on a brutality rap when the opportunity arose for a showdown with Alex's killer.

Would her killer make the same mistake as Dr. John Twist?

Faced with the Mountie, would he too misread the signs?

Something about Zinc made people want him on their side, for instinct told them he would be vicious if the knife was at his throat.

Necktie Party

What began as a necktie party would end as a necktie party.

Different definitions.

It was deathly quiet in the Athens Taverna, unlike earlier, before midnight, when the party had been in full swing. There was a party every night at the Greek restaurant, fueled by retsina, ouzo and Metaxa brandy. Belly dancers would undulate for lecherous businessmen out for a wild fling on the town, the drunkest of whom would end up thinking they were Zorba the Greek, dancing amid the tables with both arms crooked in the air...

Do-da ... do-da ... do-da do-da do-dado-dado-da ...

While George Koulelis snipped off their ties with a pair of shears.

The ceiling of the main room looked like a bed of spikes turned upside down. The stalactites—thousands of them—were all businessmen's ties. Each was pinned with the card of the diner who had sacrificed his neck phallus to the cause of the decor, and whoever had the most ties tacked up at the end of the year won a special meal cooked by George himself.

George Koulelis was a born restaurateur.

Behind the happy face, however, was hidden a well of tears,

and that well overflowed each night once the Greek was alone. A wretch of a man whose hair had bleached white from paternal grief, he sat in his smoky office behind the depleted central bar. With a stiff drink at hand, he puffed on a Turkish cigarette and calculated tonight's receipts while his heart cried for Anna. On his desk was a photo of his sweet, dead child, and though nearly two decades had passed since little Anna was raped and strangled, not a night closed in on George that he didn't mourn for her.

Drinking didn't help.

But he had to work the room.

And working the room meant sitting down to toast the regulars.

At least that's what he told himself as the booze depressed him into melancholy.

Poor George Koulelis.

The door to his office was shut against the world when the exhausted Greek caught a suspicious noise out in the taverna. Stubbing his cigarette and downing the Metaxa, he rose from his chair to cross the smoky haze to the door, where he armed himself with a bat he kept nearby just in case.

Easing the door open merely sucked the smoke from his office out into the restaurant, which was dark and inhabited with spooky shadows cast by lights intruding in from the street. George stepped through the murky cloud to look around, then froze as the muzzle of a gun was pressed into the nape of his neck.

"Drop the bat."

He dropped it.

"Hands behind your back."

Snap! Snap! His wrists were locked with a pair of handcuffs.

"Money?" George whispered. "Is that what you want from me?"

"No, Koulelis. I want the truth."

The Greek smelled garlic on the breath warming the back of his ear.

"The truth?" he said.

"What time did you get home?"

A frown creased George's forehead. He was still at work; he wasn't home. Then, like being hit with a blow from the bat, he was struck by the meaning of the intruder's question.

Should he lie?

Or should he tell the truth?

"Four-ten," he said.

"How do you know?"

"I checked my watch against the kitchen clock when I arrived."

"Is that the truth?"

"Yes."

"You got home at 4:10 and found Anna gone?"

The barrel of the pistol was cold on his scalp as George tipped back his head to nod.

"Why did you lie in court?"

"They made me."

"Who?" asked the voice behind the gun.

"The police detectives."

After all the lying he had done for almost twenty years, the father of the dead girl was all lied out. If he died tonight, it would be a blessing. If there was a heaven, Anna would be there. And if he was to join her in the afterlife, now was the time for him to unburden his soul.

"Are you the Hangman?"

"Yes," said his confessor.

"I'm tired of lying."

"And I'm sick of your lies."

"The detectives came to me after the arrest. They said there was a problem with the time I *thought* I got home. Haddon killed Anna. No doubt, they said. He was a sick monster who would rape and kill again if he wasn't stopped."

"You believed that?"

"They were the police. For what reason would they lie to me?"

HANGMAN

"The time?" said the Hangman.

"The time," echoed George.

"I want to know *why* you changed the time."

"Haddon had an alibi for 4:10. It was physically impossible for him to have snatched Anna before 4:15. If I stuck with my arrival time, they said the courts would let my daughter's killer go. We all knew he had raped and strangled Anna, so it was up to me to think hard about the time."

"So you changed it?"

"They showed me I was wrong."

"How?" asked the Hangman.

"By leading me through everything I had done that afternoon. 'How could you do all that and make it home by 4:10?' they asked. 'It wasn't 4:10. It couldn't be. The time you got home must have been 4:35, and by then Haddon had your little girl.'"

The Greek began to blubber.

He sobbed like a baby.

A flood of anguish flowed in his cry.

"They told me he was a devil. They told me he was a demon. They told me not to ask them what he did to my child. They were the police. They ought to know. I took what they told me as gospel from above. You don't know what it's like to lose someone that precious."

"I do," said the Hangman. "*You* saw to that."

George was so distraught that he didn't absorb the comment. All he could hear was Anna screaming for help in the woods.

"She was so innocent. She was my life. Anna loved animals. And she *loved* me. That's the precious child I lost to some demented monster, so I did what they told me was necessary to bring Haddon to justice. I trusted what they said. I had to have revenge. What greater burden could be laid on the shoulders of a father than the one they laid on mine? I was angry. I was trying to grieve. Her death was an emotional apocalypse for me. Unless I changed the time, her killer would go free, so I moved the time forward to 4:35. The end justifies the means, the cops told me. Oh, good God! What did I do!"

"You hanged four people," the Hangman said.

"I didn't find him guilty! Twelve jurors did!"

"If you hadn't fingered Haddon, he wouldn't have been arrested. If you'd told the truth, he would have been acquitted. And if he'd been acquitted, who would have hanged?"

"I'm sorry! I'm sorry!"

"Too late, Koulelis."

The pressure of the gun against his spine forced George forward. He and his confessor moved toward the darkest part of the taverna, a corner that could not be seen from the street. Ahead was the ladder the Greek had climbed to hang the ties he had snipped off during the necktie party. The ladder wasn't where he had left it before heading to his office to add up the night's receipts.

"Huuuh!" gasped the Greek.

Until his breath was cut off.

So dark was it near the ladder that George didn't see the noose hanging from a ceiling beam up among the jagged teeth of ties until the Hangman slipped it over his head. The gasp was cut short by a hard yank on the other end of the rope, and George went up on his tiptoes to ease the stranglehold. Never had he been so scared.

"Climb," ordered the Hangman.

The Greek scaled the ladder.

"Stop," ordered the Hangman.

George was halfway up.

The Hangman secured the loose end of the rope to the bar.

"You want a necktie party? You've got one, killer."

The Hangman gripped the ladder wobbling beneath the Greek's feet.

"It's all your fault, Koulelis. And now you must pay. Whoever raped and strangled Anna is free because of you. By fingering

Peter, you focused police attention on your home when she could just as easily have been snatched off the street. Anna was to meet a friend in the park at four. What if she arrived early and was grabbed there? No matter whether you got home at 4:10 or 4:35, Anna would not have been at your house for Peter to kidnap.

"The irony is that in spite of you, Anna's killer will probably be caught. Authorities now have his DNA from the stains on her underwear, and soon every perv with a history of sexual violence will have his genes stored in a central data bank. One day a computer will spit out a match, and Anna will have the justice you denied her."

The Hangman wrenched the ladder away to turn the Greek off like Ketch used to do on Tyburn Hill.

"I wish I could say your pain will be over in a moment... "

George kicked desperately in the air as he hanged.

"But witnesses who lie must learn the same lesson as perverse jurors."

Whirrrrrr! The motor of the hand-held cordless saw cut in.

"So I have some cutting to do."

Loophole

Vancouver
Tonight

"My lord," I announced, loud and clear, as I came in the main door to Quick Draw McGraw's courtroom yesterday morning, "I have a habeas corpus."

All heads turned.

Showtime, folks.

I had checked the case list half an hour ago and, taking note of the fact that there were other matters to be heard by the judge, had stalled until his court was in session to make my move. Slipping down to the criminal registry on the second level, I filed my papers like a thief in the night and asked the clerk to get them up to court ASAP. As I pushed open the gate between the gallery and the counsel pit, the clerk brought the file in by another door.

Again, Lyndon Wilde, QC, had donned his silky best, but whether he was putting on the dog I don't know. At Tuesday's adjournment, he did tell the judge he'd be in court on Wednesday, so I magnanimously gave him the benefit of the doubt. To show he was in chambers, he had doffed his black gown, which was draped over the back of his chair. The prosecutor rustled as he rose to his feet and fished his pocket watch from his vest to confirm the time.

"Not only is my learned friend late," he told the judge, "but he has also rudely interrupted the case at bar."

"My lord . . . "

I paused.

We call that pregnant suspense.

"Yes, Mr. Kline?"

I had the go-ahead.

"Must I refresh my learned friend on the history of habeas corpus? The writ dates from before the Magna Carta in 1215. The Latin means let's 'have the body' brought into court so we can test the legality of the prisoner's detention. There was a time in these courts when freedom was sacrosanct. A habeas corpus *always* went to the front of the line. Has Mr. Wilde become so jaded that liberty is ho-hum to him?"

The old fart bristled.

"I argued my first habeas corpus before you were born, son. I don't need you—"

Bang!

I slammed my fist on the table.

"This isn't a *game!*" I protested. "Alexis Hunt was hanged in Canada *and I can prove it*. Ethan Shaw is charged with capital murder. America *wants to kill him*. Is his fate to hang in the balance while your lordship listens to a charge of . . ."

I turned to the lawyer at the bar.

"What's your case?" I asked.

"Theft," he replied.

"Theft," I echoed. "My client waits in the shadow of the death house as my learned friend blusters about my manners in interrupting a *theft!*"

Man, I love the decorum of the law. All that "may it please your lordship" when you think he's a moronic dunce, and "my learned friend" when you're out to slit his throat.

In the philosophy of law, there are two schools of jurisprudence. The British favor positivism, the belief that law is an objective pursuit governed by statutes and previous court decisions that offer some certainty to the outcome of trials. The Americans favor realism, the belief that law is a subjective pursuit influenced more by whether the judge just had a tiff with his wife or spent the past hour in bed with his mistress.

I'm a realist.

And so was Quick Draw.

McGraw knew this would likely be the crowning case of his legal career, with more publicity than he could imagine. His finger was in the air to determine how the wind was blowing, and I knew he would side with me to make himself look good.

"Clear the deck," he ordered. "Counsel for Ethan Shaw has a habeas corpus."

"And an abuse of process," I added.

"Sheriff."

"Sir?"

"Let's 'have the body.' "

With his backbone ramrod and his shoulders squared for the media, the "brownie" went to the door that brought Ethan up from the cells, then led him with even-handed respect across to the dock. No sign of torture, as you can see.

From my battered briefcase, I withdrew the secret papers I had just filed and dropped copies of what the clerk handed to the judge in front of Wilde.

"My lord," he chuffed. "this material takes me by surprise."

"It shouldn't," I said. "As you will see."

"Once we know where this is going, I'll deal with that," said McGraw.

"My lord?" I prompted.

"Begin, Mr. Kline."

"Some background is essential for perspective. I was aboard *The North Star* the night of the hanging. My client dined with me as we sailed north from Seattle, then, before dessert was served, Ethan Shaw asked his brother, Justin Whitfield, and Alexis Hunt to join us at our table. For quiet, we later moved to a bar called the Captain Ahab, where three of us had coffee and Mr. Shaw drank. A compass built into the tabletop tracked the ship's direction.

"By then, we were cruising in the Strait of Juan de Fuca, somewhere near the border between Canada and the United States, which runs along the middle of that dividing waterway. While we were talking, two crucial things occurred.

"First, a photographer took a picture of the four of us in the bar, with the lights of Victoria, British Columbia, twinkling in the background. Next, Ethan Shaw spilled his drink on the table, and as it was wiped up by our server, she drew our attention to the direction of the inset compass. The ship was sailing *due west* in the strait.

"The documents filed to prove these truths are as follows: My affidavit—"

Wilde was on his feet.

"My young friend should know better than to offer himself as a witness in his own case."

"The affidavit of Justin Whitfield—"

"The *brother* of Ethan Shaw! Blood is thicker than water, my lord. *Res ipsa loquitur.*"

"The affidavit of John Dunn, captain of the coast guard vessel *Vector*, to confirm that the configuration of lights in the background of the photograph is indeed Victoria."

"So?" said Wilde.

"I'm sure my friend has a cellphone if he wishes to call the captain."

"Do you take issue with that, Mr. Wilde?"

"No, my lord. So what?"

"And finally, the affidavit of Diane Marsden, the bar server, to confirm that the inset compass did point due west."

The judge turned to Wilde.

"Is that in issue, Counsel?"

"No, my lord. Again I say, 'So what?' Nothing my friend has offered changes matters one whit. The ship sailed west past Victoria. I accept that. It's a fact. But even if, as this photo indicates, Alexis Hunt was alive at the time, who's to say the ship was north of the borderline?"

"Do you sail, Mr. Wilde?"

"No. Golf is my passion."

"Pity," said the judge. "I do," he added.

"Your lordship gets my point?"

"Yes, Mr. Kline."

"I fear my learned friend thinks I'm wet behind the ears. Perhaps your lordship would explain the problem to him?"

The judge nodded.

I had made him my co-counsel.

"The sea, too, has rules of the road, Mr. Wilde. And the rule of the road in the Strait of Juan de Fuca is this: ships sailing east cruise in American waters and ships sailing west cruise north of the borderline in Canada's jurisdiction."

The prosecutor winced.

He was in *big* trouble.

The kind of trouble that can turn your bowels to water in court.

Be it Canadian or American, the ship of state had taken a torpedo below the waterline.

I closed in for the kill.

"My elderly friend has much to learn about jurisdiction," I said, giving him back the line he had laid on me yesterday. "But even more troubling, he has much to learn about *ethics.*"

"I protest!" fumed Wilde.

"Careful, Mr. Kline," cautioned the judge.

These West Side wimps were virgins when it came to streetfighting. In the East End, you fight like this. First you knee them in the balls. Then, as they double over, you ram your fingers into their eyes. Then, once you have them on the ground, you curbstomp their heads against the concrete gutter.

"My lord, Mr. Wilde seeks to deceive this court. In the aftermath of what occurred aboard the ship, an unfortunate turf war developed between authorities on both sides of the border. The result was that they refused to share witness statements, and this extradition was launched to send my client to the United States so he can be executed. It is only by fortune that this information fell into my hands, because these crucial witnesses— Justin Whitfield and the bar woman—were interviewed by *American* police."

Another pregnant pause.

Let it fester.

I whiffed the stench of fear coming off Wilde.

Time for the *coup de grâce*.

"In other words, the key to jurisdiction lay within Mr. Wilde's grasp, and knowing my client is fighting for his life, counsel for the United States hid this fact from *you!*"

That did it.

The hair of the judge was on fire.

If there's one thing you never do in court, it's make the judge look like a dupe.

"Mr. Wilde, what have you to say?"

The old boy began bailing water as fast as he could heave.

"My lord, I can assure you that I knew nothing of this. My learned friend has bushwhacked me with these allegations. In all my years at the bar, I have never been a party to—"

"Judgment," barked the judge.

The court recorder sat up. That was her cue.

"Ethan Shaw applies for a writ of habeas corpus. He submits that this court lacks jurisdiction to extradite him to the United States of America to stand trial on an indictment for murder. This morning, a provisional arrest warrant was issued by this court. The death of the victim, Alexis Hunt, occurred onboard a ship that was sailing from Seattle to Vancouver. From what this court has considered in unchallenged affidavits filed by counsel for Ethan Shaw, it is now evident that the murder occurred in Canadian waters, and that there is no jurisdiction in this court to extradite Ethan Shaw to stand trial in Washington State. A writ of habeas corpus will issue. The warrant is vacated."

That's how I like it.

Shoot from the hip.

We don't call him Quick Draw McGraw for nothing.

"My lord," I said, pulling more paper out of my briefcase, "I have taken the liberty of drafting the writ. If your lordship would sign it here and now, my unjustly imprisoned client can walk out of your court a free man."

The scratching of reporters' pens was music to my ears.

"Damn!" one cursed. "I'm out of ink!"

I do believe I heard the clench of Lyndon Wilde's hemorrhoids.

"My Lord, I ask you not to sign the writ until I can have the provincial Crown re-lay a charge of first-degree murder."

It was time to curb-stomp this old fart. After I finished putting the boots to him, his cases from the Feds would dry up too.

"Enough!" I exploded, slamming down my fist. "Has this man no heart? Has this man no shame? In this same court yesterday, I submitted that there was no case against my client. I asked him for a trial in Canada's courts, and his dismissive reply was this: 'The consent required to try an American for murder committed on a foreign ship in Canada's territorial sea is a matter for the attorney general of Canada. No consent is forthcoming. Those are my instructions.' What he did was force your lordship to say to me, 'That ends the matter of the necessary consent.'

"Well"—I was building steam."—that does *end* the matter."

I whacked the table again for emphasis.

"Because this crime assuredly occurred on our territorial sea"—I pointed west toward the wide Pacific—"and without the consent of the attorney general of Canada, there can be no charge tried by the provincial Crown!"

Stomp. Stomp. Stomp.

I was breaking bones.

"Mr. Wilde has already deceived this court in an attempt to *lynch* Ethan Shaw, and now he seeks to make your lordship a henchman too."

I walked to the dock to stand with Ethan.

"This is habeas corpus.

"This isn't a game.

"Give my client justice.

"Sign the writ, my lord."

The gallery held its collective breath in anticipation. Quick Draw weighed the scales of justice in his best interest. Should he rein me in for stepping over the line, and thus make it look like he was a closet Crown prosecutor, or should he let Lyndon Wilde, QC, take the fall?

No contest.

The judge signed the writ.

"File it," he told the court clerk. "You're free to go, Mr. Shaw."

As I led Ethan out of court to reap my reward in the limelight of the cameras massed outside, I had to pass the player on the other side. Zinc Chandler stood by the gallery exit.

I could have said something nasty like "I'm sorry for your loss," but hey, I'm a lawyer who's got a soft spot.

So as my lips passed within range of his ear, I whispered in consolation, "Every noose has a loophole."

Red Herring

Sunlight beamed in through the sloped glass roof of the great hall of the law courts, but even the sun was no match for the glare of the cameras flashing at the pair of lawyers outside. Zinc witnessed the chaos from the five-story hall, an angry man seething to his core, the pain in his head worsening with every flash of instant fame.

Turning his back on the media circus to leave by the rear exit, the Mountie found himself face to face with the statue of Themis. The blindfolded goddess of justice held balanced scales in one hand, but, befitting a country that had abolished the noose, the sword of justice in her other hand had been replaced with a scroll of paper.

A flurry of paper had freed Ethan Shaw.

For an instant, in Zinc's mind's eye, the figure of the goddess was that of Alex Hunt, and in that brief moment, he relived the intimacies the pair had shared. The memories struck home with a pain so sharp he feared his heart would explode, and he grasped how profound a loss he would suffer every day for the rest of his life.

"Alex," he said to the statue, "this I swear to you: If it takes everything I have, including life itself, you *will* have justice for the injustice done to you."

From his pocket, Zinc withdrew a Swiss Army knife. Prying open a blade, he nicked the index finger of his left hand.

Blood welled in the cut.

Zinc watched it flow.

Then he touched the cold gown of the statue and let it run red.

"This I swear in blood."

The inspector was leaving the law courts by the Smithe Street exit when his cellphone rang.

"Chandler," he said, expecting it to be DeClercq. The chief superintendent, hit by a relapse, was back in bed with immobilizing flu.

"Zinc, it's Maddy."

"My favorite detective."

"Your sarcasm is cutting."

"I'm angry. Have you heard?"

"Heard what?"

"Ethan walked. All because of you. That was about as stupid a move as I have ever seen—trying to hide where the ship was when Alex was killed so you could allege she was hanged in the States to support your request that we extradite Shaw."

"You've lost me, Inspector."

"Don't play games."

"Be *specific*. Exactly what do you believe we hid from you?"

"Justin's statement."

"What about it?"

"He signed an affidavit to scuttle your request to extradite Shaw. Justin swore he was with Alex when the ship entered Canadian waters. A photo of them proved it."

"That's not in his statement."

"No? What is?"

"I'll fax you a copy."

"It's too late for that. The horse is gone. The milk is spilt."

"It's never too late. Justin is here. He's waiting outside. I'll speak to him."

"You do that. Meanwhile, now that Ethan is back on the street, let's hope the Hangman doesn't strike again."

"He already has. That's why I called. Remember George Koulelis? The father of the girl Peter Haddon *didn't* kill? I'm at the Athens Taverna. The Greek's restaurant. Last night, he was hanged and butchered in Seattle."

Seattle

While those who make murder their business went about their grisly work, Maddy stood in the restaurant with her cellphone to her ear, describing the crime scene to the Mountie in Vancouver. The Greek—or what was left of him—hanged from a ceiling beam surrounded by a colorful array of snipped neckties. The ladder used to lynch him lay flat on the floor in a pool of blood that was collecting from the stumps of what were once his arms and legs. The same shocking color had gushed down his chin from a slash across the open mouth of the face, which had turned cyanotic blue by asphyxia. The severed limbs, both arms and legs, were propped against the bar, on one side of which the killer had drawn a hangman game in blood:

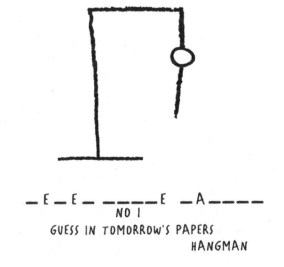

_ E _ E _ _ _ _ _ E _ A _ _ _ _
NO I
GUESS IN TOMORROW'S PAPERS
HANGMAN

"So what do you think?" said Maddy.

"The Hangman isn't Twist. The doctor was in Canada when the Greek was killed."

"Where is he now?"

"In custody. Charged with the attempted murder of me. I broke his arm during the arrest."

"Scratch him," said Maddy. "So what's your theory now?"

"Know what a red herring is?"

"Sure. A false clue."

"And the origin?"

"You got me there, Zinc."

"According to Alex, the term was in use at least as far back as seventeenth-century England. Those who abhorred the idea of a fox being hunted to death by a pack of hounds and aristocratic horsemen thought up a way to throw the dogs off track. They bought herrings at the fish market and smoked them at home until they took on a reddish color. Dragging the cooked herrings around the countryside left a pungent odor throughout the woods and fields that covered up the scent of the fox and confused the hunting dogs. Since then, a clue meant to distract a sleuth from his or her quarry has been known as a red herring."

"You smell something fishy?"

"It stinks," said Zinc.

The usual crowd of onlookers feeding off the drama of violent death had gathered on the street outside the Athens Taverna. In days of old a mob like this might have been treated to the spectacle of a public hanging, but these bland times offered little more than a body on a gurney hidden under a sheet. Maddy's exit from the building caused a stir, but they would have to wait awhile for death to appear.

A street cart was approaching to sell the mob hot dogs.

The familiar features of Justin Whitfield were in the thick of the throng. With a nod of her head, Maddy signaled him to meet her at the Starbucks a block away. By the time he arrived to sit with her at a corner table, the cop had a steaming mocha java waiting for the reporter.

"An affidavit, huh?"

"You heard," he said.

"The Mountie told me. It sank our extradition."

"Good," he said, stirring a packet of sugar into his cup. "I lost one brother to a noose. I won't lose another."

"A scoop like that? Why aren't you in Vancouver?"

Justin blew the steam away and took a sip.

"Kline's suggestion. Tactics, Maddy. He didn't want me available for cross-examination. And I don't want to be the focus of media attention. Besides, I'd have missed *this*."

Maddy nodded. "So it's a tie. Sue Frye scoops you in Vancouver. You scoop her here."

"No," said Justin. "I get *both* scoops. The *Star*'s doing a special edition that will hit the street today. Guess who got to interview Ethan and his lawyer last night? A super-scoop, since I was promised *exclusive* access until we publish."

"Quite a coup."

"With more to come. Assuming you have something for me?"

The cop slapped a Polaroid face down on the table. She kept her hand on it. "To add to your thirty pieces of silver," she said.

Justin glared. "I'm no Judas, Maddy. My affidavit did nothing more than tell the truth."

"How'd that come about? You teaming up with Kline to spring Ethan?"

"He approached me yesterday after court adjourned and asked if I'd swear an affidavit about what went on in the bar."

"To prove the ship was in Canada?"

"Yes," said the reporter.

"That's not in your statement to us."

"Because I didn't know. I had assumed we were sailing south of the line when I was questioned by police. Did you know about the rule of separation in the strait? A westbound ship sails in Canada, an eastbound one sails in the States?"

"No," said Maddy.

"Crafty lawyer, huh?"

"Not only did he stop our extradition, but he also killed the charge in Canada."

"Good," said Justin. "Ethan's innocent."

"I'm not so sure."

"I am," said the reporter.

Maddy took out her notebook. "Why?" she asked.

"Remember the piece I wrote for the *Star* the night Peter hanged? To make the deadline for the edition next morning, I had to phone the copy in to Seattle from the state prison. The editor who took it down spelled Bryce with an *I*, and that's how it appeared in print the next day."

"You were angry, as I recall."

"My brother had been *hanged,* and my paper couldn't spell his name right. Nor, it seems, can the killer, who added an *I* to the hangman game scrawled in Alex's blood on the wall of Ethan's cabin."

"Because he knew how to spell Peter's name, Ethan is innocent?"

"Yes," said Justin. "If not because we're family—he *did* leave as a baby—then because he proofread the galleys of my book. Bryce is spelled correctly throughout *Perverse Verdict.*"

"Do you think the killer got the mistake from your *Star* story?"

"I don't know. Kline used my article to raise that question with the judge. However, I do know that Ethan knows how to spell Peter's name, so he wouldn't add an *I* instead of a *Y* to the middle word of the puzzle. Nor did he lynch George Koulelis in his restaurant last night. Ethan was jailed in Vancouver."

"Answer a question?"

"Sure."

"Don't take offense."

"Come on, Maddy. How many years have we been doing this?"

"What were you doing onboard the ship at the time Alex was hanged?"

"Were you looking for me?"

"No," said the cop. "Zinc and I were in a lounge going over the case."

"You want my alibi?"

"Ease my mind."

"I was in my cabin."

"Doing what?"

"Sharing my bed with our server from the Captain Ahab bar. After Ethan and Alex left to get some air, I stayed in the bar talking with Kline for a short while. The woman gave me the eye over his shoulder, so I left to meet her outside."

"That's not in your statement."

"And it's not in hers. We didn't volunteer what we weren't asked. Ethan was in custody. The questions were about Alex."

"Why the grin, Justin?"

"I find it funny. Your suspecting the Hangman might be me. I can assure you I know how to spell my twin brother's name."

"So what do you make of this?"

The detective turned over the Polaroid lying face down between them. The snapshot was of the hangman game on the bar in the restaurant. The reporter studied the print beneath the gallows:

_ E _ E _   _ _ _ _ E _ A _ _ _ _

No I. Guess in tomorrow's papers. Hangman.

"Hmmph," said Justin. "The game has gone back a step."

"To correct the misspelling."

"And it's back to 'papers.'"

"Sue Frye must have pissed off the Hangman."

"It reads as if the killer takes exception to the misspelling of Peter's name."

"It's a demand that we get the spelling right."

"So why the game on the ship?"

"It was a red herring."

"How does that make sense?"

"Damned if I know," said Maddy. "But what we have to do in your special edition is publish, big and bold, the answer to the puzzle. Hopefully, *Peter Bryce Haddon* will end the hangings."

"A red herring?" mused Justin.

"A red herring," she said.

And suddenly, the detective solved what was going on.

Special Eye

The Royal Canadian Mounted Police has four letter sections: Special E, Special I, Special O and Special X. Special E, the outlaw biker-gang squad, is now disbanded. It was crucial at a time when bikers were rife in this city. Special I is the ears of the force. Some say the I stands for "Intercept," but that's not so. I stands for I, and no one knows why. Special O is the eyes of the force. Some say the O stands for "Observation," and that *is* true. Since they are the cops who surreptitiously trail the bad guys, the blandest-looking Mounties get posted to O. Special X is the Special External Section of the force, and its X derives from the fact it looks cool.

Image is everything.

Especially with the Mounties.

Special Eye was a play on Special I. The man who owned the security store was a tailing specialist with O back in those halcyon days when he and Zinc had gone after the Ghoul. The exodus from Hong Kong for fear of what would happen when China took over saw hundreds of thousands of wealthy Asians fly to Canada, and most of them had settled in Vancouver. What everyone knew (but was afraid to say, for fear of seeming racist) was that among those immigrants hid a horde of Triad thugs. Well, the thugs were here. And they were vicious. And their prey was other Chinese. And their favorite pastime was home invasion.

Home invasion was a nasty art. The psychology was to shatter forever your sense of security, so it would thenceforth be your *home* that you dreaded most. A gang of thugs would overpower you at the door or be waiting inside for you to return. A nifty trick was to tie you up and gag your mouth, then pistol-whip your aged parents before one eye and rape your wife and daughter before the other. Once you knew your guests meant business, you had the choice of turning over your material possessions or sitting back and watching as the thousand cuts of Chinese tradition were performed on your family for your viewing pleasure.

In this city, home invasions were a dime a dozen, and if you wanted the best there was in security, you went to see the specialist at Special Eye. The greeting above the door read "Let Special Eye watch over you."

Bill Caradon was graciously accepting a platinum credit card from an elderly Chinese couple when Zinc walked in. A lot of wealthy Asians lived in Kerrisdale, so Special Eye was on 41st, in the heart of the West Side. The amount Bill rang in had four zeros tacked on. Business was good.

Back when Bill was an operative with O, he was a scruffy cop with long reddish hair and a pirate beard, and his muscular frame was softening to fat from too much junk food on round-the-clock stakeouts. A transformation had turned him into the Rock of Gibraltar, his buffed body fighting trim from working out, his hair cut and his chin shaved commando-style. The store surrounding him was an extension of the can-do man, with hardware for every security problem on display. If you had the money, Bill would barricade you, with anti-pry guards and Lexan shields, with bulletproof glass and countersurveillance equipment, with transmitters, monitors, phone recorders, scramblers, scanners and pinhole mikes and cameras. "Spy vs. Spy" from *Mad* magazine would love the gizmos Bill sold here.

Zinc poked around until the Chinese couple left. Finally, the cop and ex-cop were alone.

"Long time, no see."

"How ya doing, Bill?"

"Can't complain. Fear grips the city."

"You always were the best. Now everybody knows."

"A rough go, eh? Sorry to hear about your girl and what went down in court."

"You have thirsty ears."

"It's my business to hear."

"I need a favor, Bill. Lend me your ears."

"You have Special I."

"I requires warrants."

"Warrants make things legal."

"Legal be damned. I've had enough legalities for one day."

"A bug without a warrant is illegal, Zinc. Break the law, and I could be in trouble. Anything overheard is inadmissible if the person bugged had a reasonable expectation of privacy. That means the only voice caught that might end up in court is that of a burglar who mumbles while he works."

"I know the law, Bill."

"Mine's the voice of reason."

"The love of my life was killed and her killer is free on the street. I think he and his brother lynched five people in tandem. They took turns hanging victims while the other had an alibi. I know it's illegal, and I'm asking a lot, but I promise no finger will point at you if you help me out."

The ex-cop stroked his chin.

The pirate beard was back.

"How far do you want me to shove the wire up his ass, Zinc?"

Blind Justice

Vancouver
Thursday, November 16 (Today)

See no evil.
    Hear no evil.
    Just speak evil.
    The verdict.
    There was a moral sickness loose in the land, and for the sake of the future, someone had to act. Switched on the TV and what did you see? A video of a black man cowering on the ground as a ring of rogue cops clubbed him senseless. The case went to court and what was the verdict? A jury that watched the same video didn't see a thing.
    Were they blind?
    O. J. beat his wife. His wife left him. O. J. blew his top. His wife was found dead. O. J. led the country on a weird car chase with a suicide gun pointed at his head. O. J. was charged with murder. The nation watched his trial. A jury heard the same witnesses as everyone else. Judging from the verdict, it seems the only word they heard was "race."
    Were they deaf?
    The flip side of those trials was Peter Haddon's case. The state had nothing against him but junk evidence. What began as an

accusation with no foundation somehow ended in a jury verdict that sent an innocent man to the gallows.

How did that happen?

The Hangman knew.

The rot set in the instant that "duty" became a dirty word.

There was a time when duty turned commoners into heroes. Watch an old movie and there is no doubt who the hero is. He or she is the one who understands duty: the binding force of doing that which is *morally* right.

Maybe it was Vietnam and Watergate. Maybe it was turning on and dropping out. Maybe it was too much *me, me, me* as center of the universe. Whatever the reason, duty waned, leaving us with a world in love with *anti*-heroes. Anti-heroes lack the attributes that make us heroes, and now we laugh at that nobility of spirit and mind that once prompted us to do the right thing. How corny, we think. Today, empty vessels are summoned for jury *duty,* so the guilty go free while innocents like Peter hang.

That's blind justice.

The Hangman was strong medicine for that disease. Hopefully, these hangings would smarten jurors up. The worst enemies of justice are those who believe it rarely fails. They are like Justice herself, willfully blind, and the time had come to rip that phony blindfold from their eyes.

See what you're doing?

Look what you did to me.

Hear the cries of your victims?

Listen to my *Scream.*

Fail in your duty, and I will balance the scales.

Someone has to put duty back in the jury room.

A trial isn't a game of blindman's bluff.

A trial is a game of hangman.

So get your verdict *right!*

Those who believed the Hangman's retribution was murder were wrong. Necessity was the defense to these hangings. Those who were hanged deserved to die, as a lesson to those of like perversity as much as for the travesties of their verdicts. Such deaths were necessary to avoid similar evil to others in future trials, and the evil to be prevented was far greater than the evil of ridding the world of these condemned. It was like sacrificing one in a lifeboat so the rest could eat.

Necessity.

If only the problem was just bad apples.

Unfortunately, the barrel was rotten as well.

So that's why the Hangman sat in this room, one hand holding the rope while the other coiled, coiled, coiled a hangman's noose.

For tonight.

Lynch Law

Vancouver
Tonight

William S. Burroughs was right.

Take it from me.

"A good criminal lawyer can sell all his luck to a client, and the more luck he sells the more he has to sell."

The phone had been ringing nonstop since I sprang Ethan from that murder charge yesterday. I am suddenly the hottest lawyer in town, and crooks and killers who didn't know I existed before are now crashing down the piss-stained door of Kline & Shaw to hurl their filthy loot at my bank account.

My bank account.

Ethan and I aren't partners.

What brought me up to the law courts on a drizzly night like this was a sizable retainer from the father of a skinhead charged with stomping a Sikh to death. A gang of them had done it— Oops, pardon me. The proper way to put it so no blood gets on your hands is a gang of them were *alleged* to have done it—and a motion for separate trials had been granted. The case against the ringleader had gone to the jury, so I came up to see if the verdict resulting from his trial would help acquit my client next month. At three hundred bucks an hour, why not spend the evening reading here instead of at home?

HANGMAN

I had told the sheriff to give me a shout down in the barristers' lounge if the jury came back. With my feet up on the table, I sat by myself in the empty room, reading a slew of newspaper stories about my Big Win! It pleased me to note that none of them had misspelled Kline.

The irony of life is how the wheel comes around. A week ago I was writing a piece on famous hangmen in the hope that it would catch the eye of the Hangman and convince him I was his kind of gunslinger. Now I was featured as the lawyer of the *alleged* Hangman, and a paper had done a sidebar on Canada's most famous hangman to background the story on me:

> No one knows how many people Arthur Ellis hanged. The estimates go higher than six hundred. Whatever the number, Arthur Ellis was a name to fear.
>
> Arthur Bartholomew English was born in England in 1864. Before he was mustered out with the rank of captain, he fought colonial battles with the British army in India, Egypt and South Africa. Kicking around, with nothing to do, he found work in the hanging trade with James Billington, who was then number one on Britain's list of executioners. Arthur's uncle was John Ellis, a hangman also on the list who later slit his own throat with a razor.
>
> A hangman gets paid by the number of necks broken by his noose, so English sought executioner's work out in the colonies. Having hanged prisoners in the Middle East, he finally settled on Canada as a good base and made his home in Montreal. For anonymity, a trade name was needed, so Arthur English, family man, turned into Arthur Ellis, hangman.

Have gallows, will travel was his calling card. A portable hanging machine, made from the wood of the scaffold that hanged the Patriotes of 1837, accompanied the hangman. Assembled with nuts and bolts, it was painted a suitable red.

From 1913 to 1935, Arthur Ellis executed Canada's killers, as well as the killers in colonies spread around the world. His weakness was a fondness for strong drink, and one night of drunkenness saw him shouting and brandishing a loaded .38 in the middle of an opera at Montreal's Orpheum Theatre.

What finished Ellis's career was the botched hanging of Thomasino Sarao. The prison told the hangman that the woman weighed 145 pounds, so he calculated a long drop. What she weighed in fact was 187 pounds, so the sound heard on the scaffold when Ellis released the trap was a squish instead of a thud. The extra weight and gravity had torn off her head.

Now, a new Hangman is on the loose.

Like Thomasino, his victims lose body parts.

The legs and arms are gone.

The body remains.

If there's another victim, will he tear off its head?

"What you reading, Jeff?"

Ethan had found me in the barristers' lounge.

"A piece on us."

"The interview in the *Star*?"

"No, I left Justin's paper at home."

"I hear you've got Suzy phoning around to secure new office space?"

"We're moving uptown."

"You and her?"

"Me, her and *you*, Eth. What did you think? That I would abandon you if I made it big?"

"You don't need me."

"Yes, I do. Every barrister needs a good solicitor."

"You can have your pick of solicitors now."

"Who am I going to choose? Some silver spoon? You think that would make me happy? Working with some West Side prick?"

"You'd really stick with me?"

"You're my right-hand man. It's onward and upward, Eth. Just one condition: The time has come for you to stop drinking."

"I drink to drown my sorrows."

"Your sorrows are gone. You drank because the assholes wore us down. That's history, buddy. We beat the fuckers. Now we're going to thrash them at their own game."

Ethan nodded.

"You'll quit the bottle?"

Another nod.

"Then it's a deal. No more puddles of piss at our door. From now on, we do the pissing."

Ethan smiled.

I gave him a grin.

We shook hands.

Kline & Shaw.

"Is this why you left the message with Suzy for me to come here?"

"No," I said. "Let's walk and talk."

I swung my feet off the table and we left the barristers' lounge. The hall lined with judges' photos was deserted at this late hour. The hum of a vacuum cleaner echoed from one of the chambers courts opposite the library. We turned in the other direction and passed through a set of doors that led out to the great hall. It was suddenly colder in this open area, where we had to choose between three routes. The staircase ahead descended to the court registry where I had filed my habeas corpus motion. The escalator ascending beside us to the right doubled back to carry those who had difficulty with stairs up to the next level. Beyond that was the great hall, reached by an entrance that yawned wide in front of the escalator.

That yawn swallowed Ethan and me.

The courts were tiered behind us as we walked into the glass wedge. Voices filled the upper reaches of the huge cavern from the level where the skinhead was being tried for murder. The main doors to our left in the side wall of the wedge were usually locked after the court day was finished, even if a jury was deliberating late. The death of the Sikh, however, was such a racial tinderbox that the chief justice had ordered that nothing be done that would make it look like access to justice was being denied. Painted on the glass beside the doors was a welcome—ALL COURTS WHEN IN SESSION ARE OPEN TO THE PUBLIC. So instead of the usual procedure of having the public enter by the back doors, the main doors remained unlocked tonight.

It was murky in the great hall. There was light up on the fifth level, where the trial was going on, but it was insufficient to penetrate down here. The government was cheap when it came to lighting public buildings, so all we had to guide us through the cavern was a few pot lamps.

The doors slid open to admit an elderly Sikh. His white turban was soaked with rain. The swish of traffic crossing Hornby Street on Nelson came in with him. Cars streaked by in flashes of white and red. The doors slid shut to exclude their noise.

Another turn right put the doors at our back. The Sikh took the escalator that rose from the U between us and the dim entrance from which we had emerged. A concrete divider separated us from him. Eth and I faced a flight of thirty wide stairs, and by the time we climbed them to reach the next level, the Sikh had left the escalator to trudge his way up the zigzag route that scaled the tiers of courts.

With the toe of the wedge to one side and the stack of courts to the other, we walked the length of the great hall while rain ran in rivulets down the sloping glass roof. So heavy was the downpour that lights glittering in the office towers looming overhead had no more definition than bright smears. So cold was it in the vault that we could see our breath. So shadowy was it at the far end that the bust of Lord Denning, Britain's great judge, could have been a mugger skulking to waylay the two of us in the dark.

"You're not out of the woods, Eth. You must keep that in mind."

"You think they'll charge me?"

"They could," I replied. "There's nothing to stop the AG from giving his consent."

"I didn't kill her."

"I know. You were framed. What we must decide is what do we do about it?"

The statue of the goddess of justice blocked our way. Blindfolded Themis stood on her pedestal, her cape flowing behind and her scales held high. At her feet stood Ethan and I.

"Twins are strange, Eth. The bond that ties them together is almost supernatural. An identical twin is like a doppelgänger, the ghostly double or counterpart of a living person. Your twin brothers had that bond, so that's why Justin is obsessed with Peter's hanging. Psychologically, he was hanged too."

Ethan shook his head.

"What's wrong?" I asked.

"Justin and Peter weren't identical twins. They were fraternal twins."

"So?" I said.

"They didn't share the same DNA. And they didn't look alike."

"Nature or nurture? They shared a *womb,* Eth. You can't get closer to a brother than that."

"What's your point?"

"Justin is sick. And we can use that sickness to help both him *and* you."

"How?" he said.

"Listen and I'll explain. Justin is the Hangman. He has hanged five people. Konrad in Seattle, because she was on Peter's jury. Curry in Vancouver, to throw the cops off track. Busby in Seattle, because he too was on that jury. Hunt on the boat, after she figured out who he was. And the Greek in Seattle, to kill two birds with one stone. Not only did hanging him avenge what he did to Peter, but hanging the Greek while you were in jail might have helped free you."

Ethan frowned.

"Now what's wrong?"

"Something I should have noticed about Justin's trip to Vancouver."

"You mean when he drove up to see your mom? And to get the page proofs from you?"

"Yes," he said. "The same night Jayne Curry was hanged in Vancouver."

"So what's wrong?"

"He *drove* up, Jeff. That's what Justin told me when he phoned from Mom's and we agreed to meet later for dinner to discuss his book. He was already at the restaurant when I arrived, and could have lynched the Curry woman in the interim. After we ate, I drove him to the airport, where we drank in the lounge until he caught the last flight to Seattle. What didn't log in my mind as a mystery before now was that if he *drove* up to Vancouver in a car, what happened to the vehicle when he *flew* home?"

"Maybe it was a one-way rent-a-car."

"I suppose."

"You can ask him when he comes up to talk with me."

"Justin's coming?"

"He will when you ask."

There was some sort of commotion upstairs, as two men got into a war of words. The term "Nazi" was used by one and the term "raghead" by the other. The trial was being retried outside the court.

"You're in danger of standing trial for a murder Justin committed. Justin's in danger of being charged with the Hangman crimes in the States. If he is, your brother will face the noose himself, so how I suggest we defuse both dangers is this.

"Justin retains me to act for him in the Hangman case. In exchange for surrendering the Hangman to the Mounties, I'll get them to guarantee to try him here for the Canadian crimes, and to make Seattle authorities promise not to seek the death penalty if they attempt to extradite him later.

"That will free you from being a suspect in the Hunt murder. When Justin stands trial for the Hangman crimes, I'll plead him not guilty by reason of mental disorder. That disorder will be that he was psychotic at the time, and was suffering under the delusion *that he was his brother.* Because of the psychic bond existing between twins, Justin thought he was possessed by the spirit of his dead brother, and Peter Haddon used him as a means to seek revenge from beyond the grave. The defense can also be raised to stop any attempt by the Americans to extradite him south to face a hangman in the States."

"How do you know he's insane?"

"I don't," I said. "But shrinks need a cash flow like everyone else, and they'll be scrambling to take part in that Cadillac defense."

"So all we need is Justin?"

"That's your job, buddy."

"I'll talk to Mom."

"When?"

"Tonight," he said.

"Time is of the essence, Eth. If they charge you with Hunt's hanging before I can work a deal, I'll be caught in a conflict of interest if I surrender him to free you."

"I'm on my way."

"Good. Call me later."

I lingered by the statue while he walked toward the stairs and watched him disappear from sight step by descending step. The cavern around me was as bleak and austere as could be, a far cry from the cozy buzz of the Rattenbury courts. I had come a long way since that day in Kinky's court when Mrs. Mudge's explosion had hooked me on the law. If there was any justice in this dog-eat-dog world, I wouldn't have been left to make my name in this shitty shell. So bankrupt of foresight were the silver spoons that they made the dumb mistake of letting the old courthouse go. Like the Old Bailey in London, it had built up respect for the law during the hangman's reign, and while the Brits had the smarts to keep that tradition going, the slicks from the West Side had trashed it here. The result was this hole, which stood for nothing in a contemptuous time, and nothing proved that point better than the fact that some malcontent had spit on the goddess of justice.

No, it wasn't spit.

It was a trickle of blood.

A red streak marring the robe of Themis.

I'll be damned.

Who did that?

"Justice is bleeding," I muttered.

Let it bleed, I thought.

My footsteps echoed in the great hall as I too walked toward the thirty wide steps that descended to the main doors. As my foot touched the bottom step, a drenched figure in a raincoat with the hood pulled up approached the law courts. The doors slid back to let it in, the swishing of the traffic beyond bursting in with the cold. As I U'd around to the left to make my way past the escalator to the hall that would lead me back to the barristers' lounge, I was followed by the dripping form.

Wet rubber soles squished on the hard floor.

Squishh. Squishh. Squishh.

HANGMAN

The shadow of the hooded figure closed around me.

The Reaper? I thought.

The shadow of Death?

Then I laughed to myself when I smelled garlic on its breath.

At least it's not a vampire out for—

Whack!

The blow to the back of my head hit as I was skirting the mouth of the escalator. The force of it dropped me to my hands and knees on the cold concrete floor, and my chin struck the edge of one of the planters that lined the escalator's base on its open side. The Hangman slipped the noose about my neck when my head bounced back.

The rope cinched tight to cut off my air. Before my senses could recover from the shock of the blow to my skull, I was caught in a desperate tug-of-war for my life. My heart was pounding, but no blood rose to my brain. I tried to gasp for oxygen, but the noose was strangling me. My frenzied fingers clawed at the rope with no success. It was buried deep in the flesh of my neck.

The shadow of the Hangman darkened the floor. It was cast by a light above the escalator. The moving steps were conveying the killer up. I thought I saw a hook at the end of the rope in the shadow's hand, and thought I heard the clang of metal striking metal, then—confirming what I feared—the noose jerked me back and up.

The rope was somehow hooked to the rising mechanism!

Like a marionette dancing on a string, I was yanked from my knees to my feet. I tried to scream, but only mewling came out. I tried to gasp, but all I heard was gagging. Dangling over the open side of the escalator, I was dragged along the floor below as up, up, up slipped the Hangman and the secured end of the rope. With one hand gouging into my flesh to get a grip on the noose, and the other hand raking the slick surface of the escalator's flank, I had to rise up on my tiptoes to keep from being hanged.

Glass...

Stainless steel...

And smooth drywall...

Everywhere my hand clutched, it failed to find a grasp.

Then up, up, up, and I too was in the air.

Bulging like those of a fish, my eyes bugged out of my head. Flopping around on my lip, my tongue stuck out of my mouth. A sign for the Law Courts Inn leaned against the escalator. I kicked it over as my feet thrashed about, snapping fronds off the ferns in the line of planters. My heels tried for a foothold on the side of the escalator, but, where it angled up to the next level, a cubbyhole was recessed into its base. The only foothold was air.

The killer had me suspended several feet off the floor and must have hit the emergency button to stop the upward glide. I was in the angle where the escalator ended at a wall, from which my spastic kicks were knocking photos of judges.

The blood engorging my head burst a vessel in my nose, and life trickled down my lip to wet my wagging tongue.

My ears filled with the surf of a calling sea, then a death rattle gurgled in my constricted throat.

I began to convulse.

I was passing out.

In my dying consciousness I must have grasped the rope, for there it was in the clutch of my clinging hands. With every fiber of strength muscled into my arms, plus that shot of adrenaline that squirts when death is at your throat, I yanked on that line like I used to do in my high-school gym.

Not many people can climb a rope hand over hand. Never had I been this glad to be an East End kid, for if you want to survive in a place ruled by the law of the jungle, you learn every Tarzan trick you can. The noose around my neck stopped pulling as I climbed the rope, and soon I was able to hold myself up with just one hand, freeing the other to slacken the strangling cord around my throat.

I slipped the noose from my head.

HANGMAN

My grip on the rope let go.

And like Tarzan in the movies, I pounced out of my "hanging tree."

The Hangman fled while I lay gasping for breath beneath the noose, scared off by a gang of skinheads coming down from the trial above.

Stalked

Vancouver
November 16 (Tonight)

Zinc was parked across the street and half a block down from where he had watched Ethan Shaw park his Ford at a meter beside the law courts. Stepping out into the teeming rain, the lawyer had pulled a hideaway hood out from the collar of his coat to protect his head against the downpour, then had run toward the rear doors of the building. It was too risky to follow him in, so instead the Mountie sat back in the driver's seat of his car to reflect on the good times he and Alex had shared. It was a memorial service of sorts, for on the floor of the passenger's seat she had once graced sat a funeral urn filled with his love's ashes. When this was over, when she had justice, he would return Alex to Cannon Beach, Oregon, and give her remains to the sea to rest in peace. Until then, she would stay with him, and the seat she once occupied would be cluttered with an array of high-tech surveillance hardware supplied by Special Eye.

Rat-a-tat-tat, the rain drummed a military tattoo on the roof.

Tapping the steering wheel in time made the cut on his finger hurt.

The Mountie mourned and waited.

The way he had it figured, the surviving brothers were in this together. For Steven Mark Haddon—Justin Whitfield—the vendetta against those responsible for the wrongful hanging of his brother was motivated by a warped sense of twin bonding. For Ethan Quinn Haddon—Ethan Shaw—the vendetta was the outburst of a ground-down drunk. Whatever unresolved turmoil made him drink, it was channeled into revenge against those who had destroyed his mom by lynching the brother Ethan never got to know.

Together, they were the Hangman.

The perfect alibi.

One or the other—or both—had used Halloween to hang Mary Konrad. To mask the fact that they were out to hang jurors in Seattle, one or the other—or both—had hanged Jayne Curry in Vancouver. Not only did that expand their spree to embrace all perverse jurors, and thus turn what began as a vendetta into a crusade, but that blind bought them time to get Bart Busby. One or the other—or both—had hanged him in Seattle while the smoke-screen distracted police.

Very clever.

Mix-and-match killers.

One could forge an ironclad alibi while the other was on the hunt, then they could reverse roles to alibi-up the one who had no alibi for the prior killing.

The Hangman was actually Hangmen.

Like the Hillside Strangler(s).

Peter Haddon's brothers were a killing team.

Ethan was the weaker link because he was a drunk, and Ethan drank too much that night on the boat. Something Alex said caused Ethan to snap, and in a drunken stupor, he killed her in his cabin. Did Justin go down to the cabin after Alex was dead and stumble upon the mess that could send them both to the gallows? With no time or opportunity to cover up, did he do the best he could with the situation? For all those reasons the lawyer argued in court, did Justin turn it into a Hangman crime Ethan wouldn't commit? Then, to put any doubts to final rest, did he hang the Greek while Ethan was in jail?

That Ethan was the Hangman, Zinc had no doubt. It was too great a coincidence that he was Peter Haddon's brother, and that he lived in the same city as the smokescreen victim, and that he was found in the cabin where Alex Hunt was hanged.

No, he was guilty.

And he was free.

And Zinc had insufficient reason to arrest him or his older brother.

But he would get it.

No matter what the cost.

Zinc sat up when he caught sight of Ethan rushing down the street, hood up and shoulders hunched against the rain, the trees on either side of the walk as bare as skeletons. The lawyer had exited from the courts by the main doors at the corner of Hornby and Nelson, not by the rear doors through which he had gone in. Was he rushing because of the rain or something else?

Something like going to meet Justin?

From pool of light to pool of light, Ethan dashed to his car. Unlocking the door, he climbed in and soon drove away. From one of the Special Eye devices on the seat beside him, the Mountie could hear his quarry breathing in the Ford ahead. The bug would catch any talk in Ethan's car.

The Ford angled east on Georgia Street and drove past the fountain out front of the old courthouse, the spray foaming with soap suds someone had tossed in for a prank. The Hudson's Bay Company and the central post office, the dual coliseums of the new library and the arena where the Canucks and Grizzlies play— all approached and passed the spattered windows of both cars. They left the uptown core by the Georgia Viaduct to reach the darker part of town: the squalid East End. Through the dismal streets the game of cat and mouse continued until Ethan's Ford finally stopped out front of a small bungalow.

Zinc knew the address.

The home of Ethan's mom.

Into which the lawyer vanished to escape from the wet and the cold.

The only light on inside was behind the window to one side of the door. No others came on. Zinc wondered if Justin Whitfield was in that room, waiting with his mother for his brother to arrive. If so, what they had to say was what he wished to hear, so Zinc pulled into the shadows directly across the street and rolled down the driver's window of his car.

From the spy gizmos supplied by Special Eye, Zinc selected the laser-bounce listening device, then aimed it so the beam hit the window at a right angle to turn the pane of glass into a microphone. Voices within the house vibrated the window, and the laser bounced those vibrations back to Zinc's car, where the receiver next to him converted them into words.

He wondered if this drizzle would play havoc with the beam?

The Hangman watched as the lawyer limped out from the great hall, and contemplated gunning him down in a drive-by shooting. That, however, would merely end his perverse career, without tying the means of his death to the motive for it. So instead of killing Kline here and now, the Hangman followed him to his car and waited for him to get in, then followed that car along Georgia Street and across the Viaduct to the East End, where it drove to a dilapidated house and parked in the driveway along one side.

The house was dark.

No one home.

Except the lawyer, who kept the headlights shining so he could see while he limped to an overgrown flowerpot beside his car and lifted it to remove the spare key hidden beneath.

Hobbling to the front door, he cranked the key in the lock, then limped back to replace it under the pot. After dousing the headlights and locking his car, Kline returned to the house and disappeared inside.

The Hangman's car was parked down the street.

Streetlights in the East End were few and far between.

While Kline was unlocking the house, the Hangman was watching him from behind the darkest tree.

Tick-tock . . .

Tick-tock . . .

The killer went for the key.

Vigilante

Vancouver
Tonight

The pistol in my hand is an eight-shot, 7.65 caliber Mauser semi-automatic, taken as a trophy off a dead Nazi in the Second World War. I have no idea who that Nazi was, nor do I know how many people were killed with this gun. Every time I see a movie set during that war, I imagine the nastiest Nazi in it carrying this Mauser, so it has built up quite a history over the years. Gram got the gun as payment for blowing a junkie war amp back when she was a young whore working the skids. It scared the crap out of several johns who tried to beat Gram up for an extra thrill, and when the angels finally called her to that cathouse in the sky, the Mauser passed from her to me.

My nerves are calm.

My hands are steady.

The walnut grip is cold in my grasp and the barrel aims at the door.

I'm waiting for the Hangman.

The end is near.

The price of winning a cause célèbre is that it brings out the nuts. No cause was more célèbre at this moment than me freeing the Hangman on a technicality, so that meant I was public enemy number one, and that drew the ire of the nuts in anonymous crank calls. Some sounded like nuts ready to crack, so that's why the Mauser was in my car—and would have gone into the law courts if not for security checks.

The gun isn't legal.

This is Canada.

The first thing I did once I had recovered enough to function after the attempt on my life was gather up the rope the Hangman had left behind. Then I limped to my car on Hornby Street and withdrew the Mauser from its hiding place. Tucking the pistol into my belt so it was close at hand, I checked the rear-view mirror as I drove away, and continued to check it as I headed east.

I was being followed.

I sensed the eyes behind.

So I led the Hangman here, and now I wait, the gun in one hand and a bat in the other, lurking in a dark nook just inside the door.

My grandmother used to have these books by Ellery Queen. She picked them up at a swap meet in the Ritter Project. *The Greek Coffin,* and *Dutch Shoe,* and *Chinese Orange,* and *French Powder Mystery.* You came to a point in each novel where the story stopped and a "Challenge to the Reader" by the author appeared. It was time for you to solve the whodunit, if you were out to beat the player on the other side.

If this were a novel, that time would be now.

But of course, it isn't.

This is real life.

My ears listen intently for any sound outside.

My eyes watch the doorknob for it to turn.

Yes, there it is.

The snicking of the lock.

The Hangman has found the key outside.

The knob is turning.

The door is easing open.

HANGMAN

A dark figure steps into the dark hall.
Another step.
The bat is in a swing.
Time to take justice into my own hands.
This is the East End.
This is my turf.
And this is what we do to fucks who fuck with us.
Too late, sucker.
Showtime, folks...

Vancouver
November 16 (Tonight)

Such were the thoughts, memories, daydreams that passed
through his brain as Jeffrey Kline relived the past sixteen days
while standing in that black hall waiting for this moment. The
baseball bat clipped the Hangman's skull and sent the intruder flying into the foyer. From the shiver up the handle and the crack of
the blow, Jeff knew his stalker was knocked out cold. The lawyer
used the handcuffs the Hangman had brought to return that favor,
then dragged the shackled killer up the foyer stairs.

It took a few minutes to rig up the gallows, but by the time the
Hangman came around from the blow, it was ready for the drop.

The house was a rundown two-story from the early days of the
city. The foyer off the entrance hall was chilly with drafts. The rick-
ety staircase ascended up one wall, then angled at the upper landing
to create a stairwell. The plunge from the narrow balcony backing
the stairwell was a good twelve feet down to the main floor.

The noose around the Hangman's neck was a double strand.
The slightly shorter length was fashioned out of piano wire so it
would yank a foot before the hemp rope, slicing the flesh of the
neck down to the bones of the spine. The hard jerk of the hemp
rope a split second later would sever the vertebrae exposed by the
previous cut, tearing the head of the Hangman off the still-
plunging body.

The drop from here to there was greater than any used by official hangmen.

This gallows might as well be a guillotine.

Kline was standing on the safe side of the upper rail. The Hangman sat slumped unconscious on the rail itself. All that kept the killer from taking a plunge into eternity was the lawyer's grip—and the urge the lawyer felt to say a few last words.

The Hangman came around.

Tick-tock . . .

Tick-tock . . .

Time was running out.

Last Words

"You've reached the end of your rope," joked Jeffrey Kline, his mouth inches behind the Hangman's left ear. "Before I let you drop to the hell you deserve, I want you to appreciate how brilliant I am. A mind like mine comes along once in a generation of lawyers. I am a *master* at the legal game."

Spill salt on the table and superstition says you should pinch a few grains and toss them over your left shoulder.

Ever wonder why?

The Hangman knew.

Because the left shoulder is where the devil sits in his endless whispering battle for your soul with the angel on the right shoulder.

The hope is that salt will blind the devil to give the angel an edge.

Well, this was like that.

Except this voice over the Hangman's shoulder was that of the devil's *advocate.*

"Hate like yours I understand. I hate, too. It's ingrained. I hate everyone who ever put me down, and I hate every silver spoon who tried to keep me down. The only pittances life ever offered me were those cast-offs I could beg, borrow or steal. I wish I'd known earlier that murder was the key.

"Love like yours I don't understand. That emotion you call love is foreign to me. I have never felt love and never will. I know what I am. I'm a psychopath. An individual who exhibits amoral and antisocial behavior, lack of ability to love or establish meaningful personal relationships, extreme egocentricity, et cetera. I face others like me every day in the courts. Those symptoms fit most lawyers to a T.

"Ha, ha.

"Get it?

"That's a lawyer joke.

"You, however, have proved Clarence Darrow wrong. What he said was, 'Nobody kills anyone for love.' What you killed for was your love of Peter Haddon. You must have loved him to death.

"Ha, ha.

"That's a pun.

"Damn, I'm funny.

"Me, I plead the defense of necessity. To make it as a lawyer, you need lawyer's luck, and lawyer's luck is hard to come by these days. You can wait a lifetime for that breakthrough case, and no way did I intend to wait that long. Not with skid-row drunks pissing at my door. So I *made* my luck in this cutthroat profession. By hanging Alex Hunt, look where I am now.

"At first, I thought the way to fame was by hooking you, so I drafted a newspaper piece to attract you as a client. That was a long shot. I had no control. A bust in the States and you would hire an American gunslinger. A bust in Canada and you would have your pick of lawyers. What were the odds that you would choose a skid-row kid like me?

"Who was I kidding?

"What a fantasy.

"But then I got an unexpected break. Ethan sought my help to solve his ethical dilemma. He suspected that his brother was the Hangman, and he asked me to meet Justin on the crime cruise so I could assess that possibility for him. If so, there was no need for me to publish an article to hook the Hangman. All I had to do was prove my legal ability. And what better proof was there than a *rigged* trial? A trial in which his brother Ethan was in jeopardy? A trial in which the outcome was never in doubt for me, because *I* controlled the evidence that went to court.

"What a setup.

"What a frame.

"It was brilliant.

"Don't you agree?

"There was only one lawyer Ethan could depend on to save his skin: his buddy Jeff.

"His childhood friend.

"That's what friends are for.

"Ha, ha, eh?

"I knew Ethan would get drunk that night. A drunk drinks, so I ordered booze. Then I suggested he invite his brother to our table, and he returned with Alex as well. For what I had planned, *any* victim would do; I was going to allege that Ethan had been framed. I thought Alex would be ideal, since her involvement with the Hangman case would make her seem to be a target, but there was no reason for Ethan to hang her. Imagine my shock when I later learned he was Peter's brother, which gave him a motive for *all* the Hangman crimes.

"The first defense I built in was jurisdiction. I had to make sure Hunt was hanged in Canada. That would allow me to act for Ethan, and it would stop the Seattle cops from extraditing him. Cheating the Washington gallows would be Win Number One.

"To that end, it was me who set up the photograph in the bar so the lights of Victoria were the backdrop behind Alex, Ethan, Justin and me. I took maritime law at UBC, so I knew the separation rule in the Strait of Juan de Fuca.

"After Alex and Ethan left the bar for some fresh air on deck, the woman serving us gave Justin the eye, and I was left alone when he went after her. That gave me an opportunity to pick up the trail and follow Alex and Ethan down to his cabin.

"Alex answered my knock on the door.

"'How's he doing?' I asked.

"'Sick as a dog,' she said. 'He's in the toilet, throwing up.'

"That's when I hit her.

"Down she went.

"Then I ambushed Ethan as he stumbled out of the john, clubbing him before he saw me.

"I used a length of rope I had cut on deck for a noose to hang Alex from the curtain rod. I slashed her arms and legs to be symbolic, but I didn't hack them off so as to avoid the blood. Then I scrawled the hangman puzzle on the wall, like the one I'd seen that morning on TV. Because the latest guess by the cops had been the letter *I*, I filled that in where I thought it fit.

"Big mistake.

"That same morning, Ethan had shown me a copy of Justin's article on Peter's hanging in which the typo Brice—with an *I*— appeared. That lodged in my brain as the proper spelling. It wasn't dispelled before we boarded the boat, since I only heard Bryce spoken for the rest of that day. So when I drew the hangman game in blood on the wall, I made the mistake of repeating the typo in Brice.

"Is that how you got onto me?

"You asked yourself who benefited from the death of Hunt, and who lacked family knowledge of how Bryce was spelled?

"You put two and two together, then came up with me?

"We lawyers are trained to take advantage of all openings, and to turn disadvantage around to help our client's case. The misspelling ended up as a blessing in disguise, for when I discovered Ethan was actually Peter Haddon's brother, I could argue the misspelling proved he *didn't* draw the puzzle. Why, if the Hangman was out to make a statement about his brother's wrongful hanging, would he lynch a victim in his own cabin and foul the answer to the hangman game by *misspelling* Peter's name?

"The logic of it was that whoever killed Alex Hunt was someone *outside* the Haddon family.

"Unwittingly, I had secured Win Number Two.

"Lawyer's luck.

"The way I figured it was this. Win Ethan's case and I would impress you, apart from the fact that that win itself would be my breakthrough. Maybe you would come to me and confess to save Ethan. Maybe you would kill again while he was in jail to prove Ethan innocent of the Hangman's crimes—both to get him off and to take back your vendetta from whoever was trying to copycat your M.O.

"No matter how you played it, I knew you'd play into my hands.

"Which you did.

"By coming after me.

"I must admit, you took me by surprise with your attack. A hanging in the law courts. That took guts. But once warned, I was ready for you.

"This house you followed me to tonight is rented by Ethan. He's off seeing his mom right now. If Ethan takes a trip, I house-sit, and that's how I know about the spare key. Tonight I'm a burglar. And so are you. Which will become evident to the cops after I smash a window and replace the key you removed from the pot to get in.

"Ethan will return to find you dead in his home. Chandler will arrest him for your murder. The Mountie has an ax to grind for Hunt's hanging. Ethan will ask me to defend him, and I'll argue that *you* were the Hangman all along.

"Which you are.

"So try this on for size.

"Mary Konrad died because she was the weak juror who sealed Haddon's fate.

"Jayne Curry died to hide that motive. You heard the Mounties were investigating her and realized she would make the perfect smokescreen. You drove up to Vancouver with Justin Whitfield and dropped him at his mom's. While he was with Ethan, you hanged the juror, then drove back to Seattle alone. The reporter caught a plane.

"Bart Busby died because he was the Haddon juror most to blame.

"Why you lynched Alex Hunt is a mystery. She was digging into the Haddon case. Were you afraid she had discovered whatever tied you to Peter, so you decided to kill three birds with one stone? That hanging not only removed any threat from Hunt, but also—because it offered Ethan as a suspect—baffled police long enough for you to kill again.

"It was a blind.

"It fit your M.O.

"It bought you enough time to get the Greek.

"George Koulelis died because he had fingered Haddon as the killer of his daughter, Anna.

"And with his death, your vendetta was complete.

"Except for Ethan.

"The grudge you nurse against Peter's brother is anybody's guess. As good a theory as any will be this submission. The false accusation of murder put Haddon through hell. First, he lost his freedom. Then he was raped and castrated in jail. Then he spent years with death hanging over his head. And finally, he suffered an end to that psychological torture in the hangman's noose.

"We know where Justin was during that ordeal. He was at his brother's side through thick and thin, and when the gallows floor dropped away beneath Peter's feet, Justin was there to see him out.

"But where was Ethan?

"Nowhere to be seen.

"Did he think Peter guilty?

"Was his blood thinner than water?

HANGMAN

"The Hangman's reason for being is to drive home moral lessons. Those who fail to do their duty suffer the same consequences. Send Peter to the gallows, and to the gallows you go. Let your brother stand falsely accused, and falsely accused will you stand.

"That's why you framed Ethan on the ship. So the Judas would know what Peter had endured. You filled in the *I* instead of the *Y* so it would look as if the drunk was trying to cover up by turning suspicion toward a killer outside the family. Hanging the Greek while Ethan was in jail wasn't an attempt to free him from the charge, but was aimed instead at causing the cops to wonder if he was half of a killing team. When I sprang Ethan so easily from that moral lesson, you set out to set him up again.

"You don't want to kill him.

"That would be unjust.

"Balancing the scales is what the Hangman is all about.

"What happened tonight is that you went over the edge. Guilt from all those murders got the better of you. A suicidal urge drove you here, so your death will have an after-effect for Ethan. You broke in, rigged a gallows, gagged and cuffed yourself, and climbed over the banister to jump into the well. You knew love and grief would drive Chandler to arrest Ethan. You hoped he'd see the break-in as a ruse, like the misspelling on the boat. Ethan will again be falsely accused, and your vendetta will reach from the grave.

"Lucky for Ethan, he has me.

"Currently the hottest gunslinger around.

"All I have to do is raise a reasonable doubt. I will plead a similar-fact defense. Because there is a nexus here between strikingly similar crimes, how can Ethan be the Hangman when several were committed at times for which he has alibis? Would he hang you in his own house so soon after being charged with hanging Hunt in his cabin? The only way your death makes sense is if it's a mad attempt to frame Ethan again.

"Who would do that?

"It must be the Hangman.

"And who is the Hangman?

"The Hangman, I'll say, is you.

"Because you really are the Hangman, when we dig deep enough we'll find the proof. Any holes in what I have theorized tonight will be filled by the argument that your mind was crumbling. Not only will I spring Ethan from another cell, but—the icing on the cake—I'll be the lawyer who unmasked the Hangman.

"See what I mean?

"A *master* of the game.

"The only downside is that no one will know the truth of how brilliantly I played this one.

"Sure, they'll see me as a great lawyer.

"But the genius is in how I set it up.

"And that, in case you're wondering, is why I am telling you.

"I must admit, however, that again you took me by surprise. As did Ethan, I thought the Hangman was Justin Whitfield. And he was so obsessed with hanging those who had hanged Peter, I thought, because *he* had raped and killed Anna Koulelis. Come to think of it, that could still be so. Maybe that will be my next cause célèbre. I'll be the lawyer who finally found out who murdered that little girl.

"Damn, I'm good.

"The only piece missing is the final link. If I ungag you, will you supply it? I'm dying to know the link between you and Peter Haddon.

"What do you say?

"Any last words?"

The Drop

Vancouver
November 16

Perched on the precipice high above the long drop into the stairwell, her hands shackled behind her back with her own cuffs, the
double nooses of wire and rope looped about her neck, Det.
Maddy Thorne listened to her hangman confess. Like every criminal lawyer she had jousted with in court, this one loved the sound
of his own voice.

Any last words?

Screw you, she thought.

Never talk to the cops is the lawyer's creed.

Never trust a lawyer is every cop's reply.

Lawyers are liars.

It's built into their trade.

A lawyer argues black is white or white is black, according to
how he's paid.

They're *professional* liars.

What a dirty job.

There was stuff she could tell him to fill in the missing link. Like
how her dad was ground to hamburger when she was two, sucked
off both feet into the blades of a jet engine. And how her mom was
living common law with Earl Haddon within a year, so the girl was

raised in Seattle with two stepbrothers from her stepfather's first marriage. Peter and Steven. Fraternal twins. And how Earl Haddon was a cruel man who belittled his sons and frightened Maddy. She was three years younger than the twins, and she loved Peter with all her heart. One summer day when she was fourteen, Maddy followed Peter into the backyard, and there, in a tepee beneath the twins' treehouse, she lost her virginity to that sensitive youth.

It wasn't rape.

Both teens consented.

It wasn't incest.

They weren't blood-related.

What it was was insecure Maddy yearning for *someone's* love.

The secret relationship grew for four years. Then Peter moved out to live on his own. The plan was that Maddy would follow when she finished high school, but within two months Peter was charged with murder. Maddy's mom quickly whisked her away from the Haddon house and its ugly scandal.

Ten years of heartbreak and horror followed. What Maddy couldn't do was visit Peter. Not because her mom said she couldn't, but because it would seal his death warrant if the state discovered that Peter had had "incestuous" sex with an underage girl. The case was too precarious to chance backing up the admission testified to by the cop driving the paddy wagon. Peter would appear to be a pedophile, and appearance is all-important when a jury is involved.

So she didn't visit.

And doubted him herself.

Could Peter rape and kill a little girl?

Of course not.

He loves me.

And when he's acquitted, everything will go back to how it was.

Then: *bam! bam! bam!* Three blows in a row. Peter was convicted. Peter was raped. Peter lost his manhood to a gelding blade.

No more going back to how it was.

What Maddy did instead was become a cop. She hoped the answer to her guilt over doubting Peter was hidden in the files of the Seattle police. It wasn't. She hoped she could do something about injustice, but the courts were a law unto themselves. Like all cops, she was sickened when she watched them work. The good guys got fucked. The bad guys got off.

"He wants you there," Justin had said.

"To see him hang?"

"No, to see *you*. He says yours is the only love he's cherished, so if you can take it, his final wish is not to die alone."

So she did it. She saw Peter off. And as he hanged before her on the state's gallows, Maddy *knew* she had lost her one true love.

This, and a lot more, she could tell the hangman who had her in his noose. Like how no other lover had taken Peter's place. And how betrayed she felt when a DNA test finally proved him innocent. If not for that perverse jury shirking its duty, Peter would not have hanged for something he didn't do, and she would have had his love through all those years. And he would be here now to see her through her fear, the abject fear she had endured for the past few weeks, since the day her doctor gave her the chilling diagnosis: the headaches were caused by a tumor in her brain.

An inoperable tumor.

The life she had left was just months.

She was going to die alone.

Thanks to Peter's jury.

All this she could tell him, but what good would it do? Kline would merely pervert it to his own dirty scheme, and use it for why she'd hanged herself tonight. Hopefully, Zinc would spot the fatal flaw in the lawyer's story: the fact that Maddy was with Zinc while Alex was being hanged. That, however, was up to him, and if he thought the Hangman was a killing team, he might think Maddy had linked up with either Justin or Ethan, or possibly *both*. He would remember telling her about Jayne Curry and Dr.

Twist when he was in Seattle the night Mary Konrad died. He would remember their cellphone conversation, when he was at the Vancouver murder scene and she was driving back to Seattle on the I-5. Curry could have been hanged by any combination of them, and Maddy's "partner" could have hanged Alex while Maddy was with Zinc.

Very crafty.

No wonder she loathed lawyers.

With so many suspects, Kline was above suspicion.

Her part in this was over. Her crusade was at an end. Vengeance was hers for the unjust conviction and hanging of her lover. The Hangman would put the scare of hell into prospective jurors, and if that inspired others to punish the perverse, then Peter's death and her death would not be in vain.

All that remained for her to do was to cheat the hangman herself, so Maddy wrenched free from the grip of the lawyer and hurled herself from the edge of the precipice into the dark stairwell.

Though muffled by the gag, "I'm coming, Peter!" were her last words.

Her death was spectacular.

A squishing squirt, caused by the constricting of the wire noose, filled the foyer below. Blood exploded in all directions from the severed vessels, and billowed up as red mist like spray from a fountain. A sharp crack followed as the rope yanked taut, snapping Maddy's neck in two as her head ripped off. Released from the weight of her body dropping to the floor, the rope sprang back up like a yo-yo. Because the wire noose had cinched tight around the neck bones, her head was still caught in the loophole that bounced back to the lawyer.

Wow! thought Jeff.

What a cool kill!

This he had to see.

What a thrill!

HANGMAN

So down the staircase he went, to the main floor, where the headless Maddy lay in the foyer at this end of the front hall. Being careful not to leave footprints in the spray of blood, Jeff stood with his back to the door to survey his handiwork.

Yes, he thought.

I can work with this.

The inspiration for the beheading was the sidebar he had read on Arthur Ellis earlier that night at the law courts:

> What finished Ellis's career was the botched hang-
> ing of Thomasino Sarao...
>> Now, a new Hangman is on the loose.
>> Like Thomasino, his victims lose body parts.
>> The legs and arms are gone.
>> The body remains.
>> If there's another victim, will he tear off its head?

The head twirling in the noose gave Jeff an idea.

Should he scrawl a hangman game that looked like this on the wall:

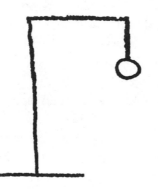

PETER BRYCE HADDON
IT'S OVER
HANGMAN

Years ago he'd seen a photo in a magazine of some poor fuck in Africa with elephantiasis. The effects of that roundworm disease were awesome to behold, for what the parasite did to certain lymph nodes was cause them to bloat to science-fiction size. The testicles of the man in the picture had grown so huge that he was shown pushing a wheelbarrow to carry them around.

That's how Jeff felt.

His balls were that big.

For what he knew in his heart was that he had it made. He would not only get Ethan off a second time, but also unmask the Hangman. All you need is one Big Win like that in your legal career and you can milk that sucker for the rest of your life.

Look what Leopold and Loeb did for Darrow.

Look what Sheppard did for Bailey.

Look what Simpson did for Cochran.

Look what Shaw did for Kline.

If he covered his tracks here and staged a minor accident to explain the whiplash collar masking the noose burn on his neck, Jeff would be securely launched on a path to fame and fortune. He had fooled the cops and he had fooled the Hangman, and what he had told Maddy was gone with his wind, so to speak. Not another soul knew the truth, and that was a small price to pay for no more piss at the door.

Not another soul...

That wasn't quite so...

For unknown to this lawyer enjoying a good gloat, his confession to Maddy *wasn't* gone with his wind. It had been caught by one of the tiny pin mikes secretly installed in the house by Special Eye, including that stupid admission that he was a burglar, which made the words transmitted to the digital recorder in Zinc Chandler's car admissible in court. And even now as Jeff tried to remember the title of that film with Cagney—Was it *White Heat?* The one in which the punk shouts triumphantly, "Made it, Ma! Top of the World!"—that car was braking to a halt at the curb outside Ethan's house, having driven across the East End from the home of Ethan's mom.

The driver's door swung open...

The Mountie scrambled out...

Zinc's blood was at a boil as the Smith & Wesson 9mm cleared the holster clipped to his belt.

Now he was charging up the walk toward the dark door, hurtling toward having it out with the guy who hanged his lover. Anger and outrage powered this six-foot-two assault, until two hundred pounds of muscle smashed against the wood.

The *CRACKKK* of the door bursting open was much louder than the crack that snapped Maddy's neck. Jeff whirled as the Mountie exploded into the narrow hall behind him. His hand went for the Mauser tucked into his belt.

"Police!" Zinc shouted.

The bug was still recording.

"Drop it!" he ordered.

The cop had the drop on the lawyer.

The eye at this end of the barrel aiming at his heart didn't scare Jeff half as much as the glare of the man beyond. He saw death—*his* death—in those eyes, so the lawyer let go of the Mauser and raised his hands in the air.

The cut that had made the blood oath to Alex was on Zinc's trigger finger. That finger pulled the trigger and the gun bucked in his hand. This was one case the courts would not screw up. When the courts fail to do justice, it falls to vigilantes. The nine-mill round from the Smith caught Kline in the chest, a little to the left of his breastbone. You might say the lawyer died from a broken heart.

Some you win.

Some you lose.

That's the legal profession.

Author's Note

This is a work of fiction. The plot and characters are a product of the author's imagination. Where real persons, places or institutions are incorporated to create the illusion of authenticity, they are used fictitiously. Inspiration was drawn from the following non-fiction and video sources:

Frank W. Anderson, *A Dance with Death: Canadian Women on the Gallows 1754–1954* (Calgary: Fifth House, 1996).

——, *A Concise History of Capital Punishment in Canada* (Calgary: Frontier, 1973).

Brian Bailey, *Hangmen of England: A History of Execution from Jack Ketch to Albert Pierrepoint* (London: W. H. Allen, 1989).

Edna Barth, *Witches, Pumpkins, and Grinning Ghosts: The Story of the Halloween Symbols* (New York: Seabury Press, 1972).

Robert Bolt, *A Man for All Seasons* (Scarborough: Bellhaven, 1963).

William S. Burroughs, *Junky* (London: Penguin, 1977).

David D. Cooper, *The Lesson of the Scaffold* (London: Allen Lane, 1974).

Chuck Davis, ed., *The Greater Vancouver Book: An Urban Encyclopaedia* (Surrey, B.C.: Linkman, 1997).

Lord Devlin, *Trial by Jury* (London: Stevens, 1956).

Diagram Group, *The Way to Play: The Illustrated Encyclopedia of the Games of the World* (New York: Paddington Press, 1975).

Charles Duff, *A Handbook on Hanging* (Yorkshire: EP Publishing, 1974).

Howard Engel, *Lord High Executioner: An Unashamed Look at Hangmen, Headsmen, and Their Kind* (Toronto: Key Porter, 1996).

Furman v. Georgia, 408 U.S. 238 (1972).

J. H. H. Gaute and Robin Odell, *Murder "Whatdunit": An Illustrated Account of the Methods of Murder* (London: Pan, 1982).

Gregg v. Georgia, 428 U.S. 153 (1976).

Reinhold Heller, *Edvard Munch: The Scream* (London: Allen Lane, 1973).

Jill Hierstein-Morris, *Halloween: Facts and Fun* (Ankeny, Iowa: Creatively Yours, 1988).

Gordon Honeycombe, *The Murders of the Black Museum 1870–1970* (London: W. H. Allen, 1983).

Roderick Hunt, *Ghosts, Witches, and Things Like That . . .* (Oxford: Oxford University Press, 1984).

John Laurence, *A History of Capital Punishment* (New York: Citadel, 1960).

Kindler v. Canada (Minister of Justice) [1991] 2 S.C.R. 779.

Peter V. MacDonald, QC, *Court Jesters: Canada's Lawyers & Judges Take the Stand to Relate Their Funniest Stories* (Toronto: Methuen, 1985).

——, *More Court Jesters: Back to the Bar for More of the Funniest Stories from Canada's Courts* (Toronto: Methuen, 1987).

Kirk Makin, *Redrum the Innocent* (Toronto: Penguin Canada, 1998).

Marge Mueller and Ted Mueller, *Seattle's Lakes, Bays & Waterways: Afoot & Afloat* (Seattle: The Mountaineers, 1998).

George L. Murray, "Manson's Last Case," *The Advocate* 42 (1984).

Reference Re Ng Extradition [1991] 2 S.C.R. 858.

Regina v. Dudley and Stephens (1884), 14 Q.B.D. 273.

Regina v. Frisbee (1989), 48 C.C.C. (3d) 386 (B.C.C.A.).

Regina v. Morin [1988] 2 S.C.R. 345, on appeal from Regina v. Morin (1987), 36 C.C.C. (3d) 50 (Ont. C.A.).

Peter Randall, *Adult Bullying: Perpetrators and Victims* (London: Routledge, 1997).

Reginald Rose, *Twelve Angry Men* (Sidney Lumet, director [1957]; William Friedkin, director [1997]).

J. C. Smith and Brian Hogan, *Criminal Law* (London: Butterworths, 1969).

Frank Smyth, *Cause of Death: The Story of Forensic Science* (London: Pan, 1980).

United States of America v. Burns and Rafay (1997), 116 C.C.C. (3d) 524 (B.C.C.A.).

The Vancouver Sun, The Globe and Mail and *The Seattle Times.*

Colin Wilson and Patricia Pitman, *Encyclopaedia of Murder* (London: Pan, 1984).

Dilys Winn, *Murder Ink* (New York: Workman, 1977).

The best Dracula? Christopher Lee. Though purists would probably argue for Lugosi.

And what about those cannibals who killed and ate the boy in the lifeboat? Did Dudley and Stephens have a defense of necessity to murder?

No, said Lord Coleridge, the chief justice of the Royal Courts: "Who is to be the judge of this sort of necessity? By what measure is the comparative value of lives to be measured? Is it to be strength or intellect, or what? It is plain that the principle leaves to him who is to profit by it to determine the necessity which will justify him in deliberately taking another's life to save his own."

In the case of *Regina* v. *Howe* [1987] AC 417, the British House of Lords recently upheld *Dudley and Stephens* as having decided that necessity is *not* a defense to murder.

America, however, offers another view.

In *U.S.* v. *Holmes*, 26 Fed Cas 360 (1842), also a shipwreck case, the court held that a drawing of lots in similar circumstances would legalize a killing. *The American Model Penal Code* includes a general defense of necessity.

The noose and necessity?

Where would the Hangman rather be tried?

When I'm at a social gathering and someone finds out I'm a lawyer, the question that usually crops up is, "How can you defend someone you know is guilty?"

That depends on your ethics.

Jeff Kline offers *both* answers.

When I'm at a social gathering and someone finds out I'm a writer, the question that usually crops up is, "Where do you get your ideas?"

Let me tell you the tale of my brush with Canada's gallows.

Sometime between midnight and 1 a.m. on March 29, 1974, Miller and Cockriell returned to Miller's house from a pub in Fort Langley, B.C. They found a beer-drinking party in progress. Something was said about the death of Miller's brother two years before, when he drove into a ditch at the end of a police chase. There was talk about shooting a policeman, during which Cockriell said words to the effect that if Miller didn't shoot a cop, he would. As he and Cockriell were leaving the house at about 3 a.m., Miller took with him a 30-30 Winchester rifle and loaded it with one shell in the chamber.

With Miller at the wheel and Cockriell in the passenger's seat, they drove to Cloverdale, a few miles away. There, the courthouse and the Mounted Police detachment were side by side in one block. To attract the attention of a Mountie, Miller drove around the block several times and Cockriell threw a beer bottle through the window of the courthouse.

Constable Pierlet was driving a marked police car. His relatives were on their way to the West Coast for his upcoming wedding. When Miller's car attracted his attention, he followed it, flashing his red light. Miller pulled onto the shoulder of the road and stopped. The Mountie pulled his car in behind, and at 4:58 a.m. radioed the license number to the detachment and asked for backup. The constable got out of his car and walked up to the driver's window of Miller's car. Miller's hands were on the steering wheel and the rifle was resting across his arms with the muzzle pointing toward the open window. The constable asked Miller to get out of the car. That was the moment when Cockriell pulled the trigger and the bullet struck the Mountie in the chest. He managed to get as far as his own car, where he fell to the ground. About two minutes after he had made the radio call, the officer was found there by the Mountie who had come to cover him. He died almost immediately thereafter.

Meanwhile, Miller and Cockriell took off. The distress call—"A Member is down!"—went out to prowling patrol cars. The fugitives led police on a wild chase for twenty miles, during which the rifle was thrown out of the car. Eventually, they were forced off the road and arrested.

Convicted of a murder punishable by death, Miller and Cockriell were sentenced to hang. Though the death penalty was still law, Canada had not hanged anyone since 1962. The summer of 1976 saw the issue reach a climax on both sides of the border. The United States Supreme Court restored the death penalty in *Gregg* v. *Georgia*. By coincidence, Canada's Parliament was to vote on whether to retain the noose on the same day that we were summoned to Ottawa to argue the case of *Miller and Cockriell* v. *The Queen* before all nine judges of Canada's Supreme Court.

Lawyers have a saying: "Hard cases make bad law." If you have an important issue to argue, you don't want it riding on a bad set of facts. In the case of Miller and Cockriell, the Crown's submission was this: The two appellants planned to kill a Mountie; they went looking for one, found one and killed him. What we were there to do was strike down hanging.

There is a tradition in Canadian law that says, "If you lose a client to the noose, you see him out." Hangings in British Columbia took place at Oakalla Prison Farm, where the condemned was dropped down an old elevator shaft. Lose Cockriell's appeal and that's what I may witness, I thought.

First came a visit to the Department of Justice, where a somber bureaucrat showed us a list of those on death row, and said that if both the vote in Parliament and the outcome of the appeal backed the noose, the government would have no choice but to hang someone. Guess whose names were at the top of the list.

June 22, 1976, was the day. The appeal began with my senior counsel rising to his feet. To the best of my recollection, what followed was an exchange that went something like this:

"My Lord Chief Justice, my lords, this appeal raises the basic issue of whether the state has the right to put its citizens to—"

He was interrupted.

"You call this a factum?" one of the judges barked down from the bench.

It was a complicated issue. Our factum was long. It had appendices.

"I'm sure if your lordship reads it—"

"Read it! I can't even *lift* it!"

"My lord, the issue is—"

That's when the chief justice jumped in.

"Come, come, Counsel. You have no defense. This factum doesn't conform to our rules."

There was a pause.

This was not looking good.

And that's when my partner leaned down to me and said, "Hang on. Those are the liberals I hoped would be *with us* on this appeal."

Good God! I thought. We're here to decide whether to hang two men, and the court's hung up on the length of our factum!

We were in the thick of it against overwhelming odds when a runner came in with the result of the vote in Parliament. He had two slips of paper. The one for retention of the noose read 133. The one for abolition read 125.

Bang!

Snap!

Thump . . . thu—

In my mind's eye, I saw our client hang.

As it turned out, he didn't die. Yes, the Supreme Court unanimously upheld the legality of hanging, but the runner who'd come from Parliament had mixed up the slips, and consequently had reversed the results of the vote.

No matter where you stand on the morality of the death penalty, the undeniable fact remains that human foibles infect fallible courts that make irreversible decisions.

This novel was inspired by that danger.

The province in which Slade resides is bordered by the two states that retain hanging. In January 1993, Washington hanged Westley Allan Dodd, who, incidentally, fought for the right to be executed.

In July 1994, while on a flight to Africa to research *Evil Eye,* I was seated beside a Seattleite. At about three in the morning, somewhere over the Congo, we passed time by playing hangman. The puzzle I wanted to pose for him was *Westley Allan Dodd,* but I didn't know whether the middle name was spelled *Allan, Allen* or *Alan.*

10 Rillington Place is a film about the Christie/Evans case, the travesty that did away with Britain's noose. Richard Attenborough played Christie; John Hurt played Evans.

I watched that film again as background for this novel. Afterwards, I was sitting in the dark before a hypnotic fire, sipping Scotch as I developed this plot within my mind, and suddenly a primal shiver wormed up my spine.

His wife was killed, his child was killed and he was framed for their murders; no one believed him when the real psycho became the chief witness against him at his trial, and the entire British legal system fell for Christie's perjury. Imagine how Timothy Evans must have felt when he met Albert Pierrepoint on the gallows and the hangman put the noose around his neck.

I didn't need to imagine.

How he felt was this:

Slade
Vancouver, B.C.